Glory in the Dust

A Civil War Novel

By

Earl Cripe

This book is a work of fiction. Places, events, and situations in this story are purely fictional. Any resemblance to actual persons, living or dead, is coincidental.

ISBN: 1-4107-9017-7 (e-book)
ISBN: 1-4107-9016-9 (Paperback)
ISBN: 1-4107-9015-0 (Dust Jacket)

This book is printed on acid free paper.

1stBooks - rev. 12/28/06

Publisher's Note: *This publication is a novel. It is designed to tell a fictional story with the American Civil War as its backdrop. Where this novel touches history the accounting may or may not be accurate; it is incidental to the goals of the author and the publisher. It is sold or distributed with the understanding that the publisher and the author are not engaged in rendering legal, or other professional service. If legal advice or other expert assistance is required, the services of a competent professional person in a consultation capacity should be sought.*

Special Sales

First Edition signed copies can be purchased from the author at www.gloryinthedust.com or by calling 1-800 878-2654.

About the Cover

The picture on the cover of this book is a partial replica of "The Railroad Cut," a painting by the celebrated Historical Artist, Dale Gallon. This painting is a special work by Mr. Gallon commemorating the 140th anniversary of the Battle of Gettysburg

The carefully researched and highly accurate historical art of Dale Gallon has been the standard by which Civil War Art is judged for more than twenty years. The Gettysburg Times, Mr. Gallon's hometown newspaper, said it best, *"Dale Gallon continues to provide collectors of limited edition prints with the reality of the Civil War that is unmatched by other artists."* We believe that "The Railroad Cut" is the finest and most inspiring piece of Civil War artwork we have seen and that is why we have chosen it for our cover

This painting, as well as others by Mr. Dale Gallon, can be seen and purchased at www.gallon.com or ordered from Gallon Historical Art, 9 Steinwehr Ave., Gettysburg, PA 17325

Dedication

This book is dedicated to Carol Lowe Smith of McComb, Mississippi. I first met Carol in Yosemite Valley, California, in 1962, shortly after being discharged from the U.S. Army. I went there to work during the summer as we often had done during our college days. It seemed a good place to get my thoughts sorted out and arrive at some direction for my future. Little did I suspect the life-changing experience that awaited me. Suffice it to say that, through our colloquy and reverie during that enchanted summer, I discovered a true friend, a brilliant mind, and a beautiful, captivating, and classic woman in every laudable sense. It was my first and only camaraderie with a southern belle of the highest order. From then on, it has been easy for me to understand the mystique and the legend.

In the fall of 1962, I went for a visit to Oxford, Mississippi, the home of the University of Mississippi, where Carol was a senior and the homecoming queen. Again, I was unaware of what was in store for me. James Merideth was being admitted to the University and Oxford was an armed camp. After a memorable evening at dinner and a day of being shown around the town, Carol confided in me that she was having trouble protecting me. Irate students and alumni of 'Ole Miss' were in no mood, under those circumstances, to extend southern hospitality to anyone from the North; particularly from

California. She suggested that I leave Mississippi and not return until the dust had well settled, since she could not guarantee my safety.

I saw her only once after that, a brief visit in Yosemite National Park in 1963, but the lovely fragrance of her memory has lingered on. Through the years, I have kept a distant contact with Carol and her husband Dr. Shelby Smith, and I am not being histrionic in saying that Carol Lowe Smith has left a lasting and treasured imprint on my life.

Years ago, I promised a novel honoring her inspiration and memory. Many seasons have come to the meadow since that pledge was made, but the artist has finally returned with his easel, and the splendid gold of the Quaking Aspens is even more inspiring than the green grasses of spring. It is fitting that this book about the inimitable Catherine Morgan provide a dedication forum to one who is herself the consummate personification of the fabulous southern belles and their grand tradition.

Foreword

By

Chester Smith

CEO of a Media Conglomerate
Country-Western Entertainer
www.chestersmith.com

There are occasions in life when you hear a song, see a movie, or read a book that you know is going to be great. There are thousands of good songs, good books, and good pictures, but the great pieces do not come along that often. Most of us could count on the fingers of both hands the songs, pictures, and books that we consider great. When they do come down, we would like to be the one to sing them, to act in them, or to write them. I have been privileged during my career to have had some involvement in that. But we also enjoy hearing them, watching them, and reading them. A measure of envy is endemic to being human, but artists recognize greatness when they encounter it and they appreciate and respect it. As a Country-Western performer for more than fifty years and the CEO of a Media Conglomerate for more than thirty years, where it is my duty to make decisions on what programming will resonate with the audience and what will not, I have an additional basis for recognizing a work of unusual quality when it comes along.

Great works, be they songs, pictures or books, revolve around subjects that are time honored and institutional. These are the simple things that connect with the heart, the mind, and the emotions of people. The subject may be love, heartbreak, courage, adventure, or danger. Very often, those subjects are associated with events of historical and cultural significance. It might be the Gunfight at the O. K. Corral, the Indian massacre of Custer at the Little Big Horn, the tragic love affair of Romeo and Juliet, Moses crossing the Red Sea or D Day, and the landing at the beaches of Normandy. Like *Gone With the Wind* and *The Red Badge of Courage,* great books, movies, and songs are drawn from the haunting and deeply emotional story of the Civil War.

When a work is based on the Civil War, the issue of success or failure resides with the author because the War has the power and drama to carry any story that captures a part of its essence with insight and skill. *Glory in the Dust* may well become one of those classic novels that are cherished through the years for that reason. It is a winsome tale about the fabulous Catherine Morgan and how her experiences changed the outcome of the war and shaped her future. The writer does not lead the reader by the hand, step by step, to the place he wants you to arrive at in the end. Instead, he paints vivid pictures on his word canvass that immerses the reader in the ambiance and romance of life in the old South before and during the war. The reader is swept along with the tide of change and deposited on the beach of the new South in its aftermath.

The author's view of the War is fascinating and unique as is the messenger he has chosen. Catherine Morgan was a great southern belle that everyone can admire. She was the original green eyed, red haired beauty that Scarlet O'Hara, and other southern 'leading ladies' have been modeled after. Her courage, character, and dedication combine with her stunning beauty to make her one of the truly great women in our nation's history. It is fitting that the author has chosen to make this book her story and to give her some long over due recognition.

Another compelling aspect of this book is the fresh and provocative way the author deals with the issue of slavery and the interaction between servant and master. The author makes them real people whose emotions, feelings, actions, and accomplishments are essential to telling this story and to the American story. Enslaved people have acted out some of history's epic dramas. Joseph, Daniel, and the Three Hebrew Children, are a few of the many examples. Not a few took place in the early days of our country. To trivialize one's life because that person was a slave is a grievous moral injustice.

But the author does not preach this message to the reader. He weaves it skillfully into the warp and woof of the novel so that you do not realize what is coming until you are suddenly surrounded by it. By then, it is too late to avoid the conflict. Whether you agree or disagree, you have to deal with it.

Harriet Tubman is one of the most unusual, if not *the* most unusual women in history. It should not be surprising then, that the author's use of her in this book is unique. The interaction between Harriet Tubman and Catherine Morgan Hill is high drama. "Powerful" is the word that comes to mind.

Through the eyes of Catherine Morgan, we see Chancellorsville, Gettysburg, and the Wilderness Campaign in a way that we have never seen them before. We also see General Grant as the South saw him and it is quite different from the ordinary "Civil War Documentary" view.

Almost unparalleled in literature is the authors characterization of the fabled southern raider, General Nathan Bedford Forrest. Like Joe Christmas in Faulkner's *Light in August*, he seems to be quintessential good and quintessential evil in the body of one person. He is a major player in this compelling drama who is sure to evoke strong reactions from the reader.

It is common for people to think that everyone in the North opposed slavery and everyone in the South supported it. In that respect, I found the views of many southerners, Robert E. Lee and Mary Chesnut among them, quite surprising. Those views are across the entire spectrum. There were people wholly against slavery, others completely for it, and many nuances and subtleties in between. It is interesting to learn that the Southern brain trust had pretty much decided, even if the South won, slavery was on its way out and a program would have to be implemented to bring that to pass. It was only after the War, during the reconstruction period, that the tension between black and white turned to bitterness and hatred. One is caused to wonder what would have happened if the South had won?

Glory in the Dust captures the romance of the aristocratic South, the idealism of the Confederate movement, the changing face of warfare, and the importance of Southern women to the cause. I will not discuss the surprising twists that the story takes because I do not want to ruin the book for you. But I cannot imagine anyone reading this book and not feeling its excitement and importance.

I have known the author well, as a fellow performer and a close personal friend, for forty-eight years. He is a man with a brilliant mind, a vast accumulation of knowledge on an extraordinarily broad and far reaching number of subjects, and a rock-solid and time-tested moral character.

In my view, Earl Cripe has fashioned a masterpiece that will be regarded as an American classic in time. From my personal discussions with him about people, the arts, and the meaning of life, I must say that I am not surprised. In high school and college, Earl was an award-winning actor who had a bright future in show business if he had wanted it. This understated son of a Missouri Ozarks horse trader and a Kansas farm girl has always been a philosopher to whom those of our circle migrated when we wanted honest answers to serious questions. He is a gifted orator and writer. In fact, this book is the very kind of transcendent achievement in the Arts that I, and others who know him intimately, have always predicted for Earl. It could have happened years go. In 1962, he told us of his decision to make a vocation of novel writing. But then things changed in his life and convictions and Earl has his own reasons for having waited until now to put out this dramatic and compelling novel. I for one am glad he did. It has come at an important time in our country when many are looking to the past for an un-shifting foundation upon which to build a hopeful future in troubled and uncertain times. I believe this book can and will perform an important function in this vital area of national life.

I highly recommend this book to any and all who like to read; who appreciate writing excellence; who have an interest in the Civil War; and who like lucid tales of adventure, romance, danger, intrigue, and suspense. If you are one who would like to know more about the fabulous Catherine Morgan, you will like this book. And if you are among the growing number who want to see the women of the War get some much deserved and long overdue recognition, you will really like this book

/S/Chester Smith
Nashville, Tennessee

Preface

The most riveting, compelling, troubling event in the history of America was the Civil War. Far more than the Revolutionary War, The War with Mexico, the War of 1812, the Indian Wars, the First World War, or even the Second World War, the Civil War seizes the emotions and rouses the passions of Americans of all walks of life. The Civil War fosters in us feelings that we do not understand and cannot explain. In spite of the fact that it was the bloodiest war in our history and played against the shameful backdrop of father killing son, brother killing brother, and friend killing friend, it is revered in a romantic—almost hallowed—light. To the black man, that may be owing to the emancipation of slaves that resulted. But to most Americans, that is simply not the reason for our enchantment.

In this book, I have not tried to answer the mystery. Like many thinking men, I have some ideas as to why it is still our greatest national story. Some day I may attempt putting those ideas to pen. But that is not my reason for this writing. Like many Americans, I have had my own romance with the Civil War. I have about thirty books on the subject in my library which include the excellent series by Bruce Catton, Douglas Southall Freeman, and Shelby Foote. I have enjoyed immensely *Sherman the Fighting Prophet* by Lloyd Lewis and the masterful work *The Wilderness Campaigns* by Edward Steere. These are only a few of the many that I have read—some of them two and three times. It is not an exaggeration to say that I am pretty familiar with the Civil War and more than a little intrigued by it.

Even so, this book is not an attempt to tell the story of the Civil War from yet another perspective. It is exactly what the title page says: a novel. I have sometimes related events as they happened and perhaps from little known vantage points, but that is incidental to the goal. It is an attempt at a historical novel that will provide the reader with an interesting and thought-provoking diversion. It tells enough history to be real and enough fiction to be fun, interesting and, as always in fiction, an escape from the trials and pressures of the real world.

In order to give the book originality and spare it from the reactions of "here we go with another one of these," I have told the story from the perspective of the women of the War. There is the remarkable Harriet Tubman. Other principle women are the general's wives Ellen McClellan and Varina Davis. Also of note are Mary Chesnut the famous diarist, the renowned woman reporter Sarah Morgan, and Tuttle the slave girl.

But the story belongs to Catherine Morgan Hill. It is her story. I chose this beautiful, vivacious, intelligent, resourceful, loyal woman as the anchor of the book because she embodies what this story is all about—loyalty to the southern aristocracy, devotion to states' rights, fierce resistance to anything perceived as unfair or unjust, and devotion to family, friends, and subordinates that knew no limitations or boundaries.

And then, another prescriptive beckoned. I am not a laureate for the modern, feminist movement. But great women have always risen above their fated course and, in so doing, have invoked the homage of all but the envious and the insecure. Sarah of the Old Testament, Cleopatra, Joan of Arc, The Fair Elaine, and Helen of Troy have ever been venerated by the most gallant of men. Catherine Morgan Hill belongs in that sanctum of transcendent women. But because the Civil War is a man's story, this glorious, courageous, incredibly beautiful woman has never gotten the recognition that a person of her stature and influence in the War deserves. Perhaps it is the chivalry in me that I have worn her colors onto this auspicious and daunting field.

I stand in a certain esteem of all the women of this book, but none half so much as the winsome Miss Catherine.

Please remember that this is a novel. The liberties that I have taken with the lives of those in the story are justified by literary license. It has not been my intention to demean, deprive, or offend anyone who is a descendant of any participant in the Civil War, North or South. Since I am neither a historian nor a philosopher, the only way I can explore and advance some of my own thoughts is in fiction. If I am wrong, it does not matter. It is a novel—a fiction—only a story.

Earl Cripe
Columbia, California
August, 2003

Chapter One

The Pride and the Prejudice

The voice barked with an authority that was unique in the annals of military history.

"Sergeant, please do not leave! I wish you to come back in and sit down."

The Sergeant stared back with a bleak, red-eyed defiance. "With all due respect, Colonel, I do not wish to stay."

As painful and unpleasant as the situation was, the Colonel held his ground. "Although I said *please*, Sergeant, that is not a request, but an order."

The Sergeant did not yield. "What does it matter if I disobey," he said, gesturing fatalistically into the air.

The Colonel tried hard to keep control, both of his emotions and the military protocol. "I am still your commanding officer and you are a soldier and, as of this moment, my personal Aide. It does matter and you know it—for you, if not for me." He looked into the face of the Sergeant with a withering gaze. But the Sergeant did not melt. He said nothing but stared back with anger, resentment, hurt, and defiance. Finally he came back inside the door, closed it and sat down.

The Colonel pushed his chair back from his desk, crossed his legs, folded his arms across his chest and leaned back. He was the picture of a soldier: erect, neatly dressed, and well manicured with his silver-gray hair and beard meticulously trimmed. A large but finely featured head rested on massive shoulders and out of his smooth but somewhat leathery face, two large, steel-gray eyes stabbed like a cold north wind.

It was the best of times and the worst of times for Robert E. Lee. His position as Superintendent of the Military Academy at West Point on the Hudson had been the high point of his life. Out of a sense of duty, he had left West Point for an assignment in the west that eventually led him to Mexico. At the war's end, Lee was given two years military leave to attend to personal business. Then he was sent to a command in Texas but Lee fully expected and hoped to return to West Point one day. While there, the war pressures mounted. States were leaving the Union and talk that Virginia would not be far behind reached Lee from many quarters. Lee counseled against it. Secession was nothing short of revolution, he warned them. Abruptly he was summonsed to Washington and offered a generalship and an army of 75,000 men. Furthermore it was common knowledge that General Winfield Scott was planning of retire and was ready to write Lincoln a formal letter requesting that Lee be advanced to General and given the command of the United States Armed Forces. The word was out that Lincoln was in full agreement and the appointment was only a matter of a little time. How much Lee wanted that position, only he could know. It would be the crowning achievement of his military life, it would be exoneration for the sins and disgraceful behavior of his father, and it would make him one of the most respected and powerful men in the world. Lee retired to Arlington to think it over.

From his youth, Lee had never believed in slavery, either as a social convention or an economic platform. Furthermore, he was sure that, if war actually came, the South could not win out against the Union. He was fully against what was happening. The problem was that Lee was an aristocrat, born with loyalty to one's parents and one's state as a basic aspect of his character—indeed, his very being. To turn his back on either was cowardly and disloyal. He had agonized through the night after having received official word of the cessation of Virginia. In the end, it was clear to him what he had to do. The Sergeant he was facing had been with him since Mexico and there was no one Lee liked any better in the service. He understood the emotional and ethical rejection the Sergeant felt toward what he knew Lee was going to tell him. What the Sergeant did not know and could not know was that Lee's own feelings of defection and disloyalty to the Union were many times greater.

Finally the Sergeant spoke, some of the anger and resentment having subsided. "I know what you are going to tell me, Colonel Lee, and I did not want to hear it from you. How can you do this to a country whose well being and defense you swore to uphold until death?"

Lee had no answer to the question and did not attempt one. "Virginia is my home state, Sergeant," he said. "My mother and father were from her. My wife and family live there. Virginia is my roots and my cradle of life. I have spent my adult life trying to rebuild the family reputation in Virginia. What good will it do me to be a great man to the world if I am a traitor at home? I have to do this, don't you see?"

The Sergeant began to talk loudly again. "You are worried about reputation and integrity back home, but you don't give a damn for the fact that you put your hand on the Holy Bible and swore loyalty and allegiance to your country."

The remarks stung Lee and he fired back unthinkingly. "It appears that this may no longer be my country, Sergeant!"

The sergeant shook his head vehemently in disbelief. "The South is wrong, Colonel. Surely you know that!"

Lee sighed wearily; then took a deep breath. He had not counted on the Sergeant being so intransigent and so hostile. "It isn't a question of right and wrong, Sergeant," he said doggedly, "it is a question of blood."

The Sergeant stared hard at Colonel Lee. "Not a question of right and wrong? My God, Colonel Lee, what has happened to you?" Lee looked down and did not reply. The Sergeant rose to leave. He turned to look at Lee again. "I hope I never meet you on the battle field, Colonel, because if I do, I will kill you."

Lee grew philosophical and tried to be conciliatory.

"I suppose it may have come to that, Sergeant," he said. "Of course each man must do his duty as he sees fit." He offered a letter across the desk. “As a last act as my Aide, would you see that this gets to General Scott?”

The sergeant did not look at Lee. “I would prefer that you get someone else to do it, Sir. Anyway, I am not your Aide anymore; you have resigned, and . . . and I am not your friend anymore, either.”

Lee tried to break the awkward silence that followed. “Maybe this is all nothing, Sergeant,” he said in a conciliatory tone. “Maybe it will be resolved shortly and we can go on as always.”

The Sergeant started out the door. “I do not wish to serve with you anymore, Sir. I dislike being in the same room with traitors.”

The Sergeant left the room and Lee called after him.

“Good by, Sergeant. I will miss you. Thanks for your faithful service, and God’s speed.” The Sergeant did not look back nor reply.

Colonel Lee sat alone in the quite office at Arlington that had once been his sanctuary. How he had loved the power, the sense of fulfillment and the ambiance that came with being a major factor in the US Army. He loved his office with the big leather chair and the polished desk. It was his retreat where he felt peace, security, and fulfillment. But now it seemed so sad, dark, cold, dreary, and unfriendly. Lee blinked back the tears. He tried not to think about the Sergeant and the deep hurt that was trying to push into his soul. He had hoped desperately for some understanding; some sad but amicable and meaningful parting with his old friend. He had really needed that . . . really needed it—but. . .

Finally he rose, stiffly and tiredly, and left his life as an officer of the United States behind forever. He walked down the stairs and out onto the great lawn. As he looked off to the Potomac River and Washington beyond, he mused to himself, ‘Dreams—what shallow, deceitful, fickle, disappointing illusions. Maybe we are better not to dream—but then . . . but then . . .’

Lee shook his head sadly and walked around Arlington. As always, his posture was erect, and his pace brisk. But inside his head was down, his step was halting and his heart was numb with stunned disbelief.

Chapter Two

And She Was Fair To Look Upon

Early morning settled gently out of the night sky upon Hopemont, the Morgan estate on the outskirts of Lexington, Kentucky. Catherine, the youngest of the Morgan children and the only one still at home, stirred from her slumbers, rubbed the sleep from her eyes, and looked out through the honeysuckle at the barnyard scene familiar to her from childhood. She felt frustration as thoughts of events, threatening her present and future happiness, crowded into her mind. Her brother, Captain John Morgan, recently married the beautiful Mattie Ready and lived on the estate in separate quarters. Yesterday he secretly confided in Catherine that war was imminent and its outbreak could not be far off.

Catherine gasped to get her breath and reached a decision. She would not start the day worrying about this. She would get up, get things going right, and take control of her life. She needed something to bring back her sense of well-being and reinstall the confidence that characterized her emotional makeup. Catherine knew exactly what would do that.

At 7:30 A.M., the chill gave way to invigorating freshness. She rose quickly, shed her flimsy night robe, turned to the bed, put one knee upon it, and began critiquing herself in the full-length mirror on the wall behind. Rich, auburn hair, which shone with a deep luster that pleased her, flounced lightly on her back to about six inches below her shoulders. Her cameo skin glowed like a classic painting in the early light. Big, bright, green eyes sparkled in a perfectly formed, accentuated, and highlighted face. A long, smooth, aristocratic neck connected to shoulders that were exactly broad enough and perfectly rounded.

Her mother, Henrietta Hunt Morgan, looked through the blinds and saw her daughter posing. She came quietly out on the porch and sat down on the bed. Catherine turned sideways to acknowledge her mother, and then she looked over her shoulder at the profile in the mirror. Her chest was just the right size to accommodate her full, firm, naturally uplifted breasts.

She saw her mother glance at her briefly and then down at her hands. Catherine knew that her mother did not want to be caught looking at her because she did not wish to encourage this curious morning ritual, the wisdom and correctness of which her mother was in doubt. She followed her mother's gaze as Henrietta looked around the old porch as if trying to discover something she had missed through the years. "Catherine," her mother said more than once, "I simply do not understand your love for this old porch. It is nothing but a place of sweat and toil to me." As if defending her point of view, Catherine looked with her.

The cobbled floor on the west allowed the laundry water to run out under the wall into the French drain. This Spartan area, with finished but un-coated wood walls, a low, beamed ceiling and a few homely appliances, looked more like a part of a commoner's dwelling than the elegant house of an aristocrat, her mother said. The old cooler kept milk and butter in the winter when there was ice. Next to it, stood apple and potato bins. A bread cabinet and another closet that housed lanterns, overshoes, boots, and rain slickers filled out the wall. The only feature on the floor adjacent to the south wall was a laundry basin. The large, round wood stove for heating water and burning trash stood mid-point between north and south, and nearer the west wall. The day bed, table, a lamp, and chair took up the floor space near the east wall. Visitors were never allowed to see this rustic part of their cherished home. Catherine's father adamantly refused to do anything with it, saying that he would not spend good money on a utility area designed for the express purpose of chores. Her mother vowed, after he died, to remodel it, but she could not, out of deference to him. Though she never told her mother, it pleased Catherine. She wanted it to stay just the way it was.

Catherine turned to face the mirror and reviewed her small waist, her flat tummy, and her classically framed navel. Shapely hips, superbly lined, devolved into splendid thighs, their gentle, artistic curves flowing gracefully into exquisite legs, cute and dimpled knees, fetching calves with refined muscles, medium long ankles, and small feet. Then she turned back to her mother, whose eyes darted away and began inspecting the porch again. Catherine studied her for a moment, and went back over what she knew of her life.

Her mother had given birth to eight children at Hopemont: two girls and six boys. Catherine was the youngest. Her father and mother knew early on, or so they said, the uncommon womanly attributes possessed by her. But it was only in the last few years that her mother began to talk to others of her brilliant and beautiful mind and marvelous character. It pleased Catherine to know that the mother felt that way and she smiled warmly to herself.

She turned again and studied her profile. Smooth, healthy arms, with a hint of farm-girl muscle but not too large, hung easily at her sides. Long hands, good sized for a girl, featured strong but very lady-like fingers. Her entire anatomy was healthy and strong but not coarse, wholesome but not indelicate, and vibrant but couched in mystery.

From the mirror, Catherine saw her mother looking at her intently. Catherine knew the routine. Her mother made her point and would not look away this time. Catherine turned to her with an impish look and asked with 'little-girl' innocence: "Mamma, do you think I am prettier than Mattie?"

Catherine could see that the question surprised and displeased her mother, though she tried not to show it. "I don't know as I have thought about it," Henrietta said. "You are both very beautiful. Do you have to be prettier than she?"

Catherine made a pout. "No, I was just wondering. I mean, I think I am prettier than she is."

This bold statement broke through her mother's defenses. Catherine saw her mother take her face out of her hands in a purposeful gesture. She gave Catherine a baleful stare. "Sweetie, why in the world would you say something like that? What has gotten into you? Are you envious of Mattie?"

"Oh, Mamma, of course not, I was just…but I like her very much. She is very sweet—even though she does have quite a temper."

Her mother shrugged. "Well, she has more of a temper than you do, but then, so does everyone else." Then Henrietta turned sober. "But Catherine, it worries me so to see you primp in front of that mirror and stare at yourself."

Catherine brushed off the criticism with a smile and a toss of her head. "I am trying to be serious, Mamma."

Her mother looked non-plussed, as if she was not sure how to answer. She looked long at her beautiful child. Her mother had volunteered to her more than once that Catherine possessed that rare coincidence of complements that made her one of the great beauties of her era. Catherine realized that her mother, a widely noted beauty herself in her day, knew about such things. Catherine smiled inside as she remembered the words she had seen on an unfinished letter, left lying on the kitchen table, written to Mary Chesnut. Her mother wrote that her inimitable physical attributes and her marvelous character made Catherine Morgan a woman for the ages.

Finally, her mother answered. "So am I, Sweetie. And yes, if that is what you want to hear me say, you are prettier than Mattie. You are prettier than any other girl in the world."

Catherine started to protest, but then decided she would be playing mind games with her mother. After all, she had coaxed her mother into saying what she did.

Catherine wondered why her mother, who was so openly vocal about her beauty, struggled over Catherine looking at herself in the mirror.

Her mother, seeming to tune into her thoughts, continued after the long silence. "But sweetheart, it's not natural. Do you think God is pleased with your preening and strutting your pretty plumage like a peacock?"

Catherine grew sober and looked at her mother like a scolded child. "Mamma," she asked in earnest, "do you really worry about me because of this? I won't do it anymore, if I am causing you distress."

Her mother moved quickly to stop any thought of personal crisis. "Oh, no, it's just that…" Her mother fell silent and did not finish, but Catherine understood the answer.

Her mother got up from the bed, crossed the wood floor, and sat on the stool near the wash basin, where she could look at her daughter from a little distance. Catherine relaxed and breathed deeply. It was a pleasant morning. The crisp, fresh air, scented with honeysuckle, was almost intoxicating. Outside she could hear the ducks and geese beginning to move around.

Finally her mother asked, in her matronly tone, "Shouldn't you put on your robe, dear?"

Catherine made another pout. "Yes, Mamma—if I am making you uncomfortable."

"Oh, Catherine," her mother replied in a frustrated tone, "you are not making me uncomfortable."

Catherine seemed pleased. "Then I think I will sit here for a while," she said. "The air feels so good on me just now."

"Catherine…" Her mother seemed to be studying if she really wanted to ask the question on her lips. Then Catherine saw the resolve come into her mother's face. She braced herself mentally for what might be coming. "Catherine, do you ever think seriously about getting married?"

Catherine studied her mother quietly for a few moments. "It is funny you should ask just now," she said. "As a matter of fact, I have been thinking about it lately."

That seemed to please her mother who asked, "Do you mind if I ask who?"

"No, I don't mind. Ambrose Hill."

"Why, Catherine! Ambrose Hill. Really."

"Yes, don't you approve?" Catherine asked, knowing that her mother did not approve. It was not that she had anything against Captain Hill. He was comfortably well off in his own right, but not wealthy by any means and not an accepted member of the Lexington society or southern aristocracy in general. But Catherine could have her pick of plantation owners, wealthy aristocrats among the merchants and industrialists or men in high governmental places. Her mother set great store by such things, but Catherine set little. She was more interested in causes than in position and status. Catherine did not really need money anyway. She knew she would inherit Hopemont and a sizable fortune with it when her mother passed on.

In any case, it didn't matter to Catherine, all wrapped up in the pride of military men. She cared little about such things. Her fascination started with the military about four years ago when Catherine, who was sixteen at the time, went with her father to New York. Her father, who had access to just about anyone and anywhere, took her to West Point. There she met the commanding officer, Colonel Robert E. Lee of Virginia. Catherine came home almost in a trance. Her fixation with the Colonel lasted so long that her father finally gave her a real hard talking to. "It's fine for little girls to get crushes on teachers and preachers and generals, but you are going way too far with this. The man is nearly thirty-six years old, he is married, and he has three daughters. Now, I want this stopped. This is no way for a good Christian girl to be acting." Catherine moped for a while, and then came out of it, but she never lost her devotion to the military. Military men counted far more with her than bankers, politicians, or plantation owners.

Her mother, after a long pause, broke into her thoughts. "Well, it is not mine to approve or disapprove, is it?"

Catherine cared much about her mother's feelings on this. They would live at Hopemont with her mother after the war, if she were still alive. If she could get her mother to talk about it, Catherine felt certain she could get her to come around. "Perhaps not, Mamma," she said, "at my age, but you must have an opinion."

Her mother sighed uncomfortably. "Yes, of course, Sweetie. Well, I think Ambrose Hill is a fine man, and he is local too."

Catherine made a mock pretense of being hurt. "You don't think he is good enough for me, do you?"

"I don't think any man is good enough for my little Kitty," her mother answered, "but that's just silliness. If your heart is set on Captain Hill, he will pass fine with me." Her mother shifted uncomfortably. "Has he asked you, then?"

"No, but he will, particularly if I encourage him. He's very much the gentleman, you know. He is waiting for me to give him a sign."

Her mother chuckled and looked at her with kind amusement, she thought. "Many a young woman has thought that," her mother said, "only to find that it was not so cut and dried."

A bit of Catherine's youthful arrogance showed through. "I know, Mamma, but I am not 'many a young woman.' He will ask me, and when he does, I am going to marry him right away."

This seemed to concern her mother. "That abruptly? Should you not wait a bit for appearance's sake?"

Catherine shook her head quickly. She wanted to dispel any discussion of waiting. "There is going to be a war, Mamma, and I want to marry him before it starts. But don't worry, I will not go off and leave you."

"Oh, pooh! Catherine, you can't…"

"I will not, Mamma!" Catherine said, her emotions rising and the tears coming to her eyes. "There is no use talking about it. I know your unselfishness and your mother's love and how you would sit here and die in your loneliness and neglect to make your children happy. But I will not do it. You have no one but me and I am not going to abandon you. I will not get married if that is to be the result."

Her mother sighed. She knew it would do no good to argue. Catherine's love and loyalty to her mother were undying. She would not change her mind. "Well, let's not worry about it now. He hasn't asked you yet, and I am getting pretty old, you know."

Catherine fussed. "You are not that old. Don't you feel well?"

Her mother answered fatalistically. "Oh, I feel okay, I guess—but sometimes I don't. Sometimes I get dizzy spells and my heart beats fast and then slow—not always, or even often—but sometimes."

Catherine frowned in genuine worry. Since a child, she dreamed of something happening to her mother and father. She despised that terrible dream, and she hated the thought. She knew that someday it would happen to her mother, as it had to her father, and Catherine could do nothing about it. She had a difficult time being objective about things she could not plan for and could not think her way through.

Her mother broke into her thoughts again. "What makes you think there will be a war? Your brother does not think so."

Catherine shifted on the bed. She squinted her eyes as she looked at her mother over her right shoulder. She did not want her mother to know Catherine and her brother had talked privately about it and left her out of it. "My brother says that because he is the one who has formed the home guard and he doesn't want to alarm people," she answered carefully, weighing every word, "but he knows; I can tell you that. The South has to fight, Mamma. We will never give up state control to the central government."

Catherine ached a little as she saw her mother shake her head in bewilderment. "Well, Catherine, I hope they don't fight over something like that—don't you?"

Catherine looked out through the honeysuckle so her mother could not see her face. "If we are going to fight over anything, it might as well be that."

"Catherine!" her mother said, the surprise registering in her voice, "Do you mean that you are in favor of the South going to war for independence?"

Catherine hesitated. She liked neither her tone nor the feelings inside of her. Still, in these desperate times, people made choices that they ought not have to make. "Yes, I am, Mamma."

Her mother groaned a bit in disappointment. "I am flabbergasted!"

"Do you think I am awful?" Catherine asked conciliatorily.

"No," her mother replied, trying to sound objective, "it's not that. It's just that I am surprised."

Catherine tried to shift the emphasis from herself to the issue. "Are you so set against war?"

"No, I guess not," her mother said, looking very vulnerable, "if that is what the men folks want, it is just that, well, my sons…"

"Oh, Mamma, of course; how perfectly dreadful of me! I am so sorry."

"No, no, Sweetie, it's all right now, I…"

Just then, the screen door opened and Emmanuel started in with the milk. When he saw Catherine sitting on the bed, he froze, his eyes dilating with terror. As she frantically tried to cover herself with blankets, he dropped the pail, covering the wooden floor with milk and foam, and fled.

Chapter Three

The Appearance of Evil

Mrs. Morgan was in a panic. "Catherine! Oh no!" she fairly shouted. "The nerve of that boy! Why, I'll..."

Catherine realized the situation and the excitement in her mother. She cut in quickly and firmly. "No, Mamma, it is not his fault. It is mine for sitting around at this time of day with nothing on. Emmanuel comes in here every morning with the milk. Usually I have the door latched when I am out here. I don't know what happened. I must have forgot to check it last night."

This did not soften her mother. "But Catherine, he saw you with nothing on. That boy will never get that picture of you out of his mind. He will die with it. This cannot be allowed. He has to be punished."

Catherine saw clearly the seriousness that could come out of this, and her mind was racing for some way to get control of the situation. "Mother, I am surprised at you," she said sternly. "Punished for what?"

Catherine did not often refer to her as 'Mother' and it meant that Catherine was ready to do battle. This brought her mother up short. "Well, at least, he will have to go."

Catherine softened a little and became philosophical. "Mamma, I am not hurt—embarrassed—but not hurt. It is one of those unfortunate things that happens. It means nothing more than we make of it. You must promise me that you will say nothing at all about this to anyone. The men of the town will be out here trying to lynch poor Emmanuel if this gets out. The hot heads will never believe that he did not do it on purpose, and he will have no one to stand up for him."

Catherine got up and began dressing in work clothes. "I have to go and talk to poor Emmanuel. He is huddling in terror somewhere. I have to find him before he runs away."

Her mother started to rise. "I'll go talk to him, Sweetie, you…"

"No, I have to do it, Mamma. Emmanuel will never be able to be around me or to look at me if I do not get to him right now."

Tension and worry sounded in her mother's reply. "Well, you be careful."

Catherine stopped to give her a look of reproof. "Mamma! Be careful of what? Anyway, it's not Emmanuel I am worried about, it's Tuttle."

"Tuttle? Why in the world are you worried about Tuttle?" her mother said, as if she wondered about Catherine's sincerity.

"Because she is a wife. Maybe she will think I am trying to vamp her husband. She knows I know that he comes in here every morning."

The remark scandalized her mother. "Oh Catherine, really!"

"Well, there's a lot of 'high yellas' running around Mamma," Catherine said, stuffing in her shirttail. "Somebody has been vampin' somebody—unless they just fell out of the sky. And before you say anything, I got that from your beloved Mary Chesnut." Catherine did not believe that white women were involved in those situations, but she wanted to get the attention off Emmanuel.

Her mother defended the virtue of southern womanhood. "You know that is all white men and Negra women."

"I suppose," Catherine replied. "Anyway, an accident can't be helped once it's done. I am sure it will not ruin his life, Mamma, and it certainly will not ruin mine." Then she went out to find Emmanuel. As she neared the vehicle shed, she saw Emmanuel dart out the back and run for the barn. "Emmanuel, stop right there," she shouted. She hated to talk to him in that tone of voice, but she knew he would keep on running if she did not. As she neared him, he had one foot in the air and a wild look of fear in his eyes. If only she could reach him before he snapped. Gently but without hesitation, she reached out and put her hand on his shoulder. "Emmanuel," she said quietly, "No one is going to hurt you. You did not do anything wrong." Slowly he lowered his foot to the ground. The wild look went away but fear remained and he was trembling. "Emmanuel," she said with gentle authority, "I want you to come with me to the colonnade. We must sit down and talk." She started to walk, then looked back. He was still standing there in indecision and fear. "Come on," she said pleasantly.

Emmanuel regained enough composure to ask a halting question. "Whose out der, Ma'am? What dey gonna' do to me? You takin' me to dat big tree wid the hangin' limb. I ain't dumb like you thinks I am, Miss Cath'n; I know what happens to black men that looks at white women in de wrong way. Hab dey got rope?"

Catherine hurt inside and wanted to cry but there was no time. The next few minutes were crucial to her life and his. "You know me, Emmanuel," she said calmly. "You know you can trust me. No one is going to hurt you; I promise you that. Now come with me, please, we cannot talk standing here in the middle of the path." She began walking again and slowly he followed.

Chapter Four

The Long Steel Rail

Catherine sat at a table in The Planters Horn, a restaurant in Lexington, having lunch with her friend Colonel Wolf. On a chilly day, the sun felt good through the window, but it was too warm for a coat. As she stood up to take it off, the Colonel rose to help her. He surveyed her light blue gingham dress, with a dark blue bodice, white linen cross laces and a splendid gold necklace with midnight blue sapphires. "My word, Miss Kitty," he said proudly, "You do wear the prettiest things." Then he grew thoughtful. She blushed as he said, "Of course, I believe a gunny sack, on you, would look like a coronation gown."

She took a bite of her sandwich and put it down. "Ummm," she said to the Colonel, "Why is it that food smells and tastes so much better in restaurants?"

The Colonel frowned. "It doesn't; not to me. But maybe that is because I eat out a lot. There is nothing to compare to home cooking in my book."

Catherine studied her friend as they sat there passing the time. In his early fifties and a career soldier, he looked so elegant in his new gray uniform with the red trim. When states began to pull out of the Union, he changed his loyalties to the Confederacy. Davis promoted him from captain to Colonel and put him in charge of the telegraph center and commissary. His ancestry was German and he looked the part. He was a big man with an expanded girth. His large head featured gray hair that was starting to bald, a round face that was jolly most of the time, and pale blue eyes that were alert and penetrating. John had told her that Davis wanted him in charge of this strategic cross roads because of his high intelligence and the ability to run an efficient operation without close supervision. He was sort of her godfather since the death of her own father, and he seemed to like that role.

Catherine looked out of the window at the loading platform. Three strange looking men moved nervously on the dock, waiting for the train to leave. Soldiers from Colonel Wolf's unit stood guard, protecting them. Catherine leaned close to the Colonel and nodded her head in their direction. "Colonel Wolf, who are those men?" she asked.

The Colonel answered in a confidential tone. "They are emissaries from President Davis on their way from Montgomery to Washington."

Catherine registered surprise. "Why are they traveling through Lexington?" she asked.

The Colonel shrugged as he answered, "It doesn't make much sense to me—part of the Davis penchant for intrigue, I guess. He gave them this indirect route because he is fearful that their mission is known, and an attempt to intercept them will be made by those whose hearts are set on war. Well, anyway," he said, "It isn't that far out of the way, I guess."

Catherine tried not to act as interested as she was. "I wonder what message they have for Lincoln?" she asked.

Colonel Wolf nodded his head positively. "Yes," he said, "Well, they are supposed to have a deal from Davis to Lincoln that will prevent the war." Catherine looked disappointed.

The Colonel looked hard at her and his mood changed abruptly. "Oh, yes," he said in a testy tone, "you young people think war is fun, don't you? Well, when you have lost a father and three brothers in one, then you will think differently. If anything will prevent war, Kitty, I am for it."

Catherine did not know what to say and fell silent for a while. His tragic story had not dampened her enthusiasm for war. At the risk of sounding calloused, she asked, "Do you know what the proposition is?"

Wolf remained silent for a moment, as if trying to regain his composure. The server brought some more coffee and the aroma was delightful to Catherine who never drank coffee at home. She sipped it while piping hot and thought she had developed a genuine taste for it. She looked up at the still-frowning Colonel.

"Yes," he said, in a delayed answer to her question, "they will offer Lincoln a guarantee of safe shipping on the Mississippi in exchange for abandoning Fort Sumter."

Catherine tensed inside as she realized the attractiveness of the offer. "Will Lincoln do it, do you think?" she asked.

Wolf shrugged his massive shoulders. "He will, if he has any sense. But the way I hear it, he will not."

Catherine tried to suppress the relief she felt inside so it would not show. She thought of another question. "How long are they to be in Washington?" she asked.

"They come back through here in three days," he said.

"Will you know if they succeeded or not?"

"Maybe," he answered.

"Will you tell me?"

"Yes, I can probably tell you that," Wolf replied. Catherine fell silent and thinking. "Better eat your lunch, Kitty, it is getting cold," he said. Catherine smiled meekly and took his advice. As she munched a carrot, she watched the train pull out, her mind following after it and the three men. She tried to envision the scene in Washington. On the way home, Catherine was engrossed in thoughts and imaginations that became more troubling as the minutes passed. Would the three men be successful? Would Lincoln accept their proposition? Was the South to be denied independence?

When she reached Hopemont, her imaginations had turned to worry and gloom. Her mother saw her dilemma. "All right, Sweetie," she said in a matronly tone, "Suppose you tell me what is troubling you."

"Oh, Mamma," she said wearily, "Important and exciting things are happening. The future of Kentucky is being negotiated by fools and all I can do is sit and try to keep my sanity in the meanwhile."

Her mother looked at her narrowly. "And just whom do you mean by 'fools'?" she asked.

Catherine gestured fatalistically into the air with one of her hands. "Lincoln and three silly looking emissaries from President Davis," she said disgustedly.

Her mother was kind but stern. "Catherine," she asked, "What good did it do to spend the time and money to send you to catechisms? The Gentleman's name is 'President' Lincoln. And when did you start judging the ability of officials on the basis of their looks?"

Catherine put her hands to her face and began to cry. When her mother did not console her, Catherine took out a hanky, dried her eyes, and took a deep breath. "I know I am being impertinent," she said, "and I apologize."

"Very well," her mother said, "Now Catherine, I want you to listen to me. You are going to work yourself up into a dither if you do not stop this undisciplined champing at the bit."

"But Mamma," Catherine said, leaning forward and spreading her hands, "At this very minute, our future is in jeopardy. How can I just sit by, do, and think nothing?"

Her mother put up her hands in a plea for calm. "That very well may be," she said, "but what are you and I to do about it? It is best left to those in positions of authority whose calling it is to make such decisions. If we try to take matters into our own hands, we will only make them worse."

Catherine sighed deeply and grew calm. "Yes, Mamma, I know. But maybe they will not do the right thing."

Her mother grew philosophical. "They are only men and it is an imperfect world."

Catherine nodded her head. "Oh, yes, I know you're right," she said like a little girl. "Now I don't know if I can sleep and this may go on for three days before I know what's happening."

"You will be able to," her mother said calmly. "God gives his little ones sleep. The best way to turn off the worry that keeps one awake and bring rest is to pray. Pray for President Lincoln; pray for President Davis; pray for the three men."

"Will that assure me that they will do the right thing?" Catherine asked.

Her mother thought for a moment. "The right thing?" she asked philosophically. "Maybe not what you consider to be right, Sweetie, but it will assure you that the will of God will be done. We can't ask for more than that."

Catherine was suddenly very tired. She kissed her mother and went up to bed. She was thinking what to ask God to do about President Lincoln when she fell asleep.

On the afternoon of the second day, Catherine was in the slave quarter putting cold rags on Tuttle's brow to bring down her high fever when a messenger arrived from Colonel Wolf.

"What is the message?" she asked the courier.

"I don't know, Ma'am," he replied. "It is in this envelope and I did not look at it."

Catherine dried her hands on her dress, sat down on Tuttle's bed, tore it open, and began to read:

Miss Kitty. The emissaries will be here sometime tomorrow morning. As soon as I know anything, I will brief you. There is no need to come early. It will be late morning or noon before I know anything. I will be at the railroad station.

Wolf.

Catherine felt the rush of excitement but this time without the anxiety and frustration. The flow of emotions was in the right direction. As she lay down to sleep that night, her mind did not want to shut down. It was not the worried, anxious fretting of recent days, but an excitement of sorts. She tried to envision the three men getting off the train and imagined what they would have to say. Would Colonel Wolf have any news about that situation?

It was there that her thoughts began to drift and become infiltrated with nonsense. Colonel Robert E. Lee and Captain Hill appeared, talking about something. Then suddenly Colonel Lee was no longer a man but a horse pulling her buggy. Colonel Wolf appeared from nowhere, addressing her as general, and asking for orders. She looked at her arms and was surprised to see that she was wearing a uniform. Then everything went black.

Chapter Five

To War or Not To War

Catherine left Hopemont early in response to Colonel Wolf's message. Against the chill morning air, she snuggled her cheeks down in the wool-lined collar of her tartan coat. Under the coat, she wore a corduroy green and tan vest over an off-white blouse with ruffles and a long, flowing gray tweed skirt. Hopemont was north of the railroad station where Catherine needed to go to meet her friend Colonel Wolf. The road, a solid clay base, was rutted a little from summer use. The highbred pacer, instinctively wandering in the road to choose the best surface, moved along easily, making only a clipping sound on the hard surface. The buggy bumped a little but the transverse spring deadened the shock and Catherine felt little discomfort. The cool, dew-laden air dampened the road and only a wisp of dust trailed along behind the buggy.

Having left without breakfast, Catherine pulled a big, cold, red apple from her pocket. The sweet-tart taste was good and it helped brighten her countenance.

It would take the pacer about a quarter of an hour to trot the distance to the train depot. To Catherine, filled with anxiety and anticipation, the distance shrank so slowly just sitting and watchingthe road ahead. She looked around at the scenery to make the time pass.

Far to the south, she saw the rugged outline of the Appalachians, their high peaks bluish-purple in the mountain mists. Closer to her, were vast fields of Kentucky burley tobacco. To the west, she looked across neat, white wooden fences to rolling fields of bluegrass, dotted with small stands of Kentucky Ash. Thoroughbred mares grazed contentedly, their foals frolicking around them. From distant farm buildings, Catherine could hear roosters crowing and the occasional barking of a ranch dog.

About half way to the depot, Catherine passed Waveland, the mansion and estate of Joseph Bryan, grandnephew of Daniel Boone. Next, she came to Ashland, the beautiful brownstone palatial manor built by Henry Clay in 1812, the year of the war. It was surrounded by huge green, thickly matted lawns and lined by magnificent stands of Kentucky Ash, from whence its name derived. In the still of the early morning, not a leaf rustled and Catherine thought they looked like majestic, silent sentinels.

As she reached the edge of town, she passed the beautiful two-story brownstone and red brick townhouses; their porticos supported by pilasters or columns featuring ornate Corinthian capitals and well-worked cast iron bases. Thick, dark-green hedges walled rich lawns. Neatly gardened flowers, Dogwoods, and Broad Leaf Maples were a common sight. Kentucky Ash lined the streets.

As she rocked along in her buggy, Catherine breathed deeply, taking in the wonderful aromas of the farms, the tobacco fields, the exotic perfume of the Dogwood blossoms, and the delicious odors of fresh-baking bread and other culinary delights that wafted on the early morning air.

As she turned on Broadway, in route to the train station, she could see the buildings and grounds of Transylvania University. Catherine swelled with pride. Her Grandfather, John Wesley Hunt and Mary Lincoln's farther, Richard Todd, helped found it. Now, in its eightieth year, it was the oldest institution of higher learning west of the Alleghenies. Jefferson Davis, John C. Breckenridge, and Edward M. Johnston were among its graduates. As she neared the far edge of the grounds, she passed the little old cabin of Robert Patterson, one of the early settlers. He built it before the town was organized in 1781.

A little farther along she looked out on the Keene property, purchased from Patrick Henry who received it as a grant from the government in the frontier days. There was talk of a harness racing track in the not-too-distant future, and it was causing a sizable controversy in the community.

She smiled as she reached Market Street and passed Christ Church. The Gothic revival building, erected in 1845, was her church, and the Episcopalians had owned the property since 1791.

As she turned on West Main Street and neared the station, she looked up at the fourteen-room mansion of the Todds, built in 1806, eight years before Hopemont, but owned by the Todds since 1832. Catherine took some satisfaction in that knowledge, though she did not know exactly why.

Catherine came back from her thoughts at the sight of Colonel Wolf standing near the station depot. She went to him and asked, "The three men—are they here yet?"

Wolf shook his head. "No, but they will be soon. They are on a siding outside of town, waiting for this train from Montgomery to pass." He paused and looked a bit worried. "But, Catherine, it will be several hours, if at all, before I know anything. There are going to be talks. I probably will not be in on them. After that, I will find out what I can. You should not have come down so early."

"I know; you made that clear. But I was so keyed up I wanted to be down here when the train comes in. Is that all right? I mean; I can…"

Colonel emitted a worried sigh. "Oh, no, I guess it's all right, if you don't mind hanging around. It just seems to me that…" His voice trailed off and he did not finish his sentence.

Catherine saw something that sparked her interest. "That man in the gray suit…who is he? I mean…I am sorry. Do you know…?"

Colonel Wolf did not wait for her to rephrase her question. "Yes, that is John Lamon, a law partner of President Lincoln."

Catherine raised her eyebrows. "What's he doing down here?"

"He's coming back from Charleston…a meeting with Governor Pickens," Wolf answered. "I am a little surprised. He wasn't supposed…well, I mean, we didn't expect him on this train."

Catherine did not want to press too hard but she must know all she could. "What was that all about? Another deal to prevent war?"

Wolf gave her a long, penetrating look and then answered. "We have a rumor that he told the governor Sumter will not be re-supplied."

"How did the rumor come to you?" she asked.

"Well…" Wolf looked around to see if anyone was listening and then lowered his voice. "We got a wire at the office last night from the train depot. Pickens was out on the town introducing Lamon and telling everyone that he had assurances the Fort would be abandoned. There was supposed to be something akin to a parade in Lamon's honor today." Catherine felt the disappointment return. Wolf gave some reassurance. "I don't think it is going to be that way," he said.

"What makes you think that?" she asked.

Wolf was philosophical. "Well, I told you we had information that Lincoln was going to re-supply it," he said. "It is hard for me to believe that the President would send a law partner to convey a message like that. Now, here is Lamon, not staying for the big celebration today. It just looks like something is amiss to me."

The train to Washington pulled out and in about ten minutes, the southbound eased up to the boarding dock. The three men got off and Colonel Wolf's men escorted them immediately to the waiting carriages. The Colonel started to leave, but then turned to Catherine. "Where will you be if I find anything out?"

"In the Planter's Horn, I guess," she said reflectively. "I haven't had breakfast yet. I can probably string it out over two hours."

The Colonel seemed to be genuinely concerned about her anxiety in the meanwhile. "Well, no doubt there will be someone coming along with whom you can pass the time of day," he said.

Catherine shook her head negatively. "I don't want to talk to anyone just now, I…"

When she did not continue, the Colonel nodded in agreement. "Yes, I see what you mean. It might be best at that."

He started to leave but Catherine stopped him. "I suppose it is silly of me to ask, but…that tall man, standing outside the smoking car…do you know who he is?

The Colonel looked down at her. “You don’t miss anything, do you Miss Kitty? Yes, he is Commander Robinson, of the U.S. Navy.”

“I suppose he is on his way to Charleston too?” she asked.

“Well, he is actually headed for Fort Sumter if our information is correct.”

“What is he going there for?” she asked. “Is he going to take over from Major Anderson?”

“No,” the Colonel answered emphatically. “He is going to discuss the feasibility of rearming the Fort.”

“Really,” Catherine said with surprise. “How did you get that information?”

Wolf looked as if he was trying to think whether to tell her or not. Then he said, very confidentially, “Major Anderson is a Kentucky boy. He got the word to us.”

Catherine reacted with annoyance. “But I thought he chose to stay with the Union. Why would he give us that information?”

“There is a real conflict in his mind, Catherine,” he said, “as there is with others. Some of these men put their hands on the Bible, swore loyalty to their country to the death, and then had to choose between that and loyalty and love for their people and their state. Until you stand on that spot, you will never know what they are going through or why they chose as they do.”

“But Captain Hill and…”

“Yes, I know. And me and Colonel Lee and lots of others. But then there are men…deeply religious men, some of them…who feel that their word is their bond and it is better not to vow than to vow and not to pay it. Some of them feel that their integrity and…and their souls, even, maybe…are at stake. Don’t forget that Lincoln is a Kentucky boy, and so was John Brown.”

Catherine felt shaken as she asked, “But Colonel Wolf, how then…?”

“Look, Catherine,” he said firmly, “I don’t want to discuss it now. I will be in touch as soon as I can. If the time drags on and I do not appear, it is because I don’t know anything, or that I can’t get away. But I will find you as soon as I can; I promise you.” With that, he was gone.

When the southbound pulled out, Catherine walked to the tracks and looked after it. There was something nostalgic, poignant, and a little haunting about looking down the long, shimmering track at a distant disappearing image. It made her feel left out, like she wanted to be on that train and going too…to wherever.

She thought about Commander Robinson and wondered what he and Major Anderson would talk about and decide…if anything. Then she turned and looked the other way. And John Lamon…what really happened in Charleston yesterday? Did he tell Governor Pickens that Sumter would not be re-supplied? And if he did, was Wolf right about his having overstepped his bounds? And what would Commander Robinson and Major Anderson decide? Would Anderson make a decision with the people of Kentucky taken into consideration? As a northern officer, how could he? She just could not believe what Colonel Wolf had said and she felt…she felt just a little anger about it. You had to be for one side or the other. You could not be for both.

The re-supply of Sumter would mean war. Everyone agreed on it. Catherine believed that if war did not come, the South would cave in to the North, and everything they knew and loved would change. On the other hand, she was not a mercenary. She also knew, or at least she thought she knew, some of the horror war would bring. She found herself both hoping that they could prevent war and that they would not.

The wind came up sharp and a cloud moved over and darkened the day, adding to her melancholy, almost eerie feelings. A hint of coal smoke still wafted on the air and her face was stinging as she stood there, her hands jammed down in her coat pockets for warmth, looking up and down the track and wondering about the two strangers that she had never seen before. Could their missions have anything to do with her destiny? Reason would say no; that she was just indulging in intrigue and mystery. But somewhere inside of her, she could not shake the feeling that it was otherwise.

An hour before dark, Catherine gave up and went home. The ride was filled with angst as each passing moment moved her further away from the center of importance. She fought hard against the desire to become angry and impatient with the Colonel for not letting her know something. Frustration kept her from settling down and she feared that it was going to be a long night.

The following day, Catherine was in the colonnade brooding when a cab arrived in the yard. A young soldier was driving. "Colonel Wolf respectfully requests your presence, Ma'am," he said. "He sends word that he is now ready to brief you on everything." The sundial in the garden moved beyond the mid-point of the afternoon when Catherine got in the cab. The trip into town seemed to take forever to a nervous and edgy Catherine, gripped in the vice of suspense.

During Colonel Wolf's briefing, the frustrations subsided but guilt took their place.

"Well, Miss Kitty, your worries were all for nothing," he said cynically. "It has been verified that Lincoln did not authorize Lamon to say what he did. Furthermore we have had word from Charleston that Robinson and Anderson have agreed the Fort should be re-supplied."

"Did Major Anderson…?" she started to ask.

"No, at least not yet," Wolf cut in. "One of the sailors that went with Robinson got liquored up and started talking."

"But are we sure, then…?" she asked.

"That the Fort will be re-supplied?" he questioned. "Not for sure, but the three men came back with tales of deceit and duplicity. Lincoln is sending out Seward to tell people one thing, and then Lincoln is reneging and saying that he gave no such assurances."

"So then, they will tell President Davis that the Fort will be re-supplied?" she asked.

Colonel shook his head negatively. "Their message from Seward is that an announcement will be made by Lincoln to Governor Pickens, informing him Sumter will be abandoned."

"When is this supposed to be done?" Catherine asked.

"It is hard to pin anything down in this strange situation," Wolf replied, "But I think it is to be in three to four weeks."

"Why so long?" she asked.

Wolf shrugged. "Ostensibly, Lincoln has to get, or wants to get, full agreement with congress and cabinet before he acts.

Catherine saw where he was headed. "And you do not believe Lincoln will do it," she said.

"No I don't," the Colonel said, "And if not, the South will be forced into action. It looks very much, Kitty, like you have got your beloved war. I just hope, young lady, that you do not forget, before it is all over—when Negras are living in your house and you are out chopping cotton—how bad you wanted it."

The Colonel's remarks stung Catherine sharply. "Colonel," she said, trying to be strong but having a difficult time, "I never said I wanted war."

"You didn't?" the Colonel, asked, not sparing her. "Well, that's what I saw on your face and heard in your tones."

"Colonel," she said defensively, "you are being very strident with me on the basis of your deductions. I never said one time that I wanted war."

The Colonel looked at her with a cocked eye. "Oh, so you are telling me that you were not disappointed at the thought that Sumter would not be re-supplied and that there might not be war? Well then maybe I owe…"

"No, I am not going to lie about it," she cut in. "But I had other feelings, too. At times, I found myself hoping that the Fort would not be re-supplied. I don't know how I feel about all this, exactly." Catherine's emotions were building as she took out her handkerchief and blew her nose. "But Colonel Wolf," she said passionately, "if we don't fight to protect our states' rights, the Government will come in and take our plantations and then we may very well have…have…"

"But Kitty," he replied in the tone of an advocate, "We may not face that. We have a way of life now and so far, there is only talk of changing it. If war comes, and it will, it is going to change, one way or the other."

"But the South will win, Colonel Wolf," Catherine said, her voice rising. "You believe that, don't you? You went with the South."

"I went with my heart, Kitty; not with my head," Wolf answered.

"What? What are you saying? Colonel Wolf, surely…"

"I don't know, Kitty," he said, his voice sounding tired. "I don't know. I am a soldier, not a politician, and there are lots of things these politicians are not taking into…" The Colonel stopped, walked to the window and looked out for a moment. Then he turned back to her with a different look on her face. "Look, Kitty," he said, "I was hard on you, and I am sorry. It's just that…I have been in war and I know what is coming. You have not been, and you don't."

"But I can't do anything about it," she said innocently, "It will either come or it will not."

"That is true," Colonel Wolf said in softer tones. "But how you feel about it and how you talk to others about it and how you feel about your enemies…those things will all be very important one day…maybe even more important than the outcome of the war. I once wanted war and…" The Colonel's eyes began to cloud. Then he said, "Kitty, let's don't talk about it any more, not now anyway. We have had our say; let's go on being friends." He paused and smiled at her, "When is your wedding?"

"In four weeks," she said.

The Colonel walked over to her. "I want to be able to look forward to that with the same joy I have always felt about my place in your life. If war comes, we are on the same side." He took her hands and lifted her out of the chair. "It's getting on toward dark and I am going to get you home."

Catherine saw his emotional dilemma. "I accept your apology, Colonel Wolf," she said. "And I apologize too. I do want to go on being friends. You are the best friend I have besides Mamma. I…oh…"

Colonel Wolf put his finger to his lips. "Enough," he said quietly. "Now you know everything I know. Go home and get some rest."

As the horse drummed its two-step rhythm and the cab rocked along the empty road to Hopemont, Catherine's mind buzzed with confusing thoughts. She hoped her mother would still be up.

Chapter Six

A Time to Wed

Hopemont shined with a glory never before seen in her fifty-year history. The famous fan-lighted doorway and the huge Palladian window were brilliantly decorated. Catherine and her sister individually polished every bauble on the massive chandelier in the great room. The white marble porch, with its ornate Corinthian columns and classic Greek capitals, was as clean and polished as the ballroom floor. The great room, the porch and the large, richly matted, closely mowed lawn were alive with gentlemen and their ladies from all over Kentucky and beyond. Rigs and unhitched horses filled the barn and the yard. Servants borrowed from neighboring estates unharnessed, fed, watered, and bedded down those staying over.

Almost as if by a signal, the hum of talking ceased and all eyes focused on the famous cantilevered staircase with elaborate woodwork, reed fluting and bulls eye design. At the head of it, on the arm of her uncle, Charlton Hunt, first mayor of Lexington, was a breath-taking sight. The radiant Catherine Morgan, her auburn hair perfectly done and shining richly in the candlelight, was making her last descent as a maiden. A murmur of surprise and awe rippled through the crowd as she started down. From behind the broad knit veil, her bright green eyes sparkled like emeralds on white sands in the clear waters of a vernal pool. Her cameo complexion glowed with a candescence angelic. Her ruby red lips parted to reveal perfectly matched, ivory white teeth, star-crossed in the candlelight. The gorgeous wedding dress, made by her mother's friend and celebrated seamstress Sally Grace of Montgomery, Alabama, was a labor of love and a work of art. Intricate embroidery and needlework perfectly matched her aura. Catherine stole a glance down at the fig-leaf hem that glided effortlessly over the polished wood of the stair and felt the gentle tug of the lovely train that followed obediently behind. Once on the floor, she stopped to face Colonel Wolf who proposed a toast to her. "To the inimitable Catherine Morgan," he said with more formality and eloquence than she thought him capable of:

"If form, or face, or charm, or grace
Of excellence, you have the most.
To your unrivaled eminence
With glasses raised, we drink this toast."

Catherine swelled with pride. Toastmasters were expected to author their own verse and it was always an anxious moment. It wasn't exactly Browning but Colonel Wolf passed with colors flying high. Because of accessibility to the fireplace, only the men of the wedding party hurled their glasses. Catherine wondered how they would get all that glass out of the fireplace.

Catherine looked at her brothers, so neat and handsome in their black tails, white bow ties, and white carnations. She smiled approvingly at her beautiful sister, resplendent in the gorgeous gown made for her by the Lexington chapter of the Daughters of Kentucky. She saw the quiet but deeply smiling face of her mother in that beautiful dress made for only her mother to wear. She glanced at the servant's door and saw the grinning faces of Emmanuel and Tuttle in the simple black suit with black tie and the plain white dress that she had made them for this occasion. They were so proud that they were about to bust wide open, and Catherine was proud that they were proud.

The altar was set up in the famous Hopemont garden. The guests sat and stood on the lawn, bathed in the shade of a stand of Kentucky Ash, planted to protect from the afternoon sun. Catherine glanced around from behind her veil. Her mother had invited most everybody who was anybody in Kentucky. Most of them were there. Each of her brothers and her sister were allowed to invite two persons without approval. Her brother Key, in Lexington, Virginia, studying under Jonathan Jackson at Virginia Military Institute, had invited Robert E. Lee, who attended. Her husband-to-be, also a Virginia man, was not allowed to whisper to her before the wedding. But he looked proudly at Lee and then at her. She told him with her eyes that she saw Lee.

Captain Hill had petitioned Catherine's mother that the service be the short variety being afforded military men these days, but Catherine, to her mother's delight, refused. They suffered through the entire hour and a half long ceremony. It was only right. Everyone should have to suffer something for anything so valuable. How much could a wedding mean if they took the easy way? By the time it was over, Parson Edwards had reiterated most of the great marriages of the Bible, giving an embarrassingly frank discussion of marital duty and they gave audible assent to each and every one. In the end, Captain Hill slipped on her finger a beautiful diamond handed down from his Irish Great Grandmother. Everyone cheered and the festivities began. The Lexington Chamber Orchestra, consisting of several violins, a cello, a flute, and making use of the famous Morgan piano with a fourth pedal giving the effect of drums and fife, provided the music. Catherine waded through the first dance with her husband as gracefully as she could. She did not care whether he could dance or not, but everyone standing aside and watching made it a little hard. Then she danced with her uncle, a very good dancer and everyone else got on the floor in the great room or on the porch and joined in. At the completion of the dance, she felt a peck on her shoulder. She turned to see the grinning face of her husband with Robert E. Lee in tow. "My Dear," he said like a little boy, "Would you honor Colonel Lee and me by giving him this dance?" The number was the Blue Danube Waltz. The Colonel danced as lightly as the gentle afternoon breeze that buffeted her cheek.

"You are a remarkable dancer, Colonel Lee," she said, trying to sound sophisticated.

"Thank you," he said easily, "but hardly your equal. Your brother tells me that we have met."

Catherine caught her breath. What should she say? "Yes," she laughed, "But I am sure you do not remember. I was with my father and I was not very old."

"I am sorry to tell you, Mrs. Hill, I do not."

"Oh, that's all right, Sir, I am not offended."

Lee looked at her with an amused twinkle. "That is not what I mean, Mrs. Hill. I meant to say that I regret on my own behalf that I do not remember you. When a man meets a woman as beautiful as you and does not remember it, that does not speak very well for the condition of his mind."

"But Colonel Lee, you had your wife and daughters to think about," she said good-naturedly. "How could you remember me?" Lee looked at her as if to say 'touché' and did not comment further.

During the evening, Catherine kept her eye on Emmanuel and Tuttle. She insisted, over her mother's objections, that they serve coffee to those who wanted it. It had not been going too well, but everyone one knew she wanted it and they were gracious.

When a tired but euphoric Catherine climbed the stairs with her husband, little remained of the night. It had been a glorious evening and one that had already changed her life forever.

A week passed following the wedding and Catherine lay on a lawn chair in the colonnade, thinking.

Hopemont never hosted a more grand and glorious spectacle. She blushed as she remembered Mattie telling Catherine that many were already calling her the most beautiful bride the South had ever seen.

Though she tried to conceal it, Catherine was deflated to learn that she had spent those agonizing months with her first and…and only crush on a man who did not even remember her. But, if true, why did he come to her wedding? She did not believe him. For some reason that she could not figure out, he thought he was serving her by saying he did not remember.

How her heartbeat quickened when she danced with him. She put her hands to her face and it was hot. Catherine scowled. How could she feel such things for another man at her wedding, and how could she spend time thinking about anyone but her husband when they had only been married a week? Catherine reasoned that her attachment to him before, his elegance and dancing grace, the war, his hero status, his name being on everyone's lips and because her husband and her brother thought so highly of him, comprised the complex answer. She knew that she did not harbor any feelings of a forbidden nature and would not do so. Her love for her husband, with whom she was fully satisfied, was pure. Love for one's husband and domestic duty were more a matter of character than emotion. By character, upbringing, and faith, Catherine was well suited and well prepared. The fact that there were other attractive men in the world did not detract from her love for Ambrose, nor corrupt it. Her life was devoted to his happiness. But she did hope—a desire that she agreed with herself never to pursue too deeply—that she would have a friendship with Robert E. Lee for as long as they both lived.

A day had passed since her husband left to join his unit. Jefferson Davis assigned him to John Magruder's outfit to guard Richmond and patrol the Potomac front in Northern Virginia. As she lay back and looked up at the tall trees, their graceful leaves fluttering and making a soothing sound in the balmy afternoon zephyrs, a cab rattled in and the driver brought her a note. She opened it and read:

"Colonel Wolf requests your presence as soon as possible. Very significant developments."

Tuttle came out with the teapot and Catherine instructed her to tell Mr. Morgan that she had gone down to see Colonel Wolf about something important.

The day was pleasant and she asked the young soldier to put down the top to the cab. The anxieties of a few weeks earlier in going to see Colonel Wolf were gone. She sat back comfortably and took in the sights and sounds of the journey. The ride into town was relaxing.

When they reached the headquarters, Catherine grinned as she saw her friend, but her smile quickly faded at the grave look on the face of the Colonel. Something was wrong.

"Well, Catherine," he said as they entered the office, "It has started."

"What do you mean?" she asked.

"Beauregard fired on Sumter," he said, "and the President has declared war."

"Lincoln, you mean?"

"No, President Davis," he replied. "But there is no doubt it is what Lincoln wanted, and he will respond with his own declaration before the day is out…maybe tomorrow."

They sat in stunned silence. Finally Catherine spoke. "Colonel Wolf, I am sorry…"

Wolf held up his hand to stop her. "No, Catherine; no. Let there be none of that. That was then. This is now. The war is on and we are in it together. You, as the wife of one of our fine commanders, are a military fellow. You may come to me at any time—for information, for support, for anything…lawful and within my power."

Catherine tried to be cheerful. "Well," she said, "we know it will not last long. When the North sees we mean to have our independence, they will let us go."

Colonel Wolf looked at her long and sadly. "You really believe that, don't you?" he said.

Catherine was shaken. "I guess I do. My husband says it and John my brother does too." She looked at him hopefully. "Don't you, Colonel Wolf?"

"I don't know," he said cautiously. "I hope it is true but…but I don't think so."

"But why, Colonel Wolf?" she asked anxiously. "All the best officers were Southerners and have gone with us."

"That is true," he said, "and that is in our favor. But Lincoln has more men, more guns, more money, many times more horses, and, most importantly of all, more factories and foundries for turning out ordinance. Lincoln is a bulldog and he will not give up. We will have to beat him down, and I don't…" He did not finish his thought and fell silent.

"But why would he do that?" she asked. "Why wouldn't he just let us go?"

Wolf looked at her kindly but sadly as one looks at a naive child. "Don't you know the answer to that?" he asked her. "Lincoln believes in his cause—believes in it just as strongly as we believe in ours. I don't know what you think of Lincoln, but he is not a quitter and he is a man prepared to die for his principles." Catherine had nothing more to say.

He was quiet for a moment. Then he said, in the one and only time she had ever heard such words from Colonel Wolf, "God have mercy on us all…man, woman and child, North and South, black and white…all of us. We are going to need it. Amen."

Chapter Seven

The Breaking Silver Cord

As Catherine neared the old house, she saw Doctor Higgins' hack in the drive. Panic almost gripped her as she jumped from the buggy, tied the horse to the hitching rack, and ran into the house. Emmanuel kneeled at the day bed wailing Negro chants. "What's wrong, Emmanuel?" Catherine asked, but he didn't hear her. She went into the kitchen and found Tuttle sitting at the table sobbing. "Tuttle, what's wrong!" she asked.

"Oh, Lawd, Missy, dear Lawd," Tuttle wailed between sobs.

Catherine looked around the kitchen and saw that nothing had been done. The lunch dishes were still in the sink and there was a musty smell in the air. She would attend to that later. She must find out what was going on. "Tuttle!" Catherine said sternly, "Please stop that and tell me what is wrong."

Tuttle mopped her eyes with the back of her hand. "It's Missers Mo'gan, Missy," she said through sniffles and sobs. "I speck she's dyin' sho nuff."

Catherine felt her pulse quicken and a wave of unsteadiness came over her. She steeled herself against panic. She must maintain control of her emotions or things would get out of hand. "Why aren't you up there with her?" Catherine demanded.

Tuttle broke out wailing again but checked herself at Catherine's glare. "Doc Higgins done tole me to git out'n dey. He say my carryin' on only makin' things wuss."

Catherine ran up the stairs just as the short, slight figure of Doctor Higgins was coming out of her mother's room. He stopped in front of her and looked down. His thin, silvery hair was limp from sweat and he looked pale. He wore the same black trousers and light gray vest with no coat that she had always seen him in. His shirt bloused beneath the vest—the tail almost out of his trousers. He had that medicinal smell about him that always triggered insecurity in her. "Oh, Doctor Higgins," Catherine asked anxiously, "is she…?"

"Dead? No, not yet, but her days are short," he said. He paused and Catherine peered hard in the dim light of the hallway to see his eyes. "There's nothing I can do for her, Miss Kitty," he continued, "It's her heart. I gave her the best I got for pain, but we've got no medicines to treat that."

Catherine tried to compose herself, but found it difficult. The friendly old house had turned cold and threatening. The wood paneling on the walls of the upstairs hallway, always so rich and satisfying, now seemed dark and depressing. The baroque patterns in the rich carpet of the hallway floor seemed busy and nerve-wracking, almost to the point of making her dizzy. She fought hard to keep control. "How long…how long will it be, do you think?" she asked in a frightened tone.

Doctor Higgins rubbed his mottled face, distorting his eyes into red, watery, grotesque shapes. "Maybe a week," he said, "maybe a month, maybe a day, maybe only minutes. She might be gone right now."

Catherine started for the door and then stopped. "Could it be months—maybe even years?"

Doctor Higgins shook his head emphatically. "No. No. Well, I say 'no', but I am not God," he said. He paused again, as if pondering a weighty problem. When he spoke, his voice sounded thin and gravely. "I suppose it could be months, but I do not think so. She was pretty bad this time." He stopped and looked at Catherine in a way that unnerved her. She listened for some reassurance in his frank analysis but heard none. "You know how these things are, I guess," he said. "She will rally up some since it didn't kill her this time. But that doesn't mean she will get back to where she was before it hit her." Doctor Higgins took out a handkerchief and mopped his brow. "I think she's goin' to be a good deal worse than she was," he continued. "She needs rest. I don't want her gettin' out of bed without me seein' her first."

"I will see that she rests," Catherine said supportively.

Doctor Higgins made a sour face. "And another thing. See if you can't stop that darkie from carryin' on so. A lot of what it takes for people to mend is happy faces and encouragement."

"Oh, it will be all right, Doctor Higgins," Catherine assured him. "Mother understands Tuttle and she is comforted having her around. And Tuttle will see to Mother's every need."

Higgins seemed disappointed and displeased that Catherine did not agree with him. "Well, I know," he said defensively, "but you people have to stop feelin' sorry for yourselves and think of your Mamma. Such takin' on makes her sad and saps her strength."

Catherine was confused. "I always thought it was best to be straightforward," she said.

Doctor Higgins looked a bit impatient, like it was not his job to hold school. He ran his fingers through his hair and shook his head. "Well, sure, Miss Kitty," he said, "That's right, when people are breathin' their last. But when they are tryin' to heal up and get better, they need cheerfulness and encouragement."

Catherine was beginning to feel discouraged. She was getting no help and no sympathy from Doctor Higgins. "But I thought you said…"

Doctor Higgins held up his hand in resignation. "Look, Kitty, she's your mamma," he said almost angrily. "I am just trying to see that she is made as comfortable as possible."

Catherine felt chastened and went into the little-girl tone. "I am sorry, Doctor Higgins."

Doctor Higgins shook his head in frustration. His voice became raspy with irritation. "It is nothin' to be sorry about. It is just somethin' to do or not do." Catherine suddenly wished that Doctor Higgins would leave so she could go to her mother. The more he said, the more confused she was getting. She thought she knew how to handle things, but now she wasn't sure. She tried to figure out the right tone and pose to strike to get out of this awkward situation. "Yes sir, yes sir, I understand. Thank you so much."

Doctor Higgins looked at her blankly for a long moment. Catherine knew now that she could depend on him for his medical knowledge and potions. But she had not known him to be so crusty and complaining. In the past, her mother called for him and worked with him and Catherine never had this kind of involvement with him before. She wondered if he had always been this way.

Doctor Higgins seemed to pick up on her thoughts. "You are not being fair with me, Kitty," he said sadly. "I can't get emotionally involved with every patient I see. What little emotional strength I have left would soon wear through. But I have given my best to this family. I spanked your bottom when you took your first breath, and I delivered you, your brothers and your sister," he said in a softer voice. "That is a very special lady to me in there and I will do all I can for her. I am only tryin' to get you to do the same." He started down the hall, and then turned to her again. "You let me know, the minute she takes a spell for the worse."

Catherine understood what he said to her and felt remorse at having judged him so harshly. "Yes, Doctor Higgins, I will certainly do that," she said as warmly as she could, "and thank you very much." She felt she was going to cry and she blinked back the tears. "I guess I am upset and not at myself exactly."

"Of course, Miss Kitty, I understand," he said in a conciliatory tone. "Let's try to understand each other. These life-and-death struggles are hard enough when people pull together."

With that, Doctor Higgins went down the stairs. Catherine leaned over the rail to watch him go. It was odd, she thought, that in all her years in that house, she had never really paid any attention to the kitchen from the head of the stairs. How different it looked from up there. It seemed smaller, the walls were not so high, and it looked quainter. Tuttle was sitting at the table, her eyes full of grief and tears. Catherine heard her ask brokenly, "Doctor, did I sho' 'nuff kill Missers Mo'gan?"

Catherine knew she had shaken Doctor Higgins' confidence in the wisdom of criticizing Tuttle. She hoped this touching scene would pierce his crusty exterior and it did. "No, my dear girl," he said to her kindly, "Mrs. Morgan is still alive—for now, at least." Catherine smiled as he took her hand, patted it, and then wiped some tears from her eyes with his handkerchief. She was regaining some of her confidence in him and it felt good. She needed that very much just now.

Doctor Higgins continued. "I didn't mean to scold you—Miss—Tuttle, is it?" he said to her, "but we must be very careful to be happy and cheerful around Mrs. Morgan. That is what she needs just now. We must wait until we are out of her sight and hearing to do our sorrowing. Do you think you can do that?"

Catherine saw the big grin on Tuttle's face as she said, "Yes, Suh, Doctor, I shore nuff think I can." Catherine watched as Tuttle followed him to the door. "Thanks to God and you, Doctor. Or, I shudda said, 'to you and God,' I speck."

She heard Doctor Higgins chuckle. "No, no," he said to Tuttle, "You had it right the first time."

Tuttle smiled broadly and Catherine saw that her eyes were clearing and she seemed genuinely happy. "Well, I am sho' 'nuff glad you wuz here," she told Higgins.

"That's just my job, Tuttle," he said pleasantly. "I've got my job and you've got yours. That's the way it works—isn't it? It's up to you now, and I'm countin' on you to do it well."

Tuttle nodded her head enthusiastically and waved him goodbye. "Lan' sakes," Catherine heard her say aloud to herself, "that man ain't nuthun' as bad as those Niggers been tellin' me."

Catherine understood suddenly that Doctor Higgins himself was shaken by her mother's condition, but he meant to do the best he could. What a difference a few kind words make, she thought to herself, even if they were not directed to her.

She did not want Tuttle to know she was eavesdropping, so she withdrew from the railing, turned, and went quietly into her mother's room. The soft, matronly character, in the presence of which Catherine had always felt so comforted and so secure, had disappeared. An emanation of frailty, weakness, anxiety, and fear had taken its place. She lay with her eyes closed but opened them when Catherine looked down at her. The tired and wrinkled face looked so vulnerable. Even her voice lacked its usual timbre and melody. Deeply shaken, Catherine wanted to burst out bawling, but she knew she didn't dare. "Catherine, I am so glad you are here," she said weakly. Her breath was heavily laden with the smell of medicine and the room was dark. That wonderful lavender scent that had always pervaded her mother's room was gone. It now smelled more like a hospital ward. A hint of the ammonia odor of smelling salts lingered.

Catherine took her hand and held it tightly but gently. "I am sorry I wasn't here when…with you…"

"No, you couldn't know it would happen," her mother said with effort. "You can't stay here day and night waiting for something to happen to me." She paused. "Catherine, would you please go over and open the shades. Doc Higgins thinks that if it is darker in here, it will keep me quieter. I find it very depressing." Catherine threw back the curtains and it helped the mood a little. "And please open one of those windows, Catherine. It smells so musty and stuffy in here." Opening the window helped too and Catherine felt a little better. She went back to the bed and sat down, taking her mother's hand again. Her mother continued. "I had Tuttle here with me. What a dear little thing she is. She took good care of me while Emmanuel went for Doc Higgins."

Catherine grew cautiously serious. "He said she was upsetting you with her crying," she said hesitantly.

Her mother's face brightened and her voice strengthened. "Oh, pooh! Why don't doctors stick to docterin'. It does me good to see that people care about me. It would have bothered me more if she hadn't cried."

Catherine agreed with what her mother was saying. It was about what she had told Doc Higgins. But she was uncertain how much of what the Doctor had said might be true, and she did not want her mother to lose confidence in him at this time. Catherine tried to be conciliatory. "Well, Mamma," she said calmly, "I think he is concerned that she not wear you out or upset you."

Her mother seemed to rally again. "Well, he can just leave me and Tuttle to our own cases," she said tartly. She turned her face up so her eyes would meet Catherine's. Catherine felt a pull at her heart as she realized her mother was trying to be stern but hardly had the strength. "And you too, Missy," her mother said. "I don't want anybody changing Tuttle. I like her just the way she is." The fire subsided and she drifted back to a meek, tired voice. "What did he say?" she asked, trying to disguise the fear and to sound detached. "Am I done for?"

Catherine thought as fast as she could. She could not try to fool her mother. It would not work and she would not do it anyhow. But how much was necessary to say? Catherine shifted uneasily in the chair.

He mother spoke tersely. "If you are trying to figure out what to keep from me, don't!"

"Yes, Ma'am," Catherine said, trying to think ahead of her words. "Well, he said that you had a bad spell and that it could have killed you, but it didn't. He said you would make a recovery, for this time at least, and that you need to rest." Catherine paused and sighed. "I suppose you and I are going to fuss over that."

Her mother shook her head in resignation and looked beaten. "No, Sweetie, we are not," she said quietly. "I am not going to lie in this bed day and night, but I am very tired and I know I need to rest." She tried to turn in the bed and seemed to experience weakness and pain. Catherine helped her get the position she wanted. "There, now, that's better," her mother said. "Did he say how long it would be before I have another spell? Will the next one finish me off?"

Catherine tried to sound hopeful and convincing. "No, Mamma, he said he did not know; that he wasn't God." She took a deep breath to get force behind her words and steady them. "It might be a short time or a long one and it might be as much as months…or even…or even…well, I asked him if it could be a year or more and he didn't…"

"Or as little as days?"

Catherine looked down at her hands on the side of the bed. She must be strong. It could undermine what little confidence her mother had left, if she broke down now. "Or as little as days—yes, Ma'am."

Her mother seemed to be spurred to a sense of urgency. "Catherine—I need you to do some things for me; will you?"

"Oh, of course," Mamma!" she said emotionally.

"Well, one of them is easy, and the other…" Her mother was hesitant and looked at the ceiling. She tried to clear her throat and coughed a little. Catherine helped her with a sip of water. "The other…I don't know."

Catherine's desire to comfort and assure her mother was almost desperation. "Anything Mamma," she said emotionally. "I promise I will do it."

"Don't promise 'till you have heard, Sweetie," her mother said. "Haven't I always taught you that?" Catherine waited expectantly and her mother continued. "I need you to go down to the bank and get Mr. Todd to come up here. It doesn't have to be today—but it should be soon, just in case…Well, and now the other thing. Hear me out before you say anything." Her mother shifted in the bed uncomfortably and Catherine suffered inside with her every movement. "I want you to see if you can get hold of John and get him here. He upset me when he was home last and I said harsh words to him." Tears came to her mother's eyes. "I can't die without seeing him again. I just can't."

Catherine was stunned. "What must he have said to you?" she asked in wonder, "You never say harsh words to anyone."

A look of worry and remorse clouded her mother's face. "I know," she said softly, "and I shouldn't have to him, but…well, it wasn't just what he said, but how he said it. He said he wished every damned Yankee in the world was dead, including his uncle and his kin who sided with the North."

Catherine did not want to argue with her mother now, but her loyalty to the South, to the military and to her husband was very vital and querulous. "But Mamma," she answered respectfully but with a frown, "we are fighting the North."

"I know that, and I know that you…but…but…but he said he had killed northern women and children and that he enjoyed it more than anything he had ever done." It seemed to Catherine that it pained her mother to talk, but she continued. "It would keep the little bastards from growing up and becoming Yankees, he said."

Catherine's countenance fell. This injected an entirely different element into the matter. "Oh, Mamma, no!" she protested. "John said that?"

"Yes and then, well, he said a lot of very ugly and unnecessary things. I was afraid for his soul, Catherine," she said in a worried tone. "He has never been a devout person like you and I don't know where he…I lit into him pretty good, trying to make him think about what he was doing. He did not take it well, and left with coldness towards me."

Catherine was indignant. "Well, the fault is his, Mother," she said angrily, "not yours. He had no right to say that to you, and if he's doing that, he is not right either. My husband doesn't like Yankees, but he would never do that, nor would he say it." Catherine was angry, confused, and worried, and she was becoming emotional.

Her mother seemed to rally up a bit as she tried to calm Catherine. "Now, there I have gone and said too much," she said in self-reproach. "I wasn't going to tell you, but I was afraid you would not go if you didn't know the seriousness of it."

Catherine's anger gave way to curiosity. "What did you say to him?" she asked.

"I said…I said…Oh, Catherine, please—no."

The dilemma was clear in her mother's face. Catherine was worried for her health and moved quickly. "I am sorry, Mamma," she said, "It is none of my business anyway. You are right not telling me. It is between you and him."

Her mother seemed relieved. "Get him to tell you," she pleaded, "if he wants you to know."

Catherine could see that her mother very much did not want her to know what she had fussed with John about. Though she would like to have known what it was all about, she disclaimed interest in the hope of putting her mother at ease. "I am not even going to let on that I know," she said as if all curiosity had passed. "It doesn't matter to me anyhow."

"Yes, you will—you will tell him to get him to come." Her mother seemed almost desperate as she said, "He is not going to want to—but he must. I cannot leave it like this." Her mother began to weep softly. Catherine bit her lip. She could never stand to see her mother cry. It took from her all sense of security and left her desolate and sorrowful. She put her head against her mother's cheek and buried her face in the quilt to hide her own tears.

Catherine left the house immediately after her conversation with her mother. She would go first to the Bank of Lexington and leave her mother's request for Mr. Todd to visit her. Then she must find Colonel Wolf. She did not exactly have a plan, but if anyone could or would help her, it was he. He might even be able to get a message across to John.

The afternoon was still and the dust boiled up around her and made it difficult to breathe. The road seemed lonely and unfriendly. Things that usually brought her pleasure now bothered her. The creaking of the buggy wheels made her nervous and the sound of the birds disturbed her thoughts. The smell of the horse was unpleasant and she could not get comfortable in the buggy seat. Catherine tried hard to get a grip on herself but felt the frustration of not being able to.

As she rode, she attempted to think. John was in Murfreesboro when she last heard, but would not be there now. Being a raider, he could be anywhere. Catherine prayed that she could find him. This life-and-death situation, so important to her mother, had enduring and future importance to her. She was fighting the desire to become angry with him. What had happened to him, anyway?

She left word with the receptionist at the bank. She did not want to encounter Mr. Todd and take the time to explain everything. Then she drove to the telegraph Center. The sight of Colonel Wolf and his steady, paternalistic voice restored some sense of order and hope to her mind. She went in and sat down as he busied himself trying to help her. She knew John was somewhere in the west—Tennessee or Mississippi—but she did not know where. Colonel Wolf spent the whole afternoon and evening trying to get a fix on John and his raiders. Finally, he came in and sat down heavily at the table. "Miss Kitty, I can't find your brother—I just can't!"

"Oh, no! Dear God!" Catherine said, struggling to keep her composure. "But you must have found out something?"

"Oh, I know about where he is," Colonel Wolf said, "but I can't reach him or contact anyone who can go to him."

"Where is he?" she asked, trying to finesse the question by him. "About, I mean?"

She did not succeed. Colonel Wolf regarded her narrowly. "Why?" he asked in a worried and suspicious tone, "What do you have in mind, Mrs. Hill?"

"I just want to know what you know, that is all." He did not move or reply, so she said firmly, "He is my brother, Colonel Wolf."

The Colonel looked at her grimly for a long moment. Finally he said, "This means an awfully lot to you, doesn't it?"

Catherine breathed deeply to keep her voice from wavering. "Oh, Colonel Wolf, it means more than you can possibly know," she said emotionally. Wolf studied her for a while longer. Catherine saw his suspiciousness give way to compassion. He shrugged his shoulders and led her to the map room where he pointed to an area between Nashville and the Kentucky border.

"He is actually not that far off," Wolf told her. "He and Forrest have been moving this way, apparently following the railroad. There is something in the wind, I don't know what…ah…I guess it is alright to tell you that—you being a Colonel's wife and all."

"Colonel Wolf,' Catherine asked, trying to sound casual so as not to arouse the Colonel's suspicions further, "if someone were riding down the tracks in that area, would the raiders be likely to see him?"

"I am sure they would," he answered, not discerning her motive, "but your brother is not likely to be riding down the tracks, Miss Kitty and anyhow, we have no way of…"

"Thank you, Colonel Wolf," Catherine said abruptly. She stood up, shook his hand, and left quickly, leaving a troubled looking Colonel Wolf standing in the door staring after her. She hoped she had not been rude or offensive, but her mind was spinning and she did not want to hear any more. She hurried to her rig and set out for Hopemont at a fast trot. As she rode, she formulated her plan. It was insane, but she had to do it. Her mother was lying helpless and needed her now. Her devotion to her mother was without limits, and her mother's well being meant more to her than her own. She could not let her down without giving it a try. She was going to ride down there and try to find John.

Chapter Eight

No Place for a Lady

Catherine had changed a lot since the days of her maidenhood at Hopemont. The war had a way of bringing those changes to an officer's wife and in a hurry. She was more mature now, less the little girl, and her candor and boldness had brought out a spirit of bravery that worried her. Catherine feared almost nothing. She would undertake difficult—often masculine—tasks. This had brought criticism from General Jackson and a number of other officers.

Her husband insisted that she learn to shoot the new northern repeating rifles, captured in battle, and he sent one home with her. She could protect the house while the men were gone but the design went beyond that. Catherine had convinced him to let her come to the front and stay with him when her mother…when Hopemont no longer needed her on a constant basis. He would only let her do it if she agreed to learn to shoot a carbine and to ride regular army saddle—and become proficient at both. One could not retreat from an invasion riding sidesaddle in a skirt or dress. Catherine did not mind; in fact, she rather liked it. She had never been a town girl or a prima donna and she only wore hoop skirts at formal affairs or when her mother or her husband made her do it. While at home, she rode daily, and went to the woods to shoot. Many of the citizens of Lexington complained about it to her mother. 'This was no way for an aristocratic lady to behave. What had happened to the lovely Catherine—pride of Lexington?'

But Catherine kept at it until she became proficient. Now she did not know whether to be glad or sorry. One did not have to consider what they could not possibly do. Emmanuel saddled up the horse while she made a bed roll and gathered up a heavy coat, a rain slicker, some food, and ammunition. Emmanuel fretted and wanted to go with her, but she could not let him. They needed him at home—and that was true. Even so, she would have let him go, but the risks for her to be seen in the forests with a black man must not be taken. She warned him that Mrs. Morgan must not know anything about this. If the horse was still tied to the rail at first light, he should come and knock softly on the screen door, which, she promised him, would be locked. Then she settled down on the day bed on the porch and waited for morning.

First light had just broken when Catherine left Hopemont and rode southwest on the road to Munfordville. There she planned to cross the Green River on the railroad trestle and follow the railroad bed south toward Nashville. If Colonel Wolf's information was correct and if she was lucky, she would encounter the raiders in the area of Bowling Green before leaving Kentucky.

It was the middle of June and the warm time of the summer, but the early morning air was crisp and fresh. Catherine breathed deeply and took in the wonderful aromas of the countryside. The Blue Grass was blooming and giving off its pleasant smell. The fields were decorated with the bluish tinge. The leaves on the gums and maples were exuding the perfume of their seeping resin. A myriad of summer flowers lined the country road and contributed a cacophony of odors to the balmy air. As she rode on, birds began to wake up and commence their morning symphony. The further south she rode, the more carbonates of lime and sandy loams combined with the clay of the roadbed to eliminate the dust and reduce the click of the horse's hoofs to a soft thud.

But not everything about the start of her journey was pleasant. Catherine soon realized that knowing how to ride military saddle and being accustomed to it were two very different things. The cost of this journey, no matter how it turned out, would be high. Her fine-blooded horse had an easy lope. She much preferred it to his trot, but her husband had warned her many times not to lope a horse more than twenty minutes out of the hour or she would soon be afoot with a dead horse behind her. There simply wasn't time to let him walk, so Catherine gritted her teeth and the horse jogged on.

At the Green River trestle, Catherine tried to ride the horse across but he was skittish. Fearful of being thrown in the middle of the bridge, she led him across. It seemed to take forever. Once on the other side, she mounted up and headed for Bowling Green.

In the early morning of her fourth day out, she awoke to find a big, powerfully built man standing over her and the most frightening eyes she had ever looked into staring down at her. She sat up, clutching the blankets to her chest. Then, remembering that she was fully dressed, she dropped them in her lap. "Good morning," she said as calmly as possible.

The man threw back his head and uttered a loud, short laugh. "'Good mornin'? Did you say 'good mornin'?"

Anger flushed in her cheeks. "Yes, I said good morning," she answered tartly. "Is there something wrong with saying good morning?"

The man did not answer. Slowly the amusement faded from his eyes and Catherine thought she had never seen a more evil gleam. "Ma'am, now give it to me straight, 'cause I ain't a feller to fool around with. What would you be doin' out here?"

"I am looking for my brother."

"Oh, you're lookin' fer your brether," he repeated in a demeaning tone.

"Yes, I'm looking for my brother," she said, her anger beginning to rise. This man was playing with her like a schoolboy pokes at a toad and she did not like it. Who did he think he was?

"Now listen, Ma'am," he said, "I may be able to help ya if ya don't get me mad, which ain't hard to do, I may say. I am goin' to ask ya again. What are you doin' out here?"

"I told you," she said indignantly, "I am looking for my brother."

"Oh, yea, so ya did. All right, the next question—who is your brether?" he asked, "And what makes ya think ya can find him out here?"

"My brother is John Morgan, and I have every reason to believe that he is in this area somewhere."

The man regarded her narrowly and his countenance softened a bit. "Mrs. Ambrose Powell Hill and the sister of John Morgan," he said triumphantly. "So you are the famous Catherine Morgan Hill. I must say, Ma'am, that your beauty has not been exaggerated."

Catherine wriggled impatiently. "See here, Sir," she said, "I am in no mood for compliments. Can you and will you help me? If not, I had best be going."

The hard, mean look returned to the man's face and the evil leer to his eyes. "That's too bad, Ma'am," he said coldly, "'cause I ain't complimented a woman since I can't remember when, and won't be complimentin' you again." The man whistled and a number of horses galloped up to the tree. "You boys put up a tent where it won't be seen, and make sure this lady stays in it 'till I get back." He turned to Catherine. "I'll go git your brether fer ya, Ma'am. I can't say how long it will be, but I will git him as fast as I can. Meanwhile you stay in the tent, and don't come out. I will leave some men nearby to watch so that you are not taken. There are Union cavalry in the area."

"Freemont's men?" she asked.

"No, Ma'am, I wish it wuz," he answered. "You'd be a lot safer. It's Custer, Ma'am. The only man in the Union that is anywhere near as mean as me and your brether."

Catherine could see that this man meant to help her and the hot glow faded from her face. "Thank you very much for helping me," she said politely, "and…and thank you for the compliment; I was rude and I am sorry."

The man looked at her for a moment, his black eyes glowing with wickedness, but he said nothing. Then he whirled and was off.

Catherine waited what seemed to her to be endless hours. It was hot in the tent and the smell of pitch from the pines did not seem so pleasant in the stuffy atmosphere. Catherine had not bathed for several days and she was also well aware of that fact. She felt grimy, sticky, and downright scroungy. On top of it all, she needed to go to the toilet. She desperately wanted to get out of that tent, but the big man had told her not to get out of the tent and Catherine was reluctant to disobey him. She decided to wait as long as she possibly could, hoping John would show up in the meantime.

In mid afternoon she awoke from a fitful nap to the sound of a soft tread nearing the tent. She held her breath as the flap opened and then broke into a grin. It was John. Quickly she bounded out of her little jail. John put his finger to his lips to quiet her. "There are enemy in the area."

"How close?"

"I don't know; maybe near—maybe far." He roughly grabbed her arm, led her to a log, and motioned her to sit down. "Catherine, I am very upset with you," he said cantankerously. "What in the world..."

His words hit Catherine like a slap in the face. Immediately she reacted. "I have been in these woods for three days," she said heatedly. "I have blisters from my soles to the middle of my bottom. I ache everywhere, I am scared, I am hungry, I am filthy from head to toe, my clothes are stuck to me like wall paper, I stink so bad I can't stand myself, and I am depressed. If you say one more word of reproach to me..."

John Morgan could see he had yanked the wrong cord. "All right, all right!" he said in a conciliatory tone, "I am sorry. Now Catherine, as calmly as you can, tell me what this is all about?"

Catherine paused, taking several deep breaths in an effort to compose herself and change her tone. "It's Mamma, John," Catherine said. "She is dying and she asked me to find you and bring you to her."

John looked away and did not reply for a while. Finally, he said, "I am sorry, Catherine, I truly am. If you could have gotten word to me, I could have saved you the trouble. I am not going home, Catherine, there is too much for me to do here. The cause of the Confederacy..."

The hostility in Catherine's actions stopped him in mid sentence as she got up and walked toward her horse. "All right, John," she said, almost shouting to keep from crying, "But let me tell you one thing. You had no right to talk to Mamma the way you did. No mother should ever have to hear that kind of talk coming from her son. Now she is dying, and instead of you going to her like you should have, she is reaching out to you. If you are so proud and so infested with bloodlust that you cannot go home and say 'I am sorry' to your dying mother, the one who gave birth to us and looked after us as good, and loved us as much as any mother in the world—if you are willing to cut off your own mother in her desperate and dying hour of need, then count me out too. You are not my brother anymore. I will not own you to anyone, you will not be welcome in my home, I will never come to yours, and I want nothing more to do with you." Catherine put her hands to her face and began to cry. Weakness swept over her, sinking her to her knees. John came, lifted her up, and carried her back to the log. "Put me down, you monster, you…"

"Catherine, stop, please. I can't stand this." There were tears in his eyes. "I will go back with you, and I will apologize to mother, if you want that so bad."

Catherine sniffled and dried her eyes on her sleeve. "I was hoping you would do it for her and for you; not just for me."

John hung his head, looking at the ground. "I have wanted to go to her, oh so many times, but I could not do it. Every time I got ready to do it, I couldn't. I was ashamed to face her. I was afraid she hated me and would tell me to get out."

"Oh, John!" Catherine said brokenly, "How could you think that of our dear mother."

"It wasn't of her; not really," he answered. "I was so terrible, so crazy and so hateful that she did not know me anymore and I thought, when she told me what she did, that I was anathema to her." John grew silent and cautious. He looked at her from the corner of his eye with his head turned from her. "Did she tell you what she said to me?"

"No," Catherine answered, "she said you would tell me, if you wanted me to know. She told me what you had said to her because she was afraid I would not go find you if I did not know her desperation and her pain."

Her brother breathed a visible sigh of relief and his mood grew much more relaxed. "Good," he said, "I am glad. I am not going to tell you either. I mean, do you really want to know?"

"No, I don't," she answered quickly. "It doesn't matter. I just want to get you back there and pray it is before mother dies."

John had dropped his defenses completely. "Well, if she dies first," he said emotionally, "she goes to a better place. It will not hurt her anymore."

Catherine shook her head negatively, with her jaw set. "I know, John," she said firmly, "but it will hurt you…and me. We must hurry."

"Are you able to ride now?" he asked.

"Oh, yes," she said with a put-on drawl. I've been lying around in that tent all day and I'm ready to hit the trail."

"Spoken like a true ranger," he said with a laugh.

They went into a lope to try to gain some distance before nightfall. Catherine was in a quandary. She was anxious to get home, but even in a lope, her blisters hurt and she was worried that they might become infected. Her bottom was so sore she could hardly bear to sit in the saddle. John told her to relax and settle down. The tension would only make things worse. Then he noticed her turning her toes in toward the horse. He told her to turn her toes out as far as she could without stressing herself. Both things helped and she made the rest of the gallop pretty well.

When they slowed to a walk, she asked John a question. "Who was that awful man who found me?"

John chuckled and nodded affirmatively. "That, my dear, was the famous Nathan Bedford Forrest."

Catherine put her hand to her face and gasped. "What? Oh, John! Oh, no!"

"You are horrified."

Catherine shook her head in disbelief. "I had always thought of Colonel Forrest as a suave, handsome, southern gentleman. Isn't he a rich planter from Mississippi?"

"That he is," John said. "He is worth a million and half dollars, they say."

Catherine puzzled this new information for a moment. Then she shrugged as if reaching a decision. "Oh, well," she said. "I am sure he is not as mean and evil as he appears. A man can't really help his looks I guess; can he?"

"You are right about the last part," John said, "but wrong about the other."

"What do you mean?" she asked.

"Nathan Bedford Forrest is one of the meanest, most cold blooded, sadistic people I have ever known," he said. "He makes me look like a choirboy."

As they rode in silence, Catherine pondered the information about Forrest, trying to reconcile the man she had met earlier in the day with the famous Nathan Bedford Forrest of whom everyone spoke with such appreciation and the image she had developed in her mind. She came back from her thoughts as she saw John shaking his head negatively. "I hope this will be your last single-handed raid, sister," he said in a worried tone. "God—if there is one—was with you on this…this…whatever it was?"

"John," Catherine asked, the alarm sounding in her voice, "did you just say, 'if there is a God?'"

John grew cautious. "I did but I probably didn't mean it. It's just language I picked up in the camps."

"Are they all heathen in those camps?" she asked.

"Oh, no," he said. "In fact, Forrest holds revival meetings weekly for the men and talks to me about the Bible just about every time I see him. But it is hard for me to take him serious. He doesn't see any contradictions in his life, but I see legions of them."

A serious scowl took over Catherine's face. "I think you need to talk about this with Parson Edwards."

"No, I will not do that, Kitty," John said, shaking his head resolutely.

"With Mother, then, I mean, if she's…"

"Um…I don't know."

"Well, with me, then?" she asked.

"All right," he said, "I can do that with you, but not now. Let's run a little more before dark."

Catherine sucked up her gut and her courage and they took off on another lope, up the tracks toward home.

Chapter Nine

There Is No Place Where Her Voice Is Not Heard

Catherine went to Richmond to spend a little time with her husband. The visit being over, Catherine prepared to return to Hopemont. The train did not leave for about two hours, and Catherine planned to walk around Richmond when a courier from President Davis brought her a message. She opened it and read:

Dear Kitty:

I met you once but you were too small to remember. I am Mary Boykin Chesnut, a friend of your dear mother.

I heard that you were in town and that you may be coming to live near Richmond soon. I want very much to get to know you and I hope we can become the best of friends. I have recently inherited a house in Richmond, and I would like very much for you to stop in on me for a few moments if you have the time.

If you will go with the courier who has brought you this message, President Davis will have you driven here and promises to get you back well before your train leaves.

Catherine looked absently at the note and frowned. Last minute things disturbed her. Having an hour or two before getting on the train suited Catherine's style. It afforded her time to wander around, rest and get relaxed. The ride always seemed so much more pleasant if she did not rush to get on.

But she would go to see Mrs. Chesnut because of her mother. Besides, Catherine had been told enough times to get to know Mary. In spite of her age and maturity, Catherine had never been away from home for extended periods, and the idea of having an influential person on her side when her husband went off to battle attracted Catherine. She sent the courier to get the cab and gathered up her bags.

Catherine liked Mary's Richmond home, christened Axley Manor, although, it was nothing like the Greek architecture of Lexington. It was a Tudor mansion built of half timber and half brick. Its three-gabled roof rose sharply, displaying three stories of windows to the South overlooking a lovely lawn and garden. Two majestic Virginia Ash stood in the back yard, shading the house from the late sun but not hiding the scenes beyond. A fine, cobbled walkway several hundred feet in length descended through three sets of brick steps, lined by three-foot high walls of brown-red brick frosted with age. Mulberry trees almost hid the carriage house and the most prominent flowers were rows of yellow and white tulips that filled gap between the cobbles and the stone walls. The tops of the walls were mortared and at intervals, there were stone flowerpots with blooms that Catherine did not recognize and lamps for after-dark passage with stone reservoirs for oil.

The air, heavier than that of Lexington, was laden with the scent of leaves, grass, flowers, and a hint of smoke from the Tredegar Iron works less than a mile away. Ash, Elm, Mulberry, and Spruce secluded the twenty-three acre estate—a little too much for Catherine's taste. They went in the house for tea in the sitting room. After a while, Varina Howell Davis, wife of the President, came in to talk to Mary about some program with the local women. Catherine was not interested so she picked up Mary's diary and leafed through it. The first part was a sort of an autobiography. This did interest Catherine. Varina would soon be gone and she wanted to know all she could about Mary if they were to spend the evening together. Catherine had been well trained. Her father had told her many times that to be a good guest, one must ask the hostess the right questions and listen a lot. Catherine settled back and began to read. The things she discovered would be most useful.

Catherine took a sip of the tea and frowned. She did not know what tea Mary was using, but it tasted bitter and she feared it would upset her, so she gently pushed it aside, looking to see if Mary was watching her. Then she continued reading.

Mary, the mistress of Mulberry Plantation, lived near Camden, South Carolina, since 1840 when she married its owner, James Chesnut Jr., at age 17. But Richmond, now the center of the new American country, better served Mary's goal of influencing the politics, economics and military strategy of the South through her writing. Her husband James, who started as the aide to General Beauregard at Sumter, now held the position of confidant on the staff of Jefferson Davis. For a time they quartered at the Spottswood Hotel, 'the place to stay' for important people coming to Richmond. Mary enjoyed that because of the opportunity to interact with the wives of generals and sometimes with the generals themselves. But a few of the wives became edgy about her doing that and she liked the idea of being able to control the situations around her. Mary wrote that, with her inherited townhouse, it was just perfect. She did not want to entertain often or to have people around much. But when she did, she could now do so at her own initiative.

Mary seemed to feel that it was important for her diary too. She could understand, she wrote, why some women thought that it a bit much for her to come down with her diary in her hand and make sure that people saw it and asked about it. Now Mary felt that she could leave it on the tea table, on a nice velvet base to give it importance and visibility, and there would be no problem getting it noticed.

The articles Mary wished to circulate were supposed to be strictly from her diary. If a woman wrote for public consumption, this did not pass with tradition. But Mary tired a little of that convention, as with many customs, and would bear some criticism, if necessary, in order to initiate change.

Catherine frowned as she read this. She looked out at Mary for a moment and thought. Mary's trickiness and her departure from conventional wisdom bothered Catherine. Supposedly, it was Mary's personal diary and no one knew its contents but she. That part of it too, bothered Catherine. Still, Mary had not asked her to read it…or had she? Catherine decided not to follow that line of thinking. She went back to reading.

In any case, people knew about Mary's diary—if they did not and it contained something Mary wanted out, she made sure that they did—and she could be coaxed into letting the right people read it. With a townhouse in Richmond, she could give an occasional party when it suited her political ambitions, she had room for many guests, and at times there would be more dignitaries in town than Jefferson Davis could house. Mary could be selective as to whom she invited as guests, and she could see great advantage for her cause to this, she wrote.

Catherine shook her head. 'I must remember that this is a very devious woman,' she said to herself. Then she continued with the reading. It startled her to discover that Mary thought she would make a better president than Jeff Davis and a better Judge than Campbell. Yet, she realized that no woman, even one of her tough hide and brazenness, could ever hold public office. But as a writer, she could express her opinions and have them known, she could perhaps influence policy, and she could let those pompous men—like Johnston and Beauregard—have it when they messed things up.

Catherine's ears were tingling. She was not used to hearing military men spoken of in such irreverent tones. She considered putting the diary down but curiosity drove her on.

Mary professed not to be a suffragette or a crusader like Clara Bowe, but about some things, she would no longer be silent. Many women who considered her a bit coarse, Mary wrote, felt that this reflected on her religious convictions. Mary expressed indignation. This was far from the truth. Her religious convictions pushed her to speak up. To dispel that myth, she wrote that she had never been afraid of Negroes, that she had never harmed any of them, and they did not seem to have any interest in hurting her. Two thirds of her religion, she said, had been taken up in being good to them.

Mary expressed her outrage at the monstrous wrong and evil method in which the white men of the South conducted themselves with respect to Negro women. They kept these women in the same houses with their wives and fathered children with them. In most instances, the mulattos one saw in a family partly resembled the white children. A lady of one household would readily tell you who fathered the mulatto children in everybody's household but seemed completely oblivious to those of her own. She apparently seemed to think that they dropped out of the sky. A white plantation owner seemed willing enough to keep his black harem with all its problems and negative consequences, under the same roof with his lovely white wife, and his beautiful daughters. All the while, he attended church, walked among others with pride, and posed as a model of human virtue. In her efforts to expose the problem, Mrs. Stowe had missed the worst of it. She made Legree a bachelor.

Catherine's face was burning from reading such bold and biting criticism. Everyone knew the truth, but talking about it broke with tradition. Drawn like a moth to the flame, Catherine skipped around in the diary to find other places where Mary had written about Negroes and slaves. In so doing, Catherine found, to her surprise, that Wade Hampton also expressed doubts and dissatisfaction about slavery. This seemed odd to Catherine since her father told her that Hampton owned more slaves than anyone else in South Carolina and maybe the whole South. She wondered if Mary had her facts straight.

As Catherine perused the diary, she found another item of interest. The direction her action and words took caused some tension between Mary and her husband. Mary expressed impatience, both to the point of scandal and guilt, about the treatment of the slaves in the South. She not only wanted to see better treatment and better working conditions but also freedom from human enslavement.

Catherine caught her breath and looked up slowly to see if Mary was watching her. She was scandalized that Mary would oppose her husband and get him into trouble and that she would advocate the abolition of slavery. Had Catherine's mother known this?

Mary did look at her now. "Oh dear," she said, "I hope I did not do the wrong thing letting you read the diary. You look pale. Are you finding it interesting?"

"Interesting? Oh, yes indeed," Catherine replied. Mary and Varina went back to their conversation and Catherine returned to the diary.

Mary's husband did not as obstinately oppose her views as some men in government. But if she expressed them in public conversation around Jefferson Davis, she would never again be allowed into a conversation when he was present. This meant as a silent listener or a participant and it might even reflect on James' position on President Davis' staff. Mary did not want to lose contact with President Davis or to cause trouble for her husband. It seemed all right as long as she expressed her views in the form of personal entries into her diary, even though they leaked out to the public as intended. But she must not interfere in the world of male politics and she must not become a noisy crusader who began to hold women's meetings. It challenged Mary to see how she might use her diary and her townhouse to establish an effective base for her activism—and Mary definitely had some ideas.

Catherine closed the diary and laid it aside. She rested her head on the back cushion of the chair and looked up at the ceiling. 'Being a friend to Mary Chesnut will not be without cost,' she thought to herself.

As it turned out, Catherine need not have worried about being able to converse with Mary through the evening. Varina had scheduled a party for the wives of the officers at the Southern White House and invited them to come, which invitation Mary accepted for them.

It was one of those elegant affairs for which Varina Howell Davis was famous. The great hall was decked with flowers of delicate, almost intoxicating fragrance and streamers and state flags were all around. It was a sit-down party, there being no men present with which to dance, and the room featured four long, beautiful, walnut tables with high-backed chairs of rich fabric covering.

Everyone seemed so gay and to be having such a fun time. The wine and champagne flowed and women talked—and talked and talked. Mary loved it but Catherine felt out of place. At this particular time, the president accompanied the Army of Northern Virginia and no one of note remained for Mary to talk serious things to, so they left early. This pleased Catherine. In the late evening, the date being July 22, 1861, Catherine and Mary returned to Axley Manor.

"Well, dear, there is nothing much to put in the diary from this night's chatter," Mary said. "I am going to bed to read a while. You do as you please."

More than an hour later, Catherine sat by the fire knitting when Varina Davis came in. She did not knock or announce herself and she moved so silently that she startled Catherine. Varina looked a bit the worse for parting, but she had a very sober countenance.

"Oh, Catherine, Dear, where is Mary?" she asked in an urgent tone.

"She is in bed reading if she is still awake," Catherine said. She followed Varina into Mary's bedroom.

Varina leaned over Mary in a familiar way of those a bit unsteady and said, almost in a whisper, "A great battle has taken place, Joe Johnston led the right wing and Beauregard the left. Wade Hampton has been wounded but not bad, it is thought. Your husband is all right, but Colonel Johnson of the legion is dead, along with Colonel Bee and Colonel Bartow. Kirby Smith is either wounded or killed."

Catherine stood tense and breathless, hanging on every word. She looked at Mary who seemed to be gripped by near panic.

Varina continued. "Bartow, rallying his men and leading them into the hottest and most crucial battle of the engagement, died heroically. My husband, the President, telegraphed me that it was a great and glorious victory for the South." Catherine was shocked to silence by the tenseness and the gratitude of the moment.

Mary spoke a little more firmly. "I am so grateful that my husband and those closest and most…yes, most important—are all right."

Varina seemed surprised by Mary's words and Catherine thought she started to say something to her, but then went on, in the same taut and focused voice, to read from a paper she held in her hand, prepared for her by General Cooper: "Dead and dying cover the field. Sherman's batteries taken. Lynchburg Regiment cut to pieces. Three hundred of the legion wounded."

Mary got up out of bed. "I don't think I can sleep," she said as she grasped Varina's arm. "Varina, you are so tired and worn. You must stay with us tonight. You should not be alone now."

Varina looked sad, worried and frustrated. "Oh, no, I cannot," she said with resolve. "I have to find Mrs. Bartow and tell her about her husband. And I cannot leave those frightened women alone. I simply must go back."

When she was gone, Mary lay ridged with tension. "Kitty," she said in a pleading voice, "What am I going to do? I cannot possibly sleep and I ache."

Catherine thought for a moment. "Well, Mamma says that the thing to do is pray. She says you will calm down and relief will come in time."

Mary nodded her head. "Yes," she said, "I feel that need, but I don't know if I can. I only pray in the morning when I rise." Catherine got up and started to leave. Mary stopped her. "Oh no, Kitty, please don't go. Stay here and talk to me."

Catherine knew that to talk about the battle would only keep Mary awake. She decided to tell her about the wedding.

"Oh, Kitty," Mary said in an excited voice. "Please get me my diary. I must get this down."

"No!" Catherine said firmly. "You are supposed to be trying to go to sleep, remember? Besides, I don't want my wedding to become a conversation piece among generals and their wives."

"Oh, all right," Mary said. With a sigh, she flattened herself on the bed with emphasis. Catherine began her review. She did not get to the part about the altar before Mary fell asleep.

Catherine got up and headed for her room. Now, would she be able to sleep? If not, she would sleep on the train.

Chapter Ten

The Gray of Winter

Three months passed since Catherine's last visit to Richmond. The strong desire to go again was secondary to the importance of being at Hopemont if anything final took place with her mother. Catherine gathered her short riding coat about her as the chill of early winter gusts penetrated her sweater and made her shiver. She looked around at the trees, many of which were now barren as the leaves had long since fallen and rains had plastered them to the ground. The fresh air of the woodland was compromised with smell of decay. It was a pithy, vegetation smell, but Catherine did not like it. In truth, she did not like winter. She had never liked it since a child.

Catherine stared, watery eyed, at the meadow before her. She thought about passing on today's session and returning to the barn but resolve and determination prevented her. She learned, from her earlier trip to Bowling Green to find her brother, that in order to be ready for life near the front with her husband, she must spend time in the saddle and must faithfully perform her drills. When the horse began to lather and her legs started aching, she dismounted, moved a good distance away from the tethered animal, and began target shooting. Her shoulder was sore from the kick of the rifle but she kept at it.

The sun had reached its apex and started down when Catherine rode out of the woods and toward home. Her pulse quickened as she saw Doctor Higgins' hack at the carriage shed. Catherine galloped the horse to the barn, handed the reins to a wailing Emmanuel without talking to him, and ran into the house. On the porch, she shed her coat and sweater and washed her hands and face. Then she ran up the stairs toward her mother's room. Doctor Higgins, who had apparently heard her on the stairs, came quickly out of her mother's room and closed the door. His hair was neat, his shirttail was in, and he looked more professional than she had ever seen him. There was a calm but severe look on his face.

"Catherine," he said with as much compassion as he was capable of, which was not much, "your mother's time has come."

Catherine thought she would panic when this time came, but, to her surprise, she didn't. "Is she gone?" she asked in an anxious but quiet tone.

"Not yet," Doctor Higgins answered, "but her moments are few. You had better go in now if you want to be sure…"

Without waiting for him to finish, Catherine slipped by him and into the room. It was quiet—almost serene. The medicinal smell was gone and the lavender scent had returned. The room was subdued but pleasant. Her mother's face was soft and peaceful. She opened her eyes and managed a faint smile. "Catherine, my precious girl, I was hoping you would come," she said weakly.

Catherine sat on the edge of the bed, took her mother's hand, leaned down and kissed her on the cheek. She tried to think of something to say, but nothing came to her. Finally, she said, cheerfully but emotionally, "I love you, Mamma."

Her mother managed a weak smile. "I know," she said "I know." After a few moments of silence, her mother spoke again. "You know, Catherine, I have thought a lot about this moment over the past months. You don't know how you're going to feel about it. There is nothing to prepare you for this experience. Yes, I am a little apprehensive, and for a while, I was a little scared. But I am not anymore. It will be all right, Sweetie; it will be all right."

Catherine knew she was expected to say something, so she repeated, "That's right, Mamma, it will be all right."

Her mother spoke again. "The words of an old hymn keep running through my mind."

When I come to the river at ending of day,
When the last trump of sorrow has blown,
There'll be somebody waiting to show me the way,
I won't have to Cross Jordan alone.

Catherine nodded. Her eyes filled with tears. She fumbled for a handkerchief as she watched her mother's face. Suddenly the breathing stopped and her mother gazed at the ceiling, a fixed, pleasant stare on her face, almost as if she looking through the roof, far off in the distance. Catherine waited for the breathing to resume, but it did not. Catherine had already seen death in Richmond. She knew what should be done. If her eyes were not closed soon, they would not close. If she wanted to stay in her mother's room for a while, undisturbed by the Doctor, she would have to do it. Hesitantly, she reached her hand toward her mother's face. Then she stopped. What if her eyelids did not close? She felt fear. Then she took a deep breath and put her hand to her mother's face. The eyelids closed obediently. Her mother looked as if she had gone into a peaceful sleep. "Maybe that is what has happened," Catherine said aloud to herself. She laid her head on her mother's breast and tried to think, between the tears and occasional sobs.

When Catherine left her mother's room, she found Doctor Higgins sitting at the kitchen table with Tuttle, drinking coffee. He did not ask her any questions. "You have lost a mother, Kitty," he said, trying to sound soft. Catherine could see the tears forming in his eyes. "I understand a little about that. I lost one too. I cannot enter fully into your grief of the moment, but I want you to know that we have lost a great lady. She was my friend, I will miss her, and I am sad."

Catherine went to him, put her arm around his shoulder, and laid her cheek on the top of his head. "Thank you so much—so very much—for everything," she said with feeling. "You have been such a good friend and helper. We have taken you so for granted and I am sorry."

Doctor Higgins pushed her gently away, turned in his chair, and looked at her. "No, Kitty," he said with conviction. His words sounded sage and Catherine listened intently. "We cannot feel as emotional, as kindly and as appreciative of each other through the years as we feel in this moment. That kind of emotional fervor would destroy us. It is life, Kitty. For you and me and your mother and your father and your family, it has been better than most. Let's leave it like that and not go back over it feeling sorry for every time we didn't do each other exactly right. There is nothing to be gained from that."

"Yes," Catherine said with conviction, "Thank you, Doctor Higgins, that helps me."

In the pause that followed Tuttle spoke up. "Well, Miss Cath'n," she said philosophically, "The Good Lawd sho' 'nuff go Hisself another Angel. Dat make two from dis house alone since I been here."

Catherine delayed the funeral as long as she could so her brothers and her sister could get home for the memorial. The day was cold and drizzly. At times, the icy wind blew in strong gusts. The service at the church was comforting. Catherine did not remember Parson Edwards ever having spoken so sweetly and with such powerful words. He concluded by reading the words of Jesus.

"I am the resurrection and the life. He that believeth on me, though he were dead, yet shall he live. And whosoever liveth and believeth in me shall never die."

His prayer was one of hope. He talked of seeing Henrietta again and of all meeting in a happier place in the new creation of the future. These were things that Catherine knew well, but they seemed to mean more now than ever. Even John was moved by the memorial sermon. She saw him engaged in a long and serious discussion with Parson Edwards while waiting for the casket to be loaded onto the spring wagon.

At the graveside, they stood under a canvas canopy that provided little shelter. The wind whipped it out of place and drove the slanting rain in under it. Those who could not get under the shelter protected themselves with parasols as best they could. Catherine was much comforted by the sight of her six brothers carrying the casket. Key, the smallest and the youngest, slipped and fell to his knees in the slick mud near the grave, but disaster was averted when Colonel Wolf, standing beside Parson Edwards holding the Confederate flag, moved quickly to grab the edge of the casket and hold it upright until Key regained his footing. Parson Edwards was very brief. He concluded again with words of Jesus.

> "Verily, verily I say unto you, the hour is coming and now is, when the dead shall hear the voice of the Son of God; and they that hear shall live. For as the Father hath life in Himself; so hath He given to the Son to have life in Himself; and hath given him authority to execute judgment also, because He is the Son of man. Marvel not at this: for the hour is coming, in which all that are in the grave shall hear His voice, and shall come forth; they that that have done good, unto the resurrection of life; and they that have done evil, unto the resurrection of damnation."

"We have not seen the last of Henrietta Hunt Morgan," he said confidently. "This is not 'goodbye forever,' but 'farewell for awhile.'"

As the crowd moved away to their rigs, Catherine stood looking at the grave and trying to envision that event. Parson Edwards saw her there and understood her thoughts. "We live by faith; not by sight, Catherine," he said wisely. "The finite mind cannot comprehend the infinite. Do not try to understand it; just believe it."

The thought helped her. "Thank you, Reverend Edwards," she said. The poet Walt Whitman, one of her father's acquaintances, was in attendance and standing nearby. He overheard the conversation. "Excuse me, Reverend," he said with skeptical good humor, "But I don't think I agree. I don't think we are required to believe anything we cannot reason out."

Catherine left them to their discussion and went to join her family.

It was a sad but a rewarding time the family spent at Hopemont over the next several days. Her sister, Henrietta, her mother's namesake, stayed for most of the week. When they were gone, she supervised the covering of the furniture and preparing the house for her extended absence. She went carefully over everything she wanted

Emmanuel and Tuttle to do. Against the advice of Colonel Wolf and Richard Todd her banker, Catherine made the decision to leave Emmanuel in charge of the estate. When she could think of nothing more to do and when her trunks were all packed, the time had come to leave for Richmond.

Catherine's baggage was too much for the buggy, so they took the spring wagon to Lexington and the train depot. Catherine sat on a cushion, but the ride was still uncomfortable. On the way, Catherine went over things again with Emmanuel to make sure he understood.

"Now, Emmanuel," she asked, "What are you going to do on the first day of each month?"

"I's g'wine to de bank," he answered dutifully, "and Mars Todd g'wine to gib me my money."

"And what are you going to do when you go to the store?"

"I gibs de man de list of things," he said, "and when he hand me de paper, I's g'wine sign my name to it."

Catherine smiled proudly. He seemed very confident. "And what are you going to do if there is trouble of any sort?"

"I's g'wine tell Colonel Wolf all about it and he g'wine send you a message ober de wire to Richmun'."

"And if you need hay or feed or the veterinarian or the doctor or anything like that?"

"I got to go after dem in de buggy. When they is done, they gives me a paper to sign and I tells dem to take it and get their money from Mars Todd."

"Very good," Catherine said. She looked at him and he became nervous. "Emmanuel," she said, "Are you sure you can handle things? I mean, I don't want to put more on you than you can do."

Emmanuel looked troubled. "Miss Cath'n," he said soberly, "I is if you don' keep askin' me. You g'wine make me think I cain't, if you keep up."

Catherine put her hand on his arm. "I am sorry, Emmanuel," she said, "but I just wanted to make sure that it isn't just my idea."

Colonel Wolf met them at the station. "When will we see you again?" he asked.

"I will come home from time to time to see that all is well," she said, "or if there are any problems. But I will not be coming back to stay until the war is over."

Emmanuel was listening carefully. "And den, Miss Cath'n?" he asked.

Catherine understood his worry. She smiled as she said, "And then we will see, Emmanuel. It is my plan to come home to stay. But don't you worry. You and Tuttle will be fully taken care of by me, whatever happens."

Emmanuel seemed relieved. She gave Colonel Wolf a hug. She wanted to hug Emmanuel but people had gathered to see her off. She felt that it would be a disservice to him, so she shook his hand.

"I don't like it, Miss Kitty," Colonel Wolf said, "You being that close to the front and the fighting."

Catherine patted him on the shoulder, smiled indulgently, and said tersely, "Let's don't start that again, Colonel. My mind is made up."

"I hear that the generals don't like it," he said.

"Then the generals will have to get used to it," she answered without concession. Catherine waved goodbye and got on board.

As the train pulled slowly out of the station and moved beyond the waving and calling out, Catherine settled back in her seat. A feeling of melancholy crept over her. There was a strong sense that something profound had taken place. An era had ended. Something that had existed was gone forever. She had no family—no ties to Lexington anymore. Only her property and her servants remained. Most of her relatives were dead or gone and her husband was in Virginia. Only her uncle, the mayor, remained, and they had never been close because of strong political and philosophical differences between him and her father. Her only tie to him was her mother and now…

She loved Kentucky and she still had interests there, but it was no longer her home—or was it? She was confused. Catherine did not weep and she was not in an emotional state but sentiments controlled her. She could not look ahead; forces greater than her will pulled her back. She thought about many things from the past and all of them touched tender spots inside of her. If she was angry or hurt, she could blink back the tears. But now her eyes were like pools slowly, silently filling up from subterranean sources. They did not overflow, but they were full to the brim and now and then, a tear spilled over and crawled softly down her cheek.

The porter, a familiar face to her, came by with a pillow. He stood over her, looking down. "Missers Hill," he said in a tone that arrested her attention, "You don't know how much of a burden you been down under of late. Now is time to git some of dat weight go off'n you. Don' worry 'bout nothin', Ma'am. You is goin' to be all right." He put his big, soft hand behind her shoulders, pulled her gently forward, and tucked the pillow in around her.

Catherine looked around to see if anyone was watching. He should not have touched her in that way, but she did not mind as long as no one else saw it. She wondered what she had done to cause him to feel that liberty. She saw him often on the train and treated him with kindness but not fraternally. His gesture expressed a kinship with which she could not identify. It projected more than met the eye, but she could not pursue it now.

The pillow eased her tensions and allowed her to relax. Her state of mind felt strange and unfamiliar to her. She had no will to do anything but sit there and let her mind take its course. In time, she fell asleep.

Chapter Eleven

The Green of Spring

Her husband Ambrose was waiting for her at the Richmond station. His orderlies took her luggage and she went with him in the cab.

"How are you, Catherine, my Dear?" he asked her in a worried tone.

Catherine regarded her husband thoughtfully. She could not quite make out the immediate cause of his concern. "Oh, I am all right, Ambrose," she said. "Do I look terrible?"

Her husband did a start. "No, not at all," he said, "You look fine. But you have been through so much. I was just wondering."

Catherine sighed and leaned her head against his chest. She suddenly realized how much she missed and needed him. So many times in recent days she had felt so alone, as if the weight of the world were on her shoulders and that it was up to her to be the strength for everyone in her world. Now she had someone to protect her and to whom she could go in times of stress. "It hurts," she said, "and I guess to some extent it always will. I owe it to Mamma never to forget her and I don't want to forget her." She stopped and thought a moment. She did not want to sound pitifulor to drag him down. "But it is life, my Darling," she continued. "It happens to everyone. I am all right. I thought it all out on the train. I am ready to move on."

The cab stopped at the Southern White House. The sight of that magnificent building inspired confidence and hope in Catherine's breast. She thought they had paused for a moment to admire. Then her husband opened the door and started to get out. "What are we doing?" She asked, "I thought I was going to the front with you."

Her husband patted her on the shoulder and smiled reassuringly. "You are," he said. "President Davis has assigned us a small house in the woods south of town and near the headquarters. You are to stay in Richmond a few days until everything is moved in and made ready."

Catherine's disappointment flashed like anger. "But Ambrose," she said, "I can…"

Her husband looked her in the eye and shook his head slowly. "No," he said firmly, cutting her off. "I will not have it. I cannot be there with you during the day, and I am not going to leave you alone in a strange place to get depressed and discouraged trying to get things arranged. I have made preparations. If you don't like it, you can change things around when you get there. But I will not let you go there until everything is ready for you to move in and settle down."

Catherine thought quickly. He seemed so determined and if he was not going to be there, perhaps it was better this way. As he said, she could do whatever rearranging she wished to once they moved in. "Very well," she said, "that seems prudent. I am to stay in the White House, then?"

"No," he said, "Varina, the president's wife, will take you to your accommodations. You will like her, I think."

Catherine was relieved at hearing Varina's name and that she was not going to spend the night at the home of a stranger. It was like suddenly finding a friend in a strange place. "I know her," Catherine said, "and I do like her, very much."

Her husband looked at her questioningly. "You do?" he asked. "How is that?"

Catherine sighed. After arriving home from the last Richmond visit, she made the decision not to tell him about the visit to Mary in her letters. She had not asked his permission to stay over and she saw no reason to mention it. Now she wished she had written him about it. "When I was here last," she said, "I got a note from one of Mamma's friends, a Mary Chesnut. I went to visit her before returning home. While I was there, Varina Davis came over and I met her."

Her husband thought before answering. He looked very sober. "So you know Mary Chesnut too?" he asked in a strained voice.

Catherine was perplexed. How could something so innocent suddenly become an issue? "Yes," she said. "Ambrose, you are not upset with me, are you?"

He did not answer immediately. Then he said, very carefully. "No, sweetheart, I am not upset with you. In fact, it is at the home of Mary Chesnut where you are going to be staying for a few days." Catherine thought he seemed in doubt whether to continue. Then he said, "But Catherine, I want you to be careful around that woman. She has some very strange ideas and she is not quiet about them always."

Catherine sensed there was some tension in this situation and she decided to hold nothing from him that would come back to haunt her. "I know about her strange ideas," she said.

Her husband looked worried. "She told you all of that when you first met?" he asked.

"No," she replied, trying to anticipate where this was going.

"Well, then how did you know about it?" he asked her, trying not to be accusative in his tone.

"I read her diary," Catherine answered. Some of the emotions she felt when she was reading it were now coming back to her and she thought she knew his concern.

"All of it?" he asked.

"Yes—well, most of it," she said.

"But Catherine, how…" He stopped and looked troubled. She could see the corner he was in. She decided to put an end to the cat and mouse game.

"Ambrose, she prevailed upon me to stay overnight and I did. I did not have an opportunity to ask you, so I used my own judgment. She was such a friend of Mamma's. While I was there, Varina came in. She and Mary Chesnut talked for several hours. During their discussion, I read her diary."

Her husband digested the information. Catherine could see that he was struggling and that what she said did not set well with him. Finally he said tersely, "I see."

Catherine was stunned. How could he be angry about this? But he seemed to be. "Ambrose," she asked, trying to keep emotion out of her voice, "you are upset with me, aren't you?"

"No," he answered dryly.

Catherine could see that he did not want to hurt her but at the same time, he could not let go of it. "Are you sure?" she asked, wanting to get this matter settled.

Her husband stared into her eyes for a long moment. Then she saw him soften a little. "Yes, I am sure, Catherine," he said quietly. "It's just that Mary Chesnut worries me and I do not want you to be recruited for her cause."

Catherine looked around before answering. The White House was magnificent, the town was beautiful, and the lovely trees and flowers gave off such a pleasant aroma. Even for a winter day, the sun was shining and it was pleasant. She had long anticipated the time when she would come here to stay with him permanently. She did not expect it to be exactly like this. It should have been a charming moment, but it wasn't; at least not just now. She knew of his unusual sensitivity before they married and that small things bothered him more than they did her. She had never paid much thought to it, feeling that it had to do with other things and other people besides her. Well, if she had made a mistake, she might as well know it. She turned and looked him in the face. "Ambrose," she asked firmly, "don't you trust me?"

He looked back and then looked away. "Yes, Catherine," he said softly, "I do trust you. But I also want to protect you. And of course, you know my position as a general in the Army of the Confederacy. I just want you to know the concerns I feel about Mary Chesnut and ask you to keep those feelings in mind as you mix with her. I will not bring it up again."

Catherine caught her breath. "A general? Did you say a general?"

"Yes," he said, proudly. "It just came down this week. I was going to tell you but we got off on other things. I am a brigadier now."

She gave him a hug, then backed away and looked at him. "Ambrose," she said reassuringly, "I know your concerns about Mary Chesnut and I feel them too. As I told you, I read most of her diary." She paused and looked for the right tone of voice. "But she was mother's dear friend," she said, "and I want to give her a chance. Maybe I can help her."

His countenance brightened and she saw the crisis pass. She put her hand in his as they walked up the long steps to the White House.

Catherine stayed a week with Mary Chesnut. She saw her husband most evenings, but he would never consent to stay the night. Finally, he told her that all was in readiness. With great joy, she moved in. At last, she was home with her husband to stay until the war was over and they could go back to Hopemont. Their little house was modest but nice. It was secluded in the woods on the southern outskirts of Richmond, about a half-mile from Lee's headquarters. Catherine loved it there because she was with her husband. He took away the loneliness that she first felt about her mother, and the homesickness for Hopemont soon passed. Catherine took to conjugal life with great devotion and applied herself to the matter of making her husband happy in all ways. When the army was in the field, Catherine went along and camped as near to the fighting as General Lee would allow. She was able to be with her husband most nights. This greatly displeased General Jackson and some of the other generals. Catherine did not care. Her husband did care, but not enough to send her back home.

At this particular time, McClellan had withdrawn to Washington and there was little activity on the Northern Virginia front. No one expected it to last long, but General Lee and her husband had returned to the permanent headquarters of the Army of Northern Virginia in Richmond, waiting for something to happen. There were things Lee needed to catch up on and little time in which to do it. Her husband approached her about helping out at the headquarters with General Lee. At first, Catherine, for some reason that she did not entirely understand, viewed this as a threat to the great oneness that they had developed in their married life. But her husband kept bringing it up and it was clear to her that it meant a great deal to him. Catherine wavered. 'Was Lee asking for her?' She doubted it, but... Finally, she agreed and before long, she found it a pleasant addition and a way to fill the lonely hours when her husband was gone. She never went to the headquarters when her husband was in the house.

Less than two months after they had moved into their new home, Catherine was with child. She returned to their home in Richmond to stay until the baby was born and was old enough to take out in the field. Mary and Varina fussed so about it being her first child and all the things that could go wrong, but Catherine never worried. The birth was easy and they had little Henrietta, a bouncing, red-haired, green-eyed girl. Catherine loved everything about her life in Richmond with her husband. She had never envisioned such peace, contentment, and sense of being where it was all happening and fully involved in the cause. The birth of her daughter meant that she would not be able to go to the headquarters for a while and she would miss that. She had developed a good working relationship with and a sincere appreciation of Robert E. Lee on the few occasions when he was at his headquarters in Richmond. He was the consummate gentleman, soldier, and leader. He allowed her to go there when he was gone and attend to a few things. It was a pleasant part of her life that would have to be put on hold.

The baby was about four months old and both her husband and General Lee were in Richmond for a little while. Though her husband was in Richmond, he was seldom at the house during the day. He was not on leave and was usually out on training exercises or planning sessions from morning until evening. As Catherine sat on the porch swing rocking her baby and singing to her, she saw a familiar figure riding up the lane. When he got near enough, she saw it was General Lee. He dismounted and stood at the foot of the porch.

"Please come up, General, and have a seat," she said, wondering what the occasion was.

He sat beside her and reached out his hands. "May I hold the baby?" he asked. Catherine hesitated. "I have three daughters of my own," he said with an amused twinkle. "I do know how to hold girl babies."

"Oh, of course," she said, "I was just trying to think if she was wet, or anything."

Lee took the baby and beamed down at her. "Looks just like her mother," he said. "Red headed, green eyed and gorgeous."

Catherine was embarrassed. "Thank you," she said.

Lee handed her back the baby. "I suppose you wonder what I am doing up here?" he asked.

"Well," Catherine said, trying to think what the appropriate answer would be, "I did wonder if there was an occasion of some sort."

Lee leaned back, crossed his legs, and pushed up his hat. "Actually, there is. I could have sent someone else up with the message, but I sort of wanted to see this baby. I have heard so much about her."

Catherine was embarrassed. "Oh, General Lee," she said, "Have you never seen Henrietta? I am so sorry that we…"

"No, actually, it is very much my own fault. Your husband has invited me to come up to the house many times, but I just…well, anyway, we have a report from intelligence that there is going to be an invasion of Lexington shortly." Catherine reacted with surprise and fear. Lee moved quickly to calm her down. "Don't get too excited, Miss Kitty, it is not supposed to be much. As we have it, it is an attempt to encourage slaves to defect to Ohio. It is not actually to be a military operation in the strictest sense of the word. But it is being led, or so we think, by a Union captain. It is a bit of a shadowy report and there are a number of questions, but I do believe we have enough to say that it is, in all likelihood, going to happen." Lee could see that Catherine's hands were trembling and he took the baby again.

"When is this supposed to happen, General Lee?" she asked.

"Well," he said, "as we have it, the early part of next week. Possibly even over the weekend."

"Will I have time to get there first?" she asked.

Lee looked surprised. "You would have to hurry," he said, looking at her gravely. "Would you do that?" he asked.

"I will if my husband will let me," she said with finality.

"But the baby? Surely you can't take her on a trip like that," Lee said as if he was about to issue an order preventing it.

"I will leave her with Varina. She loves to have her. She will be all right for a few days or a week."

Lee handed her back the baby and rose to leave. "Maybe I shouldn't have told you," he said thoughtfully.

"If you hadn't," Catherine answered with good humor that shaded but did not hide the seriousness of her words, "I would never have forgiven you."

When dinner was over, they put the baby in warm wraps and went out to sit on the porch. The air was fresh with the smell of pine, fir, and spruce. A few night birds were calling. A whippoorwill, which stayed nearby, was making its haunting sounds. The stars were out and bright. A big, yellow moon had just risen and cleared the trees, bathing everything in a magical, silvery light. The couch swung gently. Catherine thought it was such an enchanting moment that she hated to spoil it, but she must tell him.

When he had heard her out, he looked at her soberly. She could see his long, smooth face in the moonlight but she could not see his eyes. Finally, he said, "And you want to go, I suppose?"

Catherine put her hands in her lap and determined to be calm, sweet, and obedient. Even so, her words sounded tense and almost desperate. "I feel that I must, Ambrose, if you will let me."

He was silent for a while. Then he said, "I feel that you should go too, Catherine. There is too much at stake, and I doubt your servant is able to handle a crisis, though I don't mean to…" He paused, not knowing how to finish his sentence. Catherine breathed a sigh of relief. She had been prepared for the difficult job of gentle persuasion. "You will leave the baby with Varina, then?"

"Yes," Catherine said.

"You have talked to her about it?" he asked.

"No," she answered, "but I am sure she will do it. You know how she is always trying to get me to come into Richmond and leave her a few hours."

"Yes," he said, "I am sure she will."

Catherine grew sentimental. "I hate to leave her that long with strangers," she said, "but…"

"Don't worry, Sweetie," he said, "not a day will pass without her seeing her father's face." Catherine snuggled against his arm.

"Thank you so much," she said.

The magic feeling returned and they sat for a while longer and enjoyed it. "You will want to be going early and it's getting a little too cold for the baby," her husband said at last. "Perhaps we should go in."

Chapter Twelve

Let My People Go

As they neared Lexington, Catherine looked for signs of trouble but saw none. The train arrived at the station without incident. When she got off the train, she questioned the stationmaster.

"Some sort of disorder was going on in town a while back," he said, "but it looked mighty strange for a military operation. What little fightin' they was on Main Street passed a few hours ago and there don't seem to be nuthin' happ'nin' in the middle a town, Ma'am."

Catherine, no stranger to the sounds of war or the nearness of fighting, and not the least bit afraid, walked down the street toward the telegraph center to see if she could find Colonel Wolf. The smell of gunpowder lingered in the air and she saw evidences of fighting here and there—a round had broken a window or knocked a piece of brick out of a wall. Far off in the distance she could hear a rifle pop now and then. Though it was fall and the evenings were cool, there seemed to be a stickiness in the air.

Dark descended rapidly and she hurried to get to the telegraph center where Emmanuel left the horse and buggy for her. As she walked past an open lot, she heard the sound of moaning and someonecrying out. She saw several wounded northern soldiers lying on the ground. They looked to be blacks. Surely, the North had not stooped to using Negroes in its forces! She started to go in and report it to the Colonel when she heard a familiar voice say, "Miss Cath'n, is dat you? Please he'p me, I'm dyin' sho nuff."

Catherine strained her eyes and looked, not wanting to go any closer. "Who said that?" she called out. "What did you say?"

"Oh, Miss Cath'n, thank the dear Lawd. It's me, Tuttle," she heard the faint but unmistakable voice say.

Catherine made her way around the wounded soldiers and across the dark lot. The ground was slippery beneath her feet and the lot smelled of death and pollution. She reached Tuttle and looked down at the dusty, bloody face. "Tuttle! What in the world?"

"Oh, Miss Cath'n. Oh, Lawd! Oh, Lawd!"

"Tuttle! What are you doing with that Yankee cap and that blue arm band?" Catherine demanded sharply.

"Oh, Miss Kitty! Lawd have mercy!" Tuttle moaned.

"Stop that and answer me—quickly," Catherine snapped impatiently.

"Oh, Miss Cath'n," Tuttle said in anguish. "Miss Moses done come to town wid her black b'gade. She trying' to recruit darkies to jine up wid her."

Catherine was stunned by the news. "Oh, Tuttle, no!" she exclaimed. "How could you?"

"Miss Cath'n, I's de sorriest…"

"Here, give me that cap and that arm band," Catherine said. She reached down and jerked it off Tuttle's arm.

"Ouch! Lawd, Ma'am!"

"Well, it serves you right," Catherine answered without sympathy. "Now, you stay right here."

"How can I go no where, if'n I wuz to want to?"

"Well, you stay here anyway," Catherine ordered. "I am going to get you some help."

Colonel Wolf sent the medics to bring Tuttle into the dispensary. Then he came into the anteroom where Catherine was waiting. He sat down, turning his face at right angles to her and looking at her out of the corner of his eye. "All right, Miss Kitty," he said coldly, "what is it this time?"

"Why, Colonel," Catherine said innocently, "I don't know what you mean?"

"Oh, I think you do," Wolf answered in a gruff voice. "The men found Tuttle lying with injured Negra solders in Yankee uniforms. There was a rifle on the ground near her."

"They must have seen her," Catherine answered slowly so she could choose her words, "and when she wouldn't sympathize with them, they shot her."

Colonel Wolf looked hard at her for a few moments. Then he took a deep breath. "Kitty, now listen to me," he said sternly. "You know that your husband is often accused of being a Yankee sympathizer because of his past association with Mrs. McClellan. I want to help you and I always have. But I do not have the same dedication to this little black…to Tuttle. I want the truth—and don't you lie to me—and I think we can exonerate you and your husband from this."

Catherine looked hurt. "Did I ever lie to you, Colonel?" she asked.

"I never knew you to lie to anyone," he said, "and don't you start now. I must have the truth. Was Tuttle going off with Harriet Tubman? Was she joined in with these—these Negra troops?" He paused and regarded her narrowly. "There was a Yankee cap and a blue armband found in the bushes at the edge of the lot. Did you change anything when you found Tuttle?"

Catherine suddenly felt prickly with sweat and her mouth was dry. She mustered all the courage she had and looked the Colonel in the face. She hoped that she did not look as guilty outside as she felt within. "No, sir. I did not," she said, her voice cracking just a bit.

"You did not?" Wolf asked.

"I did not," she replied.

"You did not?" he asked again in obvious disbelief.

"Colonel Wolf, I…"

The Colonel held up his hand and sighed in frustration. "Miss Kitty," he said, "my men think you took that cap and band off her and threw it in the bushes. And that is what they are probably going to be saying among themselves. I may be able to stop them if I get rough enough but I hate…" The Colonel stopped and took and a deep breath. “All right, Kitty; all right,” he said with doubt and disappointment.

Catherine gathered her courage. She must not back off now. “Colonel,” she said firmly, “I want to take Tuttle home.”

The Colonel shook his head. “She cannot go now,” he said.

Catherine moved to the edge of her chair trying to appear aggressive. “Why not?” she asked as forcefully as she could.

“She needs medical attention that you cannot give her at home,” the Colonel said without conviction. She is not fatally wounded, but she is seriously wounded. She may die if you take her home.”

Catherine knew he was making an excuse to hide the real reason, so she pressed him hard. “I will take that chance,” she said.

“I will not let you take that chance,” the Colonel answered. “I know you are scared, but I have to keep her here, at least for a few days. If you are not lying to me, everything will be all right.”

Catherine did not give in as he had hoped. “Is her medical condition the only reason?” she asked.

Colonel Wolf looked out the window. “No,” he said, “she has to be questioned.” Catherine moved further out on the edge of her chair and started to protest. Colonel Wolf held up his hand and stopped her. “I can’t get around it, Kitty,” he said flatly. His voice had changed and Catherine’s hopes fell. She put on a hurt and angry face, in an effort to play on his sympathies and he tried to be conciliatory. “I am sorry,” he said, “but under the circumstances, it is better this way. If I did get around it, it would cast suspicions on you and your husband and me. The Sergeant who found her thinks she was fighting with the Yankees. He is going to put that in his report. The worst thing I could do would be to not question her.” Catherine tried not to look worried and distressed, but she couldn’t help it and she saw that is was doing nothing for Colonel Wolf’s confidence. Catherine thought he was returning to his original suspicion. “Kitty,” he said compassionately, “there’s still time to get out of this.”

“What do you mean, Colonel?” she asked with as much innocence as she could manage.

“All right,” he said, “That’s the way it is, then. We will have to go with this.” He started to rise.

"Colonel Wolf, I have to see Tuttle," she said insistently, "you do not have the right to deny me that."

The Colonel sank back into his chair. "I don't think you should," he said tiredly.

Catherine could see he was starting to weaken, if she could just keep the pressure on. "I have to, just for a moment," she said emotionally. "She will be so afraid. I have to reassure her that I am not angry with her and that it is all right. I know her, Colonel…"

"We have given her something to make her sleep," he responded. "She will not be worrying about anything in a little while."

Catherine shook her head negatively, in rejection. "But…"

"Oh, all right," he said. Her insides began to ease up. She was winning him over. "But Kitty, just for a very little while—please. Let's don't raise any more suspicions than there already are. Here," he said, "take this note." The Colonel scribbled something on a piece of paper. "Give this to the orderly. I am going home where they can't find me for a while."

"Thank you so much," Catherine said as he was leaving the room. She was light-headed and sat for a moment, breathing deeply to get her pulse rate down. Then she took the note to the corporal at the desk to the dispensary. She gave it to him and started to go on in.

The corporal reacted swiftly. "Ah…just a moment, Ma'am", he said uncertainly.

"Is there some problem?" she asked, tying to sound forceful.

The Corporal shifted uncomfortably. "I have to get the Captain's approval," he said nervously.

Catherine saw his lack of resolve and came down on him hard. "This authorization is signed by Colonel Wolf, Corporal," she said, impatiently.

"I know, but…just a moment, please." Without giving her a chance to reply, he rushed over to a second lieutenant attending to a wounded man. He listened to the Corporal, looked at the note, and then looked at Catherine.

Finally, he came over to her. "Ma'am," he said politely, "you are going to have to wait until we can get the Captain's approval."

Catherine knew they would fold if she kept the pressure on them. “I cannot wait. I explained that to the Colonel. He told me to give you this note.”

“Ma’am, there’s a problem…”

“Listen to me, Lieutenant,” she said in a military tone. “I am Mrs. Hill, the wife of General Ambrose Powell Hill. I have a note from the commanding officer of this command. My servant has been wounded by a bunch of hoodlums, and I need to see her and see her now, Lieutenant.”

The lieutenant looked at the corporal and they walked off a few paces. A captain came into view and they went over to him. He started to go up front and then stopped. He shrugged his shoulders and said something to the corporal. He came back to the desk. “I am sorry, Mrs. Hill,” he said, “you may go in now.”

Catherine hurried back to Tuttle. “Tuttle, are you awake?” she asked.

“Yes, Ma’am, I sho’ is, but I is gettin’ sleepy,” Tuttle said, barely above a whisper.

“Are you awake enough to listen to me?”

Tuttle yawned. “Yes, Ma’am.”

“All right, then listen,” Catherine said urgently, moving in very close to her face. “You only have to remember this one little thing. Go to sleep saying it and wake up saying it. They are going to question you tomorrow.”

“Oh, Lawd!” Tuttle cried, her body tensing and her eyes dilating.

Catherine put her hand over Tuttle’s mouth and then took it off. “Don’t panic, just listen,” she said, lowering her voice so no one listening outside the room could hear. “You were standing alongside the road in front of our house to see what the commotion was. Someone grabbed you and started pulling you along. After that, you do not remember anything but being shot and being brought here. Have you got that?”

“Yes’um.”

Tuttle was almost gone and Catherine was worried she would remember nothing.

“Tuttle,” she said almost desperately, “you must listen to me. Don’t say anything else. Don’t try to think anything else. It makes no difference if they yell at you and accuse you of lying, or what they do."

"Do I remember talkin' to you, Ma'am?" Tuttle asked.

Catherine was reassured by Tuttle's question and she breathed a sigh of relief. "No, you do not. Not out there—not now. Whatever they say, you do not remember talking to me. You just don't, that's all. Period!"

"Yes, Ma'am," Tuttle answered.

"Tuttle," Catherine said, "I will be back to see you as soon as they will let me in." Catherine kissed her on the forehead and left.

At the door, the captain met her. "Well, that was short, Mrs. Hill," he said.

"I have to leave soon," she answered, trying to sound casual, "and I needed to see her before I went. I don't think it did any good. You kept me waiting too long I fear. She was in a dreamy state and I don't think she even knows I was here."

The captain glanced at the corporal. "I am sorry, Mrs. Hill," he said, "but regulations, you know, and…"

"Oh, it's all right, Captain," she said kindly. "I am a military wife and I understand."

The captain seemed doubtful, as if her change of heart were too convenient. Catherine picked it up and second-guessed herself. Now she wished she had been angry and accusative. "Thank you, Ma'am," he said dutifully.

Chapter Thirteen

And A Time to Weep

Catherine left the medical center in Lexington and drove the horse and buggy toward Hopemont as fast as she dared. Catherine felt an acute need to get things under control and soon. At the increased pace, the horse's gait was jerky and the buggy swayed and bounced more than usual, adding to her sense of insecurity. The road was especially lonely this night. The trees came into her view like lurking figures, threatening her. The call of the night birds sounded like signals for an attack by troops hidden along the road and frightened her. The cool night air kept down the pleasant scents and all she could feel in her nose was the raw sensation of too much tension and difficulty breathing.

She desperately wanted to get home. At least there would be Emmanuel and his usual homespun philosophy to calm her down. But even that prospect failed her this very troubled and confusing night. As she drove in the yard, Emmanuel stepped out from the shadow of the carriage shed where he had been waiting all evening and startled her. He was in a state of mind that offered her no comfort. "Miss Tuttle done ran off an left me, Miss Cath'n," he said in a lifeless and pitiful voice. "I don't know what I'll do."

This turn of events forced Catherine to get a hold on herself and her emotions. "It's all right, Emmanuel," she said reassuringly, "we have found her."

Emmanuel started to clap his hands for joy, and then stopped. "You did? He asked suspiciously. "Why ain't she wid you?"

"She's in the military dispensary downtown, Emmanuel," Catherine answered.

"Oh, Lawd," Emmanuel cried, "dey got her a prizner."

Catherine grew cautious and chose her words carefully. She did not want to lie to Emmanuel, but she must bring some hope to this pathetic soul or he might not last the night. "No, she is not a prisoner. At least, I don't think she is," Catherine said quietly and without emotion. Then she changed directions. "Emmanuel, what got into her? I did not think Tuttle was capable of such a thing. I thought you and she had such a good life."

Emmanuel looked down, as if he was going to cry. Then he looked at her as straight as he could. "We did, Ma'am, an'…well…"

"What is it, Emmanuel?" Catherine demanded kindly but firmly. "Tell me everything. I need to know."

Emmanuel looked terrified. "Well, Ma'am. She ain't never been the same since I tole her 'bout seein' you on de porch dat day."

Catherine was startled and felt her heart rate rise again. She was ready for any answer but that one. "You told her about that? But why?"

Emmanuel pushed his hands in his pockets, kicked at the dirt, and walked around in several circles. "I had to, Ma'am, don' ya see," he pleaded. "Me and Tuttle was friends. I couldn't keep nuthin' like dat from her. It would 'a showed on my face and pushed us apart."

Catherine had never thought about it; she had determined with herself that night, after talking to Emmanuel in the Colonnade, that she would never think about it again. But now she had to, and it was clear to her why he had to tell her. It made Catherine feel very strange to think that Tuttle had known all this time and Catherine had never once considered that possibility. "But why would it affect her in a bad way, Emmanuel?" she asked, determined to get to the bottom of the problem. "Surely she did not think that I…that you…that we…"

Emmanuel staggered as if he was going to fall. Even in the darkness, she could see his eyes growing large. "Oh, no Ma'am!" he said as if being accused of something terrible. "Oh, no! Oh, Lawd, no!"

"Then what was it, Emmanuel?"

Emmanuel looked helpless, frightened, and uncomfortable. "I 'spec I know some of it, Ma'am," he said, "but I don' know as I kin tell ya."

Catherine shivered. The night air was too cold and she should go in, but she did not want to leave just now. She could hear his short, difficult breathing. "Well, try, Emmanuel; just try," she said, "I must know."

Emmanuel sat down on the step of the buggy. He was close to her and she could smell the hay and the barn on him. The poor boy had not washed nor eaten. He had been standing there all afternoon and evening waiting for her to come. "You see, Ma'am," he said, "after I tole Tuttle 'bout seein' you on de po'ch, she begins to think in her mine. 'He sho' can't think much of me, after he done seen her. How bad I got to look to him. How poo'ly he must feel in bed wit me, knowin' that I ain't nothin' but an old black rag.'" Emmanuel stopped, looked at Catherine, and shook his head sadly. "Cou'se, it ain't dat way, Ma'am, and she know it ain't dat way. But it work on her mine and it took somethin' out'n her." Emmanuel got up, walked over to the shed, and leaned against the door.

"We talked about it for a while and it he'p some," Emmanuel continued. "Then adder while, it don't he'p no mo'e. It jes' make it wuss." Emmanuel stopped and took a deep breath, as if trying to maintain control of his emotions. "I hoped maybe some day she would grow out'n it. But now I see she ain't goin' to."

A great feeling of sorrow came over Catherine. How wrong she had been in what she said to her mother. It *had* ruined his life. "Oh, Emmanuel, I am so sorry," she said. "If only I had locked that screen door."

Emmanuel jammed his hands in his overalls pockets, lowered his gaze and shook his head negatively. "It ain't' yo' fault, Ma'am," he said with conviction. "No body could be better to us than you and yo' mama been. It's jist this sinful worl', Ma'am. Hain't going be no better 'till the good Lawd comin' back and make everthin' over again."

Catherine thought perhaps Emmanuel was right, but she could not tell him so. "Emmanuel," she said, trying to be as cheerful and as hopeful as she could, "Let me tell you what I think. I think God allowed this to happen to Tuttle, today I mean, to change her mind and make her more appreciative of and dependant on you. I think this will clear that out of her head. I think Tuttle will be different when she gets back."

Emmanuel looked at her for a long moment. Then he managed a faint little smile and his white teeth showed in the light of the moon, which had just risen. "You shore thinkin' nice for me, Ma'am," he said sadly. "I sho' hope you is right, but…yes Ma'am, I sho' hope you is right."

Catherine still had the reigns in her hand. She gave them to Emmanuel, went in on the screen porch, and sat down on the bed. It was there she had always retreated when things were troubling her. But this time it brought her no relief. Her happy place had turned cold, dark, and depressing. Her mother and her father were dead; her brother was an atheist and a cruel man. There was war and killing and now the South was starting to go into a decline. Tuttle was wounded. Through one small oversight, she had ruined the happiness that Tuttle and Emmanuel felt in each other; the only thing of real value they ever had and probably ever would have in this life. And Colonel Wolf knew she was lying to him. Catherine trembled inside and gasped for breath. She had never lied to anyone. But what was she to do? She thought she was preserving Emmanuel and Tuttle—which she saw as her Christian duty. Now it appeared that she had cast a line to a sinking ship.

Beside that, Catherine ached all over. Her chest hurt, her nose and eyes burned, her legs pained, and she had a hard time getting her breath. The porch seemed stuffy. The Honeysuckle gave off no scent and the room smelled musty, like old wash water. Nothing at all was right.

She put her head in her hands and began to cry. Then she felt the bed move. Emmanuel had come in and sat down beside her. He looked like a helpless, lost frightened little child. Catherine was gripped by a strange feeling for him—like she had never known before. It was a feeling akin to pity but it wasn't pity. It was a very warm and emotional feeling like…like she wanted to nurse him as she had her baby…or something like that. She did not know this feeling and it made her uneasy. He had seen her sitting nude on that bed. Now he was sitting there beside her and she was alone with him in the dark house and not another soul within a mile. Her mother had said the image would never leave his mind. Was he thinking of that? Catherine was sure that he was not. Still, she was confused as to what to do next and uncertain what she would do next. She started to ask him to leave so she could be alone, but she knew that if she did that, this already-rejected young man would be scarred for life. It had been a brave step for him to follow her in and sit on that…that bed with her, and one certainly taken out of desperation and utter loneliness. She was the only one in the world he trusted—the only friend he had, now. If she turned on him…she could not and she would not.

Catherine put her arm around Emmanuel and nestled his head on her shoulder. Then they both cried and cried.

Catherine awoke to loud pounding on her door downstairs. Her head was still hurting and she still ached as she put on her housecoat and went down. She opened the door a crack to see who it was. The door pushed open and six soldiers came in. The Colonel Wolf facing her did not look like the friend she had always known. "All right, Miss Kitty, where is she—and this time no lies, please," he said gruffly.

Catherine felt as if she was going to faint. She groped her way to the settee. The dust cover was still on it and she dragged it off on the floor. Then she sank down. She did not raise her head or look at Colonel Wolf. "I don't know what you are talking about," she said weakly.

"We will have to search the house," he said in the military voice he had never used with her before. "We have already searched the barn and the slave cabin."

"Do as you must, I don't care," she said. Catherine pulled her housecoat tight around her and put her handkerchief to her nose. The whole house had not been lived in for months and it smelled so stale. If only she had opened some windows.

"So you don't know what I am talking about?" he demanded sternly. Wolf was nervous, agitated and upset. He paced the floor in front of her. She knew he was irritated that she would not look at him, but she could not. "You don't know that Moses creature stormed the dispensary just before dawn and took Tuttle out?" he almost yelled. Catherine sat up with alarm and then fell back in faintness, almost losing consciousness. Sometimes there were smelling salts in the end table drawer. She fumbled for them with one hand while holding the other to her face. Colonel Wolf came over to her, his countenance and his tone much changed. "Miss Kitty, have you been crying?" he asked, trying awkwardly to make the switch to tenderness.

"Oh, yes, Colonel," she said in a wavering voice, "all night. I just fell off to sleep when you came."

"Miss Kitty, you don't know anything about this, do you?" he asked.

"No, sir, I don't; not a thing," she said.

There was a look of consternation in the Colonel's eyes. He walked to the staircase and yelled upstairs. "Sergeant, tell the men to call off the search and return to headquarters. I will be along after a while. Do nothing until I get there."

They sat in silence, the Colonel looking at his nails and Catherine holding a hankie to her nose. After a while, Emmanuel came in and stood looking at her. She knew he wanted her to come out, but she decided not to be secret with the Colonel anymore. She had gotten both of them into enough trouble already. "What is it, Emmanuel?" He hesitated. "It's all right, Emmanuel, you can tell me. Colonel Wolf is my friend."

"I know where Tuttle is gone," he said with excitement.

Colonel Wolf stiffened, but Catherine put her hand on his arm. "You do? she asked. "Where, Emmanuel?"

"Missers…Misser…dat Moses done taken her no'th to Masschewsuts," Emmanuel replied.

Catherine stole a glance at Colonel Wolf's face to try to get a read on his reaction, but could not see him very well from her angle. "How do you know that, Emmanuel?" she asked.

"Those Niggers done tole me," he said.

Colonel Wolf gave Catherine a suspicious glance. "Who are 'Those Niggers'?" he asked.

"That is how the servants of one household refer to the servants of another," she replied.

The Colonel looked puzzled. "Why is that?" he asked.

"I have no idea, Colonel Wolf," Catherine said wearily, not wanting to pursue the subject, "it's just what they do."

"How do they know about Tuttle?" he asked.

Catherine was regaining her strength and composure. "Oh, Colonel Wolf," she said, "slaves know everything—everything! They know if someone is coming to see you on the train. They know if one of your relatives in another state dies or gets married. They know if there is going to be a big battle—everything."

"Really!" he answered with surprise. "I always thought of slaves as simple and dumb."

"Simple, maybe—but dumb? Not on your life, Colonel," she said. Emmanuel stood his ground. "Is there something more?" she asked.

"Yes, Ma'am," he said, unable to suppress a smile. "Miss Tuttle comin' back soon's she kin."

Catherine was trying to digest the information, but it was coming too fast for her to think. She had to stay in control of the situation. "Why would she do that? If she…"

Emmanuel was so excited that he cut Catherine off. "'Kaiz, she didn't wanna go in the fust place."

Colonel Wolf started forward in his chair and broke in. "What? You mean she was kidnapped?" he asked.

"No, Suh…well…yes, Suh…well, I don know, 'zackly, Suh. Moses done taken her 'kaiz she say if she leave Tuttle, the white folks gonna hang her to de fust tree."

"Why would they do that?" Colonel Wolf asked.

"Kaiz, she done been fightin' wid data black reg'ment," Emmanuel answered. "Moses say dem Rebels don't b'lieve Miss Cath'n."

Colonel Wolf looked at Catherine who immediately hid her face in her hands so he could not read it while she thought. The one thing, in all the confusion of last night, she had forgot to do was to tell Emmanuel about their little…little…little lie. Well, she was glad she had been caught. It was killing her. She wasn't cut out to be a liar. Maybe the Colonel would feel sorry for her and let her off easy. He was just beginning to, when Emmanuel came in.

She raised her eyes and looked at the Colonel. "Well, it looks like I made a fool of myself, Colonel. You were right all along."

"Yes, but..." The Colonel stopped as a light came on in his face. "All right, fine!" he said. "Let's leave it just like that." He rose and prepared to leave.

Catherine did not know what the Colonel was thinking, and she felt she had to find out. She stopped him with her question. "I will be going back to my husband soon, Colonel," she said. "Do you need me for anything, I mean, questions or...?"

The Colonel understood her anxiety. "No, I don't see why, Miss Kitty." Wolf stopped and looked around. Then he went over and opened a window. Catherine was very relieved. The fresh, cool air made it possible for her to breathe easy again and her head started to clear. The Colonel continued. "The way I see it, your slave joined the Yankees. You didn't know anything about it. You found her and came to me with it, even though you thought she was a victim. I put her under medical arrest, and the Yankees broke her out and took her North. That is about all there is to it, I would think. That is going to be my report."

Some strength returned to Catherine's legs and the aching began to subside. She got up, walked over, and opened the front door. The breeze came through strong now. The musty odor began to die and Catherine could vaguely smell the honeysuckle. Her thoughts went to Tuttle. Would she come back? Should she? "What will happen to her if she does come back, Colonel?" Catherine asked.

The Colonel took on the tone of an advocate. "A little black girl is standing on her porch when the hero of all Negras in the South comes marching down her road. She has an army and it looks like she is taking over the town. Thousands of slaves are responding to the Union program of encouraging defection in the border states. Tuttle gets swept away with emotions of the moment. She never really means to do anything, but before she knows if she is dragged into the movement, an armband is pinned on her, a rifle, which she does not even know how to use, is jammed in her hand, and she is soon laying in a vacant lot, wounded. I think many men will be willing to see her as a victim, especially for…for your sake."

Catherine got up, went to him, and put her arm around him as if he were her father. "Thank, you Colonel Wolf, you are such a good…"

Her housecoat was not very tightly cinched and the Colonel pulled away in embarrassment. "You get some sleep before you do anything," he said, "do you hear me? You look like you need it and you should be able to do it, now that…now that the inquisition is off."

She nodded, and he left, but Catherine was far from being at ease in her mind. "Emmanuel," she said, but he wasn't listening to her.

"Ma'am," he said exuberantly, "I jis' got to tell you somethin'—I jis' got to."

Catherine was encouraged by his excitement. "My goodness," she asked, "what it is, Emmanuel?"

"Eve'thin' g'wine be all right, Ma'am!" he said laughing. "Yes Suh Ma'am, eve'thin' g'wine be jis' dandy."

Catherine was trying to envision such a large turn of events in this situation. "Emmanuel, what has changed?" she asked. "How do you know?"

"Tuttle done asked for Maybell and she went and seen Tuttle out in the woods 'fore they left to go No'th. She said to tell me she weren't leavin' me—no, not a tall. Not for no free territory nor nuthin' else and she weren't' leavin' the Mo'gan place lessen' if she was sold or kicked out. She said to tell me she done got her eyes opened and she weren't g'wine shet 'em no mo'."

A great flood of relief swept over Catherine. She gave Emmanuel a hug and told him to take the day off and get some rest.

After he had gone, she started to climb the stairs but then changed her mind. She went out to the porch, locked the screen door, changed the bedclothes on the day bed, and lay down. She did not ache anymore and soft, gentle relief flooded her mind and body.

What was that verse she had read just a few weeks back?

"Weeping lasts but for a night, but joy cometh in the morning."

Now she could get some…now she could get…now she could…now…

Chapter Fourteen

Who Is My Neighbor

Dawn was just coming on when Catherine arose. She took the field piece from the nightstand and parted the bedroom curtains just enough to be able to survey the scenery. From this vantage point, Catherine had a good view of the grove of trees up on Bull Run Creek. She knew he was up there somewhere but still Catherine caught her breath when she finally saw him. Jeb Stuart and several other men on horseback were keeping surveillance on the house and on her and Ellen. Jeb had been in her home many times and she was indifferent to him almost to the point of pity. She now viewed him as a potential enemy, trying to bring her and her husband down, and there was apprehension and a little fear. She was struck by the difference in the way she saw him then as opposed to now. Anger flashed in her mind but she fought hard to put it down. It would do her no good and no one in the South, including General Lee, would be sympathetic with her. In coming here, she had left the safety of the ramparts and ventured into those auspicious but daunting fields where fateful forces jostle. She had no protection or protector and she had done it willfully, against her husband's better judgment.

Catherine arrived at the Marcy Estate two days earlier. She came up with her two daughters in response to an invitation by Ellen McClellan, childhood sweetheart of her husband. He refused to come along. Today, the last of her visit, Ellen was taking Catherine out, ostensibly to show her around the place. But Catherine saw it more as a desire on Ellen's part to get alone with her and see what would come of it.

After breakfast, they left the house and walked out on the lovely grounds of Mount Glenn Estate, Ellen's childhood home. It had rained during the night but the sun was out. Everything smelled so scintillatingly fresh and clean. A chill wind blew down from the Blue Ridge Mountains causing Catherine's face to smart and her eyes to water a little.

Catherine observed her hostess as much as she could without staring. Ellen had on a heavy, buttoned, dark brown sweater that highlighted her beautiful golden-blond hair. She wore a long, tan, corduroy skirt over a winter foundation, knit socks and medium brown, fur-lined, calfskin Wellingtons that zipped up the sides. Bright, pretty-blue eyes sparkled in a fair complexioned and flawless face. Ellen's bearing was refined and her disposition, while preoccupied, was easy and open. There was a courtliness about her. She was a true southern belle, among the most beautiful but not in the very top echelon, Catherine thought.

Catherine had on a plaid overcoat with large pockets into which she had her hands jammed loosely, giving her a casual look as they strolled along. Catherine wore a gray pair of Mrs. Marcy's walking boots. Her hair was tied in a ponytail, making it look longer than it was. She felt relaxed and at ease, which was strange for the very difficult situation she was in.

Ellen started the conversation. "Catherine," she asked hopefully, "do you think we can stay close…I mean, be good friends through the years?"

Catherine walked on in silence for a while. Then she answered in a detached manner. "I think that you and I can keep in touch and be friends from afar, but I don't think we can be close in the social sense." Catherine saw her flush. "Oh, dear," she said, "there I go again. My husband is always telling me…" Catherine knew Ellen was waiting for her to continue, but she did not know what else to say. She did not really know Ellen.

Finally, Ellen turned and looked at her. "Could you explain to me what you just said so I can make some sense of it?" she asked.

Catherine was relieved that they had not reached an impasse. "I will try," She said. "I hope I do not make it worse. Ellen, my husband did not come with me because he is harboring a bitterness against your father. I know it sounds small of him, and…and it is." She saw a startled expression come on Ellen's face. She hurried on, not wishing to give the wrong impression. "My husband is a wonderful man," she said. "I love him very much and I am completely devoted to his service and his happiness. But he is not perfect. Being overly sensitive is his biggest weakness. His feud with General Jackson has all but…anyway, apparently, your father at one time told him not to come here again, or so General Hill says. He has not forgotten. I may as well be candid. I cannot do anything about it. I tried, but he shut me out."

Catherine waited for Ellen to reply but she did not. The silence was awkward so Catherine started walking again. After a short while, she stopped and continued. "And then, Ambrose is a very proper man," she said. "He would think it a breach of decorum, and a sin against me, to talk about his relationship with you in the past, or to countenance a friendship between you and him in the future." Catherine paused to look at Ellen. She could see the hurt and rejection in her eyes. She put her arm around her shoulder. "Of course, I do not feel that way," she said. "I welcome your friendship. You have reached out to me—and I am touched and gratified by that. But I have tried to talk to my husband about you and he gets embarrassed and simply refuses. I do not see how, under the circumstances, we could be close—even after the war and if the end is such that breaches can be closed." She looked deep into Ellen's face. Ellen did not look directly at her but she could see that Ellen was starting to register understanding.

"And then there is another very unfortunate thing," Catherine continued. "And it is serious, at least for my husband, even though it is silly. Men have openly accused him—men in his command and other Generals—of being a Union sympathizer because of you and your father. That makes it especially hard now." Catherine was relieved to see the frown go off Ellen's face and the dark countenance brighten.

"Oh dear. That is unfortunate," Ellen said. "I was told that, but I thought it was untrue."

Catherine looked at her questioningly. "You were told?" she asked.

"At Lewinsville," Ellen replied. "When I entered Virginia, they told me that I was going to see General Hill to perpetrate espionage, but I thought they were just trying to trap me."

Catherine's concern was genuine. "Oh no, Ellen; what happened? What did they do…do to you?"

Ellen stopped and leaned back against a gate. "They took me off the train and into the interrogation building," she said. "A Major came in and accused me of carrying a forged pass."

"Oh my," Catherine said sympathetically, "what did you do?"

"I told him that it was not a forgery," Ellen said. "I told them that General Lee signed it."

"And they let you go then?"

"Well, more or less," Ellen said, warming to the story. "They held me a while and accused my father and me of running a spy ring. They said I was a regular Rahab."

Catherine shuddered. "My, my, Ellen. Did that scare you?"

"Actually it made me angry, more than anything," Ellen said. "It certainly was an ordeal."

Catherine was concerned and a little angered. "Oh, Ellen, I am so sorry," she said with emotion and conviction. "They had no right to do that. I must tell General Lee…well, I guess I should tell General Hill."

"Oh, they didn't hurt me, Ellen said. "In fact, when it was all over, it was kind of fun."

"Well, you are braver than I am," Catherine said, shaking her head. "I have been interrogated a few times by our own people, and I almost break down and bawl—and I do, afterwards—sometimes."

A look of guilt crossed Ellen's face. Finally, she said. "I did myself, later on the train, although I am not sure that the interrogation was the only or even the main reason." Catherine saw another light come on in Ellen's countenance. "By the way," she asked Catherine, "do you know a woman named Sarah Morgan?"

Catherine looked at her searchingly for some clue as to the reason for her question. "Yes, I do," she answered. "She is well known in the South. She is active in the women's auxiliary war effort. I met her for the first time several weeks ago at the home of Mary Chesnut." Catherine stopped abruptly and grimaced. "Well, how rude of me. Of course you don't know Mary Chesnut."

Ellen put her hand on Catherine's arm. "Actually," she said, "though it must seem strange to you, I do know her."

"You do? How?"

"I was at an exchange meeting in Washington," Ellen answered, "and President Lincoln had invited her over to talk about the conditions of, and attitudes toward, slavery in the South."

Catherine had a sudden revelation. "Oh, yes! I remember that," she said. "Mary came to General Lee for some passes with which to invite moderates on the subject to participate in the debates in her house." Catherine paused to laugh. "President Davis wouldn't give them to her so she came to General Lee. She didn't tell him about the President's refusal. General Lee signed them. My husband was furious. So was the President when he found out about it. I was right in the middle of it all because he asked me to make them out for him to sign."

"Did you really?" Ellen asked, almost gleefully. "It was one of the passes that got me through to my parents. It must have been your handwriting that they were looking at so long and hard."

"Yes it was," Catherine said, shaking her head slowly. "It is a small world at times, I guess."

"Well," Ellen said, "maybe there is something providential in our meeting after all." Catherine did not respond so Ellen continued on in another direction. "I had quite a discussion…I guess you would call it that…with Sarah Morgan about the issue of slavery. But shame on me for bringing it up; of course, you agree with her."

"Oh, no, I don't agree with her," Catherine said quickly, "but then, I don't agree with Mary Chesnut, either."

"What does Mrs. Chesnut believe?" Ellen asked. "I heard some of it, but I do not feel I have the whole picture of her position."

"She believes that slavery is evil and should be done away with," Catherine said.

Ellen seemed surprised. "She is an abolitionist?" she asked. "I thought she said she wasn't."

Catherine was thoughtful. "No, she isn't, or at least, so she says, and I guess that is true if you follow her thinking. She wants the North to leave the South alone and let them work it out. She doesn't want Negroes being disrespectful and organizing rebellion. But then she wants to organize an anti-slavery movement that will eventually result in slavery being eliminated."

"What do you believe, Catherine," Ellen asked, "about slavery, I mean?"

Catherine stopped walking and turned to face her so she could look into Ellen's face. She studied her for a good while. Then she answered carefully, "I believe in something somewhere in between, I think. I have two slaves. I am much attached to them. They are like children to me. I would never think of hurting them. And if I thought they would not starve, I would give them their freedom, if they wanted it. In fact, my mother and I…but they don't want it—at least most of them don't. And that is my problem with abolition and anti-slavery laws. If the North wins and abolition becomes a reality, all of these poor people will be homeless with no one to take care of them, no where to live, nothing to work at."

Ellen seemed unconvinced. "Are you sure that is the way they feel?" she asked.

The question challenged Catherine. Was she as sure? Or was that just the southern argument? She thought of her own servants. "I know Emmanuel and Tuttle would be terrorized," she said with conviction. "It just sounds like mayhem. I am not against a program that would eventually end slavery. But I think it has to be well thought out, orderly, and fair to all."

Ellen responded with the non-abolitionist northern line. "But of course in the meanwhile," she replied tersely, "the evil practice of slavery will continue and individuals will go on being held in chains while people who are not prodded take more centuries to make up their minds."

Catherine was very serious now, and very passionate. "I guess that is where I differ from you and Mary Chesnut. I cannot see that slavery is evil. I think many slave owners are evil and I think many slaves are treated evilly. But I can't see that slavery itself is evil."

"Well," Ellen answered, "that's what Sarah says."

The associating of her views with those of Sarah Morgan concerned Catherine.

"What exactly did she say?" she asked Ellen.

"She contends that the Bible doesn't say it is wrong," Ellen answered. "She argues that if it's not evil for a wife to belong to her husband and children to belong to their parents, then it is not wrong necessarily for one man to belong to another."

Catherine was not impressed with the comparison, which she considered to be a reach. "Did you tell her that was a voluntary submission?" she asked.

Ellen nodded her head. "I did," she answered.

"What did she say to that?"

"She says it is not in the case of children," Ellen answered, "and anyway, it is the 'morality' of ownership that is the issue."

Catherine was silent for a moment. Then she answered in measured tones. "Well, I don't exactly believe like her, I don't think."

Ellen turned up her palms and spread her fingers fatalistically. "Well, I am sure there is much to know that I do not and we are not going to solve it now," she said. "I thank you for giving me your view. I really am interested." Catherine was a little surprised that the discussion had ended so abruptly, but she did not reply. After a time, Ellen spoke up again. "You mentioned General Lee. What kind of a man is he? Is he the super human that they all say he is?"

Catherine made a pout. "Well, I don't think 'super human' is accurate or fair. But General Lee is a great man, or at least I think he is. I am around him fairly often when I am in Richmond. I help out at headquarters when I am needed, and if I can. He is gentle, kind, considerate and possessed of deep feelings and compassion."

Ellen was skeptical. "Hum," she said, "we hear that he is a bold, fearless and hard driving warrior."

"Oh, he is that, when in the battle," Catherine replied. "But General Lee, unlike most generals I know, can separate between the necessities of war and the decencies and amenities of social intercourse."

Ellen raised her eyebrows. "So he is not the machine of destruction that my husband thinks he is?"

Catherine put her hand to her face. "Oh, no, I don't mean to say exactly that," she replied. "His desire to destroy the enemy, which he definitely has, does not make him cruel, or want to destroy everything and everyone around him. He will send his men ruthlessly into battle and then weep when they are killed and personally write to their wives and family with great agony of soul."

Ellen seemed to be in deep thought. "Well," she said finally, "Isn't that what every good general does?"

Catherine shook her head. "It is the ability to be a warrior and still retain one's character, of which I speak," she said cautiously. "General Lee, as I see him, can do that. Whereas, Stonewall Jackson just shrugs and says that such are the vicissitudes of war."

"I thought Jackson was a very devout Christian man," Ellen replied.

Catherine paused to collect her thoughts and evaluate where the intensity of this discussion was taking her. "He is," she answered finally. "But there are different paths that devotion takes. I don't care to walk down his."

Ellen did not reply and Catherine was glad. She had spoken harshly of General Jackson and did not want to say any more. It seemed a good resting place for the subject.

Ellen gave Catherine a brief tour of the stables. "That is my horse," she said. "I haven't ridden her since before I was married. She is long in the tooth now." Just before arriving back at the house, Ellen stopped her. "Catherine," she said, "You have taken a great risk to come here, then, haven't you?"

Catherine looked out across Bull Run Creek and up at the grove of trees as she thought about Ellen's question. The chilly wind had turned icy and she suddenly felt cold all over. She rubbed her cold face with her warm hands and blotted her watering eyes with a handkerchief. She wanted to ask if they could go back to the house, but she was determined to give Ellen her moment. "Yes, I have," she said at length. "My husband was very much against it. I did not think he was going to let me come. Then finally he said he would leave it to me, thinking that I would not come. But I felt I had to."

Catherine could see that this disclosure had touched Ellen. "That was very sacrificial of you," she said. "I feel that I owe you much."

Catherine shook her head. "Well," she said, "it isn't all for you. I did it for us. I had to see you after you made the gesture. It's not jealousy of old girl friends or anything like that. It was just that it was wrong, the way Ambrose wanted to handle it. And I am so glad we came. I have enjoyed so much visiting with your mother and father. I think your father likes me…or at least, my girls."

Ellen broke out in a short, happy laugh. "Like you? My father has fallen completely off his perch over you," she said. "You have taken him captive without firing a shot. I told mother she had better ride back to the station with you. He is apt to try to steal you."

It was Catherine's turn to laugh. "You must be very proud of him…I mean, them," she said. She paused and they both grew serious. "Ellen," Catherine said slowly. "I don't know what the future holds, and we will have to see. I feel differently about it now than an hour ago. I see that we have much more in common than just my husband. Still, Ambrose will probably…but I am so glad I have gotten to know you, and my girls can't talk about anything else but 'Aunt Nellie.' You are a wonderful person, and I can see why my husband was bitter, even though now he…well, thank you so much for having us up and I truly do hope we meet again. And I do apologize for Ambrose not…"

Ellen picked up on the awkward pause. "You know something, Catherine," she said. "I am glad you came alone. There is nothing between your husband and me except to say 'hello, how nice to see you after all these years'. But getting to know you has meant so much to me, and I probably would not have been able to if your husband had come."

Catherine put her arms around Ellen and drew her near. "Be careful what you do," she said barely above a whisper. "General Stuart has your father watched. Since you have been here, this house has been under surveillance day and night. They are up there along

Bull Run Creek—no, don't turn and look, please—they are up there watching us right now."

Ellen seemed surprised. "How do you know they are out there by the creek right now?" she asked.

"General Hill will not let me travel without a small field glass," Catherine said. "I saw them from my bedroom window this morning."

Ellen's eyes grew large. "But how…were you looking for them?" she asked.

Catherine nodded her head. "I was," she said, "I felt certain they were there. They will search my baggage on the train on the pretense that you may have slipped something in it without my knowing." She turned to Ellen with an apologetic look. "I know how silly it must sound to you," she said, "but they really think this could be an intelligence gathering trip—that General Hill may be sending messages to you."

Ellen had a stunned look on her face. "Did they search you on the way down?" she asked.

"Oh, yes," Catherine said, watching Ellen carefully. It had occurred to her to wonder…but she determined that Ellen's alarm and concern were genuine.

"Oh, Catherine, no! Do be careful," Ellen said.

"It's not me I am worried about," Catherine replied. "They will not do anything to me; they are afraid of General Lee…or…and of General Hill too…unless they can catch me with something. But it worries me, what you said about the interrogation coming over. It may be harder getting out."

Ellen could not conceal her fears as she asked, "Do you really think so?"

Catherine reached a decision. "Ellen," she said earnestly, "if you really get…get hung up, get a wire to General Lee. Tell them you wish to include a message. Tell them—now listen, remember this; write it down somewhere when we get back to the house and put it in your purse where you can find it. Tell them to say, 'When the dog wags his tail, he is not going to bite.' If you do not forget that, they will send the message. If you must—please, only if you have to—tell them *I said* to put your message through." Ellen looked searchingly into Catherine's face. Catherine understood the question. "General Lee is very fond of me, though he does not think I know it. I think he would do anything…much…to please me." Ellen shook her head in good-natured reproach and mock scandal. "But I don't want that creepy Jeb Stuart to see my name on the wire unless you have to do it to save your neck," Catherine said. Ellen's mouth dropped open in awe. Catherine tried to turn this grim discussion to humor. "Ellen—what good is an ace in the hole," she said with a coy smile, "if you can't play it when you need to?"

Before entering the house, Catherine put her hand on Ellen's arm and stopped her. "When will you leave to go back?" she asked.

Ellen sighed and appeared to be thinking for a moment. Then she said, as if just having made up her mind, "I am going today, Catherine, I have been here long enough. It is time for me to get back."

"Oh, good," Catherine said, "then we can go together—I mean as far as Manassas Junction." Ellen smiled and nodded silently, as if lost in thought.

On the boarding dock at Manassas Junction, Catherine and Ellen stood and talked. The girls hung onto Ellen and begged her to come to Richmond with them. The train to Lewinsville arrived first. Catherine kissed Ellen and they locked in a warm embrace. Catherine brushed the tears from her eyes as she said, "Be careful, Ellen, and God's speed. I will worry about you all the way to Richmond."

Ellen looked deeply into her eyes. "It has been a rewarding visit, Catherine, no matter what happens," she said with emotion and conviction.

As Ellen's train disappeared up the track, Catherine looked after it thoughtfully. Ellen was in more danger than she knew and than Catherine cared to tell her. The southern military really did think Ellen and her father were passing information to the Union. The one comforting thing to Catherine was that Jeb Stuart did not think so, and as for General Lee, well, Catherine felt she could influence him. Still, she wondered what was in store for Ellen. Catherine would not rest comfortably on the matter until she knew Ellen was safely home. It would not do for Ellen to send a wire or to write a letter. There was enough suspicion on her husband as it was. But she knew how she could learn of Ellen's fate. She would get it out of General Lee somehow.

Chapter Fifteen

The Brave and the Lonely

Catherine sat on the colonnade at Mary's house, in a comfortable chair beside the glass topped tea table. Mary left her a note that she would be home in about an hour. She asked Catherine to come over early, the note said, so she could read something Mary left for her. It was very important that she read it. Catherine frowned as she picked it up and leafed through it. She did not care much for Mary's little intrigues. Mary did not want to be there so that Catherine would be sure to read the note without distraction. Everything with Mary took prime importance; it must be done her way and 'right now.'

Catherine sighed and decided to comply with the note. She began to read the paper that Mary had left for her and soon realized it as being from the diary of Mary Anna Jackson, wife of the famous Confederate general. It read like the beginning of an autobiography.

> Mary Anna Morrison was the daughter of Rev. and Mrs. R. E. Morrison, born at Charlotte, North Carolina in 1831. She attended the Marvin School in Salem, North Carolina where she was very popular with both faculty and students. She married Professor Thomas Jonathan Jackson of the Virginia Military Institute on July 16, 1857. For a wedding gift, Jackson gave his raven-haired beauty a gold watch and a dainty set of seed pearls.

> She gave birth to a stillborn daughter at Lexington, Virginia, in 1858 where her husband was a professor at V. M. I. Even so, it was a storybook time for sweet Mary Anna. Jackson bought two acres and built a cottage. Together they planted a garden that was to become beloved. There they spent so many hours together in such joy and contentment. When the war came, he ordered her to sell their belongings and their home in Lexington and move back to North Carolina to live with her parents until the war was over. Before leaving Lexington, she wrote in her diary how heartbreaking it was for her to be left to sell their beloved cottage. While completing business in Lexington, her life and her house were painfully lonely.

The document engrossed Catherine's interest. Her heart went out to the delicate, almost fragile Mary Anna who pined for her husband's company and endured with such agony the loneliness. As she read on, she now understood Mary's method. Mary Anna was in room with him this very moment at the head of the stairs in Mary's house. Catherine set the paper down and looked around very carefully as if being watched.

Soon Mary came bustling out the door. "Ah, Catherine," she said, "I am so sorry I wasn't here. I have just been so…well, anyway, General Jackson left only moments ago."

Catherine was crestfallen for Mary Anna. "So soon?" she asked. "But he just got here. Couldn't he at least have …?"

"No, I am afraid not," Mary said. "It isn't his fault this time. General Davis has sent word for him to go to Gordonsville at once. Something big is shaping up."

Catherine tensed as she thought of her husband. "Mary, what…?"

"I don't know," Mary replied, "but Jefferson said to tell you to come over and he would brief you as he has time. But Catherine, we must help Mary Anna while she is here. I have invited her to stay for ten days."

Catherine sighed doubtfully. "After reading this, do you think he allowed her to stay?"

"I don't know; I have my fingers crossed," Mary said. "She is such a solitary little soul, and seems so vulnerable. Would you mind very much going up and getting acquainted with her?"

Catherine picked up quickly on the tension in Mary's voice. "Of course I will. Is there anything more I should know before going up?"

Mary hesitated. "Well, Catherine, you see…oh, I think not. Just go up and meet her and show her some…some of your marvelous warmth and encouragement."

Catherine did not move for a moment, as she looked deep into the face of her friend. Then she thought she knew enough. She turned and glided up the stairs. Mary watched her admiringly. "What grace that woman has," she said aloud to herself.

Catherine knocked gently and Mary Anna came to the door. Catherine would not let the moment be awkward. "My name is Catherine Hill," she said. "May I come in?" Mary Anna hesitated. "You know," Catherine continued, "the wife of General A. P. Hill."

"Of course, Mrs. Hill," she said apologetically. "I am in a state of mind, having recently left my husband. Do come in." Mary Anna looked nervous and insecure. "He has agreed to let me stay," she said, "but he gave me very strict instructions. I was trying to think if having a visitor in the room…" Her voice trailed off.

Catherine looked around the room. It was clean and of good size, but very sparsely furnished. The aroma wasn't exactly musty but it was not fresh either. Catherine wondered why someone with Mary Chesnut's means and ambitions did not spend the little extra it would take to make the accommodations pleasant. Catherine's upbringing required her to appreciate frugality but not miserliness. She sat down on a small chair, one of the only two in the room, near a little old desk hardly big enough for a schoolgirl, and took the baby on her lap. Mary Anna's eyes were red and she mopped them with her hanky. "I am so sorry," she said haltingly, "I am so lonely when I have been with my husband and he has to go away. It just hurts so much."

Catherine felt pain for Mary Anna. "When my husband was attached to these headquarters," she said, "I moved here and took a house. When I can, I go out to location and stay with him. I don't see my husband all the time, but I see him quite often."

Mary Anna stopped her crying. "I would love to do that," she said, "but General Jackson will not hear of it. He is very impatient with women wanting to be near war and to know all about it. There is one woman in particular here that he disapproves of very much. He thinks she stays to close too danger, too long."

Catherine smiled. "That is me," she said.

Mary Anna looked horrified. "I don't mean you."

Catherine laughed. "Oh no, it's me," she said, "but that's all right, I don't mind. I want to be near my husband. He could be killed anytime and then how would I feel."

Mary Anna looked around as if to see if someone might be in the room listening. "Oh, Mrs. Hill," she said emotionally, "I admire you for that and I am so happy for you that you have a husband who will permit you to…permit you to…"

"To think for myself and make a few of my own decisions?" Catherine asked. "Yes, so am I. Listen, my name is Catherine. What is your name?"

"Mary Anna".

"Oh, how lovely," Catherine said. "And that is what you want to be called, not just Mary or Anna?"

"No" she said. "Mary Anna—that's what Jonathan…General Jackson wants."

Catherine liked this Mrs. Jackson and thought that she could help her. "Listen, Mary Anna," she said, "would you like to come down and have some tea with me?"

Mary Anna seemed to be reviewing her instructions. "General Jackson didn't say anything about that," she said. "I don't know…"

"Did he say you could not?"

"No".

"Well, there you have it," Catherine said. "Come along."

They sat for a while and Catherine told her about Lexington, Kentucky. Then she thought of how self-identifying she must sound. "Tell me something about you, Mary Anna," Catherine said.

"Well," Mary Anna said "We lived in Lexington when we were married."

Catherine was surprised to hear that. "Did you?" she asked.

"Yes," Mary Anna said with a sad little smile, "but Lexington, Virginia. Major Jackson—he was then—taught in Virginia Military Academy."

Catherine remembered the diary. "Of course," She said, "How silly of me. When were you married?"

"In 1857."

"Do you have other children?" As soon as she asked, Catherine wished she had not.

"I had a daughter still born in 1858," Mary Anna said brokenly, "but now God has given us this little darling to fill the loneliness." Tears came again to her eyes.

Again, Catherine remembered, from the paper Mary had given her, and castigated herself for not being more alert. She finally humored Mary Anna enough for her eyes to clear. "Listen, Mary Anna," she said with enthusiasm, "I have an idea—I mean, you might like it. How about going over to Varina's with me to see my two little girls?" Mary Anna liked the idea and they went.

Chapter Sixteen

The Changing Winds

Catherine hurried up the steps to the White House. She found President Davis alone in his study. "Knock, knock, may I come in?" she said.

Davis tried hard to smile at the sight of her but the worry on his face was difficult to displace. "Ah, Mrs. Hill," he said, "please grace my office with your lovely presence."

Catherine went in and sat down in the guest chair directly in front of the desk. "General Davis," she said with mock gravity, "may I ask you a personal question?"

Davis looked puzzled. "Of course; anything."

"General Davis, why don't you ever call me Kitty?" Catherine did not like 'Miss Kitty' but she preferred it to 'Mrs. Hill.'

Davis squirmed a bit. "Truthfully, you mean?"

Catherine was amused. "Why, of course truthfully, Sir," she replied, half-laughing. "What other kind of answer is there among friends…confederates, I mean."

Davis relaxed a bit. "No, no. 'friends' is fine. I like that more." Then he sighed and leaned back. "Well, alright," he confessed, "I don't like the name 'Kitty.' It doesn't suit you. I refuse to call you that. For me, it would be an injustice to your elegance and excellence."

Catherine blushed. "Why thank you, Sir," she replied, "and thank you for what you said about Kitty. I feel the same, you know."

Davis was interested in that. "Do you?" he asked. "No, I didn't know and I don't think others know either. I will tell…"

Catherine cut him off; a hard thing for her because she simply did not interrupt superiors. "I would rather you didn't, Sir, really," she said earnestly. "At this point it would involve my husband and Mary Chesnut and…and General Lee…it is too much trouble and there is too great a danger for misunderstanding."

Davis regarded her thoughtfully for a moment. Then he said, "Yes, I think I can see that. Always thinking of the other person, aren't you Mrs. Hill. Anyway it is probably just as well that commoners…"

"Why don't you call me Catherine then?" she asked.

Davis was scandalized. "Oh, no," he said with fervor, "it would not be proper. I could never do that; it is too familiar."

"Well, then why don't you call me 'Miss Catherine?' There are people who do that."

Davis frowned as he paused for a moment. "Well, my reason, if you really want to know, is that 'Miss Catherine' is what Varina calls you and I don't…I don't want her to think she is influencing me." He stopped and looked at Catherine for some sign of understanding but wasn't getting any. "I guess you think that is pretty adolescent, don't you?" he asked.

Catherine was determined to answer before she had time to think about it too much. "Truthfully, Sir?" she asked.

Davis threw back his head and laughed but did not answer. When Catherine did not say anything, he changed the subject. "All right, then, 'Miss Catherine' it is. But I am sure you did not come here to talk about what you want to be called."

"No, Sir," she said, "I am wondering what you can tell me about the trouble at Gordonsville."

Davis grew serious and the worry returned to his face. "Well, Ma'am, there is no trouble yet," he said. "But we have intercepted signals from the Army of the Potomac that an attack across the river, straight at Lee, is eminent—in the next few days—according to intelligence."

Catherine was confused. "But General Davis," she said, "an attack straight into our defensive positions? This is something new for the Army of the Potomac, isn't it?"

Davis nodded in agreement. "Yes, indeed, it is," he replied.

Catherine was trying to process the information and get some feel for what was worrying the president. "How many forces do they have?" she asked. "Do we know?"

Davis nodded his head. "We think we do," he replied. "Stuart says 120,000 all told."

Catherine decided to try the direct approach and see what would come of it. "We wouldn't mind that kind of a fight, would we, Sir?" she asked. "General Hill says that, on our soil and at defensive positions, the equation changes by forty to fifty percent."

Davis regarded her with approval. "That is right, Miss Catherine," he said, "and then of course, in an evened out fight, the Confederate soldier has proven himself to be far superior."

Catherine was still puzzled. Why then was he so nervous? The President got up out of his chair, walked to the window, put his hands on the sill, leaned out and looked down on the street. "I love this city," he said. "I love the sounds of it, the smells of it and the whole aura." Then he returned to his desk and sat down.

Catherine decided to address a different concern. "Why would the Union do that now, Sir?" she asked. "In the past they could probably have prevailed when they had us at disadvantages, and they always retreated?"

"Well, the reason of course, if there is one, would have to be Hooker," he said. "I remember him just coming up from my military days. 'Fightin' Joe Hooker' is what they call him. He is spoiling for a fight and I believe he will fight."

Catherine frowned. An aggressive Army of the Potomac was something they did not have to give much thought to in the past. "How many do we have?" she asked.

"Between seventy and eighty thousand," the President replied.

She felt a little presumptuous, asking all these penetrating questions, but he had invited her to come over for "briefings" any time. Beside that, he was an evasive man, who talked in platitudes.

She would go away having learned little if she did not pin him down. “Are we well equipped and well supplied?” she asked.

Davis nodded his head carefully. “For now, at least,” he said.

Catherine’s confusions returned. “Well, then,” she asked, trying to sound curious and not accusing, “why are you so worried, General Davis? It sounds to me like this is what we have been waiting for.”

Davis leaned forward in his chair as if at last having someone to talk to who understood the subject. “Because, my dear girl,” he said, “Hooker is also the most intelligent military man in the Union Army. Brighter than Lincoln, McClellan, Halleck, and…well, the smartest. He is the head of Yankee Intelligence. I cannot understand him making a blunder like this, his itch to fight notwithstanding.”

Catherine’s confusions were giving way to understanding and worry of her own. “You think it might be a feint, then?” she asked.

Davis wagged his head. “It is not a feint,” he said. “There has been no feint. But I am worried that it might be a setup.”

“You mean that the signals…” Davis nodded his head. “But how could that be?” she asked. “Wouldn’t Jeb Stuart know? Haven’t we questioned any captives?”

Davis had a crafty look in his eyes. “Yes we have,” he said with emphasis, “and no one seems to know anything. Our best spies and operatives on the other side know nothing.”

Catherine was getting befuddled again. “But General, I would think that would be a great comfort,” she said. “General Hill says the Yankees have no security and that anything that is going to take place is always known to us ahead of time.”

Davis leaned back in his chair and locked his fingers across his chest. “But that is just my fear,” he said. “Don’t you see, Miss Catherine?”

Catherine was really in the dark now. “No,” she said earnestly. “No, I don’t see, Sir. I don’t see at all.”

Davis leaned toward her, his arms folded and his lower chest resting on the desk. In low, almost confidential tones he asked her, “Why don’t these people know anything worth knowing, Catherine? Why is it that Stuart and Lee can’t get anything out of captured Yankee soldiers?”

“But I still don’t see…”

"Because," he said tensely, "maybe General Hooker, the military intelligence genius, now that he is in charge, has sealed off the leaks. Maybe no one but Northern Command knows what is going on."

Catherine drew upon what she had learned about the Army of the Potomac in her two years in Richmond. "Well, but General Davis," she asked, "how could things change so dramatically and rapidly? Does that seem likely?"

Davis leaned far back in his chair and looked at the ceiling. Catherine noted that it was a high backed, captain's chair and he was a short little man. It extended upward beyond his head for at least six inches. "All right," he said as if a line had been crossed and they were moving into another phase. "McClellan was never a team player. Lee thinks he is a great General; I think they should have left him at the training center. But whether he was or not, he had his own program, and it was no secret that he was openly contemptuous of Lincoln's authority and plans. After McClellan, there were a series of what can charitably be called Lincoln—or, perhaps more accurately General Henry Halleck—mistakes. In that kind of a circus atmosphere, you cannot seal off leaks or do anything else in such an orderly and timely manner as to keep us from finding it out. Hooker, on the other hand, may be a big ego and a braggart, but he knows how the military command works and he is a team player."

Catherine did not understand any of this build up of General Hooker. She thought the president was worrying unduly. "But I thought he was making terrible comments about Lincoln and Lincoln's own personal intelligence," she said.

The president leaned back again, gazed at the ceiling, and became philosophical. "Yes, yes," he said, "we have heard all that. But Stuart believes—and I think he is right—that his was a rouse to get informants to loosen up and be careless around Hooker."

Catherine was unconvinced. "Why would they go to all that trouble?" she asked.

She was used to military men who did not want a woman to know too much, and she thought he was looking at her as if she was drawing him into areas that he really did not want to go with her, but he answered anyway. "There is also an indication that McClellan had plans of being military dictator and Hooker, so Stuart believes, was trying to get McClellan to confide in him." Catherine looked doubtful. "Well, however that is," he said, "I do not believe that Lincoln…anyway, we do not know what can happen over there if the whole Army of the Potomac pulls together. I am afraid we may find out and it could be disastrous."

Catherine was non-plussed. Finally she asked, "Well, General Davis, why don't we put men up and down the river, at the various crossings, to stop anything like that?"

Davis looked at her with amusement, condescension, and patience. "That is the one thing we cannot do. If Hooker comes straight at us with stronger and better-fed men, better equipment and better guns, he will crush us and the war will be over. We have to assume that our intelligence is right. We need everyone…everyone in and ready to resist the push if it comes."

Catherine fell silent. Nervousness tried to break out in her but she fought it. She knew from experience that she could not function, sleep, or do anything if she started to worry. "Well, so, we are resigned to this course then?"

"Yes, Ma'am, I believe so," he said, "unless we get something firm to go on."

"And if we are wrong?"

"Catherine," he said gravely, "there is an enemy over there scheming on us and trying to trick us, just as we are them. Wars are won and lost more on the success of schemes and the brilliance of leaders than on the superiority of armies. That, of course, is our only hope. And on the whole, we have better generals and men who are naturally more wily. But that does not assure us the enemy will never be successful."

Catherine put her hands in her lap and looked down. "And there is nothing I can do to help, I am sure."

"Oh yes, there is, Miss Catherine," he said with conviction.

"And what is that, Sir?" she asked.

"You can pray that God is on the side of the Confederacy."

Catherine thanked him and left. She was a southern loyalist through and through and believed in both the cause and the inevitable victory. But she had settled it with herself before leaving Hopemont that God was not on either side. To her, God could not be drawn into the questionable behavior of His creatures. She was afraid of the opposite happening and did not want to offend God by being patronizing and have Him turn against them.

Catherine headed to Mary Chesnut's to pick up the girls. Maybe she could get her mind off this by talking to Mary for a while. There were times when she thought of herself as 'quite a military mind.' Just now, she was glad to leave it to the men folks. As she rode along in the cab, she did say a prayer for the preservation of her husband …and…and for General Lee.

Chapter Seventeen

That Which I Feared Hath Come Upon Me

Catherine exited the cab in almost unladylike fashion and had to control herself to keep from running up the steps of the White House. Once inside, she met Varina who motioned for her to come into a side room.

Catherine was dismayed. "The note said the President…"

Varina put her hands on her shoulders and tried to calm her. "I know he did, Dear Catherine, and he will, just as soon as he can. But he is at the telegraph giving orders at the moment and will be just a while." Catherine paced the floor and wrung her hands.

"Catherine," Varina asked her, "do you want me to try to fill you in while we are waiting for Jeffy…I mean, the President?"

Catherine looked at her almost wildly. "Well, yes if you know…" Catherine suddenly caught herself. She stopped, sat down at the little conference table, put her head on her arms, and closed her eyes for a moment. Then she looked up and smiled. "Varina, I am so sorry," she said softly, "I should be helping hold the line on panic instead of acting like a little girl. Yes, please tell me what you know. I promise to be calm." Varina seemed reassured. She took several deep breaths. Catherine interjected, before she began to talk. "Only, Varina, let me ask you something. Please, don't beat about the bush.

I do not need that. I can take it better if I don't have to fish for it, and if I hear it simple and terse, it makes it a lot easier for me."

Varina sat down, looking pale. "Well, Catherine, there is no easy way, I guess," she said. "General Hooker tricked Lee. He stole a march on him, came through the wilderness and has the whole Union army imposed between Richmond and the Army of Northern Virginia. Telegraphed reports, before it went dead, were that the Yankees were driving our men, almost at will, and it looks like certain destruction of the Army of Northern Virginia."

Catherine was stunned. She was not ready for this. "Is there…has anyone…is there anyone on this side of Chancellorsville?"

Varina shook her head sadly. "No one from the Army of Northern Virginia," she said, "except, of course the small contingent of home guards who are here to protect the White House, but they…" she stopped and looked away.

As they sat in silence, the door opened and Jefferson Davis came in. He looked white, shaken and thoroughly beaten. "Well, Miss Catherine," he asked, "how much has Varina told you?"

"She said that Hooker has the whole Potomac Army at Chancellorsville, between us and Lee. She said the Yankees were driving our men hard and were threatening to roll up the flanks. Is all that true…I mean…of course it is, or…"

Davis ran his fingers through his hair. "I am afraid it is, Miss Catherine," he said. "I don't know what to say. If you have any questions, I will try to answer—if that is any comfort."

Catherine thought a moment. Was there anything to ask? Then several things occurred to her. "Is General Lee up in his strength?" she asked. "Are the Yankees being stopped or slowed anywhere on the line? Are there any hopeful signs at all?"

Davis sighed. "Well, to take your questions one at a time," he said, "Lee has less than half of his men, no more than 30,000, on the line to face Hooker's 80,000 strong. Longstreet and Pickett are in the Shenandoah and will be long in getting up. Your husband is somewhat closer…he may be coming on by now. Lee had only D.H., Jackson, Ewell, Smith, Stuart, Gordon, and Hampton with him when the attack began.

"And then," he continued, "no, nowhere along the line is any order at all established. Hooker has momentum and he is pushing. There is no chance to regroup.

"As for hopeful signs," he said, "unless Hooker does something really stupid, it looks like we are finished."

Varina, her eyes wild and her voice shaking, turned to her husband. "My God, Jefferson, surely there is something for us to…"

The President cut her off quickly. "No, no, no, my dear wife," he said tersely, "this is no time to lose our faith. If we offend the Almighty, we have no chance at all, even in terms of the miraculous."

Varina put her hands to her face. "Oh, Jeffy, I am so sorry, I lost control of myself and did not realize what I was saying. Surely you…"

"I am sorry, Varina," he said, "but I cannot justify or excuse you. I can only try to forget you said it." Catherine was surprised at his coldness with Varina. "And Varina," he said sharply, "how many times have I asked you not to call me Jeffy in front of people?"

Varina started crying and ran from the room. Catherine pulled hard on the reins to keep from interfering. When she had gone, Catherine turned to Davis. "How did it happen, Sir?" she asked.

Davis sat down and spread out his hands. "It was a set up as I surmised…or at least, feared. He stole a march on Lee and by the time Lee learned what had happened, it was too late."

Catherine cast about for something to give some optimism. "But surely Hooker has no supply," she said. "He couldn't have taken a supply train with him?"

Davis shook his head sadly. "He has a supply train all the way back to the Rappahannock. He has the whole Army of the Potomac at Chancellorsville."

Catherine could not believe what she was hearing. "But that's…that's all but impossible," she protested. "How could he have done it with no one on our side knowing what was happening? Did something break down in command?"

Davis shook his head again. "I don't think so, Catherine," he said in a defeated voice. "Oh, there were little things that will have to be investigated if we…early in the day, Stuart heard rifle shots way off in the fog, but Lee had instructed him not to go too far east, so he did not. There is some thought now that it may have been pickets trying to warn us, but that is not confirmed."

Catherine shook her head in dismay. "But it seems…it seems almost impossible that he could have done this."

Davis nodded his head reluctantly. "I have already had wires from the British observers," he said, "calling it the greatest single military feat in the history of wars."

Catherine objected to any admiration of the enemy. "Oh, I don't think…"

Davis cut her off. "Well, I don't know, Catherine," he said grudgingly, "it is just incredible. I cannot imagine a man with the nerve to make a move like that and leave Washington completely uncovered in the face of Lee's whole Army." Davis spread his hands in exasperation. "I told you Hooker was a military genius and a fighting man."

Catherine nodded her head. "Yes you did, General Davis," she said, "I remember that very clearly."

They both fell silent. Finally, Catherine asked, "Well, what do we do now?"

Davis stared at her blankly. "I don't know, Miss Catherine," he said. "Go over to Mary Chesnut's, I guess. Get the women together and pray. Oh, and Miss Catherine, see if you can find my wife and comfort her. I am afraid I was hard on her."

Catherine grew sober. "Yes, I…"

Davis cut her off quickly and firmly. "Don't say it, Miss Catherine," he said almost wildly. "I do not want to hear it. We cannot allow…just see if you can find her, will you?"

Catherine found Mary and Varina. Varina seemed near shock and Mary was clearly angry. Catherine sat down and was silent for a while, not wishing to come in off the street and start giving orders. Finally, she said, "Mary, President Davis would like for us to organize a prayer vigil."

Mary looked back defiantly. "Does he?" she asked tartly. "Well maybe he ought to start one himself. It seems to me that he is the one who needs to pray."

Varina raised her head and looked at Mary pleadingly. "Please, Mary," she said tearfully, "don't say that. Jeffy was right. I don't know what got into me. I never talk like that. I was…I was almost beside myself."

Mary snorted in disgust. "Oh, nonsense," she said. "What you said was nothing. He has Jimmy Longstreet in his sacred circle who cusses like a slave trader. Why doesn't he do something about him?"

Varina wrung her hands and started crying. Catherine was uncertain how long Varina would last if she did not get a grip. She decided to try to take charge of the situation. She stood and walked over to where they were sitting. "Mary, listen to me please," she said quietly but firmly. "General Davis needs us now more than ever. He is under tremendous pressure. Please don't criticize him just now." She turned to Varina. "I don't mean to sound impertinent," she said, "but please try to stop feeling sorry for yourself. Your husband needs you to be strong. If there was ever a time to be a helpmeet, now is it. I am afraid he will crack if we don't hold him up."

Mary and Varina looked at Catherine like two little girls. It had its desired effect. "But Catherine," Varina said, "I…"

Catherine cut her off. "Varina," she said firmly, "your husband is under a lot of stress. He did not mean what he said. It shocked him to hear you say what you did. He will get over it. We can all pity ourselves later. Let's get together behind him. This place right here and we—your husband, you, Mary and me—are the only ones between the Confederacy and defeat…or so it seems. If we are going down, let it not be with crying, spiting out angry words, and sitting around wringing our hands. We must do what we can to help." She turned back to Mary. "The President asked me to come here and get your help. If you do not want to help us, then we don't need you. We will go to Varina's house, or to my house, or somewhere."

Mary was defiant. "Catherine Morgan Hill, you can't talk to me like that. I knew your mother before you were…"

"It is no time to be talking about who you know and how long you have known them," Catherine said sharply. "All that is meaningless at the moment. Can we use your house? Will you help us?" It was the only time she had ever seen Mary cry, and it shook Catherine so badly she wanted to cry herself, but she knew she couldn't.

Finally, Mary answered in a broken voice. "Yes, Kitty," she said. "Of course you can count on me. What do you want us to do?"

The second day, after the women had gathered and were sitting having tea, Jefferson Davis came in. Catherine knew immediately that something had changed for the better. His face was grave but something was radically different. He went to the settee and knelt down. Varina rushed to kneel beside him and he put his arm around her gently. "Jefferson," she asked, "what has happened?"

Davis got off his knees and sat up. He looked at the women in the room. His eyes were moist with emotion. "I will try to tell you…but if I get too emotional…" He stopped and dried his eyes. Then he continued. "Well, Hooker lost his nerve," he said. "First he sent off his cavalry."

Catherine was astounded. "But why would he do that?" she asked.

Davis shook his head in wonderment. "No one knows, Catherine," he said, "not even the captured Union soldiers. It is almost a miracle."

Catherine was skeptical of where Davis was headed. She still did not believe that God took sides in war during the New Testament era. "General Lee would call it military incompetence…or…well…so would General Hill."

Davis shrugged. "Yes," he said, "that is what it is being called, of course, but don't forget that a house full of women have been over here praying for two days." Catherine frowned and Davis decided not to pursue it. "Well, anyway," he went on, "that happened on the first day. Next, Hooker issued an order for all his generals…Meade, Reynolds, Hancock, Baldy Smith…all of them, who were driving our men almost at will, to quit, pull back and throw up a ring of defense around Chancellorsville."

Catherine was agitated in her excitement. "What! Why? That is almost unbelievable."

Davis nodded his head knowingly. "I know, Miss Catherine," he said, "but that is what he did. Today, Lee waited until early afternoon for the regrouped attack that would still have had him at a great disadvantage, but it never came. Finally, Lee decided to go on the attack. The situation is far from settled, but there is every reason to hope now, that we will live to fight another day."

Cheering broke out in the room and the hall rang with laughter. Finally, Davis held up his hand. "I have been under great pressure these past few days," he said, "and I apologize to any of you with whom I may have been too harsh, starting with my dear and lovely wife." Varina, who was seated where he was standing, kissed his hand and put her head against his side. He looked down at her. "But sweetheart, please never swear again, in my presence or out of it."

Varina looked up with a radiant face. "I promise Jeff…Jefferson."

The president looked at Mary with a kind but firm face. "And Mary, please do not take it so personal. There are some of us who are very sincere about our faith and our responsibilities of leadership in that regard." Mary smiled a meek smile and looked down at the floor. "And Miss Catherine…dear precious Miss Catherine. You have been a trooper. I truly do not believe I could have made it these past two days, without your strong, wise, and active support." With that, he bowed and left, taking Varina with him.

Catherine went out on the colonnade, sat down at the little glass-topped tea table, and put her face in her hands. Mary Anna followed her out. "Oh, Kitty, isn't it wonderful," she said. Catherine looked up. "Why Catherine, you are crying. Isn't it funny? You are the one who is always trying to get me not to cry."

Catherine nodded her head and dried her eyes. "I know Mary Anna, and I apologize for being a fool," she said. "For the first time in my life I have felt pressure I could not cope with and I now know how important a good cry can be." Something about that revelation struck Mary Anna as funny and she began to laugh. Catherine began to laughing too, and it felt good. They laughed so long and so loud that Mary came out to see what it was all about and was soon laughing with them.

Chapter Eighteen

How Are the Mighty Fallen

Catherine, Mary Chesnut, and Mary Anna were sitting on the veranda having tea on the beautiful April day. Mary leaned to Catherine and whispered emotionally, "Did you ever see such simple, heartwarming loveliness?"

Catherine studied the quiet beauty of Mary Anna. With her very white complexion and her jet-black hair, she looked like a classic painting one might see in a museum. Happily, some of the sadness had faded from her pretty face and a radiance was beginning to come on. She was laughing and smiling and Catherine had reason to wonder if this girl had ever known light heartedness before. It was almost like watching one of her daughters with a new rag doll. "No", she answered finally and with conviction, "I do not think I ever have." She had grown very attached to this vulnerable and needy woman in the past few days and hoped that after the war they could be friends.

It was pretty clear that she would not be seeing Mary Anna around Richmond any more. Catherine had gotten to know the great war hero a bit, as he came to Richmond or when she was near the front with her husband. She was singularly unimpressed with Jackson. He was colorless, humorless, and cruel, even in his avid fundamentalism. She wondered how a delicate flower like Mary Anna had ever fallen into a thorn patch like him.

And yet Mary Anna loved him with a devotion that had no flaw and a zeal that knew no languor. Catherine thought she could understand a little of it. She had made the same commitment to Ambrose Hill and had the same devoted love for him, though she had seen serious flaws she did not know he had when she married him. Why was it we pitied others for things that we took for granted in our own lives? She felt guilty for pitying Mary Anna, who found great joy in her marriage to Jackson and she did not pity herself.

Yesterday, General Davis called them to the Whitehouse and announced that the great battle at Chancellorsville was going well for the South. Mistakes by Hooker after going into defense and quick action by Jackson, Lee, A. P Hill, and Picket had brought some stability to the campaign. The outcome was not determined yet but the early predictions of disaster to the Army of Northern Virginia, though frighteningly accurate at the time, were definitely past. Mary Anna began by wringing her hands with worry, but the 'we've been through this before' attitudes of Mary Chesnut and Catherine rubbed off on Mary Anna, who was a quick study. She had begun to relax with them as they awaited further news.

Catherine was the first to see Varina Davis come around the corner of the house and mount the steps. The zest was lacking from her walk and her proud head was down. Catherine knew instantly that something was badly wrong. She approached the little glass-topped table and sat down quietly. All looked at her in anticipation but no one said anything. It could be bad news for any one of them and they knew it. Varina turned to Mary Anna. "General Jackson has attacked the unprotected right flank of Hooker at Chancellorsville and inflicted great damage on the Army of the Potomac. As a result, Hooker is beginning it withdraw. Hooker is too strong and a very good tactician, they say. The President does not feel that he can be destroyed in retreat or that Lee should pursue him. A wounded bear is dangerous. In this miraculous campaign, we are going to let him get back across the Rapahannock. The thing to remember, and to point out to others, is that he is leaving and it is a great victory for the Confederacy."

She paused, took a deep breath and looked down at Mary Anna. "But, in the fighting, General Jackson has been wounded and is calling for you."

Catherine waited for the explosion of tears from Mary Anna. But it never came. Mary Anna was very calm and attentive. "He is calling for me? Oh, then I must go to him at once. Where is he?"

"He is in a house at Fairfield—the Chandlers; I believe you and General Jackson stayed there recently. Mr. Davis knows all the details. He is arranging your train. You must go prepared to stay."

Catherine was surprised to note the pleased look on Mary Anna's face as she answered, "Of course; I will stay with him as long as…he will let me." She paused. "Is he bad? Do you know anything about it? Oh, but of course you don't; I am sorry."

Varina put her hand on Mary Anna's shoulder. "I know only that his left arm was shattered and it has been taken off. He is reported to have come through the…the…the amputation!" Varina shuddered and almost lost her emotional composure. "Yes, the amputation—I don't know why I detest that word so—he came through it very well. Expectations for his recovery are good, but it will be a long convalescence at home, the President feels."

Mary Anna arose. "I will go at once." Catherine got up. "Thank you both so very much for your friendship and your kindness. I cannot possibly tell you how much this has meant to me. I think…I think it may have saved me from death by loneliness—is there such a thing? I don't know if I could have faced going back home—to be alone again." She paused and looked down. "I prayed to be able to stay with my husband. Be careful what you pray for, they say."

When she was gone, Catherine talked to Mary about it. Mary had sage words. "The poor woman has been left behind and left out by the war. She has felt unwanted and unneeded since she was sent home. Now the man she loves needs her. He has sent for her and he is dependent upon her—for the first time in their marriage, I am sure. Losing a child can make one doubt her self anyway. She has her baby now, but it takes a while, sometimes years, to get over the damage of losing a child, particularly a still-born and your first—oh, my!" Mary fought to keep her composure.

"Other wives, like you and me, are out here helping and supporting our husbands, but her husband does not need and does not want her here." She paused and the impact of her words hit Catherine hard and made her feel very sad. "It is bad for General Jackson, but I believe it is the best thing that ever happened to Mary Anna."

Catherine knew that Mary Chesnut was right, but it still bothered her. How the war twisted everything. And how glad she was that she had come with her husband and stayed with him until mortal danger drove her out. It must be tragic beyond understanding to feel as Mary Anna had for the past two years.

Catherine went up to help Mary Anna get her things and carry them over to the Whitehouse. When they came up, President Davis walked out, shook Mary Anna's hand and consoled her. Then he turned to Catherine. "I would like for you to do me a favor, Miss Catherine. General Jackson has been moved from the field to the Chandler home in Fairfield. I want you to ride there with Mrs. Jackson on the train. There has been some trouble on the line but it is cleared up now. I just don't like her riding alone at a time like this. And then I don't know what she will find at Fairfield. If everything is all right for Mary Anna, you will please come on back without delay. I do not wish to incur the anger of your husband by your staying there. You know that he and General Jackson…well…"

"Yes, of course, but my children…"

"Varina will see to them…if that is all right. We are keeping the Jackson baby too. Mary Anna just cannot take her out there under the circumstances. And then, you know how we look for chances to have those lovely children of yours."

Davis produced a cab that took Catherine to the house to get her daughters and bring them to the Whitehouse. Then they boarded the train and started on the journey to Fairfield.

. . . . .

In Fairfield at the home of the Chandlers, Mary Anna was shown directly to General Jackson's bed. Catherine followed. When Jackson saw Mary Anna, he rallied. She sat on the bed and took his head in her lap. He looked up at her with a rapt expression. "Mary Anna, my darling, you have come to me."

She looked down at him, her face radiant, happy and strong. "Yes, Jonathan. I am here. All is going to be well." He closed his eyes and fell asleep. She looked over to Catherine and said with calm steadiness. "Thank you, dear Catherine. You have been such a friend. You may go back now. I can manage here."

For some reason, the train could not go back down the track to Richmond and a coach was arranged. As Catherine started the long, bumpy ride back to Richmond, she pondered the past few day's. Mary Anna had been a lost, frightened and lonely woman, forced to go back to her parents and leave her husband with whom she longed to be. In a few days she became bright and friendly but still very vulnerable. But the woman Catherine had just left was a matron of strength and confidence, in full control of herself, her husband and the situation. It was evident that Mary Anna was well prepared for where she was and what she had to do. Catherine had worried much what would happen to Mary Anna if her husband died. Now she realized that Mary Anna would be all right if he died in her arms. She would mourn and she would miss him but it would be different. It would only destroy her if he had died on a faraway field while she was sitting alone, shut out, and helpless to share in his moment of trial and need.

Catherine thought she had learned a lesson she would not forget. A woman who is born to love, to serve, and to care is lost when she is not needed. She cannot hold her capacities in reserve. She is not a reservoir behind a dam; she is a flowing stream. She gives what she has and she is what she does. When she gives nothing, she has nothing and when she does nothing, she is nothing. When men try to protect women like that, they inadvertently destroy them.

The understanding and empathy she had for Mary Anna moved Catherine. A few big tears crawled slowly down her cheeks and left spots in the dust on her vest. She looked up and said a silent prayer of thankfulness for never having been lonely, left out, and un-needed.

Chapter Nineteen

Pride Goeth Before a Fall

Catherine sat at the breakfast table across from her husband in their little house on the outskirts of Richmond. He had been sent on a short leave to be with Catherine and the girls for a few days. Now he was preparing to return to the front. Her brow was furrowed with concern as she studied her husband reading over his orders. She always knew when he was worried about something. Finally, he looked up and she used the occasion. “Honey, what’s wrong?” she asked.

Her husband sighed and tried to look matter-of-fact. “Oh, nothing really, Catherine,” he said. “It’s just the war, I guess. It has dragged on so long.”

“But there is something particular, isn’t there?” she said anxiously. “I mean you look so worried.”

Ambrose shifted uneasily and thought for a moment. Then she saw him reach a decision. “Oh, well, Catherine,” he said, “I never have wanted to keep anything from you—not that I could have anyhow. This is something I am not supposed to discuss with you, but I am going to anyway. I do not think the command has the right to tell a man what to discuss with his wife. Lee is planning to take the Army across the river into Pennsylvania.”

Catherine sat up straight and hugged her arms to her chest. “What? Oh, Ambrose, why?”

Her husband made a face and looked thoughtful. "Well," he said slowly, "there is no certainness of this answer, but I think it is because he is still trying to exorcise the ghosts of Chancellorsville."

Catherine studied her husband carefully. Did he mean what he was saying? Why would General Lee do that? "But we came out of that with a victory of sorts," she said.

Her husband nodded his head. "Yes, Catherine," he replied, "but with no thanks going to Lee."

Catherine was defensive. "General Davis says Lee fought valiantly, courageously and intelligently to turn the tide of battle," she said.

"Yes, of course there is no denying that," he said. "But the point is that, in Lee's mind—and I am just giving my version of the answer to the question 'why'—he was the recipient of good fortune and luck. As a military commander, he cannot take credit for any of it. Do you see what I mean? Can you be objective where General Lee is concerned?" Catherine fought hard inside herself to put down the disappointment she felt at hearing Lee criticized. "I think so, yes," she said quietly.

Her husband looked at her with a quizzical look that made her uncomfortable. Then he continued. "And then, Lee has egg on his face for letting himself be tricked," he said, "and letting Hooker steal a march on him and get the Union Army into this position to begin with."

"But Ambrose," she said, "everyone agrees it was not Lee's fault—that it was a brilliant military feat by Hooker and that Lee has no culpability in the matter. Isn't that true?"

Her husband nodded his head. "That is exactly right and that is the point. Old 'Fightin' Joe' deserves all the credit in the world. But, after his discussions with President Davis, Lee feels that he should have seen the same warnings. I don't see how he could have. I would not believe that Davis saw these things until after the fact if it had not been for what you told me."

Catherine relived the discussion with the President. Did General Davis not warn Lee of his concerns? But why? She was about to ask when her husband continued. "Lee now feels that he has to prove himself," he said. "If Hooker did it to him, Lee can do it to Hooker."

Catherine was alarmed and disappointed. "But that kind of thinking is not objective," she said with emotion. "It seems dangerous, doesn't it?"

Her husband nodded. "Oh yes," he said, "I think it is very dangerous."

Catherine put her elbows on the table and her face in her hands. "So that is what is worrying you?" she asked, trying to keep from worrying herself. She wanted to hold him up, not drag him down, but it was a struggle just now.

"That is only that part about why he is doing it," he said. "What he is doing worries me more than why."

"What is he doing that is so bad?" she asked.

Her husband sighed, leaned forward, and changed the cadence of his speech. "I want to shorten this up if I can," he said. "Candidly put, he is going out of our territory, with a very long and tenuous supply line, to fight offensive battles. We have never done that before. We have fought defensive battles on our own territory, where their supply lines were long and ours were short. In this way, we were able to minimize the imbalance in forces and equipment. Now we are going to exaggerate them, it seems to me."

Catherine got up, walked to the window, and looked out to the trees down at the creek. It was so cheerful out there. All the trees were leaved out this time of year, the birds were making their delightful chatter, and there was a pleasant breeze blowing. Catherine breathed deeply and took in the myriad of scents and aromas that she loved so much about the wild woods near their house. She wanted to forget all this, take him by the hand, go down to the creek, and dangle their feet in the cold water. But she had to know the rest of it. It was her lot as an observant person and the wife of a fighting general. She struggled against fear as she looked back to him while still standing at the window. "I see what you mean, Ambrose," she said. "Has anyone tried to talk to Lee about it?"

Her husband got up, wrapped his arms around her from behind, and rested his chin on her shoulder. "Oh, yes," he said. "Longstreet has gone round and round with him, but apparently to no avail. I was there on one occasion."

Catherine shook her head in bewilderment. Now her husband was aligning with one of his archenemies against General Lee. Was her husband going to become one of Lee's critics? It would not do for her to pursue this line of thinking—at least not now. "What did he say to General Lee?" she asked.

"He said, 'General'…well, actually he said 'Bobby' but of course I do not approve of that form of address. That is just one of the things that…anyway," he said, "I have a feeling that this is a great mistake'."

Catherine breathed a little easier. "What did Lee say to that?" she asked.

"He was very hard and impatient," her husband answered. "He said, 'General Longstreet, we cannot sit here on our own soil forever and fight those people. They have more money, more horses, more supplies, and more men. Eventually they will wear us down'."

Catherine thought on that for a moment. Then she asked, "Was that the end of it?"

"Oh, no," her husband said, "it went on and on; I can't tell you all of it. Next, Longstreet says, 'I think you're wrong, Sir. The war is beginning to be very unpopular in the North. People who never thought it was a good idea to begin with but went along because they were sure it would soon be over are now convinced that the North can never dislodge us from the South. After a few more bitter campaigns, I expect the pressure to stop will be so strong on Lincoln, he will have to do something'."

The logic of what Longstreet said impressed Catherine. "That must have given General Lee some pause," she said.

Her husband shook his head. "No, Catherine," he replied, "not a bit. Lee shot back without a moment's hesitation. 'No, I don't see it that way, Jim. Lincoln believes in what he is doing and will never give up as long as he is president and that is for a few more years. I don't think we can sit and wait a few more years.'"

"And Longstreet…"

Her husband emitted a short, cynical laugh. "The man is stubborn but not without diplomacy. He hung on nicely I thought. 'Well', he said, 'they sure took a hit at Chancellorsville. I don't see Hooker lasting long, what with the feud between himself and Halleck. We know both of those people very well, General. Neither of them is ever going to come across the river and attack us with relentlessness and courage.'"

"And what did General Lee say to that?" she asked anxiously.

Her husband returned to the table and sat down. "He didn't really say anything to it directly. They got in a big discussion of who Lincoln was going to replace Hooker with."

Catherine turned from the window to look at her husband. She was interested in the matter. "Ambrose, do you think Lincoln will replace Hooker?"

General Hill shrugged and looked unsure. "I don't know, Catherine," he said candidly, "I am not good at those sorts of things. But Longstreet, who is, thinks they will."

"With whom?" she asked.

"Reynolds."

Catherine tried to process that information quickly. "So he thinks Reynolds will be the man?" she asked. "Would that not be better for us than Hooker, the genius?"

Her husband shrugged. "The consensus of opinion among our generals is that it would not be," he said. "Everyone I know has high regard for John Reynolds."

Catherine poured herself some tea, came back to the table, and sat down. "So Longstreet thinks that General Reynolds would be the best man and all of the rest of you…"

Her husband cut her off. "Actually," he said, "Longstreet does not think he is the best man Lincoln has, but he thinks he will be the man."

Catherine was very interested now. She thought she knew about the Northern Generals and wondered who would be better than Hooker or Reynolds. "Who does he think would be best?" she asked.

"Longstreet thinks Grant is their best man," her husband said, "but he is needed at Vicksburg."

Catherine almost dropped her teacup. "Grant!" she said with surprise. "Really? I hear that all he does is…"

Her husband cut her off sharply, with a little iron in his voice. "All he does is 'win', Catherine," he said tersely, "everywhere, against everyone, and all obstacles. Do you realize that, in this war, Grant alone has never lost a battle?"

"But Shiloh…"

Her husband held up his palms and spread his hands. "Shiloh wasn't a sterling performance," he said, "but he still won, Catherine, when no other Union general would have and few…"

Her husband let his sentence hang. Catherine felt her way cautiously. "Ambrose," she asked, "what do you think of Grant? What would happen if he were made the head of the Army of the Potomac?"

Her husband put his palms over his face and rubbed his eyes for a few moments. Finally, he squinted, shook his head to clear it, and looked evenly at her. "I would dread that day, Catherine, very much," he said with conviction. "If it had been Grant at Bull Run, Antitam, Malvern Hill, on the James or at Chancellorsville, this war would be over, and we would all be working for Yankees."

His answer sent chills up and down her spine and she did not know why. Finally, she regained her composure. "So, did they ever get back to the discussion of the planned invasion of the North?"

Her husband nodded as if to acknowledge his digression. "Yes, they did," he said hesitantly. "Well, it was kind of a transition, actually. Longstreet predicted that Grant would eventually take over the Army of the Potomac. Then Lee says, 'That is all the more reason for us to cross the river and end the war before that happens'."

Catherine was impressed with Lee's answer. "Well, that was a sharp comeback," she said. "What did Longstreet say to that, or did he say anything?"

"Oh, yes!" her husband said with amusement. "The fireworks, such as they were, were yet to come. Longstreet says, 'General Lee, an army smaller in size, quicker, and with better fighting men should never fight an offensive battle. We should wait for the enemy to attack us. Every time we have done that, we have won. We have only suffered when we have attacked them'."

Longstreet's logic seemed irrefutable to Catherine. "Well, Ambrose, that makes sense, doesn't it?"

"Yes, of course," he said, "and I really thought for a moment it had driven home with Lee. He acted like he understood the point. But then this strange look that I have been seeing in his eyes lately returned and he started arguing. 'General,' he said to Longstreet, 'you saw what Hooker almost did—and certainly could have and should have done—at Chancellorsville. There is no reason why we cannot do the same thing. They will be less likely to expect us to go up the Shenandoah and attack Pennsylvania than we were that Hooker could go through Wilderness. If we can get behind the Army of the Potomac, we can march into Washington and end this war. They will not be able to do anything but follow along behind and nip at our heels."

Catherine looked at her husband with new admiration. "You are right, then," she said. "He is still smarting about Hooker. That is what it is all about." Catherine was thinking hard how this decision, which she was now very concerned about, might be changed. "Maybe if General Longstreet really stuck his neck out, Lee would…"

Her husband was shaking his head, so she stopped. "He tried that, Catherine," he said, "and it didn't work. Longstreet got up. Walked up to Lee, put his face close to his and fairly shouted, 'It is suicide, General'!"

Catherine put her hand to her throat as she tried to envision anyone having the courage to do that to General Lee. "Oh, my!" she said, "That was intrepid! What did the General do?"

Her husband grew very somber; almost sad, she thought. "Lee's face darkened," he said. "He looked very angry. 'Maybe,' he shouted back in the loudest voice I have ever heard him use under roof, 'but we are going to do it, and we are going to start now, so get that negative attitude out of your mind and let's start the planning of the campaign that will end the war'."

Catherine and her husband sat for a long while in the stillness of the kitchen. Finally she spoke. "So then what does this mean?" she asked.

"It means," he said, "we are headed for Pennsylvania. We are to begin at once to prepare. Those are the orders I have just been reading."

"Can anything stop him?" she asked anxiously. "Is there a chance something will change?"

Ambrose shook his head in resignation. "What is that quotation from the Bible your mother used to say," he asked. "'A live dog is better than a dead lion because where there is life, there is hope'? I suppose anything is possible, but I do not think so, Sweetheart; I truly do not."

"What about General Davis," she asked. "Can he stop him?"

Her husband stared distantly at her, lost in thought. Finally, he answered, "Davis will not stop Lee, my Sweet. Let us just leave it at that."

Catherine was thoughtful. "When will you go?" she asked. "As soon as you report back to command?"

Her husband wagged his head. "No," he said, "I hear there is going to be six or seven months of preparation. Lee has already arranged to move the Army north to the Shenandoah with a series of slow moves, reverses, and subterfuge. I, that is, my command, will not be involved in that. I will be left at Fredericksburg to pose the constant threat of a campaign that would cross there and attack Washington from the south and east.

"Stuart is to be left in the area of Culpepper to be able to gather intelligence and also to assist those who were moving east through the Blue Ridge Mountains and over into the Valley. He will also be putting out false information about a major cavalry attack of as many as twenty-five thousand mounted men." Her husband stopped and shook his head with emphasis. "I really do not know how they expect to fool a smart man like Hooker with that one. Where would we possibly be able to find fifteen thousand additional horses?"

Catherine started to say something and then did not, so he continued. "So, you see," he said, "we will be in Virginia for some time yet."

Catherine was trying to take it all in. "So I will not be hearing from you for a good while, then?"

Her husband shook his head sadly. "No, that is one of the reminders in the orders I particularly didn't like. This new security net of Lee's and Stuart's will not let any of us wire or write anyone. We are supposed to tell you not to send us mail. I don't like it, Catherine, but I don't know what else to say."

Catherine was aghast. "So I am to have no word about you," she said emotionally, "for seven months or a year—possibly more? My goodness, Ambrose…"

"Well, there will be wires to Davis," he said, "and you will be able to get reports from Varina—in your case, I guess, directly from the president—at times."

As Catherine watched him leave, she stood on the porch and felt a slow gloom trying to settle over her. Something was wrong with what was happening and it was going to change their lives...maybe...she couldn't be sure. The day was warm but she shivered as she went back into the house. Unlike Mary Anna Jackson and other generals' wives she knew, Catherine never pined when her husband was away. But just now, she felt utterly alone.

Chapter Twenty

For Want of a Nail

In the weeks that followed, Catherine occupied herself with trying to gather information about what was happening with the Army of Northern Virginia. She abused General Davis' invitation to come any time. She hung around his office until it was evident that, if she did not leave, she was going to be asked to do so. Catherine almost camped at the telegraph office and used all her charms that decency permitted in order to find out what was coming in. She felt that she had done pretty well for herself as she reviewed what she knew:

In a few months, Lee moved up and down, across the Blue Ridge into Shenandoah and then back again. In six months, Jackson was in the Shenandoah with Heth, Ewell, Strasburg, and Longstreet. The Union General Milroy was in his front, maintaining a small force, and holding both Berryhill and Winchester. At about the seven-month point, Ewell was putting pontoons across the river for Lee's entire army to cross into Pennsylvania.

It was not much, but it comforted Catherine that she knew something. As she relaxed in the sitting room of the White House munching a sandwich, the President came in. "Catherine," he said. jocularly, "I understand you are becoming quite the intelligence gatherer."

Catherine stopped eating. "Am I in trouble?" she asked.

"Oh, no, no," he said, turning serious. "I don't see how you women put up with it, but then Lee feels he must have absolute security on this."

She offered him half of the sandwich, and to her surprise and delight, he took it. "Where is my husband going now that he is across the river?" she asked.

Davis ran his fingers through his hair. Catherine hoped he would not shut her off and he did not. "He is to join Lee at Chambersburg on the 27th," he responded. "Something big is shaping up. I can't tell you what just yet."

Catherine thought she was pleased. "Well, then, so far, so good?" she asked.

Davis looked down at the table. "Not all together, I am afraid," he said softly.

Catherine knew there was no major defeat in battle and it had nothing to do with her husband, so she did not panic, but she grew very sober. "And what is that, Sir?" she asked him.

Davis looked out of window at the town. "Oh, that Hooker," he replied, "he is a sly one. He has seen through us. He has stolen a march on Lee again, put his whole army back across the Potomac and is in Lee's front."

This was news to Catherine and she sat up rigid. "Is that big trouble, Sir? Does that ruin our whole plan?"

Davis stood up and prepared to leave the room. "Well, it certainly changes it," he said. "I don't like it. But…I will keep you posted." Then he flashed a rare smile. "Or you keep me posted, which ever one of us finds out first."

Two days later, Catherine was having tea with Mary Chesnut at the mansion when Varina came hustling in. Catherine was going to ask the question but Mary beat her to it.

"Big news, Varina?" she asked.

Varina was not tense, so Catherine relaxed. "Umm…not big news, no…well, it could be, I guess," she said. "Anyway, Lincoln has replaced Hooker with Meade. Everyone at the White House—ours, that is—is practically having a party."

Catherine remembered her discussions with her husband about this very subject. "With General Meade, you say? Not with John Reynolds?"

Varina turned to her with a smile. "No, Catherine," she said, "not John Reynolds, and that is what has everyone so delighted. The change was not unexpected. Hooker and Halleck have had their fight so out-in-the-open that the whole world knows about it. But everyone expected Lincoln to appoint Reynolds. Jeffy says this may just have lost him the war."

Catherine shivered. "Well, let's hope so," she said.

As they sat, sipped tea, and chatted about the news, Jefferson Davis came in looking very grave. They all knew this was something that was big. Catherine waited for Varina to speak but she did not, so Catherine asked: "President Davis, what is it? What is wrong?"

Davis was ashen again as he turned to them. "A great battle has started at a little place called Gettysburg," he said reverently. "It's our whole Army against theirs. On this could hang the outcome of the war."

Catherine saw that Mary and Varina were too stunned to talk so she continued. "What has happened so far," she asked, "or do we know?"

"Well, the first day…actually less than half a day…is over," he said, "and we think we got the best of it."

Catherine was worried about his tone. She had heard much hopeful thinking in the past and that is what it sounded like. "So they haven't been able to drive us out of our positions, then?" she asked.

Davis took out his handkerchief and wiped his sweating brow. "Well, actually, it is a case of our trying to dislodge them," he said. "They are in defense and we are on offense. That is what worries me."

Catherine caught her breath as she remembered her husband's account of the discussion between Longstreet and Lee. "But General Davis," she asked emotionally, "why would General Lee go on offense so far from home against superior numbers?"

Davis trembled slightly and sat down on the settee. "I don't have an answer that makes any sense," he said in an unsteady voice. "We just have to trust General Lee to know what he is doing."

Catherine seemed heartened at the reminder by the President that Lee was a great general. "Yes, Sir, that is right," she said. "And I am sure all of his men feel the same."

Davis squirmed uncomfortably. "Well, not all of them, Catherine," he said.

Catherine's alarm was rising swiftly. "What do you mean, General Davis?" she asked.

The President hesitated, struggled, and then shrugged. "Oh, I guess there is no harm in telling you. You have the right to know I am sure," he said. "I had a wire from General Longstreet asking me to countermand Lee's orders to attack Gettysburg. He says Lee has lost his mind. He says it is suicide. He says that the Union is entrenched in strong defensive positions and there is no possibility of rousting him out."

They all sat in silence. Finally, Catherine asked. "What did you tell Longstreet?"

"I told him…I told him I would over look the fact that he was guilty of mutiny," he said.

Catherine left her daughters with Mary, who reluctantly agreed to keep them and stayed at the White House, going home only for a few hours to sleep and bathe. Varina was there with her most of the time. Late on the second day, the President came out looking very pale and grim. He tried to speak while standing, but could not, so he sat down. Catherine moved in close so she could hear the faint words. "It is over, my friends," he said fatalistically. "Oh, God forgive me for what I have started and have not been able to finish."

Catherine burst in. "What is over, General Davis? Please do not be evasive. What has happened?"

Davis seemed to rally up a bit. "Lee and the Army of Northern Virginia have suffered a crushing defeat at Gettysburg," he said with as much strength as he could muster. "Our men are killed, wounded, and routed. Lee and the Army cannot possibly get back across the river. Meade has only to come after them to destroy our army completely." He paused and shook his head sadly. "And there is no doubt he will do it," he said. "This is not Chancellorsville. They are on their own soil and our army is not able to fight on. There will be no miracles this time. Within a week, the Army of the Potomac will be in Richmond. There is no doubt of it." Davis fell back in the chair and held his hand to his head.

Catherine was impatient with his dramatic decline. Her mind raced to think what to do. Finally, she decided on a way to proceed. "General Davis," she said with resolution, "Until General Lee surrenders, we are still alive as a nation. Let us resist any tendency to be defeatist. We will stand with you. We must console and encourage one another, pray and keep our spirits as high as we can. There is a whole city and a whole nation that will despair if we do not keep our composure."

Davis took his hands from his face and looked at her through misty eyes. "That is right, Miss Catherine," he said, "I know it is. I will do the best I can. Maybe there is one more miracle for us in God's mercy."

Catherine was not sure that God's mercy had anything much to do with the outcome. If they were to survive this, they must do so on the basis of character, strength, and determination. But they did need prayer for themselves and the safety of their fighting men.

Three days passed since the debacle at Gettysburg. Varina and Catherine sat conversing together and waiting for the confirmation of either the army's surrender or its destruction. Soon the door opened and a grinning Jefferson Davis came through. "Lee is back on Confederate soil," he said almost deliriously. "The miracle did happen. Meade sat on his big fat…horse…and let him limp all the way back across the river. We are still alive, ladies. We are still alive."

As Catherine watched him, she wondered if she had been wrong all these months. Was God really on the side of the South after all? What other possible explanation could there be for this turn of events. She did not know General Meade or General Hooker personally, but one thing she did know…or thought she did. No one could be such a coward or a fool as to let this happen deliberately. Something strange had to be behind it…or did there? She was confused and tired and decided that she did not need to figure it out now. She put her arms around the weeping Varina, wept with her, and felt the floods of relief flowing through her body.

Catherine bounded out of the house at the sound of her husband's coach stopping in front. She threw her arms around him and held him tightly. How she had missed the feel of him, the smell of him and the aura of security in his arms. Finally, she looked up into his strong, smooth face and bright blue eyes. "Oh, my darling," she said, "I never thought I would see you alive again."

He nodded in agreement. "I did not think so, either," he replied. "It is only by the grace of God."

The next morning they sat at the breakfast table where they had first discussed the invasion of the North. Catherine looked at him questioningly. "I suppose you do not want to talk about Gettysburg with me?"

Her husband was thoughtful for a while. Then he said, "No, actually I don't mind discussing it with you. In fact, I rather like the idea." Catherine was caught off guard and looked surprised. "Well," he said, "it is really a strange thing, Catherine. No one wants to talk about it. Longstreet is clammed up and will not say a word. Ewell seems to have gone into shock over it, from which he has not recovered. Pickett will talk, but he is a raving mad man on the subject, and I do not want Lee to know I have been talking to him about it. Lee will not talk about it; neither will Stuart, D.H., Gordon, or Hampton. I have never seen anything like it." Her husband paused and then changed directions. "You know Lee resigned?"

"Yes," she said, "President Davis showed me his letter."

Her husband was caught off guard. "He did?" he asked in a surprised tone of voice. "Well, that seems irregular."

Catherine clapped her hands to her face. "Oh dear," she said. "I wasn't supposed to tell that. But to you, my husband…"

"Yes, of course," her husband said. "That would certainly be proper." He left that subject and went on. "Well," he said in a worried voice, "I hope Lee changes his mind. We need him now more than ever."

Catherine was full of questions and did not know where to start. "Will Lee…can Lee go on and be a good leader now?" she asked.

Her husband nodded his head as if fully understanding her concern. "I think this was tragic for the South, and I am not sure if we can ever fully recover," he said. "But for Lee, I think it was good."

Catherine could not discern his meaning. "In what ways, Ambrose?" she asked.

"As I see it," he said, "Lee has to trust his generals and he cannot take it out on us, his anger at Stuart."

Catherine picked up on one of her pet peeves. "Did General Stuart do something again at Gettysburg—are you saying?"

Her husband reluctantly nodded his head. "Oh yes," he said, "Jeb is largely responsible for the defeat. If Lee had known the whole Union army was on the other side of the hill, I really think he would have listened to Longstreet and gone around."

Catherine wanted to take off on Jeb Stuart, but her interest in Gettysburg pulled her back. "But that even makes it worse judgment on Lee's part, doesn't it?" she asked, "like Hooker in…"

Her husband nodded. "Yes, I think so," he said soberly.

Catherine leaned forward and started to say something, then leaned back again and thought. "All right—well, there is so much," she said finally. "What did really happen, Ambrose?" she asked.

He looked sad, shrugged his shoulders and said, "General Lee marched us right into one of the strongest defensive positions I have seen an army in. We never had a chance, Catherine," he said with a trace of emotion, "never a chance. And the hardest part of it is that Longstreet pleaded with him not to do it." He paused, took out a handkerchief, wiped his eyes, sighed deeply, and continued. "He sent us right into the middle—wave after wave after wave—and never even tried the right until the outcome was settled. When it was clear we could not push the Yankees out, he just kept sending our boys." He paused, the emotion building in his voice.

Catherine took the occasion to ask, "Were we beaten as bad as Davis said?"

Her husband shook his head in slow disbelief, almost as if reliving the experience in his mind. "Probably worse," he said tiredly. "It was unbelievable. Lee would not retreat and back off. For some completely illogical reason, he thought if he kept at it, they would break. Instead, it completely broke us. We were a mess."

Catherine was startled to learn the truth. "My goodness, Ambrose," she said, her own voice choked with emotion, "I thought the stories were exaggerated. How did you get away and back to the South?"

Her husband looked exasperated. He shook his head and took several deep breaths. "It is the most ridiculous thing you ever heard, Catherine," he said. "Meade just sat there on his horse for three days and let us drag back across the river."

Catherine found it hard to accept. "Well, maybe there was something that did not meet the eye," she said defensively. "Maybe Meade and his generals were wounded. Maybe they were out of ammunition. Maybe…"

Her husband stopped her. "No, Catherine, it wasn't any of those things," he said. "One of our men had been captured by the cavalry and he was in tow when Pleasanton, the cavalry general, met Meade on the field. 'I will give you half an hour to show yourself a great general,' Pleasanton said to Meade. 'Order the army to advance and I will take the cavalry and get in Lee's rear, and we will finish this campaign within a week.' Our man heard it all."

"What did Meade do? What did he say?" she asked.

Her husband laughed, to keep from breaking in tears, she thought. "Well, according to our man who was there and heard it, Meade said, 'A wounded bear is known to be the most dangerous. Lee is still in good condition and able to make a fight. My army is too beaten up to fight any more just now.' Pleasanton, our man said, stared angrily at Meade, shook his head in disbelief and looked like he was going to go after him."

"Were you still able to fight?" she asked.

"I just told you, Catherine," he said, "we were beat to death. We fought till we were out of everything and could not fight anymore."

Catherine could not comprehend what she was hearing. "But was Meade…?"

"Of course not," he said, anticipating her question. "It was a hard fight and there were plenty of casualties over there, but we have gone out to battle in worse shape than the Union wound up that day. They could have just rode up and taken us, Catherine. We were done…I mean, done!"

Catherine was stunned to silence. Finally she asked, "Ambrose, was it a miracle, do you think?"

Her husband looked at her and narrowed his eyes a little. "I thought you were the one who did not believe that God took sides in war," he said in a tone that cradled between glee and disappointment.

"Oh, I don't," she said, "but Chancellorsville and now this? Everyone is saying that God stopped the mouth of the lion. Is there any sensible explanation?"

Her husband looked at her for a long time as he thought about the question. Finally, he cleared his throat. "All right, listen my sweet, and I will tell you how I see it," he said. "Chancellorsville was lost because Hooker, in a moment of euphoric victory, sent off his cavalry. From there on, he was blind. He did not know who was in front of him, who was coming at him, where they were…anything. He was far from home, far away from supplies, and there were no other troops in the area to call on for help if he got cut off. Chancellorsville was a defeat for Hooker because of gross mistakes in judgment." He paused, waiting for her reaction but she had none, so he went on.

"The same is true of Gettysburg. Lee and our army had no business over there at all. Lee had been listening to Jackson too much and got to believing that God was on our side and that we were invincible. The North got into position because Meade was not there but Hancock, Reynolds, and Bufford were. If John Reynolds had not been killed the first day, the war would be over now. But he was, and Hancock did not have the authority that Reynolds had. He did keep Meade from running, but he was not in a position to give the order to go after us."

"How do you know that?" Catherine asked.

"Intelligence—captured soldiers who were there—Okay?" Catherine did not respond so he went on. "Another one of Lincoln's pitiful appointments lost his nerve when the pressure was on him and froze up. He had not won the battle, his men had, and he was mortified. All he wanted to do was get out of there. We were not destroyed because of the cowardice and incompetence of Meade.

There is a lot that is strange about this, Catherine, but nothing that is mystic. They dropped the sword and we lucked out; that is all."

Catherine was glad for that explanation. She had been around the wrong voices too long. All she needed was to hear it from her husband and now she was back to earth. "Well, Ambrose," she asked, "where does the war go from here?"

"We stay on our own territory," he said, "we let them come to us, we continue to fight defensive battles and we pray that Lincoln continues to listen to Halleck and does not bring in Grant. I don't think they can ever beat us with that bunch they have over there if we do that. The war will die of attrition and the South will go her way."

"And if they bring in Grant?" she asked.

Her husband was thoughtful for a while. At length, he answered grimly, "Then disregard everything I just said."

Chapter Twenty-One

When the Quail Calls

Varina Davis requested Catherine's presence at the White House. The appointment was for two o'clock and it was now just past lunch. It was a nice day so Catherine decided to walk. She had not gone far when a horse clopped up beside her and stopped. She looked up into the grinning face of Jeb Stuart. He doffed his English hunting hat and said, "Good day, Miss Kitty."

Catherine felt the heat building up around her neck. "General Stuart," she said with firmness that was just a bit cross, "Have you been watching for me?"

Stuart hesitated. "Well, Miss Kitty," he said, "actually, I was just riding…oh, yes I was, Miss Kitty, that is a fact. I have something important to tell you."

"General Stuart, you are always trying to tell me something important," she said with no effort to conceal her impatience.

Stuart groped for words. "Please call me Jeb, Kitty," he said, "all the rest of…"

"I will not call you Jeb, General Stuart," she said hotly, "it is too familiar." She softened a bit at the sight of his pitiful look. "And, please, Sir, I would like to be called 'Miss Cath…Miss Kitty by you. My husband objects to too much informality."

Stuart sighed. "All right, Miss Kitty," he said. "You really don't like me, do you?"

Catherine chose her words carefully. "I do not dislike you, General Stuart," she said, "and I appreciate very much your war effort on our behalf." She paused to think if she really wanted to continue with what was in her mind. She decided that she did. It was as good a time as any to set the record straight. "But Sir, I do not want to be a confidant," she said, "and the thought of being familiar with you is altogether objectionable."

Stuart ran his fingers through his wavy hair and frowned. "I am not sure exactly what you just told me, Miss Kitty," he said. "Could you be more plain about it?"

Catherine set her mouth. He had asked for it. "I will not flirt with you as you want me to, and I don't want to give you even the slightest excuse to tell stories about me and you around the campfires," she said, her voice rising in pitch. "The thought of me being regarded as 'one of Jeb Stuart's women' is repulsive to me."

Stuart forced out a weak laugh. "Well, I didn't have anything like that in mind, Ma'am," he said. "Your interest in intelligence among the women is well known and I just wanted to tell you that I am on my way to Maryland to receive a piece of information that could change the face of the war."

Catherine did not want him to know that she was interested. "I see," she said blandly. "And what would that information be about, Jonathan?"

"Well, of course I will not know that until I hear it, will I, Miss Kitty?" he said.

"And from whom are you going to get this information?" she asked.

Stuart hesitated. "From Lilly Parran," he said weakly.

"And she is?"

"An operative of mine," he said. Catherine continued her hard stare at him but did not blink. "She is a widowed friend—or was a friend—of Fitz Lee," Stuart said.

"Ah," Catherine said scornfully, "One of the famous Jeb Stuart Women."

Jeb squirmed in the saddle. "Miss Kitty, please," he said, "these women are very important to the war effort, that is my interest in them."

"I see," Catherine replied, "and that is all, I am sure."

Stuart shrugged. "Well," he said, "of course they are people and you have to keep them…"

Catherine cut him off sharply. "General Stuart, I do not want to hear this!" she said in almost a shout. "Please stop right there."

Stuart broke out in a smile. "Of course, Miss Catherine," he said too politely. "I understand and I am sorry for…"

Catherine felt the need to rein in her emotions. She was getting almost angry. Yet, she had to set him straight. "Why did you call me 'Miss Catherine' all of the sudden?" she demanded.

Stuart shrugged. "Well," he said, "that is what you just said you would like to…"

Catherine was incredulous. "I did not!" she replied heatedly.

"Well, but you started to," he said, "so I thought…"

Catherine shook her head in amazement. "My goodness, General Stuart," she said, lowering her voice, "I really have to be careful around you, don't I?" Stuart grinned and looked as if he might be preparing to ride on. Catherine wanted to know more, so she asked quickly, "Where do you meet these…these contacts? How do they know you are coming and that you are there?" She could see the confidence rising in Stuart. She hated to give him the opportunity, but she really wanted to know.

"Well, this one…that I am going to see now…Lilly Parran…works in a fashionable eating and drinking house on the outskirts of Baltimore. There is a hill on the east," he said. "She leaves the window open when she knows I will be coming. Periodically she walks over to the window and listens. I give three quail calls, then wait thirty counts, and call again. I do this three times. Then she meets me at her…at her house."

Catherine thought the story odd. "A quail call can be heard by a woman working in a noisy tavern?" she asked.

"It is not that noisy," Stuart said. "It's a nice place. Anyway, she waits until the noise is down before she goes to the window. A quail call is high pitched and shrill. It can easily be heard over dull background noise if one is listening for it and knows when it will be coming."

This sort of thing had always intrigued Catherine. "But how does she know for sure," she asked, "I mean…"

"She knows it will be precisely when she is at the window," Stuart answered.

Catherine tried to envision that scene. "All right, I see what you mean," she said. "But why all the subterfuge? I understand security is so lax you can almost walk in and out of the North un-abused."

Stuart shook his head negatively. "That was true with the Pinkertons," he said, "but not any more. Since Hooker took over intelligence from McClellan and put Captain Sharp in charge, it is a dangerous business to get information. They almost had me the last two times I went over."

Catherine had heard enough and was ready to end the discussion. "Well," she said in a changed voice, "so the outcome of the war may hinge on a quail call."

Stuart shook his head in disappointment. "Make fun if you want to, Kitty…" Stuart stopped and reiterated facetiously…"I mean, Miss Kitty…but…"

Catherine's eyes snapped at the cavalier treatment. "I ought to tell General Hill that you are stopping me on the street and being insulting."

Stuart looked amused. "But you will not, will you Miss Kitty?" he said. "One feud is about all you can handle, I hear."

Catherine stamped her foot. "You rascal!" she said. "Don't be so sure. I will not be in your influence, General Stuart. Or, I may tell General Lee."

She noticed the paling in Stuart's face. "Whatever," he said, lazily, trying hard to sound casual, she thought. "Why don't you post it on the bulletin board at the White House? 'Southern lady talked to by one of her Generals and a frequent visitor to her home as she walked along the street in public at high noon'." He stopped and straightened up in the saddle. "Do you want me to let you know what I…"

"Oh, no, thank you," she said coldly. "I will find out through my normal channels."

Stuart turned the horse in the street and looked hard at her for a moment. "Boy, you are tough, aren't you?" he said. Then he shook his finger at her. "You'll see, and you'll be sorry," he said with mock indignation. Then he rode on.

A week passed since Catherine had her encounter with Jeb Stuart. Mary told her that Davis wanted her for a briefing. Catherine walked briskly up the steps to the White House, wondering what sort of vital information he had for her this time. The President met her at the door of his office, all smiles. "Well, Miss Catherine," he said airily, "Grant is moving his men into the wilderness on his way to Chancellorsville."

Catherine gave him a doubtful look. "Oh no, not again," she said, "and it's Grant this time. But…but…is this good news, Sir?"

Davis put on his statesman's face. "It is never good news, dear girl, when you are being attacked by Sam Grant," he said. "The war has changed a good deal since Lincoln brought Grant up as the Commander of the Union Armed Forces."

Catherine looked down at her hands. "Well, that is something that every general in the Confederate Army has been afraid of for some time, isn't it?" she asked.

Davis nodded absently. "Yes, and of course the fall of Vicksburg was not only a great military achievement for Grant but also a devastating blow to us," he said. "It looks like Longstreet was wrong about this one. Vicksburg has put new life in Lincoln's re-election effort and of course, if Sherman takes Atlanta…but there is one thing that puzzles me. What do you make of Lincoln dumping Johnson and putting Grant on the ticket?"

Catherine was surprised. "I guess I didn't know that he had," she said. "When did this happen?"

Early in the week," Davis replied. "I am sorry; I thought everyone knew. Any way, you are the perceptive one around here; what is it all about, do you think?"

"I really have no idea, Sir," she said. "I am not good at political things." In fact, Catherine had an idea why Lincoln had done it, but it was vague and philosophical and she did not want to get sidetracked on the subject. She paused and looked at Jefferson Davis who seemed to be in a cheery mood. "But back to Grant and the Wilderness," she said, "I don't understand. You seem almost to be pleased."

Davis shrugged. "As I said, Miss Catherine, no action by Grant is to be taken lightly," he replied calmly. "But in this case, thanks to the work of the one of the greatest soldiers in the history of wars, it is a whole lot better than it might be."

Catherine breathed easier, even though she did not understand. "Yes, Sir," she said, "I think we all have that high opinion of General Lee."

Davis paused a moment and then continued. "General Lee—of course," he said, "there is none better. But it is not Lee of whom I spoke."

Catherine was cautious, something nibbling at the edges of her mind: "Then who gets this high praise from our esteemed President?" she asked.

Davis feigned a blush. "None other than the great Jeb Stuart," he said proudly. Catherine sat quietly and did not answer. "You would not believe what he did, Catherine," he went on. "He stole into Baltimore, met with an informant right under the noses of Sharp's men, barely escaped capture, rode all night and the next day and got to General Lee in time to warn him. Lee will be at the Orange Court House to surprise Grant when he gets there. With any luck, Lee can hold him off until the whole army, which is already on the move, gets up."

Catherine was silent for a long moment. Finally, she asked, trying to sound casual, "How did this information come to you, President Davis?" she asked.

Davis looked at her with surprise and a bit of disapproval. "What do you mean, 'how did it come?' It came by telegraph, of course," he said.

Catherine was befuddled and knew she should keep silent. "Yes, of course," she said, "but I mean, did General Stuart send the message?"

Davis laid his pencil down sharply on the desk, turned sideways, crossed his legs, and looked at her from his right shoulder. "Catherine, what in the world is this all about?" he asked.

Catherine had a sinking feeling. Why hadn't she kept her mouth shut? "Well, you see, Sir," she said haltingly, "General Stuart has been pestering me lately and just before he left…oh…well, I think he is trying to impress me."

Davis held up his hand for silence, looked angrily at her, and then looked down at the desk for a good while. Finally, he raised his eyes to her, pity showing in his face. "Dear Miss Catherine," he said with cold compassion, "I realize it has been hard on the ladies of the Confederate Army, hearing all the tales about the escapades of the dashing, handsome, brilliant General Stuart and the unfounded rumors about 'Stuart's women'. I know that the war has left you lonely and trying to imagine what all is going on. But, my dear, we must not let things get out of hand. Please try to control your thoughts. You have a fine, noble, handsome husband of your own."

"But Sir," she said, "before he left…"

Davis cut her of with a kind but firm interruption. "Miss Catherine," he said tersely. "This message was from General Lee. General Stuart is not trying to impress you, Ma'am. I am sorry but…I am going to forget we ever had this discussion, but please try to not let your imagination get out of control. Go home, sit down and write a letter to your husband."

Catherine's face was burning and she wanted to get out of there as quickly as possible. He stopped her at the door. "And Catherine," he said sternly, "if I ever hear anything like this out of you again, these briefing sessions are going to stop."

As she walked slowly along the street toward Mary Chesnut's, trying to allow time for her feelings to subside and her red face to go away, she muttered to herself, 'Never again; never again.'

Three days later, Catherine was back at the White House for another briefing by the President. She expected to find that their last meeting had affected their relationship, but if that was true, it did not show. He looked up from writing something, with a worried frown on this face. "The Battle was a stalemate," he said, "and Grant has evacuated the wilderness. Grant fought hard and came very near to breaking through, but another comedy of errors and valiant fighting by Lee held him off."

"And my husband?" she asked.

"He is all right," the President said, "but Longstreet was wounded seriously. Just how serious is not yet known."

Catherine was quiet for a time and then she said cautiously, "General Davis, you confuse me. When Grant was on the attack, you were all smiles. Now that he is in retreat, you look so worried."

Davis stared blankly at her face and she knew he was not seeing her; his mind was far away. Then his gazed snapped back into focus. "I did not say he was in retreat, Catherine," he said grimly. "I said he had abandoned the Wilderness. Grant turned right on the orange plank road. Grant and his entire, well-supplied army are heading our way. Grant is not going to retreat, Catherine. He sent a message to Lincoln there would be no turning back."

"Is that for sure?" Catherine asked. "Do we know that is not a rumor?"

Davis shook his head affirmatively. "New York reporters are not the best conveyors of messages if you want to keep them secret," he said. "Lee is going to have to beat Grant in order to stop him."

Catherine felt anxiety welling up within her. "But General Lee can do that, can't he?" she asked. "General Grant is on our territory and always before…"

The President's face was ashen. "It may take a Grant mistake, Catherine," he said, "which is about as rare as hen's teeth with that man, or…" He looked at her impishly and continued softly, "Or a miracle."

Catherine had no heart for taking the bait. After the last visit, she was on her best behavior. "But Grant made mistakes, you said, in the Wilderness."

Davis shook his head. "I do not think I said that," he replied. "I said there were errors made."

"But isn't that…"

Davis shook his head slowly but with conviction. "Lee doesn't think it is the same," he said, "and neither do I, I fear. First of all, Meade took the Cavalry to the rear and left the right flank up in the air. You can bet that Meade will never have any control over Sheridan again as long as this war lasts. Grant is not a head-lopper but he is a problem fixer. And then, Burnside apparently sabotaged the effort by not filling the middle as he was supposed to."

Catherine was shocked. "My goodness, General Davis," she asked incredulously, "how could any general do that to his own army?"

Davis shrugged. "Bitterness, I guess over feeling that he was kept from trying the Wilderness and told that it was a hair-brained scheme," he said.

Catherine was scandalized. She could not imagine such a thing. "Why, he should be shot, General Davis!" she said gravely. "That is a court martial offense, isn't it?"

"The rumor is that Burnside is headed for one," he said.

Catherine noticed she was wringing her handkerchief and she stopped. "So…" She could not think of how to continue.

Finally, the president said, "It is a new day in this war, Catherine; a new day. And a dangerous and desperate one for the Confederacy, I fear."

Chapter Twenty-Two

The Lady From Baltimore

Dinner was long over and the discussion had lapsed into a slow reiteration of old subjects. Catherine was fussing with her knitting and talking intermittently to Flo Stuart. It amused her that Flo was watching her husband Jeb like a hawk and he could not steal his usual glances at Catherine. Catherine smiled as she realized that, when Stuart invited himself over, he did not count on his wife Flo coming along. Catherine did not mind Jeb Stuart in the house. Since her awkward and embarrassing day in the President's office, she decided that the best policy was to pay no attention to him at all, one way or the other. He was company for her husband and, for some reason—although Stuart was not one of her husband's favorites and though he told her about Stuart's 'women'—he never developed the suspicion that Catherine was the attraction.

She knew what he was trying to do. He wanted her to warm up to him, to be his friend and to flirt with him innocent ways. Jeb Stuart did not need her as an intimate but he did need her to notice him. Sometimes Catherine thought the easiest thing would be to give him that. She had come to regard Stuart as not as repulsive as she first thought. But she remembered the warnings of her mother about women of unusual beauty and desirability like hers. 'You owe it the men in your life who will be friends not to lead them along. It is cruel and it will destroy friendships. You must always be proper and brutally frank if it comes to that.'

Besides, Catherine did not trust Jeb Stuart. Mary had told her that he had the reputation of being smoother than he seemed. If you opened the door wide enough for him to get his foot in, you could be in trouble. Catherine came to realize that he was a man to be noticed if you let yourself think in that way. Her policy was that if she did not want to mix it up with them, she must leave them strictly alone. And, of course, she had never, would never, and could never think of intimacy with any man but her husband. She felt sorry for poor Jeb, in a way, but it had to be like that.

When the knock on the door sounded, both Stuart and Hill were visibly relieved. Catherine went to the door, opened it, and found herself looking into the apologetic face of General Lee. She could not possibly imagine what he had in the large box he was toting.

"I am so sorry to be bothering you at this hour, Miss Kitty," he said.

"It is never a bother when you come calling, Sir," she replied sweetly.

"I…I need a place where I can put this box for opening," he said. Catherine showed him to the table and they all gathered round in anticipation. Lee apologized. "A bad time, I guess, Jeb," he said to Stuart, "to be passing on gifts from admirers. But I know you are going on assignment in the morning and I thought maybe there was a message in this."

Stuart looked around cautiously. "What is it?" he asked. "Where did it come from?"

"Captain Conrad, ace spy of the Confederate army, came in a few minutes ago," Lee said, "looking like he had been living in a swamps—and smelling like it to. He pounded on my window like he was trying to break in. I almost shot him."

Jeb Stuart scratched his head and glanced at Flo. "Who is it from?" he asked.

"I do not know," Lee replied. "It is supposed to have a message for you in it."

Flo opened the lid of big package and saw a beautiful uniform and a magnificent sword lying on top of it. Everyone held their breath as

Lee took it in his hands. Catherine was the first to speak. "My goodness, have you ever seen anything so beautiful," she said. Her husband and General Stuart had the sword out of its sheath, inspecting it.

"Is that for me?" Stuart asked.

Flo took the card out of the envelope. "No, the uniform and the sword are for General Lee." She raised her eyebrows and looked at Catherine knowingly. "From a lady in Baltimore, General?" she said. "Who is this mysterious lady from Baltimore? Tell us about her, General."

Lee was embarrassed. "I don't know any lady from Baltimore…that I can think of…honestly I do not," he said sheepishly. "Anyway, I am sorry, I thought this package was for General Stuart; that is what Conrad said."

Catherine spoke up. "Wonder if it fits?" she asked. "Why don't you try it on?"

It was obvious to her that Lee wanted to try it on. "You think I should, then?" he asked.

"Of course you should," Catherine said, "Honey, show him where he can change." As Lee gathered up the suit, Flo said, "Oh, look, there is another smaller package. Maybe that is for Jeb." Flo opened the box and gasped so that her husband and General Lee stopped and came back to look. Flo whistled through her teeth as she took, from the beautiful velvet lined hard wood case, a pair of spurs. "Wow, are these really gold?"

Stuart hefted them. "Shore feels like it," he said.

Flo sat down in a chair and put them on her boots. She always dressed like she was ready to ride off with her husband when she came to see him, and would have, Catherine thought, if he had let her. While she was doing so, Lee went into the bedroom to try on the uniform.

"What's the message, Jeb?" Flo asked.

"There's no message, Sweetie," he said. The General just said that maybe…it only says from a lady in Baltimore."

Catherine saw the suspicious look she gave him. "Hum," she said, "and who is this 'Lady from Baltimore'?"

Catherine was amused at Jeb's answer. "She's a contact in the network; an older woman of means."

Flo laughed with good-natured doubt. "An older woman?" she asked. "How old?"

"Um…forty," Stuart said, "maybe forty-five."

Flo laughed again. "Shame on you, Jeb Stuart," she said.

Catherine braved a question she could not resist. "Is that Lilly?"

Stuart looked at her oddly and said, "Yes, as a matter of fact it is."

Flo stopped what she was doing and looked first at Catherine and then Stuart. Lee, coming back from the bedroom with uniform and the sword back in the box, saved the moment.

"Oh," Catherine asked quickly, "didn't it fit?"

Lee's eyes were almost misty. "It first perfectly," he said emotionally, "just perfectly."

"I would like to have seen you in it," Catherine said.

Lee shook his head slowly. "No, Miss Kitty," he said with fervor, "I will never wear that uniform except at war's end or some other great and unusual occasion." He turned his attention to General Stuart. "And older woman about forty-five, is it?" he asked. He was giving Jeb that you-never-know-what-I'm-thinking look.

Jeb seemed uncomfortable. "Now, Flo," he said, "without women like this, we would never…"

Flo laughed lustily and Lee laughed with her. Jeb Stuart never bothered to finish his sentence. Lee and the Stuarts headed off to their houses with Flo still wearing the spurs. "Well, when you see her again, darlin' husband," Catherine heard her say, "tell her I said to thank her very much for the spurs. I never had a gift like that before." Then she laughed again and so did Jeb, but Catherine thought there was a hollowness about it—not like the melodious ringing laugher that she usually heard coming from him.

From their porch, Catherine and her husband watched them go. "What do you make of all that, Catherine?" he asked her.

Catherine turned up her palms and spread her fingers. "I have no idea what to make of it," she said. "It is…it is…I don't know what to call it…strange, I guess."

Her husband nodded his head. "Well, Lee came at the right time," he confessed. "Stuart was not his usual entertaining self tonight. He was boring me to tears."

"Yes, of course, well, because..." She barely caught herself in time. "I mean, I really don't know what ailed him. His wife, I guess."

Her husband looked at her oddly, as if he wondered what she had just said. Then he shrugged and started back inside. He stopped at the door. "Who is Lilly?"

"One of General Stuart's operatives in Maryland," she said.

He gave her a funny look. "How do you know that?" he asked.

Catherine tried hard to sound casual. "President Davis told me about Stuart receiving the tip that saved the last Wilderness campaign," she replied. "It was she who gave it to him." She tensed a little as he looked thoughtfully at her. She did not want to tell him about Stuart accosting her on the street. Would he see the disconnection and force her hand?

He did not. "Hum," he said, and went in.

Catherine stood for a while, looking into the darkness wondering about General Lee and the woman from Baltimore and what the rest of the evening held for General Stuart.

Chapter Twenty-Three

Follow the Drinking Gourd

Catherine opened the letter from Emmanuel and read it again. It was highly unusual and a bit disapproved for a servant to write a letter to the mistress of the manor, but the situation emboldened Emmanuel to do it:

"It's about Tuttle, Ma'am. You muss come by mundee mornin', or we is lost fo' ebber."

Catherine could barely make it out, but she did and she smiled proudly to herself. Emmanuel had said he would learn to write and her mother had helped him some. Catherine never believed he would be able to do it, but he had—sort of. It took Catherine a while to figure out what it was all about, but she finally did. Harriet Tubman was bringing Tuttle home.

Catherine wanted to know all she could about this notorious woman, but she did not want Mary, Varina, or President Davis to know why. She fabricated an interest other than her real one to get their help. Varina had managed to obtain for her a lengthy piece on Harriet Tubman and the Underground Railroad written by William Lloyd Garrison, an editor from Boston. As the train rocked along, Catherine decided to read what time would permit. It was a biography of sorts, though it was short. Catherine wasfascinated by her story. It started off with a strange, disturbing tale of one of Harriet Tubman's trips on the Underground Railroad.

They heard the hounds coming toward them. At first, they seemed to be off to the West, toward the river, but as they neared, the conductor knew that they were right in the path. The parcels had been instructed what to do in this case. They applied the oil and the pepper, found the lowest spot they could and covered themselves over with foliage. One of the women crawled in a hole at the very edge of the path and put some branches over her. When the dogs passed by, several of them went right over the top of her. They waited until the sound died away in the distance. The pursuers would not retrace the same ground, so slowly the conductor roused them from cover and they proceeded on toward the Kentucky bank of the Ohio, opposite Cincinnati. As they neared the bank, the conductor saw the signal: an orange and a blue light created by lanterns wrapped in different colored cloth. The conductor gathered up the eleven parcels, the largest cargo she had ever transported on the Underground Railroad, and directed them to the spot at which they were to wait for the boat. During the tension of the waiting period, the woman, over whom the hounds had run, lost her nerve. She began to sob.

"I can't go 'head wid dis no mo'e. I's g'wine stay yere. Y'all go on 'thout me." The conductor clamped a strong hand on her shoulder.

"You hush that talk, girl. You're goin' on, jest as planned. 'No turnin' back, Lord, no turnin' back,'" she sang with a big white smile, trying to settle her down. The woman started to wail.

"I can't! I can't! Oh, Lawd, why'd I ever do dis?"

The conductor spun her around and she looked in to the big, alert, dangerous eyes of a hard face with one squinted eye and a long, deep scar over it. The conductor jerked a pistol from her belt and shoved it in the woman's face.

"If you ain't goin' with us, you ain't goin' no where no more. Dead Niggers don't tell no tales. You go on, or you die!"

The woman sobered quickly. "I be all right, ma'am, I's jist skeered."

"Course you are. We all scared, Dilsey, but we got to go on. The beginnin' of the Promise Lan' lie jest over dat river."

Catherine stopped her reading and looked out of the window at the passing countryside. The story was disgusting and yet it stirred sympathy and a little admiration in Catherine's inner being. How could any woman, even one who was nearly a savage, have that kind of courage, daring, strength and resourcefulness? She continued to read.

In 1861, a few months before Sumter, Harriet Tubman, the famous 'Moses' of the Underground Railroad, made one of her last missions leading slaves to free territory and mostly on to Canada where Harriet had her home. Though the slaves were not emancipated for several years, the outbreak of the war made it no longer possible to operate the Underground Railroad, except in a few cases involving Maryland and Kentucky, and not involving Harriet.

The Underground Railroad had been in operation in some context since 1750. No one knew for sure how it got its name, but one legend was in general belief. In 1831, a slave named Tice Davids ran away in Kentucky and made his way to the Ohio River with the owner in hot pursuit. The master saw Davids plunge into the river. Keeping his eye on Davids, the owner went to a boat and rowed directly toward him. Davids reached the shore near Ripley, Ohio, with the owner close behind him. Then, to the owner's consternation, Tice Davids disappeared from sight. The owner scoured the countryside and the anti-slavery town, but he could not turn up his runaway slave. The owner concluded that Davids must have escaped on an 'underground road.' Because of the advent of the steam powered trains following the invention of the *Tom Thumb* in 1830, the story of Tice Davids soon had it that he got away on an underground *rail* road.

Harriet Tubman first became acquainted with the Underground Railroad at a time when she did not even know of its existence. She was born on the Edward Broadus Plantation, Dorchester, Maryland, in 1821. At age ten, she received a life-changing injury. A slave tried to escape and the overseer was after him. Harriet got in the way of the overseer, trying to block his pursuit. The overseer threw a brick at the escaping slave, but it hit Harriet in the head high above her left eye. From the injury, Harriet had spells of unexpected loss of consciousness for the rest of her life. In 1848, she married John Tubman, made a 'free black' by the death of his master. Harriet knew that she might be sold to the deep-south slave market at any time. She tried to discuss running away with her husband, but as a free black, he had no sense of urgency and did not want to think about the trouble. He threatened to turn her in to the master if she continued to talk about it. From that time on Harriet, now afraid of the husband with whom she had been so happy, never discussed it with him again.

In 1849, Brodas died and the estate dissolved. Two of Harriet's sisters were the first to be sold at the Louisiana auction. This was the ultimate bad fortune of a slave. The further North one was, the more she could realistically think of freedom and the better, in general, the treatment of slaves. Harriet expected to suffer the same fate soon. The window of opportunity for her to escape could close at any minute. She feared trying to escape alone because she might pass out, so she convinced three of her brothers to go with her. At the appointed time, they made their departure, but her brothers lost their nerve and returned, forcing Harriet to return with them for fear of being punished because of her absence. Two days later, Harriet learned that she and two of her brothers had been sold, not to the Louisiana auction, but to a Georgia slave trader who would take them south on a chain gang, a fate as bad or worse.

"I reasoned it out in my mind that there were two things I had the right to: liberty or death," she said. "If I could not have the one, I would have the other; for no man should take me alive; I should fight for my liberty as long as my strength lasted…"

After work on the day she found out about the sale, Harriet returned to the slave quarters singing the song that told her black brothers and sisters her decision.

"When that old chariot comes, I'm g'wine to leave you."

Catherine paused in her reading again. She was experiencing a growing excitement and found herself hoping that Harriet would be successful. 'Maybe I should not be reading this,' she said to herself. She weighed the matter for a few moments and decided that there was nothing disloyal about feeling empathy for this tragic woman, so she continued to read.

She sat up that evening until her husband John fell asleep. Then she took ashcake and a piece of salt herring, put it in a bandanna, and was gone. Once off the plantation, she headed for a certain woman's house on a farm near Bucktown. The woman had stopped on the road one day and asked how Harriet had gotten the scar on her head. When she heard that Harriet had tried to help a runaway, she told her that if she ever needed help, she could turn to her. Harriet certainly needed help. She knew she was taking a chance, but she had no choice. She went up to the door and knocked softly. The woman did not seem at all surprised to see her. Harriet did not know then that the woman was one of the 'depots' of the Underground Railroad. She gave Harriet the names of two places where it would be safe for her to stop. Harriet learned later that those who thus opened their homes to 'parcels,' or 'passengers' were known as 'stationmasters.' A frightened and weary Harriet made her way through the woods and arrived at the closest of the houses the following morning. The woman fed her, handed her a broom and told her to sweep the yard so it would look like she belonged there in case anyone had seen her come in. That night the woman's husband hid Harriet beneath blankets on top of produce in a wagon and started for somewhere. Harriet did not know these people, and all knew the treachery of white accomplices in capturing and returning runaways. Could she be headed back to the Brodas Plantation and an awful whipping? Too tired to think or worry about it, she fell asleep.

A few hours later the wagon stopped and the man told her to follow the river to the next place. He told her to rest and hide during the day and travel only at night. There were patrols out in the area looking for her. Harriet followed those and subsequent instructions.

It took over a week to travel the nearly hundred miles and reach free territory in Pennsylvania. The first day, she rowed for miles up the Choptank River by a white man. At night, she hid in the attic at a Quaker farm. The next night, she hid in a haystack on a farm belonging to a German immigrant. She spent a whole week hiding in a potato hole in a cabin belonging to free blacks. She had spent nights in the woods and had patrols pass so close to her that she had to fill her stomach with wild berries to keep it from growling and giving her away, not knowing when she would fall down foaming at the mouth for having eaten something poisonous.

"I looked at my hands to see if I was the same person," she later recalled. "There was such a glory over everything. The sun came up like gold through the trees, and I felt like I was in heaven."

Harriet always appreciated her freedom and never regretted having run away. But she had not reached heaven—not yet. Harriet returned to the South as "Moses,' the deliverer of her people. The twelve thousand-dollar price on her head would rise to fifty thousand dollars before the demise of the Underground Railroad. On that occasion, she went back to get her husband John. She forgot the fear and remembered fondly the many happy days with him. She hoped there would be many more. When she arrived at the Brodus plantation unannounced and opened the door of their old cabin, she found John in bed with a new, younger wife. When she told him why she had come, he laughed at her and again threatened to turn her in. That laugh hurt her very much. She had risked her life and freedom to come get him and he laughed at her. That laugh haunted her the rest of her days. Harriet left with a heavy heart but not in vain. She took a small party with her, which she led to freedom.

Harriet was unable to find or to do anything for her sisters, but by 1858, she had led her three brothers, her mother, her father, and an estimated fifteen hundred other slaves to freedom over the Underground Railroad.

Jarrolds the Porter, the one who had befriended Catherine after her mother's death, came by with a face cloth and a towel. Catherine covered the little book with her hands so he could not see what she was reading. "No, thank you," she said, "not just now." When he left, she continued to read.

In the fall of 1858, she gave her first public speech in Boston. John Brown contacted her after that, several times. He had an elaborate plan to free thousands of slaves in Virginia by arming them with ordinance from the arsenal at Harper's Ferry and leading them in a rebellion and exodus to free territory. Harriet was drawn to the scheme and suggested to Brown that he plan it for Independence Day 1859, to gain the added benefit of high spirits and preoccupation with revolution to freedom. But Harriet held back from helping Brown as much as she wanted to because Frederick Douglass, her newfound leader and counselor, did not like or trust Brown (though after Brown's death, Douglass praised him highly). Brown, who had no more use for Douglass, realized this and did not contact Harriet again. The result of Harper's Ferry caused her much anguish. Contrary to the feelings of Douglass and most of the others, she saw it as a basically workable plan that could have been successful if it had been carefully drawn and accurately executed. Because Harriet excelled in planning and execution, she survived long on the Underground Railroad. She had great instincts. She knew what to do, when to do it, and could conceive and carry out a new plan virtually on the run.

On one fateful day, Harriet sat in the living room of Frederick Douglass. On her right sat the elegant, courageous Anna Murray Douglas, wife of Frederick, who had been as successful as a conductor in the other major arm of the Underground Railroad as Harriet had been in hers. To the right of her was Thomas Garrett, a Pennsylvania Quaker who had lost his fortune and possessions in his participation as a stationmaster in the Underground Railroad. Then there followed (all famous and effective abolitionists and supporters of the 'Railroad') Laura Haviland of Michigan; Jarmain Wesley Loguen and his tall, willowy and fearless daughter Helen Amelia; and William Still.

"I believe that we are all here," Douglass said. "This is an historic occasion, or at least in my view. First, let me pay tribute to the most beautiful sister the black man has ever known. Excepting John Brown, of sacred memory, I know of no other who has willingly encountered more perils and hardships to serve our enslaved people than you have." Harriet knew some of the honors she would receive in this meeting, but she did not know about this. She was not an emotional person. The sorrow, tragedy, and stark reality of life had taken from her the ability to flush with embarrassment, to preen or to weep. But she had that big, white, famous smile, which she displayed without forethought, device or gloating.

"The midnight sky and the silent stars," Douglass went on, "have been the witnesses of your devotion to freedom and your heroism."

"The time has come for the Negro to enter the war as a full participant. Black troops, under the command of Colonel James Montgomery of the 2nd Carolina Volunteers, are being sent to the area around Lexington, Kentucky. The reason is mainly to enlist Negroes in this and other border states to desert the Confederacy, either to join the army or to come north to escape slavery. This is a most important step, in my view. Certainly, it can be undone if the South wins. And it might be unnecessary if the North wins. But then again, it might not. There are many pro-slavery politicians in the North, and Lincoln, much to my chagrin and displeasure, has said nothing about emancipation. It might be the last chance for Negroes of the border states like Kentucky to escape slavery. If the South appears to be winning, they can flee to Canada or take passage to England.

"At the head, because of courage, intelligence, experience and privilege earned, is going to be Captain Harriet Tubman."

I, William Lloyd Garrison, editor of the Boston anti-slavery New Paper *The Liberator*, went to Cincinnati to see her and her troops jump off into Kentucky. I stood with tears in my eyes as I saw the diminutive figure of Harriet Tubman, the woman with whom I have worked so long in the Underground Railroad, leading them out. I swelled with pride and listened with fascination as the deep melodious voices of the young Negro soldiers wafted on the brisk December air:

John Brown's body lies a-molderin' in the grave,
But his soul is marchin' on.

Catherine now knew the story behind the raid on Lexington that took Tuttle away. She laid aside the book and sat transfigured. It would never do for anyone, not even Mary Chesnut, to know it, but Catherine felt admiration and concern for Harriet Tubman. What a noble, courageous, wildly free, and sacrificial person she was. Catherine was brave, gritty, and resourceful, but she tried to imagine herself doing such things and could not come close to it. She thought about Harriet's frustrated married life and it made her think of Emmanuel and Tuttle for some reason. She felt sad for Harriet and was angry with her husband for what he had done to Harriet.

Chapter Twenty-Four

Moses in the Bush

Catherine was still engrossed in thought about Harriet Tubman when the train pulled into Lexington station. She wanted to stop for a visit with Colonel Wolf, but something told her to get to Hopemont as soon as possible. She took a cab and arrived at about 11:30 A.M. Emmanuel sat on the porch anxiously waiting. He ran out to greet her with a smile of great relief on his face. He began chattering like a jay.

She had been away long enough this time that she could not pick up his speech, so she held up her hand for him to be quiet. "Emmanuel, don't say anything except to answer my questions." Emmanuel nodded and looked scolded. "Now, tell me…tell me where Tuttle is and why today is so important." Emmanuel started to chatter again. "Emmanuel, slow down," she said. "I can't understand you. Please, speak slowly and try not to get excited."

Emmanuel stopped and swallowed a few times. "All right ma'am," he said, "I'll try. Tuttle is with Moses. They is out in the trees. Moses won't bring her in 'cause she's skeerd of bein' 'rested. I can't go to her, 'cause she sez they apt to foller me. You got to go to her. She won't come out a hidin' for nobody else. If nobody come by dark, she goin' back no'th and takin' Tuttle wid her."

"How do you know all this?" Catherine asked.

"Those Niggers done tole me," he said.

"How do those…how did they find out?"

"I dunno, Ma'am," he said. "Somethin' bout folks in town used to be conductors on de un'ergroun' railroad."

Catherine thought a while. It sounded pretty folksy to her. What if it was only a rumor? But of course, she would not know until… "All right," she said. "But what am I supposed to do, Emmanuel?"

"You 'spose to get in de buggy an' take the Cheetum road to'wd de ribber," he said. "You jess keeps goin' till Moses stop ya."

"All right, well, then get the buggy ready."

"De buggy out an de hoss standin' in de traces."

"Well, I guess—let's go and see what happens," she said.

Emmanuel looked troubled. "I can't go wid ya, Ma'am," he replied. "I sho wish I could."

"Oh, that's right," Catherine answered, "you said that." The reason was clear enough to her. A distance of several hundred yards, in plain sight of town, separated the road from the trees of the wild wood. If there were any rumors going around or any one watching, Emmanuel's presence could draw attention.

Catherine started out with trepidation. Unknown and strange adventures, where she could not reason things out, were uncomfortable for her. There was no telling what she would run into. If Harriet Tubman and Tuttle were out there, she was in no danger. Harriet had chosen a little traveled road. The Cheathams, old family acquaintances, lived out there. No one would be suspicious of her going out that way.

When Catherine reached the woods, she experienced the eerie feeling of being followed. She stopped several times and looked as deeply into the trees and brush as she could but saw no movement nor heard any sound. "I know you are in those trees," she said loudly. "Come out and show yourself!" Her voice sounded strange as it died out and the almost eerie silence returned. She had the sense of something being strange. Then she knew the answer. There were no birds singing and no woodland creatures making their peculiar noises. There was someone out there! Catherine, not one to be afraid, felt the tension and fought to keep control.

She thought about calling out Tuttle's name but decided against it. She had almost reached the river when a rock came bouncing out in front of the buggy. Catherine stopped and looked slowly around.

Finally, she saw the short, stocky figure of Harriet in the brush. She wore the uniform of a soldier, medium green like the scenery, but with no markings. She did not wear a covering. Straight, jet-black hair hung between her ears and the top of her shoulders. The big, brown, piercing, frightened, dangerous eyes bored into Catherine's face. Harriet motioned for her to pull the buggy off the road and into the seclusion of trees and brush, where it could not be seen from the road. Then she came up to Catherine. She was a short woman and her head was about as high as Catherine's lap. Catherine started to dismount.

Harriet spoke in an even, cold tone. "You git out if you want to," she said, "but we got to make this quick."

"You are Miss Harriet?" Catherine asked.

Harriet turned and looked at her with disdain. "You can't call me no 'Miss,'" she said. "I'm a Negra and a runaway slave."

Catherine was hesitant. "All right…then, 'Moses'."

Harriet was unrelenting. "Not dat either," she replied. "I'm Moses to peoples in bondage who is lookin' fer deliverance."

Catherine was uneasy in the presence of this awesome person on whose head there was a price that had now reached $50,000. "What shall…what may I call you, then?" she asked.

"You got to call me anythin', call me Cap'n Tubman," Harriet answered coldly.

Catherine was glad she at least had found out how to communicate. "Captain Tubman," she said. "I want to thank you so much for bringing Tuttle back."

The cold, indifferent mask stayed firmly in place. "I ain't doin' this for you, Ma'am, and I wouldn't' do it for you," she said in a scolding tone. "So don't go thanking' me for somethin' I ain't done. I'm doin' it for Tuttle."

"Well, that's…"

"I told her she's a fool," Harriet interrupted, "and I tried to talk her out of it, but she think she owe somethin' to you and to 'Man'el'."

"But you risked your life and freedom bringing her back," Catherine said with feeling. "Surely you will let me…"

Harriet cut her off again. "I let you do nothin' Ma'am, nor Tuttle neither," she said with finality. "I took her 'way against her wants, so

I got to bring her back; habben't I?" Without waiting for Catherine to answer, Harriet called out softly, "Tuttle, you come on out here, honey. Here's you b'loved slave master." Her remark stung deeply but Catherine saw that protest was a waste of time. Of course Harriet felt that way; how could she feel any other?

Harriet gave Tuttle a hug and a slap on the butt. "Y'all get up in that buggy and git," she said. "We been here too long."

Impulsively Catherine grabbed Harriet and gave her a hug. "God bless you," she said with emotion. Harriet was rigid but did not push her away. She smelled like brush and river water…and lots of other wild things. Catherine, who could not stand uncleanness—particularly in women, thought how strangely wonderful the smell was.

She released Harriet who stepped back and looked her in the face without changing her expression. "God blesses me, all right," she said defiantly. "But you ain't got no right to wish me God's blessin'—you bein' lovely, white, rich and free. When me and my people are free like you, then you come and bless me."

Catherine was wounded to the depths. She looked at the proud, notorious, defiant, brave little woman and her heart went out to her. "Oh, Harriet," she said, blinking back the tears, "if you only knew—you are freer than all of us. I hope some day you will realize that."

Harriet was not impressed. "Would you trade places with me if'n you could, Ma'am?" she asked. Catherine did not answer and she felt confusion in her mind. She had meant what she said. Harriet Tubman was free…in a way that she or few other people have ever known or ever would know. And yet, she would not trade places with Harriet if she could. Harriet waited and then continued. "Just tell the people of the South to give us our nach'al freedom, Ma'am, and we be happy wid that," she said, her tone softer than before. "The other kine' can wait."

Catherine was driven by impulse but also by things she and her mother had talked about many times. Perhaps now was the time. "Harriet, if you wait here," she said, "I will go and get Emmanuel. You can take them both back with you, if you want to."

Harriet's expression changed to one of reflection. "She don't want to go an leave her b'loved Mistress and her 'Ole Kentucky

Home', Ma'am," she said facetiously. "That's the big problem we got now. It's gonna take whole lot of gen'rations to get this servant's mind out'n black peoples."

Catherine sighed. How much she would like to help Harriet not make the mistakes of overreaction and wrong reactions. "Oh, Harriet," she asked passionately, "are you sure you want to do that?"

Harriet looked at her with contempt. "You got a servant's mind in you, Ma'am?" she asked.

Catherine was quick to react. "Yes," she said. "Yes I have—at least I think I do. I believe God wants us to, and I feel that it is part of…"

"Maybe you have," Harriet cut in, "but you got choice; we ain't."

"Yes, but…"

Harriet held up her hand for silence. "I don't want to talk about such things wid you, Ma'am, least ways not now and not here," she said. "I'm getting that worried feelin'. It's time we all be goin'." Harriet turned quickly to leave. At the edge of the small clearing, she stopped and looked back. Catherine smiled and waved her hand. A hint of softness came to Harriet's face, almost as if she wanted to smile back but could not do so without betraying the code that had driven her to such remarkable achievements. She raised her hand from her side to above her belt and Catherine saw her fingers move slightly. Then she was gone.

Chapter Twenty-Five

Down By the Riverside

Catherine studied Tuttle as she sat as far to the outside of the buggy seat as she could without falling off. Her hands were clasped in her lap and she did not look up. Catherine thought she looked very clean and neat for someone who had made a journey of many miles though river bottoms, through woods, and across fields. She was nicely dressed in a piece that Catherine did not recognize.

"Tuttle, you look so nice for having traveled so far," she said. "I am very…"

"Missers Doglass gave me a new dress to bring wid me," Tuttle said without looking up. "Jes' 'fore we met up with you, Moses taken me down to the ribber and like nigh scrub de hide off'n me. She say I got to be purty for Miss Cath'n."

"But how did you get the wrinkles out of it?" Catherine asked.

"Moses biled some water and held the dress in de steam," Tuttle said. "Den she smooth it out on a big rock."

"Hum!" Catherine said, "I will have to remember that." She reached over and put her hand on Tuttle's shoulder.

Tuttle stiffened with fright. "You gunna whup me hard, Ma'am," she asked. Catherine felt sympathy and guilt. "Oh, Tuttle, of course I am not going to whip you," she replied. "Anyway, when have you ever been whipped—I mean, by the Morgans, that is?" Tuttle did not answer. "Well?"

"Marse John whupped me once," she said, "real good…well, not 'zackly hard."

Catherine had not heard this story and she was shocked. "What?" she asked. "When was that?"

"Jes 'fore he went away to the wars."

"You never told me that," Catherine said, a little reproachfully.

"He say he whup me good sho' 'nuff if'n I ebber tell you or Missers Mo'gan."

Catherine was curious now. "What did he…what was it all about?" she asked.

"I tole dem Niggers he got drunk one night and was 'shamed to come home so he sleeped in the hay in Marse Todd's barn," she said. "Den he done foun' out 'bout it."

"How did you know he got drunk and slept in the Todd barn?" Catherine asked.

"Those Niggers done tole me," Tuttle said.

Catherine recognized an old frustration. "Well, Tuttle, if they told you and you told them, and they told John you told them when they were the ones who told you to begin with…oh, never mind," she said with a sigh. "Anyway, I am not going to whip you. I am glad to see you home. After more than two years, I didn't think you were coming back."

"I was woun'ed serious, Ma'am," she said, almost proudly, "and got wuss adder that hard scurryin' out'n here. An' den, dey wa'nt g'wine let me come back. A'ter while I run a way, but I got loss'. Moses foun' me and bring me back. She tell the udders, 'nuff a dis, now, I's takin' Miss Tuttle back home.'"

"Where were you all that time, Tuttle?" Catherine asked. "Where did you stay?"

Tuttle's eye lit up. "I stay at de house of a man dat looked jis like God," she said dramatically. "And dat won'erful woman—lan' sakes; she must be de mudder of all black people."

Catherine was confused. "You stayed at the home of White people?" she asked.

Tuttle pouted. "No, Ma'am," she said indignantly, "dees wuz Negra folk."

"I see. Did this black god have a name?"

Tuttle spoke with reverence. “Yes, ma’am. His name Fred’ick Doglass.”

Catherine shook her head in bewilderment. Tuttle, her little house servant, spending two years in the home of the most famous and infamous black man in the world and being brought home by the most notorious black woman of all time—how the war had scrambled everything. “You stayed at the home of Frederick Douglass?” she asked. “My word, you were traveling in high society, weren’t you?”

Tuttle was genuinely proud. “Yes, Ma’am, I was,” she said.

Then a concern crossed Catherine’s mind. This kind of publicity could bring unwanted attention. “Tuttle,” she said, “it might not be wise to tell those…all your friends that your were at the Douglasses.”

“Yes, ma’am, I knows dat,” Tuttle said as if being talked down to. “Fo’e I lef’, us had ‘tellignece meetin’s. Dey tole me lots a things not to say.”

“Did they tell you things not to tell me?” Catherine asked.

Tuttle did not hesitate. “Yes, Ma’am, some dat too.”

Catherine wondered if that was going to be a problem and decided not, for now at least. “Well, then, you had best not tell me,” she said.

Tuttle was very serious. “No Ma’am, I’s not goin’ to,” she said. “I cain’t. Moses done say she come adder me lack a houn’ dog adder a possum if I tell sec’ets.” Catherine chuckled as she tried to bring up that picture in her mind. In any case, she was sure she could understand Tuttle’s concern. Catherine would not like to have Harriet Tubman on her trail with vengeance in her heart. “Anyway, Ma’am,” Tuttle said, “I dunno no sec’ets that’d do nobody no good no way.”

“Did she tell you to say that if anyone questions you?” Catherine asked.

Tuttle nodded her head enthusiastically, as if relieved to see that Catherine understood. “Yes Ma’am, she did,” Tuttle said innocently. “Den they cain’t get nuthin’ out’n me so dey ain’t gonna to’cher me none.”

Catherine felt amusement, pity, and sorrow. “Well, let’s hope,” she said reassuringly, “that no one is going to be…”

Catherine stopped in mid sentence as she became aware of riders on both sides of the buggy. Her fears subsided when the big horse with the partially bald face and wild, ringed eye turned facing the buggy, with General Forrest looking down at her. She still had trouble keeping the evil gleam from sending chills up and down her.

He doffed his hat. "Afternoon, Miss Kitty,' he said. "I figger you'd remember me."

"Oh, yes, General Forrest," Catherine said, "you leave a deep impression."

Forrest tipped his hat. "I'm flattered Ma'am," he said.

"What brings you to Kentucky?" she asked. "I thought you and General Morgan had enough of these parts a few months ago."

Forrest made a face. "Yea, that didn't work out as planned," he said. "Well, I'm here to see you."

"How did you find me?" she asked. "Did Emmanuel…"

"Ma'am," Forrest said with a pained expression, "if a ranger like me can't find a purty woman like you in her own hometown, I better go into some other line."

"Yes, of course," she said, "But how did you know I would be in Kentucky?"

Forrest looked mockingly at her. "They got this new-fangled thing they call the telegraph, Ma'am, it…"

Catherine blushed. For a general's wife, the questions were not very well thought out. "All right," she said defensively, "you needn't make fun of me." She paused to regroup her thoughts. "But how did you know I was out here?" she asked, "I guess that is what I wanted to know."

"We been followin' you ever since you came into the woods almost an hour ago," he replied.

So! She was right after all; there had been someone out there. For some reason it comforted her a bit to know that. Then concern set in. "You mean…"

"That's right, Miss, Kitty," he said, "we saw it all. But don't worry, I won't tell your husband you was huggin' a…"

Catherine reacted quickly. "General Forrest, please!" she said, glancing at Tuttle.

Forrest sneered. "Oh, yea," he said disapprovingly, "you are one of these…well, what does it matter to me, I guess."

Catherine stiffened with fear. "Miss Har…Captain T…Moses…the woman? Is she is any danger?" she asked.

Forrest did not sneer this time. "Oh, that woman…or whatever she is…is always in danger," he said, "but not from me and my boys. Anyway, I didn't come here for that."

Catherine sighed to relieve her tensions. "What did you come for, General Forrest?" she asked. Forrest motioned for his men to stay where they were; then he led the buggy on ahead about fifty yards. He looked at Tuttle. "Oh, it's all right," Catherine said, "she's family."

Forest took off his hat. "I am pained to tell you, Ma'am," he said with a poor attempt at softness, "that General Morgan is dead."

Catherine caught her breath and prepared to cry, but for some reason she did not. Maybe it was Tuttle, maybe it was the presence of Forrest, but her tears would wait. "Oh, dear," she said, wringing her hands, "this is what you fear the most." Catherine was silent a moment. Then she asked, "How did it happen, General, in good military cause, I trust?"

"Well, sorta, I reckon," Forrest replied. "He was down to Atlanta, trying' to help Hood. The big fight was over and Sherman had all ready took the town. There was a little ruckus near the border as he was headin' back to Tennessee…and that's when he got it."

Catherine shook her head slowly. "Poor Mattie; does she know? Oh, but of course she would."

"Yea, I told her 'fore I did you," he said, "She's takin' it hard, but she'll be okay. She's a hardy gal, with lots of inner thoughts."

"I must…" Catherine started to say and then decided that her comment about writing to Mattie would be out of place here.

"I didn't show this to her, though," he said, producing a letter from inside his jacket. "It's just for you, Ma'am."

She took the envelope and opened it. Forrest stood his ground. She looked up at him. "Is it…of a private nature?" she asked.

"Ya mean, did I look at it? he asked. "No, but I know more or less what's in it. We talked about you and it a lot. I'll stay till ya read it, if you'd like, maybe you will want to ask…"

Catherine did not think she wanted to read the letter in front of Forrest and Tuttle. "I thought I would wait until I get home," she said, her voice trailing off.

Forrest looked uncomfortable. "Up to you, Ma'am," he said, "but if you want to know anythin' from me, you'll want to read it here and now."

Something in Forrest's words made her feel she should do that. She opened it and began to read:

Dear Little Sister:

If you are reading this, I am dead. I know your concern for me and my soul. I want you to know something. In February of '64, General Nathan Bedford Forrest and I sat on the banks of the Mississippi near Natchez where a little tributary makes a sort of small inlet bay. Again, he told me of the dangers of war, of the shortness of life, of the sinfulness of men, and of the need to be prepared to meet one's God. The timing was right. As you know, I was taught this by our parents and by the Church. I have had thoughts and doubts all my life and they were accelerated by my hatred and excuse for vengeance at the beginning of the war. But after our last talk and my visit with Mamma before her death, and largely due to Parson Edwards' sermon at Mamma's memorial, I have been thinking a lot about such things. I never cared much for religion. Finally, in talks with the man who is probably looking down at you now and whom you consider to be such an evil fool (I did too, when I talked to you last, but some of that changed at the last), it got through to me what the Gospel is all about and there isn't much religion in it. I got down on my knees in the wet sand and repented. You will be proud to know that Reverend General Forrest baptized me in one of the mightiest streams of them all—the Mississippi River. It wasn't the Jordan, but it is the best we have in this part of the world. General Forrest has affirmed to me (he does not believe in swearing) that he will deliver this letter to you personally, along with any assurances you need about the genuineness of my conversion.

God bless you for your prayers and your concern. I love you dearly, you precious little girl, and even though I am your brother, I admire you for your courage, your wisdom beyond your years and your many faceted beauty that is equaled only by my dear Mattie. Now you can be sure that we will meet on the other side.

Your brother John

March 12, 1864, at Natchez, Mississippi.

Catherine folded the letter in her lap and looked down at her hands. It was comforting but very sad at the same time. Was she going to cry? No, not now. She looked up at Forrest. For the first time the evil gleam was gone from his eyes, and Catherine felt that he had rustic and wild good looks without it. "So," she said, taking a deep breath to steady her voice, "my brother was sincere, then? He was honest before God?"

Forrest puffed out his cheeks and thought for a moment. "Sincere? Yes, he was sincere," he said. "Honest before God? Only God knows that for sure, Ma'am, but as much as one man can know another, I would say yes."

Catherine saw the man in an entirely different light than she had seen him before or heard and thought about him. "Thank you so much, Nathan," she said with warm sincerity. "I know it was for my brother that you did it, but thank you."

Forrest balanced his mind on his jaw. "For your brother, yes," he said, "but also for you Ma'am." Catherine wanted to pursue that but decided not to. "You see, Ma'am," he continued, "when you came all the way up that river by yourself, woke up looking into the face of the most feared man in the war and then got back in my face and chewed me out—well, that burned in my mind an admiration for you that will be there as long as I live. Nobody ever did that to me and got away with it—man or woman."

Catherine was unsure of how to respond. "Oh, well, I…"

The evil gleam returned and the face became frightening again. "But don't' ever do it again, Ma'am," he warned. "You never can tell."

Catherine put her hand to her throat. "No, Sir, General Forrest, I will certainly not," she said with great sincerity.

Forrest threw back his head and laughed. "If the same thing happened again, you would do the same thing," he said. "That's what makes you what you are." He spurred his horse and started off. Then he stopped. "Miss Kitty," he said soberly, "be careful. There's somethin' goin' on around here."

Catherine caught the alarm in his voice. “What is it, General Forrest?” she asked, her eyes growing large.

“I don’t know, Ma’am,” he said. “I ain’t got it figured out yet. Just keep your powder handy.” With that, he was gone. His men moved up and formed a line on either side of her. She looked at them questioningly.

“General’s orders, Ma’am. We aim to see ya safely out of the woods.”

At the edge of the woods, the men stopped and Catherine continued on through the open fields toward home.

Chapter Twenty-Six

To Set My People Free

"What dat man mean, tellin' you to keep your powder close by? Such goin' on to a ma'am," Tuttle said in a pout, "you ain't habben' no powder, Miss Cath'n."

Catherine looked at her with amusement. "I haven't?" she asked. "Don't be so sure of that. Anyway," she said, "it's just a military expression. Those are the only ones General Forrest knows. He was warning us to be ready for anything."

Catherine saw the fear spreading over Tuttle's face and into her eyes. "What you think is g'wine to happen?" she asked.

"I do not know, Tuttle," she said, "and if General Forrest doesn't know, there is no use scaring ourselves with imaginations. Let's not think about it."

That seemed to pacify Tuttle. Catherine saw her thoughts going in other directions. Catherine would like to have known what she was thinking. She did not have to wait long. "Moses say you g'wine to be payin' me money soon," Tuttle said.

Catherine expected anything from Tuttle but this. "Moses…Harriet said what?" she asked sharply.

"She say you g'wine pay me and 'Man'el a dollar a month."

"What on earth are you talking about, Tuttle? Who gave Harriet Tubman leave to start spending my money for me?"

"She say the No'th g'wine win de war for sho'. Den the darkies g'wine be set free. If'n we stay to your house, you g'wine pay us a dollar a month an' fowm."

Catherine nodded absently. "I see," she said. "Well, anyway, Tuttle, the word is 'found.' Can you say that? 'found'."

Tuttle looked frustrated. "Dat's 'zackly what I say, Miss Cath'n," she replied. "Fowm."

"Okay, never mind," Catherine told her. Then she paused to change the mood of the conversation. "Well, we will talk about that, when the time comes," she said.

Tuttle began to scold. "I tole her, 'Miss Cath'n ain't habben no such money as to be payin' us no dollar a month." Tuttle turned and looked cautiously and questioningly at Catherine. "Hab you, Miss Cath'n?" she asked.

Catherine mused to herself: 'Look out, Confederacy, here it comes.'

"Oh, I suppose we have if it comes to that," she said. "We will see, but let's not talk about it anymore just now, shall we not?" Tuttle acted as if she had just discovered gold. She took hold of the front handrail, bounced in her seat, and smiled from ear to ear. The sight was almost amusing to Catherine—almost.

As they neared the house, Catherine saw a rig and could make out the big frame of Colonel Wolf. She thought back to their conversation of two years ago about Tuttle coming home. She hoped that it still held. When they reached the drive, Catherine saw another man she did not recognize in a captain's uniform. He was a little, slight built man with an air Catherine did not like at all, even from afar.

As she pulled up, the Captain gave an order to one of his men. "Arrest that slave and put her in chains," he said.

Catherine lashed the soldier with the buggy whip and he jumped back, putting his hands to his face.

The Captain whirled on her. "See here, lady," he said in a cold and ugly tone, "You are interfering with government business."

Catherine ignored him and turned to Colonel Wolf. "What is this all about, Colonel?" she asked. Catherine did not like the sad and helpless look in his eyes.

"This in Captain Skinner from Louisiana," he said. "He has a letter from President Davis. He has apparently been chosen to patrol the Border States and try to stop the exodus of slaves across to the North. He has been authorized to arrest any runaways and take them with him." Catherine stared so hard at the Captain that he looked away. "I am sorry Ma'am," the Captain said, "but these people are property, and…"

Catherine cut him off. "If this girl is anyone's property," she said angrily, "she is mine!"

The Captain was ready with his line. "There has been too much *looking the other way* by owners, now that the outcome of the war is in doubt," he said. "In most cases, in border states, returnin' a slave to the owner, is just a delayed trip back across the border. President Davis has decided to take matters into his own hands. He is going to personally deal with every runaway as a matter of the violation of law."

Catherine wondered who, in Richmond, had blown the whistle on her and how they had found out about Tuttle. Now she knew. It was Davis himself. Catherine did not want to think about that just now. "And what does he plan to do with them?" she asked.

"In most cases, if it is obvious that the owner is not going to comply with Southern slave tradition," the Captain said, "they will be sold at auction in the South to new ownership far from the borders. In this way, money can be raised for the Southern cause."

This outraged Catherine, who tried hard to control her temper. "I know President Davis personally. My husband is General A. P. Hill. You need not worry, Captain, I will take care of it," she said.

The Captain shook his head triumphantly. "That will not work, Ma'am, the authority in Kentucky is in the hands of the governor. The President does not want notable persons pressuring him," he said with mock politeness. "The authority I possess," he patted his inside coat pocket, "will not be circumvented by the President."

"Let me see your letter, Captain," Catherine demanded.

The Captain pulled out the letter but did not hand it to her. "I will read you what it says, Mrs. Hill," he said.

By the bearing of this letter with its official signature and seal, authority is granted to Honus B. Skinner, assigned the honorary rank of Captain, to avoid complications with the military, to take and make disposition as instructed, of any and all runaway slaves that are apprehended either in the South soil or by kidnapping from the North. In conjunction with Congress, it is the policy of this government from this day forward, that neither the President nor the Congress will interfere with Captain Skinner, nor those bearing similar and verified letters, in this work.

Any owner who feels he is being unjustly treated may apply to the governor of his state. The governor will, in turn, in the face of sufficient reason, contact and consult with the government in Richmond, Virginia. The disposition of those in Mr. Skinner's control will not be delayed by the legal process. If an owner prevails in complaint, the Government shall make the best possible effort to recover the lost property to the prevailing owner. If that cannot be done, other slaves or like amounts of moneys will be proffered to the owner; in some cases, because of the severity of the war effort, after the conflict has settled and the government is in better monetary circumstances.

The bearer of this letter is not entitled to confiscate free blacks. If he does so as an honest mistake, he will not be held liable. It will be for the free black to produce papers establishing his freedom. If the free black is intellectually unable, he may appeal to his employer to protect by all legal means his non-bound servants or apply to the government of his state to obtain the release of same.

Jefferson Davis
President
July 4, 1864 At Richmond, Virginia.

"I wish to see the letter for myself, Captain."

Colonel Wolf intervened. "It says exactly as you heard, Catherine," he said. "I have read it."

"Then I wish you to take it in hand again, Colonel," she said. The Captain handed the letter to Colonel Wolf. "Colonel," she said confidently, "I call your attention to the sentence that says, 'It is the responsibility of the users of free blacks to protect their servants, and that this man has no right to confiscate free blacks if he is informed and knows that is what he is doing.' Do you see that?"

"Yes, Miss Kitty, I see it," Wolf said. "It isn't just exactly like that, but..." He turned to the Captain to confer.

Catherine beckoned for Emmanuel who came quickly to the buggy. "Listen, the both of you, and listen carefully and fast," she said sharply. "I do not want you to say one word; not to anyone at all. Answer no questions, not even if they hit you. Do you understand?" They both nodded their heads, their eyes dilated in fear. "Now you are going to hear some things that are going to surprise you very much," she told them, "but do not say one word. Your place here and your well-being depend on your doing exactly as I have told you. Not a word to anyone. Not Colonel Wolf, not anyone."

The Captain came up to the buggy. "See here, Mrs. Hill," he said, his feigned politeness gone, "if you are advising this girl to make a run for it..."

Catherine pushed the Captain out of her line of vision. "Colonel Wolf," she said, "these two people are free blacks. I gave them their freedom nearly five years ago. They are working for me of their own will and receiving pay of one dollar per month plus found."

The Captain was irritated. "Mrs. Hill," he asked in disgust, "do you know how many people have tried this on me, I..."

Colonel Wolf put a heavy hand on the Captain's arm. "Miss Kitty," he said, looking at her very soberly, "you will have to produce their papers establishing their freedom *prior to Tuttle's arrest today.* Can you do that?"

"Yes, I can, Colonel," she answered without hesitation.

Colonel Wolf looked doubtful. "Then...then you had better do it," he said. "Where are they?"

"In the house...in my strong box," she told him.

The Colonel looked puzzled. "Will you get them?" he asked.

"Yes, Colonel, right away," she said, "but you must take legal charge of these servants and keep them right here until I return."

The Captain lost his superior pose and sounded alarmed. "How long is she going to have to go in there and make up something, Colonel?" he asked.

Catherine sensed victory and her courage rose. "Captain, I told you already I am the wife of A. P. Hill and the personal friend of President Davis," she said firmly. "Are you accusing me of dishonesty and illegal behavior?"

"Mrs. Hill," the Captain said, desperation beginning to sound in his voice, "anyone can throw hastily together a letter stating anything, but…"

"Including the signature of her mother who has been dead for two years," Catherine said, "and the signature of the President of the Lexington branch of the Bank of Kentucky, who witnessed and notarized it?" The Captain looked crestfallen.

Colonel Wolf spoke up. "Catherine," he said, "if you can produce such a document…how long will you be?"

"I don't know, Colonel, ten-maybe fifteen minutes," she said, trying to sound as convincing as possible. "I have not seen the document in years; I will have to find it among my papers."

Skinner was agitated. "Why didn't you give these…people this paper long ago, Mrs. Hill?" he asked.

"Because my servants can neither read nor write, Captain," she said, "and I did not trust them not to lose it."

The Captain was dogged. "You say you pay these people. How?"

"How? With currency, of course," she said disparagingly. "Do you think they have a bank account if they cannot read nor write?"

The Captain turned to Tuttle. "Is this true?" he asked. "Does this woman pay you?" Catherine hoped Tuttle would not hang her head. She didn't. She put her head in the air defiantly and looked down at him out of the corner of her eyes, but did not say anything.

Catherine breathed easier. Thank God for two years in the house of Frederick Douglass. She turned to Colonel Wolf. "Colonel, I answer for my servants," she said. "They are poor, helpless, unlearned people who can be easily taken advantage of. I have told the Captain I pay my servants. I do not want him questioning them. I resent the insinuation that I am lying."

The Colonel was beginning to get on board. "The Captain will not question your servants any more, Miss Kitty," he said, "and you have my word they will not leave the position in which they are now standing—or sitting—until you emerge. If you will just get the certificate…"

The Captain had one more ploy. "I am going to go with her, Colonel," he said, "to see that all is done…"

The time had come for Catherine's calculated anger. She flashed her green eyes, the surging blood turning her cameo face dark pink, and spoke with emotion. "Colonel, this awful man is not going into my house," she said in almost a shout. "I would not allow him in there nor be alone for a moment with such white trash."

The Colonel intervened quickly. "Miss Kitty, Miss Kitty," he said in a conciliatory tone, "calm down." He turned to the Captain. "The woman has told you that the document is signed and notarized," he said with authority. "If that is true, she cannot duplicate it. If it is not then, she has hoisted herself on her own petard."

Catherine went into the house and quickly found the metal box. She found the certificate near the bottom. She took it out quickly, found a blotter and a quill, and sat down to try to fill in the blank date as near the other strokes as possible. The document had to be dated before today or it would not help Tuttle. It was hard, white bank paper—the worst kind for ink to dry on. She watched the clock on the wall as she blotted and blew on the wet ink. She considered holding it over a lamp flame but was afraid it would 'black.' In fifteen minutes, the Colonel called to her. She came to the door.

He looked worried. "Miss, Kitty, have you found it?" he asked hopefully.

"Yes, your timing was perfect," she said, "I have it right here." Catherine came out holding up the certificate triumphantly, turning it to the breeze, and hoping for any last drying. The Captain reached for the certificate, but Catherine held it from him and gave it to the Colonel.

The Captain protested. "I would like to examine that closely, if I may."

Catherine did not wait for the Colonel to respond. "You may not, sir," she said testily. "It is the Colonel with whom I am concerned. He is the one who will determine the voracity of it and send you on your evil way. Don't let him have it, Colonel Wolf. It would be like him to tear it up."

Colonel Wolf looked at her narrowly. "Miss Kitty, must you?" he pleaded. She held her breath as he rubbed his hand lightly over the slate and the signatures. If only he did not touch the date. Eventually he drew his hand across the date she had filled in. Oh, Lord, no! He registered no reaction. When he removed it, she could not see a smear on the paper. She breathed a great sigh of relief. The Colonel turned questioningly to the Captain. "Captain Skinner, the document is in order, is it not?" he asked. "These two people are free blacks, given their freedom by Mrs. Morgan and her daughter shortly after the death of her husband. I may tell you, from having known them for most of Miss Kitty's life, that it does not entirely surprise me. I see no further business for you here."

"Ah, but I do have further business here, Colonel," he said with a crooked and evil grin.

Chapter Twenty-Seven

The Strong Man and the Captive

The Captain looked beyond Colonel Wolf and to the open field. Catherine tried to make out what was happening. Across, the field a number of men on horseback were coming. When they drew near, Catherine saw what it was and her heart sank. She immediately sent Emmanuel and Tuttle into the main house with the instructions to lock the door, stay in there and not to open the door for anyone but her. Harriet Tubman, who had her hands tied in front of her with a rope being pulled by a horse, was stumbling and trying to keep her feet. If she fell, she was dragged until she could get to her feet again.

The Colonel sidled up to Catherine. "Miss, Kitty," he said professionally, "I can't help you here."

"Don't leave me alone," Catherine pleaded, "with this…this"

"I will not, you can count on it," he said, "but I want you to know I can't help you or her."

The men brought Harriet into the yard with a lurch so that she was pitched on her face in the dirt. Catherine ran to her and helped her up.

Beneath her arm, Harriet whispered hoarsely to her. "Don't try to help me—you will only hurt me and yourself. I'll get out of this; I been in these spots before. It's better you say nothin' at all." Catherine heard the fear in her voice. How could she possibly get away?

Captain Skinner grabbed her by the arm and pulled her back. "Get away from that murdering slave-thief, Mrs. Hill," he said in a hateful tone. "Do you want to get contaminated with her filth?

Catherine had to ask, though she did not want to. "What…what will you do with her?"

"This one goes straight to the slave cells at the Louisiana auction," he said, softening a bit, "the farthest from the North and the safest from abolitionist raiders. First, I will collect my fifty thousand dollars, but we may not want to sell her. We may want to have a public whipping and—if she lives through it, which she will not if I have the whip—maybe a hanging."

Catherine felt nauseated. She went to Colonel Wolf. "How could anyone be so inhumane?" The Colonel held her loosely around the waist.

"I am afraid I am not with you on this one, Miss Kitty," he said unsympathetically. "This woman has made more than eighty raids into Southern territory. She has led, by some estimates, fifteen hundred slaves to the North. That is against both Northern and Southern law. She has led military raids, one as you well know, on this town in which many people were killed. She is much more than a prisoner of war—she is a war criminal." Catherine looked at him with sad and disappointed eyes, but he did not soften. "Anyway," he said, "She has chosen this life. She didn't have to come back down here."

Catherine did not want to get angry with her friend, but he was testing her. "But she got caught for bringing Tuttle…"

"Yes, whom she kidnapped against her will—by Tuttle's own words," he said coldly.

"If she had left Tuttle here, she would have been lynched," Catherine said emotionally. "You know that."

The Colonel looked long into Catherine's face and then shrugged. "For that, I am sorry she got caught," he said. "But there is no injustice here, she…"

Catherine watched as if in the midst of a bad dream as Harriet was put in manacles, linked to a chain, and hooked to a trace between two horses. Terror gripped her as she considered Harriet's fate. "All the way to Louisiana alone between two horses and no one with her but a bunch of sadistic bullies," she said aloud.

The Captain came near, peered into her face, and snarled, "What's your interest in this woman?" The Colonel pushed in between them and led the Captain away.

Catherine felt as if she was going to vomit and she did not want to do so in front of her tormentor. She walked quickly out to the large elm tree near the road. She was almost run over by the big, bald-faced horse. Forrest stormed into the yard with full compliment of raiders. Catherine ran back to see what was going to happen.

Forrest rode up to Captain Skinner, his horse almost touching him. "Where you goin' with the Nigger, Captain?" he asked.

"Louisiana, General, I reckon," he said.

Forrest stared down with his withering evil gaze. "I reckon not. Captain," he said forcefully. "Take the irons off her."

"General, I…"

Forrest pulled out his knife and placed the wicked point on the Captain's chin. "I believe you got a hearin' problem, Captain," he said.

It was Colonel Wolf who spoke up. "The Captain has papers from President Davis to take her," he said.

Forrest withdrew the knife and turned his head to look at Colonel Wolf. "You're a friend of Miss Kitty, ain't you?" he asked.

"Yes, I am proud to say," the Colonel answered.

Forrest brushed aside his words. "You better be proud," Forrest said, "and while you're at it, you better thank your lucky stars."

Wolf looked perplexed. "But General, there's got to be…"

Catherine saw Forrest look away from him and to the Captain. "A paper from Davis, have you?" she heard him say. "Let me see it."

The Captain took out his letter. "I'll read it to you," he told Forrest.

"You seem to be a captain that needs to learn how to talk to a general. Give me the letter." Skinner stood his ground.

"I would rather not." Forrest pulled his rifle from its boot.

"The next time I say it, I will say it to one of my men take it out of your dead hand." The Captain handed the letter to Forrest. He looked it over for awhile. Then he folded the letter and tore it in eight pieces.

He started to throw it on the ground, then thought better of it and put it in his saddle bag.

"There we are, Cap'n. Now you ain't got no letter from Davis and you ain't on no special assignment. You're just a cap'n bein' insubordinate to a general officer. A man can get shot for that in time of war."

"I will see that President Davis..." Forrest put up his rifle, rode up to the Captain and pushed the chest of the big horse against him. The little Captain, whether through fear or unwise valor, tried to stand without being unbalanced.

"Captain, let me tell ya how bad you're skeerin' me. I wouldn't give you a dead coon dog pup for Davis. If I had that little dictator-fool here I'd put him in those irons and drag him myself."

"I will tell President Davis..."

"You be sure you tell him...and while you're at it, tell him to ask his Nigger General Bragg what happens when people try to push me around. Now you get those irons off that girl before I put 'em on you and drag you to Louisiana."

"General Forrest, you, Sir, are committing treason. You are aiding and abetting and collaborating with the enemy and helping a prisoner of war escape."

Catherine took note of two things. The Captain, whatever else he was, was not a coward. He had courage and was not intimidated by Forrest. And, he was alive because of it. It was the one thing Forrest admired and respected. Forrest got down off his horse and walked up to the Captain. Catherine braced herself for what she thought was coming. "Skinner, you got a scar on you that looks like it was made by an Indian lance," he said to the Captain. "Was you ever in Indian territory as a soldier?" Forrest asked him. Catherine wondered what this line of questioning was all about.

"I have been," the Captain answered.

"Have you ever seen a chief come up under a flag of truce and ask for a pow wow?" he asked.

"Yes," Skinner said, "but I still..."

"What happens then?" Forrest asked him. The General did not wait for an answer. "Everybody stops fightin' 'til the truce is over," he said, "Then they go back to their lines and the war begins again."

"Yes, sir, but..."

"Jest hold your horses, Cap'n," Forrest said. "You don't seem to be able to see nothin' so I'm going' to lay it out for ya. This woman is the enemy all right, and a bad one too, but she come down here this time under a flag of truce. She didn't come to steal or to kill or to destroy. She come to bring back a runaway slave." Catherine felt warmth spreading over her body. She knew now that Harriet would be set free to return north. She thought the Captain would give up now, but he did not,

"Apparently," he said, trying to keep his case alive, "she did not bring back a runaway slave. This woman is a not a..."

Forrest did not give him a chance to say it. "Well, whatever she is," he said, "this woman brought her home. Now Cap'n, just like the rules of war says, we're not going to fire on her till she gets back to her lines. Then, if she comes down here on another mission, I'll help you track her down. I'll whip her 'till she don't know she's bein' whipped, and then I'll hang her, right on the spot. She's cost me as much as anyone else in the South. But we can't let ourselves lose our Christian character, Captain. She's here under a flag of truce, and she has to be allowed to get back."

Catherine had thought of Nathan Bedford Forrest as daring, brave, tough, and dangerous. She now knew something else about him. His backwoods ways and speech belied as cunning a mind as she had ever known. But did he really believe what he was saying and doing, or was he...was he doing it just for her?

Colonel Wolf, who had been quietly standing by her side, suddenly came to life. "By God, Forrest," he almost shouted, "I see now. Of course. It isn't right to nab her when she's..."

"Now you got it, Colonel," Forrest said. He turned to Captain Skinner. "You see what we got here, Captain? A General and a Major trying to protect people on missions of mercy under a white flag from a trigger happy captain who don't know the difference. Enemy is enemy to him," he said.

Skinner still did not concede defeat. "But General Davis..."

Catherine saw the fury in Forrest's face and she feared for the Captain. "I told you already about Davis and my feelin's," he said angrily. "Don't throw Davis at me again, or I'm going to get mad, and then, Cap'n…well, jest don't do it." Forrest went to Skinner's men and directed the freeing of Harriet.

Catherine was watching Captain Skinner. He did not seem to be as defeated as Catherine thought he should be. He kept stealing glances toward the woods. "Colonel," she said, "the Captain is…"

"I see him, Miss Kitty," he replied. "I wonder what's out there."

"Is it an army, Colonel?"

Wolf looked at her, smiled, and shook his head negatively. "Not likely to be an army," he said, "but he may have a few men. They know where Harriet…where her trail is."

Forrest came back to the Captain. "All right, now," he said, "be on your way, Skinner. The men you keep lookin' for are tied to a big oak tree about a hundred feet into the woods. When I leave here, I will set 'em free and send 'em to ya. My men will be guardin' the woman's trail, so forget about followin' her. Now you start off right down that road south and you keep goin.' A unit of my men are going to be followin' ya for a few days. If you turn back, they have orders to shoot."

The Captain shook his head in bewilderment and became submissive at last. "I need to go to Richmond," he said, "to see what Da…what I am to do now."

"You keep going to Frankfurt," Forrest ordered him. "You can wire the President from there. If you get new papers, Cap'n, don't come back to Lexington. You see that red haired girl right there? She is Kitty Morgan, sister of my dead partner, John Morgan, and this here where you're standin' is the Morgan place. I made a dyin' promise to him that I would look after her health and property till the War is over. My men will have this property and these two darkies under surveillance from now on. If I ketch you or any of your men hangin' around here, your number is up. I ain't got time to play games."

Forrest went over and mounted the big, wild looking, bald-faced horse. He turned and offered his hand to Harriet. She looked up at him defiantly.

"I can walk," she said defiantly.

Forrest shook his head and gave her a look that frightened Catherine. "I ain't got time fer ya to walk," he said. "Now look, little woman, I got you out of those chains' I can put ya back in 'em. I said, get up here!"

Catherine prayed in her mind. "Get up, Harriet," she said to herself, "please get up. If you don't, you are going to be on your way to New Orleans." After a long staring session, Harriet finally offered him her hand and he pulled her up behind the saddle. Catherine stood and watched them all the way to the woods. She sighed and rubbed her arms to get rid of the goose bumps.

Suddenly she realized she was standing there with her back to Colonel Wolf. She turned to him and said, "Oh, my goodness, Colonel, I am gong to quit coming home. Each time it is worse. What an ordeal."

"I can't argue with that," he said. Then he looked at her and shook his head in amazement. "God, Miss Kitty, you've got nerve for a woman."

Catherine grew thoughtful. "Colonel," she asked, "do you think there is any chance Captain Skinner will come back and try to spirit Tuttle away?"

The Colonel shook his head negatively. "He can't take her now," he said, "she's a free black." The Colonel looked at her with a puzzled expression. "Why didn't you make this known before, Catherine?"

Catherine had anticipated this question coming up and she had thought it out. "Why do you think, Colonel?" she asked. "I didn't want the whole town mad at me."

"Oh, of course," he said. "I see what you mean. That makes sense. Well, I had best be getting back to my office. I don't see that I am needed here." The Colonel offered Catherine his hand. As she looked down to take it, she saw the ink stain on his palm. He noticed her looking at it. "Oh, my word," he said with embarrassment, "How did that happen, I wonder?" He was very straight faced. She wondered if he was putting her on or if he really didn't know. She wanted to ask him but she decided not to. Sometimes it was best to let things lie.

After warning Tuttle and Emmanuel not to tell those…friends of theirs…about being paid, she gave them a dollar and told them to get food and supplies at the store and Emmanuel to sign for them as usual. The bills would be sent to her as always and Mr. Todd would pay them. The dollar was theirs. Catherine marveled that one dollar could create so much joy and excitement.

That made Emmanuel think of something. "Miss Cath'n," he asked in a hurt tone of voice, "how cum you tole that Cap'n I cain't read nor write? Din't you get my letter?"

Catherine smiled. "I did, Emmanuel," she said, "and it was very good; I was so proud." Then she grew sober. "No, I told him that because I didn't want him talking to you," she said. "I wanted him to think you were helpless like little children."

Emmanuel was bothered. "But dat ain't what you think, Miss Cath'n?" he asked.

"Heavens no, Emmanuel," she said, realizing she had hurt his feelings. "You know how I rely on you and your knowledge of things. I leave this place in your care, don't I?" Catherine put her hands on both their arms. "I was afraid he would trick you into saying that you were not free blacks," she said. "Then he would have taken Tuttle away." Emmanuel seemed to be satisfied.

Tuttle was still shaken. "How could he try to take me away from you, Miss Cath'n?" she asked in a genuine pout. "Person cain't 'pend on nuthin' no mo'e." Catherine was too weary to take it up.

"Well, he didn't and he will not bother you anymore," she said, "so let's don't think about it any more just now." Catherine thought of a question she had often wanted to ask. "Emmanuel? Tuttle?" she said, "Those…those Niggers…you know…what do they tell you? Are they treated well?" Emmanuel put the dollar in his pocket and grew sober.

"Most of 'em is, Ma'am," with a hint of sadness, "but some ain't. Some gets cussed and beat and pushed around—worked too long and too hard and fed too little and fo'ced to wear poor closin'." Catherine found herself becoming less and less patient with slavery and yet she knew, from Tuttle's recent experience, that legislated emancipation and hostile enforcement would only create hundreds and thousands of situations like the one Tuttle had been through the last two years. She wished Mary Chesnut were here so she could talk to her about it.

They all got in the buggy and Emmanuel drove to the Station. It seemed to Catherine that an inordinate number of Negroes were out waving to Tuttle and Emmanuel as they passed. It must be from seeing Tuttle at home, she reasoned. Once on the train, she found herself a seat at the back of an almost-empty car and sat near the window. Then she took out her handkerchief, slumped wearily, and released the rein on her emotions. It was now time. She hoped she would not cry all the way to Richmond. She had not wept long when she fell into a sound sleep. The Porter came by with a large, soft pillow. He put it gently under her head and covered her with a blanket. Ever so carefully, he wiped the tears from her eyes and the streaks from her face. Then he looked down at her, smiled broadly, and shook his head approvingly. The word had already gotten around.

Chapter Twenty-Eight

Spurs That Jingle

Catherine mounted the steps of the White House and went to President Davis' office. He had sent for her on some matter that the courier described as urgent. As she stood in the open doorway, he looked up gravely.

"Please come in and sit down, Miss Catherine," he said in a sad and tired tone, "I need to talk with you."

Catherine knew that the war was going really badly and she did to know what to expect. "What is it, General Davis," she asked quietly "You look so depressed?"

Davis rubbed his eyes and peered at her with an expression she had never seen on his face before. "I have something of the utmost tragedy to tell you, Miss Catherine," he said, "and I hope you will take it seriously."

Catherine was bemused. What could he possible mean by telling her it was that serious and then saying he hoped she would take it seriously? This was very strange indeed. "Of course I will take it seriously, General Davis," she said.

"I hope so," he replied. Then, before she could say anything else, he continued. "Well, I might as well quit stalling and tell you. General Stuart has been mortally wounded and he is dying."

Catherine was not ready for this and she sat in silence, trying to look grave while she thought how to act and respond. Finally she asked, "How did it happen, Sir, and when?"

"It happened in a corn field near Yellow Tavern," he said, "on May the fourth, which was…uh…well, just yesterday, of course."

"Oh, dear," she said, "well, was it a battle or an ambush, or…"

"No, it was a full fledged battle. With Sheridan's men," he said. "Poor Jeb was so badly outnumbered, and of course that General Sheridan is practically a devil. Bragg was supposed to provide reinforcements, but he did not get them there in time." He stopped, mopped his brow and looked very sad and forlorn. "Actually, there weren't any to send," he said quietly.

"It was in the fury of battle then? Does any one know for sure how he was hit?" she asked.

"Yes, we do know," he said. "There was a lull in the battle. Jeb and Major Venable went out to find the break in the line and see what they could do about restoring order. They found the break on the left and were trying to devise a plan to close up when they were attacked hard by the Fifth and Sixth Michigan. The attack was not designed to 'drive home,' but it was so fierce that it pushed the whole left and part of our center four hundred yards back to a ravine. Typically, the courageous General Stuart stood his ground as the Michigan boys sped by, drawing his revolver and emptying it into the surging troops. The Blue Coats were thrown back and soon disappeared out of sight. At that moment, a Federal trooper sneaked along the fence row and shot Jeb."

"Oh my," Catherine said, "and it was—well, of course you said it was serious."

"Yes," he said tersely, "Dr. Fontaine came up immediately and saw the seriousness of it. He ordered the men to get Jeb off his horse and they had a devil of a time doing it. Stuart was on that one-man horse of his. It became unruly when they tried it lead it and they almost could not get him to the ground. Stuart told Captain Dorsey to prop him against the tree and to leave him there, but of course the captain disobeyed that foolish order. Fitz Lee arrived on the scene and had Stuart taken back to a place he felt was safe from attack. Wheatley found an ambulance and Venable ordered the ambulance to remove Stuart from the field but dear old Stuart did not give over the command without yelling, 'Go back and do your duty, as I have done mine.' As they moved off, the men heard him shout, 'I had rather die than be whipped.' Dr. K. B. Fontaine reached Stuart while the ambulance was still on its way. He had Stuart gently turned on his side so he could inspect his back. He then saw that Stuart had been shot through the stomach and would not live. He recommended that Stuart take a drink of whisky but Stuart refused saying that he had promised his mother he would not take even a sip of the stuff.

"To avoid capture the ambulance had to make numerous detours, going down bumpy lanes, on its journey back here to Richmond." Catherine saw that tears were creeping down the President's face. "He left his horses to McClellan, and Venable." Davis stopped to think a moment. He seemed to regain some of his composure. "And he left his golden spurs to Lilly Parran of Baltimore. That bothers me," he said. "Why would he do that, do you suppose?"

Catherine started to answer him and then thought better of it. "You say he is here in Richmond?" she asked. "Is he still alive?"

"Yes, he is at least at the moment," Davis said, "though he does not have much time. And that is why I called you in. He is asking for you, Catherine. I would like for you to go with me to see him. Will you do that for him?"

Catherine knew that she did not have time to think this through. She would have to answer now. What would it mean if she refused? And what would it mean if she went? He was a dying man, but who would be there and what would come of it in the way of rumors? Catherine decided that going was the only way out.

"Yes, I will go with you, General Davis," she said, trying to sound respectful and soft.

Davis breathed a large sigh of relief. "Oh, thank God," he said emotionally. "I was so afraid you would not do it."

When they reached the infirmary, Jefferson Davis took Stuart's hand. "How do you feel, General?" he asked earnestly.

"Easy," Stuart answered in a calm voice, "but willing to die if God and my country think I have fulfilled my destiny and done my duty."

"I have brought someone to see you, General," Davis said. Catherine realized that Stuart could not move his head so she walked around in front of him.

Jeb Stuart broke out in a big grin. "Dear Catherine," he said in a poor attempt to sound resonant and strong. I am so glad you came. I cannot tell you how much it means for me to die knowing that you are not my enemy."

"Why General Stuart," she said, tying to sound cheerful, "Whatever are you talking about. I have never been your enemy." Stuart smiled and closed his eyes and the Doctor motioned for them to leave.

The next morning Davis sent for her again. "During the night Stuart had fits of delirium, shouting orders and reliving dramatic battles," he said, much more composed and at peace than he had been the day before. At 7:38 he rose up on his bed and said, 'I am going fast now. I am resigned; God's will be done.' Then Jeb Stuart rode off with other horsemen to glory on different fields."

Catherine was silent for a while. Then she said, "I hope that is true, General Davis."

Davis sounded displeased. "Why Miss Catherine, why would you say that? Of course it is true."

Catherine sat for a while longer. When the silence started to become awkward, she rose to leave. "Well, then General Davis, I guess…"

Davis interrupted her. "Catherine, I have one more thing ask of you. It means so very much to me. Please do not refuse me." Catherine steeled herself against what might be coming and did not reply. Finally Davis said, "Catherine I want you to go with me to Jeb's funeral service."

Catherine had no answer but neither would she commit her self as he had to going and seeing him in the hospital. "When is his service, General?"

"Tomorrow morning at 10:00 A. M.," he said hopefully.

"General Davis, I will have to think about that," she replied. "If I decide it is something I can do, I will come and meet you there."

"It will mean so much to the other officers," he said, "and…to me."

Catherine left without saying anything more.

Catherine made her mind up during the night to attend. Talking with Mary had helped and she knew that her husband would not mind; in fact he would want her to do it. Her concern was that no rumors get started about her and Jeb Stuart but Mary had shamed her and said that no officer and gentleman would make anything out of an officer's wife going to the memorial service of a fallen fellow officer. Catherine laid awake most of the night thinking about Jeb Stuart. She had actually come to sort of like him in recent months. And, for all his bravado and pomp, he was a good soldier and had done much for the Confederate cause.

Catherine wore her black dress and it set off her red hair and green eyes very well. As she left Mary's house where she had dressed, she picked a white rose and decided to lay it on his casket. At the grave site she spotted General Davis and Varina and went to stand with them. Thankfully the oratory was brief. Before the casket was lowered and the grave was filled, Catherine went up and laid the rose on the coffin. "Goodbye, Jeb," she said audibly, "I will miss your long evenings with General Hill and your many adventure-filled stories." When she started to move back, she almost stepped on Varina, Mary, and Mrs. Gordon who had come to the grave with her and were standing close behind her.

"How very nice of you, Catherine" Mrs. Gordon said, "I wish I had been so thoughtful."

As she approached Jefferson Davis, he grinned broadly and gave her a hug about the shoulders. "You don't know how much this means to me, Miss Catherine," he said enthusiastically. I will never forget this. I know you did it for me."

Catherine looked at him evenly and smiled pleasantly. "Yes, for you, General," she said with conviction, "But also for General Stuart—and maybe a little bit for me too." She excused herself and moved off leaving the president standing there with a pleased but confused look on his face. As she walked up the street toward Axley Manor, a sense of well being and comfort spread over her whole being. She knew that she had faced head on and overcome one of her greatest personal trials and she was pleased with herself. Doing the right thing was always so large when one looked forward at it and so small when she looked back on it. It was a lesson she was determined to not soon forget.

Chapter Twenty-Nine

Your Enemies…Your Household

As the train pulled out from Richmond Station, Sarah Morgan and Catherine Hill sat together and Mary Chesnut sat in the seat in front of them studying her speech. Sarah talked to Catherine in low tones.

"Kitty, what is she going to say?" she asked.

Catherine shook her head. "I don't know; she will not tell me," she said. "It's all very secret. She says we must wait to see."

Sarah looked concerned. "I hope she doesn't embarrass us," she said with a frown.

Catherine studied Sarah for a moment. She wished that Sarah had not come. Mary would almost certainly embarrass Sarah. Catherine understood, from talking to Mary, that Sarah knew what she was getting into by going with them to Washington for the exchange forum. Now Sarah appeared to think Mary would uphold the traditions of the majority opinion in the South. Catherine could see Sarah being very upset with both of them by the end of this trip. Still, maybe these kinds of heated exchanges would help in the long run.

"Was it your idea to go, Sarah," Catherine asked, "or did Mary talk you into it?"

"Oh, no," Sarah said, "she wasn't keen on it. But I wanted to go and see for myself what this effort at *mutual understanding* is all about." Sarah rolled her eyes. "It seems quite silly to me," she said.

"Here we are at war and our women are going back and forth talking to each other as if we were friends."

That raised a question in Catherine's mind. "Sarah," she asked, "you do know that we are meeting Ellen McClellan?"

"Yes, I know that," Sarah replied. "Where are we meeting her?"

"At the station," Catherine said. "You will like her."

"Yes, I have already met her and I find her tolerable," Sarah said. She looked at Catherine curiously. "But how do you know her?"

Catherine was thinking fast. Was there anything here she was not supposed to be talking about? "Oh, she knew General Hill quite well before the war," Catherine said.

"Yes, so I heard, but how did you meet her?" Sarah asked.

"She invited my husband and me down to her father's estate for a weekend," Catherine said.

Sarah got out her diary and warmed to the subject. "Really?" she said excitedly. "Tell me about this; it sounds interesting."

Catherine did not want to say anymore about Ellen for fear of reprisals against her father. She resorted to her oldest and most successful tactic—candor. "Listen, Sarah, I hope I do not offend you," she said firmly, "but I really do not want to talk about that occasion or anything about Ellen."

Sarah pouted. "Oh, rats," she said, "I would really like to hear that story."

Catherine moved on with haste. "But I do think Ellen is a very nice person, don't you? You said you met her."

"Oh, she's nice enough, I guess," Sarah said without enthusiasm, "but she has her head full of that typical Yankee trash. You know: free the slaves, it's immoral for one man to own another, and so on."

Catherine did not answer and they fell silent. Catherine was turned in the seat where she could study this beautiful, fiery, energetic, talented, very Southern, fiercely loyal woman. Where was she born? What had been her upbringing?

"Catherine, you are certainly staring at me," Sarah said after awhile, "what are you thinking?"

"Am I? I am sorry," Catherine replied. "I was just thinking how lovely you are and wondering how you have managed with all you've been through."

Sarah rolled her eyes again. “Look at who’s calling who lovely? You know you have the reputation of being the most beautiful woman in the South.”

“Oh, pooh, Sarah,” she said. “I don’t know any such thing and neither do you. There are many women in the South more fetching than I.”

Sarah looked coy. “Well, there might be some women who would agree with you,” she answered, “but I have yet to find the man.”

Catherine was scolding. “Sarah!”

“You know what Francis says?” Sarah asked with an amused twinkle, “He says you should pose in the…well…pose for a sculpture of Helen of Troy.”

Catherine was getting embarrassed. “Can we talk about something else?” she asked. Sarah did not say anything. Catherine waited a moment and then continued. “Sarah,” she asked, “you know what Mary Chesnut is trying to do, don’t you?”

Sarah sighed and looked out the window. “Oh, yes I do, Catherine,” she said reluctantly, “but the thing I cannot reconcile or accept is that she is doing it at a time when criticism of the South and its policies, especially its racial policies, seems almost treason.”

Catherine was on alert at the sound of the word ‘treason.’ “I guess I have really been misled,” she said, trying to keep Sarah from working herself up. “Listening to Mary, I thought you two got along.”

Sarah squinted her eyes and spoke in a strained voice. “Ah, well, I guess we do, but it is an uneasy truce. Truthfully, Catherine, I am suspicious of her.”

Catherine wished she had not started this conversation at this time and looked for the way to get out of it. She shrugged and said lightly, “Well, she probably feels the same about you.”

“Oh, she does. She has told me that I am little more than fodder for Henry Clay’s cannon.”

Sarah was driven to silence and to thinking. Catherine was glad. The discussion had reached a point where the next level was going to set off fireworks.

Upon arrival in Washington, Ellen and General McClellan met them. Sarah looked him over narrowly when introduced. “So you are the notorious General McClellan?" she asked with the cheekiness of a reporter. "You don't look so frightening to me."

McClellan laughed. "Well, Miss Sarah," he said, "I guess Lee didn't think so either. That's why Grant is fighting Lee and I am escorting beautiful ladies."

Sarah started to say something cutting but did not on a sharp nudge in the ribs from Catherine. "Please Sarah," she said quietly, "We are guests of Washington and of Ellen."

Ellen had made them arrangements at one of Washington's best hotels. Sarah remarked that it was the plushest hotel she had seen north of New Orleans.

When they entered the large auditorium, it was thirty minutes before commencement and the place was less than half full, but it was filling fairly rapidly.

After sitting and conversing for some while, Sarah became very agitated. "Would you look at that!" she hissed. Catherine looked up to the stage and was startled to see the figure of Harriet Tubman walk out on the stage and take a chair. Sarah turned her anger on Catherine. "You didn't tell me there was going to be Niggers involved in this exchange or whatever it is!"

Catherine was almost speechless. "I didn't know about it, Sarah."

Sarah was slightly mollified. "Well!" she said with great emphasis.

At that moment, Harriet looked down and saw Catherine. She got up from her chair and started down the aisle. When she got about three quarters of the way, she broke out in that grand, white smile for which she was noted. Catherine was thinking fast. What was she to do? If she acknowledged Harriet with friendship, there was no telling what it would do to Sarah. If she did not, it would be an embarrassment to Harriet. Catherine refused to think about it. She would do what she would do and bear the consequences later. She rose, stepped out in the aisle, and went to Harriet. Catherine slipped her arms around Harriet and gave her a warm and affectionate hug.

This time Harriet did not stiffen but responded. "I'm glad to see you here, Miss Cath'n," she said smiling.

Catherine's eyes filled with tears. "Oh Harriet, I am so glad to see you…so very glad," she said brokenly.

Sarah grabbed Catherine by the arm and spun her around. She was talking loudly and people had turned to listen. "You Nigger-loving little…You just wait! Oh, you just wait!" Sarah shouted and stomped out of the auditorium with her head in the air.

Catherine turned to Harriet. "Harriet, I…"

Harriet smiled again. "It don't matter, Ma'am," she said. "I know how that woman is. I'm used to such talk from her kind. It's you I care about, Miss Cath'n. If you had ignored me, that would have mattered."

"Harriet, I am so glad to know you are all right," she said. "When you left with General Forrest…well, he is so mean and he said such ugly things about you."

"I don' worry 'bout men like Gen'l Forrest either, Ma'am," Harriet answered. "I know where he is. He ain't got the same rule as I have, but at least he's got dog enough in 'eem to pertect his own bones."

"Well, Harriet, I…"

"Miss Cath'n," she said soberly, "I have to tell you somethin'. I did that delib'tly, knowin' that it was goin' to put Miss Mo'gan in a strut."

"You did?"

"Yes, Ma'am."

"But why?" Catherine asked her.

"'Cause you don't know where you stand about things," Harriet said. "You got slaves that you treat like your own chil'en. All the while they were slaves, you done set 'em free but you didn't tell them 'bout it. You ain't for abolition, but you risk your life and your husband's rep'tation to help me and Tuttle."

"Yes, well that may all be true," Catherine said. "But Harriet, I don't see…"

"Because, Miss Cath'n, people ain't what they thinks about and talks about; people is what they does. Now I know where you stand 'bout all this, and maybe it'll help you get a better understandin' of where you stand too."

On the way back to the hotel, Catherine thought about what Harriet had said. She knew that a part of it was the drive that was being put on by the free blacks to force those who supported them to come out and declare themselves. But she knew there was something more that made the proud Harriet Tubman run the awful risk of public rejection in the auditorium. There was something deeper than just the struggle and the politics. A bond had forged between Catherine and Harriet in the events of the past three years. Harriet had responded to the kindness Catherine had shown her. After all, it was Catherine who had hugged her and spoke words of admiration to her down by the river. Harriet had not asked for it. She knew about private expressions that disappeared in public and disappointed those who hoped. But it had happened at Catherine's initiative and Harriet had responded to it. The poor, lonely, tragic, noble, honorable, friendless Harriet had responded to an act of kindness that she had, at the time, judged as genuine. It meant enough to her to run the risk she had taken. Catherine felt guilt at having opened herself to Harriet. Could she live up to the promise of hope that she had given Harriet? And if so, how? She was very confused. As they walked along, Mary tuned in to her thoughts.

"It's not a perfect world, Catherine," she said. "If you try to get any closer to that girl, you will destroy you and her both. It is enough that she knows you are her friend and willing to acknowledge that in public."

"But Mary…"

"No, Catherine," she said firmly, "you must not think like that. In time, things may change; even now, they are changing. Any overt action on your part would direct the kind of attention and animosity toward Frederick Douglass and his program that they do not need right now. You got the wrong signal. The girl was not trying to get you to come and follow. She knows who you are and how impossible that is. She was trying, for her own peace of mind, to find out if the things you did were really acts of love and friendship or if they were just typical reactions of a strong-minded, brave, willful woman who is not going to let anyone push her around, or anyone she takes it upon herself to protect. You gave her what she needed, and a very brave and selfless act it was, if I may say so. Let it go at that for now. In the past, you helped her by being a friend in the spontaneousness of the moment, when your character showed through. Do not ruin what has been done by scheming up something that is not real and then going out and trying to make it happen."

Catherine was not sure what all Mary had said, but she did know it made her feel better. Yet, not all was at peace in her mind. "Mary, what is going to happen when that story runs in the Charleston paper?" she asked in a strained voice.

Mary looked grave. "I have thought of that," she said. "I do not know. General Davis will be furious at me and will not let me come here anymore. I don't expect General Hill will be any too happy with you."

Catherine sighed. "No, I don't think he will," she said.

"Or General Lee?"

"Um," Catherine said, "I don't know about that."

The train passed Manassas Junction and moved well on its way to Richmond before Sarah spoke. "I don't think you are going to like the headlines in Charleston's paper," she said tersely.

Catherine refused to be drawn into the fray. "Sarah," she said quietly, "if you think that you are doing the cause of the South a service by that, then do it. I can't stop you and I do not intend to try."

Sarah was almost spitting out her words. "That…that…that black woman, in case you don't know, it, is public enemy number one in the South."

"I do know it," Catherine said.

"Then Kitty, why in the world…"

"I can't explain it to you," Catherine said, "and I don't intend to try."

Mary Chesnut had been listening very intently. When Catherine lapsed into silence, she spoke up. "The reason is that one of Catherine's slaves ran off and got lost up north. Harriet Tubman found her and brought her back to Hopemont Estate."

Sarah thought for a minute. "She brought her back…just like that…how much did you have to pay her?"

"Kitty didn't pay her anything, but she helped her get back to the North when Captain Skinner tried to take her captive."

"Well, if she was caught," Sarah said, "and…"

"Sarah," Mary said curtly, "sometimes, due to the disorientation of war, people do things they would not ordinarily do. Don't I understand that you signed an oath of allegiance to the North to get food for your family?"

Sarah was taken off guard. She started to answer, then hesitated and then started again. "Well, but you cannot compare that," she said. "I did not hurt anyone."

Catherine held up her hand for silence. Then she began speaking very slowly, carefully and with feeling. "Sarah, you have written some very dramatic and beautiful things about the war and the people and the dislocation that has taken place and how things are all turned upside down. I remember one piece you wrote in August of last year, entitled, "Gone Was My Small Paradise." In it you described how everything had changed, been scattered, and was in disarray and how sorry you were. Then you stopped and said, 'Bah, what's the use of describing the scene. Many have suffered along with us.'

"Things have changed since the war, Sarah. As Mary says, we all have been thrown up against, and have had to react to, things that we Southern women were protected from before and never had to deal with. Now our men are gone and we are left to mind the farm, and we have to learn too fast about the real world. I have had to make decisions under fire with no teaching to guide me. I have done the best I could, and I know it has not always been right. And the end is not in sight; things are going to change some more.

"But one thing I hope will never change with me. I saw a brave, courageous, dedicated woman who has done things that no general in either army could do—things that make the exploits of Jeb Stuart seem as child's play by comparison. She hates white people more than we ever thought to hate blacks. But out of her own moral code and sense of decency, she risked her neck to bring back Tuttle whom she took away, thinking she was protecting her. When she saw she was wrong, she corrected the situation by crawling through river bottoms on her belly for a hundred miles—though territory crawling with snakes, scorpions, wild animals and patrols of Confederates. I appreciate her for it, and I have learned to feel respect for her. If that offends you, that's your problem. And if it offends the South, then that is their problem. I have all I can do coping with my own problems. I cannot and will not order my life to try to please narrow minded people who make their decisions based on tradition only and have no ability to feel fairness or human compassion. Changes are taking place—maybe good, maybe bad—but changes that we are powerless to stop. I will never be in the vanguard of these new social morés. But we must make some accommodations or be left behind in an old world that does not exist anymore and never will again. I have my southern traditions too, and I have no intention of abandoning them. But my traditions do not rule me and they do not fit every situation."

"You don't really want me to print that," Sarah said patronizingly.

"I told you before, print whatever you want," Catherine said brokenly. She was overcome with emotion and began to sob.

After awhile, she felt Sarah's hand on her shoulder. She looked through the distortion of eyes filled with tears but could still make out the softening in the lines of Sarah's face, and hear it in her voice. "I will write nothing of this business, Kitty. I don't agree with you, but I respect you for your convictions and your courage. I have heard so often that you have guts, but I could never see it behind that gorgeous facade. Now I do, and I am impressed. I am not going to ruin your life over this."

Catherine could not respond, but Mary Chesnut did. "Or yours," she said kindly but firmly.

Sarah looked at her long and hard. Then she leaned back, stared at the ceiling of the car and thought. Finally, she nodded her head. "Or mine," she said, "but…"

She left the sentence unfinished. They rode the rest of the way to Richmond in silence.

Chapter Thirty

Mississippi, My Happy Home

The day was well spent and Catherine was just coming down the steps of the Whitehouse when a cab pulled up in front and stopped. Varina got out, looking very much not herself.

"Hello, Varina," Catherine said cheerfully.

Varina looked in her direction, nodded and gave her a very forced smile. "Catherine," she said distractedly.

Catherine was gripped with concern. Varina was always so in control. "Are you all right," she asked, trying not to sound worried.

Varina stared are her blankly for a second, and then seemed to come to herself. "All right? Oh yes, dear Catherine, I…I have to go in now and see the president. Forgive me. He does not like for me to be late." With that she was gone,

Catherine stood for moment and watched her go up. Something was very wrong. She turned and headed off to Mary's house where she was spending the evening. She would have to ask Mary; maybe she would know. Or…perhaps it was best to say nothing.

Varina sat in the upholstered armed chair and waited for the President to acknowledge her. As she did, she studied her husband. He looked so pale, so tense, and so drawn. Jefferson Davis had always been a feisty, emotional man but he had at once possessed the ability to control himself when he wanted to and to exude confidence, even in the face of plain evidence of impending doom. Now he was losing that capacity. The pressures were getting to him and he seemed to no longer be concerned about appearances, which had at one time been his principal obsession. He was a harassed, haunted, hunted, harshly criticized man. Everyone knew it and any attempt to ignore, deny, or create an impression of indifference was a waste of strength of which he did not have much left. Varina had at one time wished that he could let some of the starch out of his britches so that he would be more real. Now she saw that was a mistake. Every man was what he was. Her husband was a politician, an orator, and an actor. When he faced grim reality with no emotional and theatrical defenses, he was a pitiful, little, frightened, uninspiring man. She saw now why he had been as he was and she felt guilt for having personally judged him pretentious. Varina thought back over her life and their lives together.

Varina Howell Davis had been born on May 7, 1826 to William B. Howell and Margaret Louisa Kempe of Virginia at Natchez, Mississippi. Her grandfather, Richard Howell, had served as governor of New Jersey for eight successive terms. After a series of governess', Varina was advanced to Madam Greenland's School for Girls in Philadelphia.

She met Jefferson Davis in 1844 and married him the following year, making her home at "Briarfield," a country plantation-estate outside of Natchez. In the same year of 1844 her husband was elected to Congress. Varina went through an assortment of roles thereafter. She was soldier's wife when he was in the war in Mexico, a senator's wife, and a wife of a cabinet member when Jefferson was Secretary of War under President Pierce. From 1856 to 1861 she was a senator's wife again. Now she had been wife of the first President of the Confederacy for more than four years.

Varina was thirty-five years old and the mother of three children when she became First Lady of the Confederacy. William Howard Russell, an English war correspondent, was attracted to Varina and made a point of noticing many things about her. He described her as "a comely, sprightly woman, verging on matronhood, of good figure and manners, well dressed, ladylike and clever." Varina was often seen with a red rose in her deep brunet hair and she looked most striking in her gorgeous white silk dresses, of which she had a number. She was tall but not too, had great carriage, and looked most impressive when her hair was simply done so as to not detract from its length and the richness of its body and sheen. She was said to be overflowing with the nectar of life.

Little things bothered her husband and Varina found it hard to understand. He had never quite forgiven her for not being in Montgomery, provisional capital of the Confederacy, for his inauguration. In a voice that could not conceal its hurt, he had said to her, "I thought it would have gratified you to have witnessed it, and have been a memory to our children."

Varina and Jefferson had three children. When she arrived in Montgomery, Maggie was six, Jeff Jr. was three, and the baby Joe was less than a year. The White House was a charming two-story affair. She had brought enhancements from home to make it warm. Over the mantel of Jefferson's den she hung a sampler which read, "Thy Will be Done." The White House was the site of much partying and camaraderie. There were grand balls, luncheons, and dinners. Like her counterpart in the Union, Varina had been trained at Madam Greenland's to hostess and her experiences in the ensuing years had sharpened that ability. Unlike Mary Lincoln, Varina was very popular with the women and much in demand. But Varina was not a shallow or frivolous person. She insisted on going with Jefferson on dangerous trips to survey the defenses along the ocean and the northern river sector. She understood the importance of keeping wives and girlfriends of soldiers informed and that was her most effective role.

When Varina arrived in Richmond to become mistress of the gorgeous, elegant, spacious house purchased for them from Dr. John Brockenbrough, a former president of the bank of Virginia, her popularity had reached its zenith. The newspapers became almost grandiloquent.

"Mrs. Davis is a tall, commanding figure with dark hair, eyes, and complexion, and strongly marked characteristics which lie chiefly in the mouth. With firmly-set yet flexible lips there is indicated much energy of purpose and will, but beautifully softened by the unusual expression of her dark, earnest eyes. Her manners are kind, graceful, easy, and affable, and her receptions are characterized by the dignity and suavity which should very properly distinguish the drawing-room entertainment of the Chief Magistrate of a republic."

Another Englishman, this time a minister and not a reporter, was somewhat less windy and more to the point. "Mrs. Davis is the right lady in the right place." This was very well stated.

But Varina was not without her foibles. Like Mary Todd Lincoln, she had a quick wit and a sharp tongue. As the conflict wore on, the mistakes of her husband became more evident and frustrating, and things began to lose their Southern charm, Varina used these weapons on an increasing number of men and women alike. Like Mary Lincoln, Varina was interested in and learned about politics. She could argue with men and hold her own. Unlike Mary, she did very well at it during the war, and was often sought out by men who found her a fascinating forensic adversary. Even so, she was accused of meddling and of being extravagant in purchasing goods from blockade runners at inflated prices. The aristocrats in the East criticized her because she was a "Westerner" but much of that criticism ceased when they saw her talent for throwing extravagant and grand socials in a Southern style that none of them could best. Still, her popularity was definitely on the decline. She had not sunk to the level of her husband in popularity, but she was not the darling of the Confederacy that she had once been.

Finally her husband looked up from his papers. "Varina," he said with gravity, sternness, and apology, "You simply must stop hoarding flour, salt, coffee, and other staples. People know about it and it bodes very ill for our image. Just today I have entertained complaints from a number of our generals, most of them passed on from wives, of course."

Varina sighed. "But Jeffy, what are we to do? We must have food to entertain, and food in reserve if things get bad!"

Davis laid down his glasses and became very frank. "It is seen as hoarding, Varina," he said, "and we simply cannot have that, with the suffering going on around us." Varina was stung by his criticism. She had recognized in herself the vice of thinking that, because of their position, they were entitled to things that others were not and was angered to find that others resented these things to them now. In better days, nothing was too good for them and every one wanted their first couple to have more and better than the common folk. Now greed was striping them of their honor and privilege.

But what concerned her more was the inconsistency and hypocrisy of her husband. While chiding her for hoarding food, he was hoarding a fortune of the Confederacy's gold—money that had long been needed to buy army munitions, horses, and other military things. But Davis did not see it. He argued with her that they could not spend the gold because of the embargo, even though he knew full well that they could always buy from northern contrabands if they had gold. His position was no different from her own and it involved millions instead of a few lousy dollars worth of coffee and salt and flour.

"Very well Jefferson," she said formally, "I will turn in my hoard of staples and you turn in your hoard of gold."

Davis threw his pen down on the desk and angrily raised his voice. "Are we going to start this again?"

Varina rose to the occasion, the steel edge coming into her tone. "No, *we* are not going to start it," she said. "*Thee* hath *already* started it!"

Davis was pulled up short. Usually his anger brought meekness and contrition from her. He saw now that she was ready for a fight. "Varina, please do not question my judgment," he said in a voice soften by pleading. "I must provide for you and for us if anything happens to the Confederacy. I cannot go out and work or live like a common person. I must be able to go into exile and live in aristocratic comfort. I have earned this. I have given my all for this cause and have neither been properly assisted nor appreciated. I have a right, as President and chief financial officer for the Confederate States, to make this disposition of some of its wealth."

Varina became calculating. Deep within herself, she understood only too well what he was saying. She wanted to chide him but not to the point of deterring him from his course. "So, then, we are entitled to live luxuriously in exile but not to eat decently now, is that your message?"

Davis could tell from her tone that she was giving in. "Varina, my dear sweet wife," he said, "please do as I say. It will all be over soon and we will go far away and do our best to forget. I am thinking of England or France, perhaps."

"Are you then telling me that the cause of the South is lost?" she asked. "I have never heard you admit that before."

Davis changed sharply. "I am saying nothing of the kind," he replied with the hardness back in his voice. "I am still very hopeful of victory. In my last conference with General Lee, he assures me he is still anticipating striking Grant a fierce blow. If he can defeat Grant, we can prevail, all other things not withstanding."

Varina got up to leave. "From all the talk I hear," she said chidingly, "the chances of Lee beating Grant are none too good—in fact, if what one hears is to be believed, they are virtually non-existent."

Davis put on his official face again. "Don't discourage me, Varina, please," he said. "You know how much I need your spiritual support."

Varina left the President's office with a clear picture of where he and they were. Still she knew that there were a number of people who were aware of the hoarded gold and at least one had threatened dire consequences if he did not release it soon for the war effort. Her husband had defended his decision by saying that he had to keep it in reserve to prevent the Confederate notes from completely losing their value. There was enough logic and truth to what he was saying to stall them for now, but with the worsening conditions, she did not know how much longer. Varina had a sense of foreboding about her husband and what he was doing. It was a dangerous game for high stakes with enemies who were on the edge of violence and rebellion.

Varina left the White House and sought the refuge of her friend and confidant, Mary Boykin Chesnut.

Mary was in by the fire writing in her diary and Catherine was in the sitting room knitting when Varina came in. She did to look any improved from when Catherine had seen her earlier.

"Catherine, Dear," Varina asked hurriedly, "where is Mary?"

"Why, she's in by the fire with her diary."

Varina started to move off in that direction. “Oh, forgive me, Catherine, but I feel I must speak with Mary. It…it’s…well.” He voiced trialed off.

“Of course, I understand,” Catherine said quietly, “May I come in, or…”

Varina looked as if she was thinking that over. Finally she said, “Oh, of course, Catherine, please do.”

Catherine felt awkward. “Well, if…”

“No, no,” Varina said quickly. “No, you are part of this…this…do come along.”

Catherine got up and followed wondering if she was doing the right thing intruding. Something was bothering Varina and who knew that it might be. But Catherine really wanted to know if it involved the fortunes of the War, so she did not think about it too long. The thought that Varina might want to talk to Mary alone did not offend her at all. Catherine knew that Mary was one of Varina’s staunchest defenders and greatest admirers. She felt that Varina, more than any other single person, had kept the morale of the Confederacy high. She had also, in Mary’s’ eyes, kept the wives feeling involved and a part of the effort by her skillful handling of the matter of information and helping the women to understand the patience and courage that was required of them.

Varina went to the settee. Mary laid aside her diary but did not move from her chair. Catherine took a chair behind them where she could hopefully listen without being a distraction.

“What in the world is the matter with you?” Mary asked Varina. Varina sat down and did not answer. Catherine thought she looked like she was struggling with the whether or not to tell Mary about her meeting with her husband? Surely that was at the heart of the struggle Varina was having. Catherine was surprised and a little disappointed that she did not. What they did begin to talk about took Catherine off guard.

“Mary,” Varina asked, “What will happen to me if my husband is killed?”

“Varina!” Mary scolded.

"Well," Varina replied calmly, "we have to think about these things, you know, and what about you? What would you do if your husband was killed?"

"Oh, I would be alright," Mary said. "I have properties that are salvageable. Sherman raised the devil with our plantation in Camden, but most of the servants are still there and they say it can be resurrected. I don't think this house will be destroyed. When Lee leaves the trenches and heads for the Carolinas to join Johnston, the Union will not bother with Richmond. That is not General Grant's style. He will go right on past us in his pursuit of Lee. I don't think Richmond will ever be shelled. And then, I have some money—a good bit in fact—in Canadian banks."

"Do you?" Varina said approvingly. "How every clever of you." Catherine thought it was clever too and made a mental note to pursue that with Mr. Todd when she was back in Lexington.

"You're truly worried about this, aren't you?" Mary asked Varina. "Do you know something I don't?"

"Yes…well, no…well, you know, threats have been made on Jefferson's life and some of his enemies are getting very angry. Assassination is far from out of the question. We have Briarfield in Natchez, if there is anything left of the house, but I don't know how I could go down there without Jefferson and re-establish myself." Catherine was a bit surprised. This sounded more helpless than she though of Varina as being. You could not think like that; you just had to do these things if it came to it!

Mary brought her back from her thoughts. "Well, listen Varina," she said gently. "If anything happens to your husband, you and your children are to come here immediately. I can help you get situated and see that you have the things you need. Or, if that is not possible, I have the means to take care of you in a style that will befit your station. You know how I feel about you. I want you to promise to do that, and to know that you can do it. It is not good for a woman in your position to feel that she has no security."

Catherine thought that this assurance visibly relieved Varina. "Thank you so much, Mary." She said. "You don't know how much that means to me."

Mary tried to put Varina's mind further at ease. "I think it is all worry for nothing. I don't think anything…"

"I don't," Varina said tersely. Catherine saw Varina give Mary a very serious stare and there was soberness in her face and tone. "I have the feeling that I am going to be a widow before long—I really feel that."

Mary's countenance changed quickly. "A woman's intuition, you mean?" Mary asked.

"No—not exactly that strong;" Varina replied, "just a definite feeling. If the Yankees don't get Jefferson, I fear that his own people might. He has so many hateful enemies, Mary."

Mary put away her diary and went over to sit on the settee with Varina. Before sitting down, she looked back at Catherine. "My dear," she said, you must sit with us. You look so left out back there by yourself." Catherine came up and sat down with them. Mary took Varina's hand and they all sat for a long time and stared into the dying flames.

Chapter Thirty-One

To Thine Own Self Be True

Catherine sat in the drawing room at Axley Manor and waited for Mary and General Lee. She picked up a periodical and began reading a piece by Francis Warrington Dawson, editor of the Charleston News and Courier and "Fiancée" of Sarah Morgan. Some of it amused Catherine and she smiled often. But on the whole, it was a serious piece. She read:

By early 1865, desperation is setting in all over the South. Unthinkable things are being suggested that would get someone shot or hung in peacetime. One is that women cut off their hair and sell it in Europe. Estimates of the rewards of such a measure, no doubt founded, run as high as $40,000,000. Women and girls are generally for it as a way of contributing to the war effort, but men view this suggestion as unbiblical, unholy, and demeaning to their women. Other more practical men argue that even if it were done, there is no way of getting cargo out through the blockade and no way of getting the money back if it did get through, so it will never be done.

Of note is the fact that General Robert E. Lee has been encouraging the revival of an idea first put forth by Pat Cleburne last year after the debacle of Missionary Ridge. In that proposal, slaves would be freed and used as soldiers. It is being turned down out of hand at this time as "revolting to southern sentiment, southern pride, and southern honor," and as "monstrous." But now that Sherman has made his march through Georgia and Grant is at the gates of Richmond, it seems far less objectionable to many to at least discuss and think about.

Catherine laid down the article and shook her head slowly in bemusement as Mary Chesnut came churning in with the Commander of the Armies, Robert E. Lee. She sat him at the table and hurried over to Catherine. "Now you just sit with us and don't say a thing. I will take care of the talking—this is actually a scheduled interview. I want you to listen carefully and then we will discuss it when he is gone." Mary towed Catherine to the table. "You know Miss Kitty, of course?"

The General rose, nodded politely, faintly registering surprise, she thought, that Catherine was there: "Oh, yes, quite well," he said.

Catherine volunteered a reply. "How do you do, General Lee?"

"Quite well, Miss Kitty," he said, "and you?"

"Oh, General," she replied, "I am never better or better served, than when at the home of Mary Chesnut."

Mary smiled and looked down at Catherine's designated chair. Catherine took the hint and sat without being asked. Mary followed suit and then Lee. "It was good of you to make a few minutes for me, General," Mary said. Catherine watched Lee shift uncomfortably. She felt she could read his thoughts. Lee was wondering what he was there for. Mary Chesnut, a designing woman, did not ask even the Commander to teas without a motive.

Finally, he answered slowly and carefully. "I am happy to be able to drop in, Mary, but you realize that I haven't much time. I am just here for a short visit with the President. I must get back at once to Headquarters."

Catherine saw Mary glance quickly at her to see if she had picked up his betrayal of her claim that this was a scheduled interview. She had, but tried not to show it. Catherine hoped that Mary would take the hint and get on with it. General Lee could not be finessed like Beauregard or Bragg. Mary did pick it up and got to the point very bluntly.

"General Lee," she said, "you want the slaves freed, I want them freed and so do others, so…"

Lee cut her off. "Ah, yes, Mary," he said diplomatically, "but for two very different reasons."

"But what difference does that make?" Mary asked.

Lee was amused and flicked a glance to Catherine. "I cannot for the life of me see why you would not think it makes a difference," he said.

Mary did not hesitate a moment. "General, you would not free the slaves to fight," she asked, "and then enslave them again after the war?"

Catherine's interest was mounting fast as Lee pondered the question. "I would not, but others would," he said. "I never believed in slavery, but you must not write that."

"But, General, surely…"

Lee continued quickly. "The brain-trust of the South is viewing it as a way to replenish the forces and questioning what good it would do not to free them if we lost," he said. "I can tell you that they are not thinking of it as freeing the slaves—in terms of giving them social freedom forever."

"But General…"

Catherine knew the General and could tell that he was thinking as he talked. He cut her off as he nodded his head. "Well, Mary, of course I can see your point," he said. "Obviously, if we freed them to fight, then if we won the war, we could not enslave them again, could we?" Catherine wanted very much to inject her thoughts at this point but Mary had instructed her to stay out of it.

Mary reacted expansively as if having won a major concession. "Exactly, General Lee," she said, "so, it seems to me that you and I, no matter what Davis and others think, have a common goal."

Lee thought a moment. Catherine was sure he was looking carefully for the trap before he answered. "I believe that may be true, yes," he said. "But it is probably not going to matter. Those who believe we can still win the war are not going to let it pass the legislature."

Catherine saw the light in Mary's eyes. "Can we still win the war, General?" she asked.

Lee hesitated. "This does not go in your diary, does it?"

Mary made a pout. "Let me get to what I am thinking and then you have the option of telling me what not to write down," she said.

"Very well, that seems fair," Lee said. He paused to look quizzically at Catherine and then continued. "No," he said emphatically. "Without a major infusion of manpower into the ranks, we cannot win this war. We may not win in any case, but we cannot win without it." Catherine was surprised at his answer.

Mary clasped her hands in front of her bosom and was almost gleeful. "All right, General Lee," she said, "I think I can help you get this amendment, or whatever it is, past the legislature."

Lee looked doubtful. "And how can you do that, Mary?"

"General, I know this will come as a shock to you," she said, "but wives have a great deal to say about how their husbands vote."

Lee shook his head and laughed. "Oh, no, Mary," he said, "that is no surprise to me at all."

"Very well, then here is what may be," she said pompously. "I have been working very hard on the wives to get them to see the inhumanity of slavery as generally practiced. But they always come back with arguments that it will ruin the economy, that their husbands know more about it than they do, that it is not required by the Bible, and that there are no reasons other than the moral ones to make an issue of slavery at a time like this. But a good, strong, clearly worded statement from you on the subject, that you could and would stand behind, would push a lot of these people and their husbands off the fence." Catherine sucked in her breath. This was getting tense and she had lost the ability to predict Lee's answers.

Lee did not hesitate. "But, Mary, I have never made an issue of slavery," he said firmly, "although I am personally against it on philosophical grounds, and I am not prepared to now."

Mary smiled primly. "I know that General," she said, "and I may say it is one of the great disappointments of my life—I do idolize you so and wanted you to say what you once said at West Point before the war. But what I want you to say now is that you are fully and unequivocally in favor of freeing the slaves so that they can be enlisted in the war effort. I want you to say that our chances of prevailing would be greatly enhanced by such an action and that, without it, our chances are apparently non-existent. We can leave the rest out." Catherine began an involuntary shaking of her head negatively but stopped when she received an icy stare from Mary.

"What will you do?" Lee asked thoughtfully. Catherine could not believe it. Was Lee really thinking about doing this?

"I will take your statement with me," she said, "and reveal it, over a cup of tea, as a matter of sharing inner thoughts with a friend. I will make sure that every wife in Virginia and the Carolinas knows it within a week. Then I will get hold of Sarah Morgan and see that it spreads throughout the South as soon as possible." Catherine was stunned! Sarah Morgan? Mary must be out of her mind?

General Lee put her thoughts into words. "Sarah Morgan? he asked with astonishment. "Is my intelligence that poor? Sarah Morgan is a true Southern patriot who defends the beliefs of the South, including the right to own slaves, to the nth degree—or at least so I have believed."

Mary laughed. "Indeed she does, General," she said, "and when she finds this out, it will go through Georgia, Alabama, Mississippi and Louisiana like a dose of salts."

Lee, to Catherine's amazement, seemed ready to do this or so it sounded in his reply to Mary. "It might not be good if it appeared that you are telling something you promised to keep quiet," he said.

"No, I will not say that, but if some people get that impression, I will not be unhappy," Mary replied.

Lee frowned in confusion. "Why would that help our…your…our cause?" he asked.

"Because some people, upon hearing it, will guarantee that this is my invention and that you never said such a thing," Mary said. "Then when you verify it, the impact will be greater and more likely to succeed."

Lee shook his head in wonderment and mock reproach. "Mary Chesnut," he said, "you are a diabolical woman. Give me pen and paper please." She motioned him to her secretary where he sat down. As he thought for a moment, Catherine fought desperately with her insides, trying to keep from saying or expressing anything. Finally, he said, writing as he spoke, "You may write that General Lee says:

'I am for an amendment calling for the freeing of the slaves and for Negro recruitment. We must decide whether slavery shall be extinguished by our enemies and the slaves used against us, or use them ourselves at the risk of the effects, which may be produced upon our social institutions. My own opinion is that we should employ them without delay. I believe that with proper regulation they can be made efficient soldiers'."

He blotted it and handed it to her. "Is that good enough for what you want, because it's about all I can..." Mary gave Lee a hug and did a little dance.

"It is perfect, General," she said gleefully, "just perfect!"

"Very good," he said. "That being the case, I simply must be off."

When Lee left, Catherine turned on Mary. "I have always shared some of your feelings about slavery, but this...this is anti-confederacy. I am surprised at General Lee," she said sharply.

Mary seemed crestfallen at Catherine's response. "But Catherine," she pleaded, "don't you see? It is either this or lose the war."

"Yes, perhaps I see that, but Mary," she said, "that is not why you want the slaves freed. You are using this misfortune to support your crusade."

Mary was quick to respond. "If the slaves should be freed to fight, then they should be freed as a matter of moral and political integrity," she replied. "If you say 'free them to fight, but don't free them for any other reason', then you are the one who is the opportunist, not me."

Catherine mused for a moment. "Yes, I suppose I can see that, but...I don't know. I can't say anything about this now; I have to think about it," she said.

Mary sighed. "Oh, Kitty, I was so hoping you would try to bring over your husband."

Catherine was startled at the thought. "But, Mary, I...Oh, I don't know," she said.

"Just talk to him about it, Kitty."

"How?" Catherine asked with a weary sigh. "About what? Something I don't know if I believe in?"

"You are not an abolitionist?" Mary asked.

Catherine was bemused. "No!" she said. "At least I certainly don't think so," she said.

"Well, then you had better be careful, Kitty," Mary replied, "because the word is out in all the border states among abolitionist Southerners that you are one."

Catherine was stunned. "Mary!" she said, "How would anyone get that idea?"

Mary looked at her questioningly. "You really don't know?" she asked. Catherine did not answer. "Well," Mary continued, "I am not clear on the rumor, but it has something to do with you helping Moses escape General Davis' personal slave catcher."

Catherine was alarmed. "Oh, no!" she said anxiously. "But that was a matter of…well, if I am an abolitionist, so is General Forrest."

As soon as she said it, Catherine knew she had erred. "Oh?" Mary said, "Tell me more!"

"Don't try to confuse me, Mary," Catherine exclaimed. "Listen, I really have to get back to Petersburg. I have duties about which I have to meet with General Lee this afternoon."

"General Lee?" Mary said. "Excellent! Talk to him about it."

Catherine hesitated. "Oh, I couldn't do that," she said. "How would I bring it up?"

"Of course you can." Mary replied. "It's all ready up. He knows you were here and heard the whole thing."

Catherine was thoughtful. "Well, if it comes handy, I might do that," she said, and left in a preoccupied daze.

Chapter Thirty-Two

Something Old—Something New

Catherine stood in front of the mirror in a light green dress with a gray vest and laces. She examined herself for order: collar out and in place, buttons all buttoned, frills on the sleeves not tucked under, no smudges on her face. Then she turned as far around as she could in both directions to get the best possible rear view. Her petticoats were not showing and everything seemed to be in order. Since childhood, men did not intimidate Catherine, but something about going into General Lee's office with just the two of them made it all different. The soul of propriety, she never caught him staring at her like Jeb Stuart did. But she always felt a little conspicuous—as if something might be showing. Satisfied with the results of her checklist, she went in. They reviewed records of hospital turnover and some supplies that she had brought back for the commissary. She asked for a nurse's uniform for herself and he reluctantly said she could get one once he saw she would not be deterred. Finally, during a lull in the conversation, he looked at her in that way that always made her feel like she was blushing. He looked right into her face with those big, searching, expressive gray eyes. It was not a leer but it made her feel undressed. Sometimes, when he gave her that look, she clutched her hands to her bosom as if covering herself up. She felt so foolish when she realized what she was doing, but if he ever noticed, he never let on.

Finally, he spoke and she trembled a little at the sound of his voice. "Well, Miss Kitty, it is evident that you have something on your mind, so why don't we talk about it."

Catherine reacted coyly. "Oh, no, not really, General," she said weakly. He did not move nor change his expression. "Well, since you asked," she said, "there is something I would like to feel you out on. The discussion today at Mary Chesnut's about freeing the slaves for enlistment purposes…you did mean that, obviously?"

"Yes, I did," he said. "I almost did not go through with it when I saw you were there. I am sorry if you find that offensive, but I have a war to win, and I am not going to win it without more men."

"But if we use Negras in the war, why do we have to free them?" she asked.

"Miss Kitty, you cannot ask men to fight for the cause of freedom who are not themselves free," he said. "That is overt immorality and hypocrisy."

"But there are many good Christian Southerners who do not believe we should do this," Catherine replied.

Lee nodded indulgently. "That is true," he said, "but those who argue that way themselves agree that if slaves will make good soldiers, then we have been completely wrong, anthropologically speaking, about black people. If slaves can fight for freedom, then they are human beings who deserve freedom. Most of those who are opposed are scared to death that the slaves will make good soldiers and they will be proved wrong."

"And you believe they will?" she asked.

Lee did not answer her question directly. "Miss Kitty," he said, "I would rather make changes in our social structure than to throw away the Confederacy and our freedom for pride and ideology." Catherine was silent because she had nothing to say. At length, Lee continued. "Mrs. Hill, let me ask you a question. Do you think the slaves are human beings?"

Catherine turned the question over in her mind. "I don't know that I can say, Sir."

Lee's eyes seemed to sharpen and bore in on her. "Miss Kitty, that woman that you helped escape last year—why did you do it?" he asked.

Catherine was taken off balance. "How did you…?"

"Colonel Wolf made a detailed report," he replied, as he watched her closely. "Don't look so betrayed," he said. "He had to do it in answer to accusations made by Captain Skinner. But the question, Kitty—why did you do it?"

"Because she was bringing back a…a…slave," she said. "It would have been immoral to take her; it was like shooting at a person carrying a flag of truce."

Lee nodded. "Yes," he said, "I heard about Forest's argument, and I thought it a good one, and I truly believe that is why Forrest did what he did, though Davis does not. But I also believe that neither you nor Wolf had even considered that until Forrest brought it up, or is that correct?"

"Well, yes, I guess it is," she answered.

"All right, so why did you do it?" Catherine felt trapped. "Miss Kitty," he said, softening his tone a little, "I am not trying to accuse you or condemn you, but you wanted to discuss this subject and I am trying to get you to think without your traditional blinders on. I really want to know why you did it and I want you to think about it."

Catherine counseled with herself. Why was she being evasive? She had brought the subject up and he was trying to have a frank discussion with her about it. She took a deep breath and settled into her normal manner. "I guess I did it out of gratitude because she brought back Tuttle," she answered.

"All right, and I will move on," he said, "but I just want to ask you one more question about that Moses woman. Did you have any feelings for her? Did you admire her at all? Was there any nobility in her that you responded to?"

"Well, yes, General Lee," she said, "I guess there was, but I wouldn't want…"

"Miss Kitty, this is a conversation between you and me and it will not get out of this room on my account," he said with great sincerity. "Now the girl Tuttle, is she a human being?"

"Oh, General Lee, Tuttle is my…my servant. She has been with us for eight years," she said. "Tuttle is family. I love…I am very fond of her."

"I didn't ask you all of those things, Catherine," he said firmly, "I asked you if she was a human being?"

"Tuttle? Why, of course—Tuttle—yes, I would say that she and Emmanuel…"

"And Moses?" he asked.

"Yes, I guess…well, yes, I know she is," Catherine answered.

"And what, then, about all the other Negras in the South?" he asked. "Are they human beings too?"

Catherine was feeling brow beaten. "General Lee," she asked, "what is the point…"

"The point is," he said, "that if Moses deserves to be free because she has fought for freedom and you admire her, and if Tuttle deserves to be free because you know her and you love her; then how can we ask other Negroes to fight for freedom and not let them partake in the freedom for which they fight? And how can we deny them and ourselves the right to fight for freedom, when we know they are human beings?" He paused for her answer and she did not have one. Besides, she wanted to hear what he would say. "We have always argued in the past that things were going along good as they were, and we would deal with these issues some other time," he said. "Well, now things are not good—not good at all—and there is all the reason in the world to face this issue. If the black man helps us win our freedom, then he has every right to partake of that freedom. I will not fight for the freedom of one Southerner and not for another who has spilled his blood for the same cause as I."

Catherine was confused. She did not know what to say. "Well, General," she said, feeling guilty as she said it, "I didn't know that you were an abolitionist."

"I am not," he replied quickly. "I am a general who is trying to win a war and am unwilling to stand on what is soon to be an outdated social tradition and let three hundred thousand able and willing men who can help me win it, sit idle while we lose the war."

"But you wind up in the same place," Catherine protested, "even though you come down roads from different directions."

Lee grew reflective. "That is right, Miss Kitty," he said with conviction, "and that, which you consider to be a contradiction, I find to be a profound truth."

Catherine did not cave in. "But General, I am just not sure about the issue of slavery in general," she said. "I don't know how all of this bears on it."

Catherine thought that Lee was looking at her like a general views the enemy when he knows he can move in and crush him. "Miss Kitty," he said with almost an amused gleam in his eye, "you gave Tuttle and…what is his name…Manual, their freedom so that, if something happened to you, or if men like Skinner tried to get control of them, they would not suffer like most slaves do. Why did you do that, if you believe in slavery?"

Catherine knew she was cornered and she tried to bluff her way out. "But General, I don't see the point…"

"The point is, dear Miss Kitty," he said indulgently, "that we in the South have cared for these people, and done things like this for many years, but we never had to face the decisive question. As long as we took care of them, protected them, gave them some liberties and they were happy, we did not feel a crisis. Now we can no longer do that. We have to make a choice. There is a desperately good reason to free the slaves and enlist them in a common cause. But we have to face this issue. Are they fellow human beings? Do they deserve to be free? Necessity is the mother of invention, Kitty. I need these people and I have faced the issue. I say, give them their freedom, let them pay the price of freedom with their blood, and then let them share in it. Then once you make that decision, it is a small step to see that if they are human beings now, they were human beings all along, and the life that we have enjoyed in the South has been paid for more in their blood than in anyone else's. There is more than one way to suffer and to die for a cause. It does not have to be on a battlefield with someone over there in the woods trying to shoot you. It can be out in the cotton fields with the blood running from different kinds of wounds."

Catherine had never been talked to in this way by any person, though she knew it may well have been the way her father felt, and she was beginning to feel faint. "General Lee, I…I think I want to stop this conversation now and get to my work."

Lee grew soft and concerned. "I trust that I…"

"Oh, no, sir,' she said, "I asked for this, but it is enough for me to think about now. Perhaps in the future, we…"

"I think not," he said with finality. "I have taken liberties in the extent to which I have gone already, and I really don't have much more on it."

The children were in bed and Ambrose and Catherine had settled down in front of the fire. It was the most fulfilling time of her life when she could snuggle against the man she loved and feel the security of his nearness. Ambrose looked down on her face.

"You seem to be preoccupied with something, my dear. Tell me about it." Catherine sat up and turned on the lounge so she could look at him.

"Ambrose, what do you make of this talk of freeing the slaves and enlisting them?" Hill shook his head in disbelief.

"I think it is a perfectly silly idea. Here we are almost exhausted from four years of war, and we are talking of turning about and giving up on the reason for which we are fighting."

"But there is such a need for men."

"Yes, but who says the Negra can fight. I don't think you could make a fighter of him in a hundred years."

"Well, General Lee says…" Her husband's eyes snapped.

"You have been talking to General Lee about this?"

"Well, I…"

"And you did not ask me or talk to me about it first. Don't you think, as your husband, before…"

"Ambrose, don't be silly, I only learned about it today."

"When and where did you talk to Lee about this?'

"This afternoon, in his office."

"In his office? Just the two of you?"

"Well, I didn't go there for that, we were going over records…"

"I have wondered…"

Catherine cut him off sharply. "Ambrose, no! Don't say things to hurt me, please, I was only…".

"Well, you have said things that hurt me."

"If so, I did not mean to. It was unintentional, I was just trying find out if Mary Chesnut…"

"Ah yes—Mary Chesnut! How many times have I warned you to beware of that woman? Maybe the other generals are right; maybe you should not be up here, this close to the front. We shall have to talk about..."

"Ambrose, please I was only...".

"I don't wish to discuss it anymore," he said tersely. "I am going to bed. I must be up early." With that, he left and went into the bedroom. Catherine sat staring at the fire. She was terribly shaken. She and her husband simply did not fight. He had gotten hurt by her at times for not taking his side against Jackson as enthusiastically and vocally as he had wanted her to. But this was something new to her. He was genuinely angry and she could see that he had been thinking more about her being there and her interaction with Lee and the women in Richmond than she had realized. It had shaken her sense of well being with her husband.

Catherine hovered by the lonely fire and reflected on their five years of married life. He was one of the best generals in the army. He consistently commanded larger forces than any other Southern general because he was a better and more careful planner and could handle men. He would have been much more honored by the Confederacy had it not been for his feud with Stonewall Jackson.

Jackson intended to crush her husband until he simply faded away into anonymity but he had picked on the wrong man. Ambrose would not take it passively. He would neither be crushed nor go away. His sensitivity and acute devotion to justice led her husband to demand Jackson to charge him or that Davis transfer him. It had nothing to do with stability but Davis interpreted it that way. In the Army of the Confederacy, such a reputation never went away. His emotional stability continued to be unfairly questioned. Ambrose had made demands on Jackson, Lee, and President Davis that continued to tarnish his image two years after Jackson's death.

Tears welled up in Catherine's eyes as she thought of the injustice of it all and the trouble it had caused their marriage. Then her tears of regret turned to tears of frustration. Whether by deeply held conviction by Lee that Jackson had been right in their personal struggle or some other reason, Lee assailed her husband at North Anna some while earlier. Like most of the soldiers of the Northern

Virginia Army, her husband held Lee in a reverence that came close to worship. There had been much criticism of Catherine's presence with her husband so near to the fighting so often, but he had ignored it. He wanted her there, so General Lee, who privately if not publicly also wanted her there, could make use of her services. This had honored her husband. For Lee to want his wife in camp and to make use of her gave her husband a great sense of camaraderie with Lee.

But then the scene between her husband and Lee had occurred at North Anna. Lee was wrong and if he had just had the grace to say so, it would all have been forgiven and forgotten, but it was not Lee's way. Because of that, her husband's devotion to and appreciation for Lee had eroded with time.

Now it had reached the breaking point. Her husband no longer trusted Lee with her. He did not think her in danger of any moral turpitude from Lee. Her husband did not believe Lee capable of that. But he did now believe that Lee might subtly plant doubts in her mind about her husband's military judgment and behavior on the battlefield. He saw Lee's influencing her in a matter of importance that he knew her husband felt differently about, as an indication of it. Catherine knew Lee would never do that intentionally, but she suddenly understood that her husband did not. He had only the memory of Lee's biting words to dwell on. Her husband's one weakness was the inability to forget personal injury from fellow officers in the cause for which he had given his all. His confidence in his own excellent judgment freed him from self-doubt. If accused when not wrong, it hurt him deeply and he simply could not and would not let it go.

He did not possess the resplendence of Lee or Marauder or Stuart, but she cherished his long smooth face, his high cheekbones, his dark red shoulder-length hair, full beard, and his deep blue eyes. Her education in the ways of married life, in spite of her mother's disapproval, had paid rich dividends, and she found great emotional fulfillment in her marriage. She wanted to be with him all the time and she had absolutely no interest in any other man. She would never share the loyalty and closeness they had with another. They were one and nothing could have meant more to her. She believed he knew she felt that way, but he had said things tonight that had shaken her.

Catherine thought she knew why. He felt she was sharing and accepting the view of Lee and siding against him. Catherine believed she would have felt the same if the situation were reversed and her conscience smote her. She should not have brought up her conversation with Lee to question him. She had asked for his views and she should have been content with that. But that introduced another problem. She did not want to have conversations with Lee that she had to keep secret from her husband. She had not thought well of Lee for his treatment of her husband, but that had long since passed with her. Lee was a fine man whom she enjoyed being around. She had never harbored doubts about him as her husband did, but then Lee had never hurt her as he had her husband. As she sat there turning it all over in her mind, it came clear to her that her special friendship with General Lee had come to an end. She was sorry for that, but her duty to her husband came before friendship—even the special friendship of the great general. She hoped she could work that out and still stay in Petersburg and be with her husband.

Catherine knew she could not sleep if they did not get this breach repaired. She went into the bedroom. "Ambrose, are you awake?" she asked.

"I must get some sleep, Catherine," he said tersely. "Tomorrow is a hard day that starts early with a most difficult meeting with Lee and the staff."

"It is not late," she said emotionally. "I need to talk to you."

"I think not," he said, "we will talk in the morning."

"You have to leave early, you said."

"Are you not getting up with me then?" he asked.

"Of course I am, but…Ambrose, please, you simply have to turn over and talk to me. Ambrose, I am sorry I angered you. You are right, I had no leave to talk to General Lee without asking your permission. I did not mean anything by it, but I see that now, and I am sorry." Her husband turned in the bed to look at her. Finally, he took her hand and pulled her to him. "Ambrose, you must forgive me, we have never gone to sleep angry with each other. My husband, I need you especially this night. I am frightened."

"Why are you frightened?" he asked.

"I don't know," she said sadly, "the war is not going well, the South is just about on its knees, and any day now I expect to hear that you…"

Her husband pulled her to him. "Hush, my little darling," he said. "You are forgiven, and you must forgive me for being cross with you. Shall we go back in front of the fire? As you say, it is not late."

"No, I shall come to bed now."

At four in the morning, the little house shook from a pounding on the door. Lee wanted Hill out early. Something at the front demanded immediate attention. They ate a hurried breakfast and he kissed her goodbye.

The early knocker was Hill's Chief of Staff William H. Palmer. "The enemy has invaded the trenches near Rives Salient," he said in a tone that could not conceal the excitement and fear. "Nothing has come in from Heth or Wilcox during the night to indicate that the problem is widespread, but there is no confirmation of conditions."

Hill rode rapidly to headquarters at the Turnbull House in Edge Hill. Lee and Hill discussed how to hold the line. They had reached no decision when Colonel Venable broke into the room. "Army wagons are being driven wildly toward Petersburg," he blurted out frantically. "Federal skirmishers have driven our men from their post inside the lines!" Hill sprang into action to find and rally his troops. He discovered that Unionists were indeed inside the Confederate lines. No one was available to oppose the federal intrusion but an idle battery of artillery on a nearby hill. Hill sent Venable over to place the guns in a useful position and begin firing. Hill continued on across the fields and through the copses where Federal troops might be encountered at any moment. His Chief Courier George Tucker tried to stop him. "Please excuse me, General, but where are you going?"

"Sergeant, I must go to the right as quickly as possible. We will go up this side of the branch to the woods, which will cover us until reaching the field in the rear of General Heth's quarters. I hope to find the road clear at General Heth's."

They crossed the Boydton Plank Road and followed the edge of the woods for about a mile. Hill felt that he had to get to Heth and establish the right. Grant would pour around them like water over a dam if he did not. But he was apprehensive of their position and told the courier to report to Lee at once if anything happened to him. When they entered the field at the edge of the woods, they encountered Federals. They swung to the right and followed the woods again. About two thirds of the way to cover, they saw eight Federals lurking in the trees. They tried to bluff. The Sergeant rode toward them. "If you fire," he declared to the Federals, "you will be swept to hell. Our men are here—surrender!" Hill echoed the sergeant's command. "Surrender," he shouted.

"I can't see it," one of the Federals shouted. "Let's shoot 'em." Two shots were fired. One went wild. The other struck Hill in the hand, tearing off his left thumb, and entering his heart. Hill fell to the ground dead.

The news deeply disturbed Lee, as much or more for Catherine than for Hill. He instructed Col. William H. Palmer to break the news to Mrs. Hill gently and then to move her and her two children out of the path of danger across the Appomattox.

Catherine was singing as she went about her housework. The night had been as sweet and as fulfilling as any they had spent together in their married life. How truly it was written in the Bible, "Let not the sun go down upon your wrath." She was thankful that they came together and he did not go away in hurt and bitterness. She could see the importance of mending such tears at once. If you let it go, you might harden and then, who knew for sure what a day would bring forth. She did not hear the Colonel enter the house, but she heard his soft footfalls on the floor. "The General is dead," she said in a voice strained with emotion and fright. "You would not be here unless he was dead."

Order was restored over the next few days with great confusion and dire cost to the Army of Northern Virginia that was in no condition to endure it. Could the end be far away?

Chapter Thirty-Three

The Glory and the Grandeur

General Robert E. Lee sat at a small desk in his room at the White House and looked out at the deteriorating town. The pale of doom pervaded the landscape. Desperation stalked the streets Richmond bringing severe malnutrition and starvation. Through the window came a stench of decay that was so foreign to the grand old Virginia city that it seemed almost unreal—as if from another world. The neatly trimmed, thick matted, green lawns had turned a burnt brown-gray from lack of water and ragged for want of care. The once neat and colorful roofs were checkered with places where shingles and tiles were missing. The city, once humming with the sounds and bustle of life and enterprise, was silent as if gripped in fear; drab and morose like a draped casket.

But Robert E. Lee saw none of those things. As he looked out the window, everything seemed inviting and cheerful. An inner excitement gripped him. Lee tried to remember when he last felt that way and he could not. Perhaps he never had.

The War made it difficult to think and put things in perspective, but he tried. It had been two months since his daughter wrote him the news of the death of his invalid wife. Lee took time off for the funeral but was perplexed by his state of mind. He had felt sorrow but not deep regret or remorse. His life with Mary Anna Randolph Custis, since their wedding in June of 1831, was never a happy one.

It was not stormy and violent like some marriages he knew, nor was it tragic so that he felt pressured to stay away. Yet it lacked magnetism and he did prefer being off on assignment to life at home, though guilt kept him from admitting that to himself. He had read about the sensual delights in the Song of Solomon and wondered if anyone ever really had that kind of marriage. He certainly had not. He was father-confessor to his generals and only Ambrose Powell Hill even hinted of such domestic oneness. Lee felt that such marital ecstasy was probably reserved for the lower classes that had little else in life. It must be that gentlemen and gentlewomen were simply too reserved and their lives too closely watched by others for such adolescent frivolity. Still, deep within his being, he longed for that kind of a marriage relationship and felt empty and unfulfilled. It was not something that nagged at him. He viewed life objectively and bore it with dignity. Lee delighted in his daughters and felt that was probably the real purpose for marriage. But the little boy in him went back once in a while to the dreams of youth.

The one woman who stirred those kinds of feelings in Lee was Catherine Morgan Hill. 'Miss Kitty' was, without a doubt in his mind, the most beautiful woman Lee had ever seen. She possessed an ideal height of five feet, four inches and a splendid figure, perfect in every observable detail. Her auburn hair, her green eyes, her cameo complexion and her charming disposition made Lee think of Helen of Troy and Sarah of the Old Testament. She was intelligent but not forward, brave but not brassy, and wise but not bossy. In person, at least, she was everything that any man could dream of. Lee thought she must be the consummate woman.

As an analytical person and a pragmatist, Lee had watched her with modest scrutiny when he had the opportunity. When he did see her, which was not infrequently, there was a closeness and an interaction. Her dedication, which most generals disapproved of, drove her to spend much time with her husband, General Ambrose Powell Hill, as possible. She stayed in camp until the very eminence of danger drove her out. Some generals regarded her behavior as possessiveness while others saw it as recklessness. But Lee understood and he deeply admired and appreciated her for it. Kitty was a woman entirely devoted to her husband. She wanted to be where he was and involved with him as much as possible. A discerning woman, she knew the temporal and fickle life of a military man these days. As she had said to him more than once, she did not know the day when her husband would be killed and she wanted to spend all the time with him she could have.

Lee's relationship with Kitty Hill was special. She came to him with her concerns because he was the commanding general. Inasmuch as she was a lady and he was a gentleman, their friendship existed on the highest level. Still, Lee could not deny the strong attraction he felt toward her and he believed, perhaps willfully, that she liked and respected him.

Now General Hill had been dead for two weeks. He had expected Catherine to go home to Hopemont in Lexington, Kentucky but she had stayed on in Richmond, determined to do what she could to help the apparently-doomed war effort. He believed, rightly or wrongly, that part of her reason for doing that was because of him. Lee knew that what he was about to do was extremely risky. In the South, perhaps in any society, it was not approved. Some would consider it crass, and some immoral. But he also knew that if she ever left Richmond, he would never see her again, or if he did, the circumstances would be so changed that any closeness they might have, or any dependence on him that she felt, would be gone. The chance was great but he simply had to take it. If there was any future for Catherine Hill and Robert E. Lee, it was now or never. It was the boldest non-military thing he had ever done, but he had decided that he could not let the opportunity pass. The War had stripped him of just about everything. Lee felt certain that the success of his future happiness depend on the success of the next few hours. If it did not work out, at least he would not have to live the rest of his life with the remorse of not having had the courage to give it a try.

When General Lee walked out of the White House that morning and down that path that led to the modest cottage of Catherine Hill, he was his radiant best in the splendid dress uniform received from the Lady in Baltimore and never before worn. It was of rich cloth, splendidly tailored and on the man destined to model it. No one but Robert E. Lee could make the red and gray look so much like the robes of a king's coronation. The magnificent sword that had accompanied it from Maryland swung elegantly at his side. The few people he passed on the way nodded to him and then lingered to look after him in admiration.

Catherine stood at the sink finishing up morning chores. The girls were with Varina Davis. She tried to spend as much time with them as possible in the two weeks since their father died but Varina wanted them today and she let them go. The day was glorious. She opened the kitchen window and the flowers and leaves gave off a sweet aroma. She frowned as the stench of the dying city began to mix in with it. What a paradox; the scent of new life and the pall of death floating on the same fresh air together. She thought maybe it was nature's parody of mortal life.

From her neat little hilltop house that President Davis assigned to her after the death of her husband, she looked out over the city. Everywhere there seemed to be the pale of doom.

Paradoxically, Catherine's spirits soared today, almost as if the enemy threw their worst at her but left her standing. Even so, she could not envision a happy conclusion to her fate with the death of her husband. She possessed lands and wealth. Confederate script fell to ridiculously low values but she had gold in the bank if the government did not confiscate. She did not think that anyone but she and Mr. Todd knew about it and he never conveyed anything to the Davis government, which he openly criticized.

Catherine knew she needed to return to Hopemont. She had been away far too long this time and she was concerned about Emmanuel and Tuttle. She had communicated nothing to them about her plans and she knew they must be worried sick. It certainly seemed that she could take care of her family and affairs, but she did not look forward to spending a solitary life at Hopemont with just her children, soon be grown and gone and gone, and her servants. Many events in the past several years tarnished some of her golden memories and she could not envision living there, even though she loved it, alone with no family around her.

She found one thing to cherish in this drab war—the intimacy of body, and spirit that she had enjoyed with Ambrose. True, the camaraderie of soul left a little to be desired, but then nothing in this life is perfect. Now she faced long months of mourning, she would not think about another man and could not imagine who it would be if she did.

This took her thoughts to General Lee, a widower now, but she had not heard a word from him since Ambrose's death. He did not call her in to work. She stayed on, wanting to help to the end and thought her work with Lee would be one shade under which she could rest, but something had not worked. After her husband's death, she went through a period of feeling guilty about the day she spent in the office with Lee just prior to it. Was she being punished? Mary and Varina had helped her to see it as natural soul searching and regret that every woman went through after a tragedy. She wondered perhaps if General Lee went through the same thing. Maybe he felt wrong about having her back to work. She hoped not, but something misfired somewhere. The work needed to be done. Maybe he thought she did not want to do it any more. If so, she must think of some way to get word to him. If the war ended and Catherine went back to Kentucky, she would likely not see him again, or, if she did, the circumstances would be so different that nothing would be the same. But that part of it could not be helped at the moment. She could not countenance any leanings toward him now. It would be an affront to her husband's memory and would not be accepted by her peers. The lot of a widow in the aristocratic south was a severe one indeed.

She went back to the kitchen window and looked out. She saw a small Negro boy dart across her lawn and dive into the bushes of the neighboring yard. Catherine took off her apron and went to the door, intending to investigate this odd event. As she did, she found herself face to face with Robert E. Lee coming up her walk. She stood transfixed as she beheld the sight. He had on the glorious uniform, a gift from a mysterious woman in Baltimore, and at his side hung the magnificent sword. Catherine knew him to always be neat and well manicured, but she had never seen him so polished, so suave, and so elegant.

He walked up to her and bowed. "Morning, Miss Kitty," he said politely. May I come in?"

Catherine came back to reality and searched for her composure. "Of course, General," said absently. "It is my honor." As she led him and showed him a chair at the kitchen table, she remembered what he had said that evening at her home: 'I will never wear this uniform except at war's end or to commemorate some very special occasion.' It was not her imagination. This was more than an official visit. "Would you like some tea, General?" she asked.

"Yes, of course," he said, trying a little too hard, she thought, to be casual, "that would be nice."

As she fumbled through the setup, her mind was racing. 'What should she say?' She sat down across the table from him and tried to look, act, and sound natural. "To what do I owe the pleasure of this visit, General Lee? Are my daughters and I in any danger?"

Lee looked at her with a gaze that was a little different from the ordinary. It seemed…softer, somehow. "No, not any more than usual," he said "We are probably all in danger these days, but nothing new has happened."

"So, you are just looking in on me. That is so like you, General," she said. "Your thoughtfulness and care has always been…"

"Catherine,' he cut in gently, "It isn't just a social call. There is something else."

"Oh, I see, well…" As he collected his thoughts, Catherine knew a different kind of anxiety. What if, by some chance, he proposed to her? She could not accept…not now. What should she do? She continued thinking as she listened to him.

"I know the we in the South have traditions, but the war has changed many them. We have been forced out of our way of life and most of that has been to the bad. Our aristocratic women have been forced to live in tents, to wear military uniforms made for men, to abandon sidesaddles and ride like men, and to east rations for the common soldier. Plantations have been commandeered and turned into military headquarters and even barracks. Many such things have happened that our traditions do not allow but we have accepted them because of the war and in contribution to the effort. Maybe it would be forgivable if we were to try to use this unsettled time to our benefit. Catherine, I am wondering…"

She now knew for sure and what she had to say. "Robert," she cut in quickly, "The war has changed our traditions as you say, but it has not eliminated them and we must not allow that. Some of them have to do with decency and character. If those go away, we might as well lose the war; what do we have left? My husband has only been gone for two weeks. I am required to mourn for him; it is expected of me. I want to mourn for him; I require it of myself. I must mourn for him; morality demands it. I cannot consent to think of any other man …in…in that way. Her face softened and a warm look glistened in her eyes. "Not even…not even your, Sir…not now…not yet." She paused. He continued to look at her softly but did not say anything. "But I will hold you in my…my mind…in my heart. When an appropriate time for mourning has passed, you may call on me…if you still wish to."

Lee rose gently from the Table. "And what is an appropriate time for mourning, Catherine?" he asked.

For some reason, he offered her his hand. She took it and held it. "I don't know, Robert…I will have to…" She did not know how to continue.

He bowed, released her hand, and started for the Door. As he opened it he turned and asked, "Where will you be?"

"Well, I guess, here working at the old…or at Hopemont."

He nodded. "Thank you, Catherine, I will do that."

As he started out, she said impulsively, "A year, General…let's say a year."

Lee tried to restrain a broad smile. "A year it is, then." He turned and then stopped again. "I didn't know and I could take the chance, but what you said just now…the reports are far behind. You will be in tomorrow?"

She hoped she would not cry if she answered. "Yes, my General, I will be in tomorrow. But…"

He stopped her with the wag of his head. "No, not for a year…we agreed. If I am not a man of my word, best you find it out now."

He turned and moved down the path with the dignity that had characterized him since she had known him. She opened the blinds and watched him. He turned to look at the window and she released them. She thought he saw them close and she could tell that he was smiling. Through a slit, she followed him down the street. Catherine smiled to herself and enjoyed the warm flow of relief about the future of herself and her daughters. The time had come when she could admit it to herself. After she, at age sixteen, had met him in New York, she vowed to herself that she would love him forever. When her father explained reality to her—that he was married with children and it was a thing that was never going to be—she had tried to put him out of her mind and move on. But she had never completely lost that…that…that special something that she felt for Robert E. Lee. She had always loved him—not carnally, not dishonestly, not disgracefully, but in the deepest ethical and…aesthetic sense. Now she knew why.

Catherine prepared to turn from the window when she saw a curious thing. The little Negro boy, who had darted across her back yard, followed him from bush to bush, trying to stay out of sight. Catherine realized what it was all about and shook her head with an indulgent smile. Mrs. Gordon had her intelligence network going. By nightfall, it would be all over town. Well, let them talk; she didn't care. "A silver lining in every cloud," she said aloud, "but there is time to think about that later." She put on her coat and scarf and headed over to the Whitehouse to get her girls. A cab would bring them home in an hour or two, but Catherine felt like getting out, walking, and talking to someone. Varina fit the need perfectly. No secret ever passed her lips and no one understood so well.

Chapter Thirty-Four

When Devils Collide

Catherine got out of the cab and went up the steps to Mary's front door. Mary opened the door before she got to it. Catherine saw the excitement in Mary's eyes. "You were waiting for me at the door," Catherine said with surprise.

Mary acted as if she could not get her breath. "Oh, yes I was, Kitty," she said. "I am so keyed up, I am about to bust."

Mary stood in front of Catherine fidgeting. Catherine felt a bit awkward. "Should we go in?" she asked, "or…"

Mary put her hand to her head. "Oh, of course, forgive me for my poor manners," she said. "Do come in and sit down. Would you like some tea?"

Catherine studied Mary while stirring her teacup. She had never seen her like this. It didn't seem to be tragedy, but Mary looked as if she would faint at any moment. "Mary," Catherine asked, "what in the…"

Mary put out her hand pleadingly. "Oh, Kitty, please don't say anything—please!"

"Don't say anything?" she said with astonishment. "But Mary."

"Kitty," Mary said dramatically, "you must promise not to repeat what I am about to tell you to anyone."

"Mary," Catherine said, shaking her head slowly, "I don't think I can make a promise like that."

Mary seemed desperate. "Kitty, please, I can't tell you if you don't," she said, "and I have to tell you."

Catherine did not know what to make of it. "Mary, this is silly," she said. She let Mary squirm for a few moments. "Oh, all right," she said at length, "I will not tell a soul. What in the world is it? Tell me before you die of something."

Mary put her hand on Catherine's Arm and squeezed it tightly. "Forrest and Hampton have killed Sherman and destroyed his army."

Catherine stared long and hard at Mary. She seemed nearly out of her head and this appeared to support that diagnosis. "Mary, Mary, Mary!" Catherine said, "where did you hear anything like this?"

"General Hampton sent a rider with a sealed letter for me," Mary said.

For Catherine, this seemed odd too. "But why would he tell you?"

Mary shook her head doubtfully and sighed. "I don't know. He said that someone in Richmond must know if things go wrong," Mary replied, "and I am his best friend and…and the South Carolina thing…you know."

Catherine sat in silence as she thought. Who would make up a story like this and why? Could it possibly be true? Catherine did not think so. "Does General Davis know?" she asked. "Does General Lee know?"

"No," Mary replied tensely.

"But why…"

Mary cut her off. "Forrest will not allow it," she said. "He says everything depends on Lee, and particularly Davis, not knowing. Hampton says that what Forrest is doing is completely irregular. He says that Lee and Davis would put a stop to it in a minute. Forrest has put Johnson and Beauregard in arrest and has taken over the forces in the Carolinas."

This tested Catherine's ability to listen to any more and she wished she had not promised to be silent. "But Mary," she said reproachfully, "that is mutiny—if it is true. We cannot…"

"No, Kitty!" Mary almost screamed, "You promised!" She calmed down and tried to move on. "Hampton says that Forrest is the cleverest man he has ever seen." Mary paused to collect herself.

"Kitty," she said, as if about to burst into tears, "they have stopped Sherman. Our whole interior army could not do that."

Catherine forced herself to calm down and to think. When she did, the skepticism returned. "But Mary," she said scornfully, "everyone would know if that had happened. The telegraph…"

Mary leaned close to Catherine, put her hand on Catherine's arm, and said in a loud, raspy whisper, "Forrest has destroyed every telegraph line between here and the Carolinas."

Catherine tried to gather her wits. She did not believe this crazy tale, but how could she get hold of it and discuss it sensibly with Mary? "All right, Mary," she said, "let's…let's…how is this supposed to have happened?"

To Catherine's surprise, Mary began, very cogently, to describe the plan. "They laid a trap for Sherman just inside the North Carolina border, adjacent to the Wateree River," Mary said. "There is a three-mile stretch of road with a bluff on the riverside. Our boys had artillery on high ground at both ends and 50,000 troops in hiding." Mary stopped to steady her voice and take a few deep breaths. "When Sherman's whole army got up on the three-mile stretch," she continued, "they opened on him with the big guns. He could not go forward or backward and he could not get off the road. After shelling him for awhile, the infantry came out of hiding and destroyed, scattered and decommissioned what was left."

Catherine wanted to get on board, but she couldn't. "Sherman is smarter than that," she said, shaking her head negatively, "No one has been able to even slow him down."

"Well, Hampton says that he was careless after leaving the destruction of Camden and heading over to take the surrender of North Carolina from Governor Vance at Greensboro, in exchange for no destruction," Mary explained. "Hamp' said Sherman wasn't expecting any resistance at all. It took him by complete surprise."

Catherine turned it over in her mind and another glaring weakness in the story appeared. "But Mary," she said, "they did not have that kind of artillery and manpower in the region."

Mary nodded her head positively. "Wade says they did," she replied. "He said that in South Carolina confronting Sherman was a small force consisting of 13,700 troops, commanded by Lt. Gen. W. J.

Hardee at Charleston. It was Conner's Brigade—the famous old Kenshaw command. Then there was Beauregard's small troop of about 2,500—they went south, though, and never got involved—Braxton Bragg's army of less than 10,000 and about 20,000 under the command of Joe Johnston," Mary said, counting on her fingers. "10,000 loose and drifting east from J. B. Hood's defeated and scattered forces had to be rounded up. The force awaiting Sherman was more than 50,000. Hardee, Bragg and Johnston all had artillery and some cavalry horses."

Catherine did not want to be a fool. She simply could not afford to be taken in by such a tale. If this kind of thing were circulating, it would get out from someone and they would be the laughing stock of the town and the army in a few days. She continued to look for flaws in the story. "A 60,000 man army could not all get on a three-mile stretch of road," she replied negatively.

"Yes, they could," Mary said. "Sherman forages and does not carry a supply train; he only has caissons. Most of his men are foot soldiers. Sherman did not allow straggling when on a purpose march. Four abreast and in ranks, it only takes about a mile for 60,000. Then they had some Cavalry, artillery, and wagons that took up less than the other two miles. Forrest had it figured out when they hunted the spot for the ambush."

Catherine mused. She did not expect Mary to have sensible answers. "But how could they get them all together is such a short time," she asked, "and make a fighting unit out of them?"

Mary answered without hesitation. "Wade says they started three weeks ago," she replied. "He says you would never believe it unless you had watched Forrest in action. He says the man is a marvel. He thinks…Hampton thinks he may not even be human."

"But why will they not tell Davis and Lee?" she asked. "I would think that if…"

"Because" Mary said, cutting her off, "Forrest has a plan to defeat Grant and it all has to come down shortly and with no interruptions, delays or interference. It must happen before Grant finds out about Sherman. Lee has to be told and Forrest is on his way to do that now. But Davis would stop the whole thing, rearrange his army, and put

Forrest away for mutiny. You know how Davis feels about him since that affair in Kentucky at your place."

Catherine put her hand over her face and rested her chin on her chest. Assuming it to be true, what did Forrest have planned? "What are they going to do next?" she asked. The answer disappointed her.

"I am not sure," Mary said. "All I know is that Hampton is putting all the troops and ordinance on train cars and heading for Virginia to join forces with Lee. Forrest is supposed to be on his way to find Lee." Catherine just sat there shaking her head. "Aren't you happy, Catherine?" Mary asked.

Catherine thought about what she had heard. She tried to look at it in a light in which it could possibly make sense, but found it hard to do. "Well, Mary, if it is true, 'yes', I guess I would be—about Sherman and the victory." She shook her head sadly. "But all this breakdown in command…I just don't see that as a good thing at all."

"Hampton says that Forrest's idea is to beat Grant and win the war," Mary said. "Then he is out of it."

Could Mary and General Forrest think it would be that simple, Catherine wondered? "But General Davis will never let him just walk away," she said, shaking her head.

"That is what General Hampton said," Mary replied, "and Forrest just laughed. He would take care of Davis, he said."

Catherine sighed. "Oh, I heard him say that in Kentucky," she replied, "but I don't believe he knows General Davis as well as he thinks he does."

Mary looked calm now. "Well, anyway, that is the story, Kitty," she said. "I feel better for having told you."

Catherine shook her head slowly. "Yes, well, I am glad of that, I guess," she said with dubiety, "but I am not sure I feel better for having heard it."

"What are you going to do, Catherine?" Mary asked.

"Do? Nothing!" Catherine said fatalistically. "What can I do; I can't tell anyone. I guess we will just have to wait and see what happens, Mary."

Mary gave her a narrow look. "And you think nothing will happen, I take it?" she asked.

Catherine paused to think again. “Well…” She stopped and sighed loudly, puffing out her cheeks. “I don’t know,” she said uncertainly, “if Nathan Bedford Forrest is really involved, I would not be surprised at anything.”

Chapter Thirty-Five

The Strange Encounter

Catherine drove a surrey out to Petersburg but no one was in the office. Lee, she learned from some hands at the stables, had gone down to the trenches, which he tried to do often to keep up what little morale was left. Catherine drove down toward the front and then off to the east. She knew about a little meadow, a kind of secluded spot where her husband often met her, from which she could see some of the trenches. She did not want to be seen, so she tied the horse about a quarter of a mile away and walked down the banks of a little stream that flowed through the meadow.

As Catherine neared the little clearing, she stopped and ducked behind a tree. There was a mounted Confederate officer in the meadow. He was just sitting there, with his back to her, looking down the line. Finally he rode out and she moved on down. She was at the very edge of the clearing when she heard him coming back. Catherine took a seat on the grassy bank beneath the low, thick branches of a tree. She was not sure how well concealed she was, but she did not have time to get any further away. Catherine strained her eyes and tried to figure out who it was. In the saddle, he sat a lot like Stonewall Jackson. She tried to think what officer stationed at Petersburg looked like Jackson.

While musing on the matter, the rider dismounted, led his horse into the trees, and climbed upon a rock at the side of the trial.

Catherine could get a look at his front now, and the hair began to rise on her neck. Another rider coming into the meadow broke her concentration. This one, she had no trouble identifying. It was General Lee. She could not figure out what was going on. It looked like the first man meant to jump off the rock and onto Lee. Should she call out and warn him? Something told her not to.

She watched Lee ride into the meadow, look to the right and left, and then turn to leave. He put his hands to his face and it looked to her like he was laughing. Then the man came down off the rock and Lee started to dismount. Catherine looked back up the stream to see if she could get away without being seen. Her hair rose again. Sneaking across the stream, circling around behind her and climbing upon a big rock was a man who looked for all the world like…and was…General Nathan Bedford Forrest.

She turned back to the meadow and nearly panicked. Lee and the other general were walking straight toward her. Catherine tried to think of what to say if they discovered her. They sat down on the bank of the creek, not more than ten or fifteen feet away and turned their backs toward her.

Catherine pinched herself to see if she was awake. This was an eerie place and she had an eerie feeling. It was more like nightmares she remembered than anything real. And suddenly she knew it could not be real. The man with Lee was Stonewall Jackson. If it had not been for General Lee looking exactly as she had seen him yesterday, she would have thought she had wandered into the valley of the dead.

She listened as Lee and Jackson began to talk. "See here, General Jackson," Lee said, "I'm not much good at this 'fanaticism and miracles' stuff. I was at your funeral. I saw you dead. I saw you in the casket. I saw you buried." Catherine started to get frightened.

She heard Stonewall Jackson laugh. It was like him to think this was humorous. "No, you didn't General. You just thought you did," Jackson said. "Who you saw was a Union Colonel who had died that night in the dispensary. My wife commented on how much he favored me. Dead people always look some different. It was then that I got the idea."

General Lee was still very emotional and she said a prayer that he would not break down. "What idea, General?" he asked.

Jackson continued his weird tale. "I couldn't stand the pity, General. I could not stand the men waiting around like vultures. I got over the pneumonia crisis. The fever broke that night, but I knew that I would be long in recovering. And I was not sure that I ever could, or ever would want to, return to the service. I was numb in my mind about loosin' my arm—the one that always kept me upright in the saddle. I didn't know what I wanted. I thought I might go into traveling evangelism."

Lee was getting his strength back now, she thought, and he sounded a little angry, though Catherine was not satisfied with the force behind his words. "But why would you do this to us, General?" he asked. "Why would you put us through this grief? Why would you demoralize the men?"

Jackson was argumentative. It certainly sounded like he was alive, she thought. Dead men surely wouldn't argue. "I saw it differently, General Lee," he said. "I felt that as long as I was laying here, helpless, the men not knowing what to expect, there could be no healing—no moving on. It would be bad for morale. I thought it best if I get out of the picture. Then if I got well enough, I would come back."

"But you appear to be well," Lee scolded, "and you did not come back."

Jackson had an answer. "About the time I got well, Grant gave you the slip at Cold Harbor and pinned you down at Petersburg. Sheridan destroyed Early and took over the Shenandoah. Jeb Stuart was dead, Sherman was running wild in the South, and I saw the Army of Northern Virginia was in a losing siege. I decided to take on a new identity, sneak into the North, get into the Union lines and find out what I could. We have to know where and when and how Grant can be beaten. If we do not, we are going to lose."

Catherine wondered if Jackson thought he was telling Lee anything he did not already know. As if listening to her thoughts, Lee answered. "Well, Jackson, Sherman has destroyed South Carolina, and is heading for North Carolina. Governor Vance is offering to surrender the State to Sherman in exchange for no destruction."

"I know, I have heard all about it," Jackson said. "Can Hampton do anything?"

"One can hope," Lee said, "but I do not see how."

"What about Beauregard and Johnston?" Jackson asked.

"No; nothing," Lee said sadly. "If they ever were good generals, and they may not have been, they are not now. The war has passed them by. They are finished emotionally and mentally—like I feel sometimes. They're like jackals, fighting over leftovers." Catherine was shocked. She had never heard Lee talk about a Confederate general like that before. Maybe Forrest knew what he was doing after all.

Jackson continued. "You don't see much hope then?"

"Not much, General Jackson," he said. "We are out of ammunition, out of weapons and out of food. I cannot get rations for the men; Sheridan has me cut off from just about everyone."

"Can't the cavalry get him off your back?" Jackson asked angrily.

"What cavalry?" Lee replied. "I have no cavalry anymore, General, except for Wade Hampton. And if he does not stay where he is and try, we may as well surrender now."

Catherine tried to digest what she had heard as they paused for awhile. General Lee lay back and looked up at the trees. Then he turned his head and looked right at her. Could he see her through the branches? It was sort of dark in there. She did not believe that he could. She was reassured when he turned away and did not pay her any more attention.

Lee began to talk again. "But back to your venture, General Jackson; what did you find out behind enemy lines? Did you find that special something you were looking for that will bring us victory?"

"Yes, I did, General," Jackson said, "but in talking to you, I am not sure it will do us any good."

"What do you mean?"

"I mean that Grant thinks if he could get you out of these trenches and into the open, he could attack and put an end to the war," Jackson said.

"Is there any doubt in your mind that is what would happen if I left the trenches, General Jackson?" Lee asked.

"No, I am afraid not, General Lee," Jackson said. Your men are too few and too weak and not well enough armed. Beside all that, we would need substantial artillery. If we had men in waiting—if we could surprise Grant with a force that was able to strike him a massive blow, we could take that Army of the Potomac."

Catherine's heart ached for Lee as she heard him say, "Well, there is no good day-dreaming, General. We do not have that kind of force available. And what about Sherman? He will be here in a few days. And if we do not get some rations for the men, it is not going to matter in any case. They are sick and anemic and many of them are beginning to die now."

"I know," Jackson said. "It is just so sad. The opportunity has finally come and we cannot make use of it."

Catherine realized that the situation was worse than any of the women were being told. She had never heard this dismal an evaluation. She watched General Lee leap to his feet. What was it, she wondered? A racket was coming from the direction of the big rock. Nathan Bedford Forrest came half running and half sliding into view.

"Ah, but we do have men and artillery, generals," he said loudly. "Wait until you hear what I have to tell you."

Catherine listened with interest and fascination to Forrest's tale.

When Forrest had finished, General Lee spoke out. "General Forrest," he said, with the iron of old days in his voice, "do you not know the penalty for issuing false orders to your superiors and usurping command? Why did you do such a thing?" Catherine winced as she thought Lee serious, but apparently, he was not.

"Cause I am a rebel, Gen'l," Forrest said with humor, "and I don't like West Point Yankees tellin' me how to fight." Then they all lit up the night air with a hearty laugh that had a ring of hope in it, and anticipation.

Catherine wanted to stay and hear the rest of the plan but it was her chance to get away. She found her way back to the rig, got in it, and headed for home. There wasn't much light left, but she could make it if she hurried. As the pacer trotted along, she thought how accurate the story Mary told her had been. Things were looking up. What was Forrest's plan? She wished she had been able to stay and hear it.

Chapter Thirty-Six

A Strange Man with the Strangest Plan

Catherine was a little uneasy as she got out of the cab and started toward General Lee's office. She entered the lobby, hung her coat, and went in. Lee sat at his desk writing. He spoke to her but did not look up immediately. She stood, waiting for some indication of what to do.

"Oh, Miss Kitty," he said absently, "I am sorry; please sit down. Well, I may as well just jump into it," he said. "Miss Kitty, I saw you in the meadow yesterday afternoon."

Catherine breathed a sigh of relief. This concerned her far less than the other possibilities. Then she realized she should say something. "Oh, I see," she said. "I am sorry, General Lee, but I went there before you came in and I did not know a rendezvous had been set."

"There had not been, actually," he said. "You did not see Jackson, then?"

Yes," she said, "but I didn't know who it was. I tried to identify the man. Then I stayed too long and could not leave without being seen. I couldn't believe the story Jackson had to tell. I kept wondering if he were really alive."

Lee nodded. "I know." He said with understanding, "I did too. It is one of the stranger things I have encountered. But what about the information Forrest brought us? You must have found that harder still?"

Catherine could not wait for an answer from her thoughts. "Oh, well, General Lee, in truth I already knew about it," she said.

Lee started forward in his chair. "You, what? Catherine, I am starting to get that eerie feeling again," he said anxiously. "How could you possibly already have known about it? Are you psychic?"

Catherine locked her hands together and gazed at the ceiling. She had told Mary she would never breathe a word. Would she stir something up that would hurt her relationship to Mary? Well, she had to tell him; that was all there was to it. "General Hampton sent a courier with a sealed letter to Mary Chesnut."

Lee regarded her narrowly as he digested the information she had just given him. "Why would he do that, do you think?" he asked.

"She said he said it was because he wanted someone in Richmond to know what was going on if anything went wrong with the plan."

"What plan would that be?" he asked.

Catherine shrugged. "I guess he meant Forrest coming to find you while he loaded everything on train cars for Virginia."

Lee nodded. "Well, so you know that much. Will Mary Chesnut say anything to anybody?"

"No."

"Are you sure?" he asked warily.

Catherine nodded her head very emphatically to dramatize her words. "I am very sure," she said.

Lee raised his eyebrows. "She did to you," he replied.

Catherine hesitated. "I know," she said, "but that…that is different. She had to tell someone."

"What about Varina Davis?" he asked.

Catherine was very firm. "Particularly not Varina," she said.

Lee looked at her for a sign of doubt but saw none. "Okay, so you know that part of it too." He paused for a dramatic change. "It is very important that Mary does not leak it…ah…let the cat out of the bag. This plan depends on absolute secrecy."

Catherine frowned in worry and disapproval. "I don't like not telling President Davis," she said soberly.

Lee sighed. "I don't like it either—not at all," he said, "but I do see Forrest's point. If we have a chance of winning the war, this may be it."

"I didn't hear that part of it," she said. "I ran when you all broke out laughing."

Lee nodded. "Yes, I know," he said. "That is why I had you come in. Now that you know about Forrest and Jackson—I did not realize you knew about Sherman—and since you are my private secretary and I may have to rely on you in this connection for the next several days, I want you to know the rest of it—that is, if you want to know?"

Catherine scooted her chair toward the desk in anticipation. "Oh, yes, of course," she said. "I am very interested. Once a general's wife—always a general's wife, I guess." Catherine realized what she had said and flushed deep pink. "Oh, no! I did not mean to say that. I am so…"

Lee held up his hand for her to stop. "That is quite all right, Miss Kitty," he said, "don't be embarrassed. I knew exactly what you meant." Lee got up, went to the windows and closed them, walked through the office door to the building entry, opened it and looked both ways. Then he came back and sat down. "All right," he said, "here's the plan."

"We have sent a Mississippi man to tell Grant that I am quitting the trenches on Wednesday morning at 10:00 A.M. and making a run down the Appomattox to Jetersville. There I am ostensibly going to load my men and equipment on rail cars and head for North Carolina to join up with Johnston."

"Will Grant fall for that?" she asked.

"Well, we will know soon," Lee replied. "I believe he may well. Captured pickets and spies tell us that Grant is almost as sorry for my men as I am. This is not his kind of war. He wants desperately to get me out of the trenches. He knows he can crush me if I make that mistake."

"But I thought you said…'"

"Yes, but Grant does not know it isn't a mistake," Lee replied. "Everything we have said to him through the operative makes sense to Grant, the thinker. 'The South is beaten to its knees.' 'We are out of rations, ammo and all other ordinance, clothes and replacements.' 'The Southern soldier feels that the longer the war goes on, the more his family will suffer and that the outcome has to end one way.' 'It is the idealism of Davis and his generals that is keeping it going.'"

Catherine was confused. "But then, I don't see…"

"Well, that is all background," he said. "Let me tell you about the plan and you can ask as we go along. We're going to have a trap set for Grant. It is Forrest's 'Double Envelopment and Frontal Attack,' so called."

"But that isn't in the manuals," Catherine said. "I have read them many times and I don't remember anything like that."

Lee looked apologetic. "No, it isn't, Miss Kitty," he said, "and I…but Forrest has often used it successfully during the war without a single loss."

Catherine sounded as if she was a general reviewing war plans. "So where will everyone be?" she asked.

Lee smiled. "Miss Kitty," he said, "if women are ever allowed to be officers, you…All right, General Hampton and his men will mass in the meadows south of Drewry's Bluff. When ready to attack, he will move down the Railroad and join the southernmost of his forces with Forrest's northern contingency at Petersburg. If Grant takes our lead, he will be several miles northwest of Hampton, along the road that follows the south fork of the Appomattox River. Guns and units will be deployed as marked on this map and will be in waiting for Grant to retreat towards Petersburg."

"What about General Forrest?" Catherine asked.

"He will be on a siding, waiting back up the line," Lee answered. Sheridan has been snooping around and has already seen tracks on the road west of Burkeville. He may be back out tomorrow looking around some more."

Catherine studied the map. "What about the rest of his people?" she asked. "How and when will you get them up?"

Lee studied her approvingly as he nodded. "They will transfer at Burkeville on Tuesday night and move into position about halfway to Petersburg on the Southside Railroad," he said. "They will wait there until Grant moves down the river road after me. Then they come up by train and rendezvous with Hampton at Petersburg."

Catherine shook her head in doubt. "Will there be time for all this moving?" she asked.

"Yes," Lee answered, "the artillery is already off and will be in position, except for that which Forrest is going to leave on train cars. The cavalry will be on the ground. It will take about three hours to get to Petersburg and get his 7,000 infantry off the train and into position."

"And the Army of Northern Virginia?" she asked.

"General Jackson and I will be about five miles up the Appomattox," he said. "On the way in, Forrest scouted an excellent place for the infantry and guns. There is an area where Grant will round a bend and will be in a river valley—which we are calling 'the bulge' for simplification—with a narrow on both ends. We will be in the hills waiting to open on him with canon and mounted rifles. Then we will fall on him with the infantry and drive him back through the narrow entrance where Pickett's batteries will do him much damage. The infantry will chase them out of the bulge and back into the arms of Forrest and Hampton. As soon as they are visible, we will open on them with artillery."

Catherine had discussed military operations strategy many times with her husband but never sat in a planning session. She was impressed by the cold ruthlessness of it all and it made her shiver. Lee continued. "General Jackson will halt our people in the cover of the mountain until we have shelled them to the point of infantry attack," he said. "Then we will fall down from the west and Forrest-Hampton will come up from the east and crush Grant in the vise. Forrest will have men on the south side to keep them from making an escape. He will leave enough men back to be astride the Southside Railroad to patrol the entire south side of the trap."

Catherine knew the right questions. "What if they try to escape to the north?" she asked.

"They will not be able escape to the north," Lee aid confidently. "They have no pontoon bridges out to cross the Appomattox. If they try a slow crossing, we will destroy them from three sides."

"What if Grant doesn't bite?" she asked.

"Then the Army of Northern Virginia will be out of its siege. Sherman will not be behind us. We can regroup in the hills and fight on. With Sherman defeated and the entire southern interior virtually free of meaningful northern armies, we can fight on a good while." He paused and looked very sober and very tired. "But we cannot prevail over time if that happens," he said. "Grant knows how to reorganize fast, he has the reserves, and he will do it. To fight on, we must have men, food and supplies, which we will not be able to get in sufficient quantities. Our one and only chance to win this war is right here and right now. Grant must be beaten."

Catherine was still in doubt. "Well, I don't know; it all seems so odd," she said. I wonder what my…what General Hill would think of it."

"Your husband would not have agreed, Catherine. He was a careful and cautious General. That was his strong point and at once…well, his strong point. He wanted to be sure of winning before he put in his troops."

"You mean like at North Anna?" Catherine asked and was sorry as soon as she had.

Lee fell to silence and studied her face. Finally, he spoke in saddened tones. "At North Anna I let my frustrations, my fears and my ill health goad me into a very lamentable mistake. I wish I had found the grace to apologize, but I have never been able to do that with my generals." He paused, "But, Catherine, let us stay with the problem at hand for now."

Catherine was relieved to hear him say words that eased her only real sore spot toward him. But there was no time to dwell on it now. Catherine was a military wife. She knew she had heard the final word. She dropped her military face and resorted to womanliness. "Well, I am sure you know what you are doing, General Lee," she said submissively. "I have all confidence in you."

Lee nodded. "I know, Miss Kitty," he said, "it is Forrest in whom you have no confidence, but…".

"Actually, General, that is not true," she replied evenly. "I have great confidence in General Forrest—great confidence!"

Lee looked at her strangely. "Do you?" he asked. "That is interesting."

Catherine was not anxious to talk to Lee about Forrest and changed the subject. "General Lee," she said firmly, "I want to watch the battle."

Lee was alarmed. "Oh, Miss Kitty," he exclaimed, "I don't think that is possible."

"But, Sir," she said, "there is a high hill east of Dunlop's Station."

"You mean the other side of the turnpike?" he asked.

"Oh yes, a half a mile, maybe," she said. "It is just south of Swift Creek at the very top of a steep canyon falling off to the north and into the Creek. It overlooks both Swift Creek and the Appomattox River from Petersburg to Jetersville station. It's a great vantage point."

"But how will you get up there?" he asked.

"Oh, it isn't that steep from the west," she said. "I can drive a rig to the top. I have gone up there several times to watch the fighting in Petersburg. Do you know the one I mean?"

Lee was thinking. "Yes, I do, but…"

"No artillery will be aimed up there, surely?" she said.

"No, but…stray fire from one of the high powered northern repeater rifles could reach there."

"But General Lee," she said, not giving an inch, "stray fire could have reached my house in Petersburg just as easily. You know I have never been afraid of war."

Lee sat silently for a few moments. "I know you are not afraid of war," he said, "But it would be a pity if you were killed now that…now that…now that the war maybe so nearly over." Catherine looked as disappointed as she could. "Well, Miss Kitty," he went on, beginning to weaken, "I cannot—at least, will not—forbid you to do it. All I can say is 'be careful'. If anything begins to land close, get off of there in a hurry."

Catherine thanked him and left. As she neared the rig, she saw, on the ground, a twisted handkerchief she had dropped. She picked it up and mused on it philosophically. How differently this morning had gone from what she thought when she drove up. Catherine mounted and started the drive for her home. Her jaw was set with grim determination. He had better not come up with anything as an afterthought. Nothing would keep her off that hill on Wednesday morning.

Chapter Thirty-Seven

Nor The Battle to the Strong

Catherine shivered against the cold in the early morning air. The horse trotted briskly up the little-used buggy trail and the wind created by the movement made her eyes water. She wore nothing heavy because she expected it to be a mild day. There were blankets in the back of the rig in case she had to stay all night, but Catherine did not want to stop and get one out to put around her.

She left the girls with Mary, which made it a little more difficult. They did not much like to go there, but Catherine could not risk anything by leaving them at Varina's. Varina must not know, General Lee said. The girls saw the picnic basket and wanted to go along. They cried when she would not let them and that bothered Catherine. Why should innocent children be hurt because of the subterfuge of grownups, Catherine mused to herself? She thought about taking them, but the chance of danger dissuaded her…and besides, the secret would be out. Varina Davis would know all about it within a day or two.

Catherine found the level spot beneath her favorite tree, spread her blanket, threw out her cushions, and drug out the chair. She set up the telescope that her husband had left her. A glass so powerful could be nerve-wracking and frustrating for someone who did not know how to use it, but Catherine did. One could not follow the action with it.

You had to focus it on an area of interest and wait for activity to come into focus.

With the naked eye, Catherine could see into the town of Petersburg, the trenches, and Fort Stedman, but Blue Ridge mist made clear vision very difficult. Catherine kept her fingers crossed. She set up her little sundial as her husband had taught her. By nine o'clock, the mist burned away and left the air pristine blue and crystal clear. She poured herself a cup of tea and settled in. It was only tepid now, but it still tasted good. As the shadow inched toward ten o'clock, the anticipation began to mount. She could see a few riders coming to Grant's headquarters. No one left. Something was going on. She wished she could tell Lee, but then, of course, he already knew as much as she did and more.

Her breathing stopped as she spotted Jackson and Lee on a little knoll east to the railroad, behind some trees. She decided the best way to watch the beginning, if it happened today, was to focus on them. When the shadow touched ten o'clock, she sat at her field glass and glued her eye on Lee. Would anything happen at this first deadline? She saw Jackson turn to Lee and nod his head. Lee gave a hand signal of some sort. Almost instantly, a wave of human bodies rose from the trenches, and started running across the tracks and toward the Appomattox River trail. Catherine held her breath as she moved the scope to Fort Stedman. Would Grant come out after them, or had he taken the bait? Would he give them the time to get free of the trenches? She watched for ten minutes until her muscles began to ache and her eye watered from strain. Nothing happened. Grant had fallen for the scheme. She lay back in the chair and rested. "Dear God," she said aloud, "Let this be a success. Well, not because you are on our side, but because…well…help us all. Help me. Oh…not my will but thine be done." She breathed easier. It wasn't so hard, once she said it.

Without the scope, Catherine could see the men streaming up the river at a run. "Those poor men," she said aloud, "where are they getting the strength to run?" By ten thirty, Lee's Infantry was halfway to the bulge. Catherine could see down into it and saw some artillery pieces not too well hidden from above. She looked back to Fort Stedman just in time to see Grant's cavalry charge out, followed by a briskly marching infantry. Catherine waited for the artillery but, to her surprise, none came. How could Grant watch Lee move out with artillery and not take his own in pursuit? Then she remembered General Lee telling her Grant thought that crushing the Army of Northern Virginia would be simple, once they were out of the trenches. Grant thought Lee was racing toward Jetersville to load his artillery on the train. It was evident that they did not expect an artillery battle and Grant had no place to deploy along the river road. Catherine mused aloud, "Little does he know what he is in for."

When Grant's army cleared the Weldon and Richmond tracks and started pursuit up the Appomattox River road, Catherine judged that the rear guard of Lee's Army was two miles ahead, and the van neared the bulge so that the 70,000 men stretched out over a distance of three miles. Such cavalry as Lee had took positions in the rear to minimize the havoc that Sheridan could wreak on the foot soldiers. Catherine focused her attention on Lee's infantry. The men, who started out in double-time, slowed to a fast march about halfway to the bulge. It required another forty-five minutes by her dial for the rear to pass out of the canyon and into the widened river valley of which the bulge consisted. She thought several hundred casualties had been inflicted by the harassment of Sheridan, whose large cavalry troop could not be held off by the meager horsemen of Picket. When the last of Lee's infantry passed in, she guessed Grant's army a mile behind. With her field glass, Catherine determined the leader of Grant's troops to be General George Meade. She had scanned the field but did not see Grant.

It did not look like Meade tried to close too fast. This told her that they still did not suspect anything. Meade probably thought he could corner Lee at the railroad station and preferred to fight him there, rather than out on the river trail.

Sheridan did not follow Lee's cavalry into the bulge, but chose to direct all of his efforts toward the Southern cavalry who had purposely scattered, hoping to lead him away. Catherine saw this as a break for Lee. Had Sheridan ridden in, he would have seen the Southern soldiers taking cover in the earthworks, and might have discovered some of the artillery batteries. The trap would have been exposed and the Northern army might have retreated toward

Petersburg. Catherine did not believe that, along with Sheridan, the large army could not have been contained by Forrest and Hampton and could probably have returned to the safe quarters of Fort Stedman.

She watched as the Confederate infantry continued to move up the Appomattox River road toward the Danville and Richmond railway. Meade and his commanders—she recognized Baldy Smith and Hancock; the other man must be Warren—picked up the pursuit and closed to with a half mile of the rear guard. At a little after 12:00 noon, the Confederates swung uphill to the southwest and took to the earthworks prepared for them by Longstreet and Daniel Hill on Monday and Tuesday. At the same time, seventy Confederate guns opened up from positions that stretched along the ridge from a mile ahead of the Union van to its flank. Catherine never witnessed this kind of carnage before and she felt weak. The devastation stunned her. The Union had nowhere to go and no cavalry to charge up the hill to disable any of the guns. Some units, under the general she thought was Warren, tried to charge the earthworks to find shelter and a place to make a stand but got pushed back by heavy Confederate fire and a murderous rain of canister shot. Other units succeeded in overrunning a few of the batteries but could not use the big guns to their advantage. In less than thirty minutes, Meade seemed to see the trap he had been lured into and signaled an orderly retreat. At 1:15, the bluecoats were out of the bulge and back on the river road to Petersburg. As they moved about two hundred yards out of the bulge, Pickett's batteries, that had left Petersburg with Lee and taken position on the south end near the river, opened up on the Union rear. As they broke into a run to escape the rain of death from the sky, Forrest moved his artillery into position and began to fire from the east. Meade was caught in a cross fire from the front and the rear. In desperation, he ordered his men up the bank and into the woods to the south. But Jackson had mobilized the guns in the bulge. They streamed down the mountain on the backside and into the area where Meade had hoped to make his escape, cutting Meade completely off. Sheridan could not come to his aid because Forrest and Hampton were attacking him from the south and the east. They were being shot like cattle at a slaughterhouse. Catherine saw the Union commander order his troops back to the river, where they tried to cross it the best way they could. But Jackson was ready for the move. He ordered the artillery to cease firing and moved in with infantry and cavalry. In a hopeless position, the commander raised the white flag of surrender, much to Catherine's relief.

She was amazed to see Forrest ignore the surrender and continue to charge with his men and his cavalry. Then he saw an even more troubling sight. Jackson too ignored Meade's attempt to surrender and continued the blood bath.

Catherine saw the Union cavalry general, Sheridan, it must be, make a suicidal charge from Forrest's rear and into the center where he and his men picked up Meade, Warren and Hancock, and made a run for a small breach to the south. Miraculously she thought, Hancock made it out and raced for Petersburg. Warren and the horseman who had picked him up were shot and killed. Catherine saw the horse shot out from under Sheridan and he and Meade go sprawling on the grass. Then she saw Forrest race toward Sheridan with his sword drawn. Sheridan managed to wrap his jacket around Forrest's sword and pull him from his horse. Catherine watched in breathlessness and anxiety as Forrest and Sheridan locked in a death struggle. She expected Forrest to win easily, but it wasn't turning out the way. It looked like Sheridan had the upper hand when one of Forrest's men rode up and shot the Union cavalry general in the head.

Catherine saw a general of the Confederate Army, Hampton she thought, ride into the center of the fray, swing General Meade up, and carry him to safety in the rear. Catherine gasped as Forrest and Jackson continued the slaughter. It was clear to her that they did not mean to stop until they killed every soldier in the Union army. Catherine became very angry. This is not war; it is murder. She looked frantically around for Lee. Why didn't he do something about this? Surely, he did not approve! Finally, she saw him riding into the fight. He drew near Forrest and seemed to calling to him. Forrest ignored Lee and pressed the men on to the fight. She looked back for Lee and did not see him. Then she saw him ride up to Jackson.

Some sort of a shouting match ensued. Jackson started to ride away and General Lee charged his horse, Traveler, into Jackson's mount. Jackson shouted something at Lee, then spurred his horse and rode over to Forrest. When Jackson got Forrest stopped, a long, heated conversation took place. She could only imagine the conversation.

When the shooting stopped, the remnant of Grant's Army of the Potomac sprawled on the hilly ground south of the river. Hampton came up to General Lee with Meade in tow. Meade jumped down from Hampton's horse and went over to Forrest, yelling at him and shaking his fist. To her surprise, Forrest turned and rode away.

Meade next charged Lee. Much animation and waving of hands followed. Finally, Lee rode off.

A weak, emotionally spent, and nauseated Catherine sat for about an hour before gathering up her things and starting home.

"Oh, my goodness," she said aloud herself as she rode down the hill. She could not get the image of Forrest and Jackson shooting unarmed boys, trying to surrender, out of her mind. Her contempt for Jackson did not take much stirring, but Forrest presented a different challenge.

The cool evening air revived her. She knew she would feel differently tomorrow when the horrible images began to fade. "I wish I had not gone up there, today," she said and rode the rest of the way home in silence, consciously trying not to think about anything.

Chapter Thirty-Eight

The Death of a Giant

Catherine stood at the glass-toped tea table and looked wearily down at Mary Chesnut. "Can we go inside," she asked quietly, "I…it seems so cold out here to me."

Mary gave her a concerned look. Without answering, she rose and led the way. Once inside, she directed Catherine to the stuffed chair near the fireplace. "You had best sit here, Miss Kitty," she said. I will stir up a little heat." The day was not that cold and Mary made small fire. "You must have caught a touch of something up on that mountain," she said.

Catherine sighed deeply. "Oh, I don't think it is that, Mary," she said wearily. I am just so drained. If feel like I am past going."

Catherine knew Mary wanted to hear about everything but hoped she would not push. She didn't. She waited a while and then asked calmly, "It was really hard, then?"

Catherine nodded. "Much more than I thought possible," she said.

Mary was fussy. "Why didn't you just come out and tell him the whole thing? She said. "It might be the best for us in the long run."

Catherine shook her head slowly but with conviction. "I thought about it Mary, but I soon saw that would be the worst thing I could have done. You know how President Davis is; so emotional and so easily hurt." She closed her eyes and leaned back. Then she opened them again and sat up as if startled. "I cannot do this," she said firmly. “I will be asleep in two minutes.” Catherine put her hands to her face and rubbed her eyes as she continued. “Oh, Mary, I did not say anything that was untrue but I think lied every time I opened my mouth,” she said.

Mary looked worried. “What did he ask you?” she wanted to know. “What did you say?”

Catherine was reluctant to relive any of the pasts several hours but knew she had to. “He told me he knew that I had spent three hours with Lee two days before the battle and he did not want any lies. I knew something, he said, and if I would come clean and tell him what it was, he would get me off with a severe reprimand.”

Mary was wringing her hands. “Oh dear,” she said. “What did you tell him?”

“I did not say anything,” Catherine answered. “I was determined that, if he got anything out of me he was going to have to drag it out.” She shifted in the chair. “First, he asked me if Lee had told me about Sherman.”

Mary’s eyes grew big as she fussed with her hair and wrapped it tightly around her finger. “What did you say?” she asked.

“I said ‘no’.”

Mary put her hands to her breast. “Oh, Catherine,” she said in awe, “I could never lie like that with a straight…”

Catherine put her arm on Mary’s arm. “Lee didn’t tell me,” she said without conviction. “He asked me what I thought of Forrest’s story. I had heard it from you and from Forrest, but Lee never told me.”

Mary sounded jubilant. “Oh, Catherine, how clever of you,” She said. Then she grew sober. “What happened next?”

Catherine drew a deep breath as she thought. “Well, then he asked if I knew Forrest was in the area.” She said. Mary looked with anticipation but did not say anything. Catherine continued. “I told him I did, but did not see anything strange, necessarily, about a Confederate General being in Richmond.”

“What happened next?” Mary asked, fighting to keep clam, Catherine thought.

"He asked me how I knew Forrest was here. Had I seen him? I said I saw a man I thought was he when I was in the area of Petersburg. But he did not see me and did not say anything to me."

"Did he accept that?" Mary asked.

"Not exactly. He came and stood over me and said, "So you never heard him say what his plan was?"

Mary looked pale. "Oh, Catherine!" she said dramatically.

"Well, I answered sharply. 'General Davis,' I said, 'I told you Forrest did not see me and did not say anything to me. I never heard Forrest talk about any plan."

Mary seemed to be scandalized. "But Catherine, you did really," she said.

Catherine was evasive, even with Mary. "No, I did not," she said doggedly. "I left the meadow before Forrest had time to tell it. General Lee told me what it was, but I never heard Forrest say anything about it."

"Oh, Catherine, my goodness, you did have a terrible time of it, didn't you?" Mary said in an astounded voice.

"Well, it just went on and on like that. 'Did Lee tell me that he was planning to attack Grant?' 'No, sir, he did not,'" Catherine said.

Mary shook her head in admiration. "And all the while, he had told you," she said.

Catherine scolded her. "No, Mary he had not," she said impatiently. "Lee did not attack Grant, Grant attacked Lee."

Mary sobered a bit. "I see," she said with some confusion.

"Then he wanted to know," Catherine continued, "if Lee told me he was expecting to be attacked by Grant and did he say what time this was to happen."

"And you said?"

"I said no," said weakly. "I do not know what Mr. Davis thought but my answer 'no' was to the question, 'did he tell me what time?'"

"But I thought you said…"

"Lee said he did not know," Catherine answered, becoming irritated. It could be any time over a two-day period and it might never happen." Mary opened her mouth, but did not say anything. "Anyhow, Mary, it was all about General Lee abandoning the trenches and making a run for it. It was not about Grant attacking. How could Lee know what Grant would do?"

Mary stopped asking questions and sat in nervous awe. "Oh, Catherine, my, my," she said, shaking her head in sympathy.

"Yes, Mary, it went on and on. I thought he would never stop," Catherine said. "But I did find out some interesting things from him."

Mary perked up. "Oh, this will be easier to hear," she said. "What did you find out?"

Catherine counted on her fingers. "Lee has presented Lincoln with a surrender document. Davis does not know what it says, but Lee claims it is almost a replica of what Davis offered Lincoln on the James."

Mary smiled. "Well, at least he should have been happy with that."

Catherine shook her head "Oh, no, he wasn't at all," she said. "In fact, I think Lee's making an offer to Lincoln that Davis had not seen made him angrier than anything that happened. Anyway, Lee has given Lincoln until tomorrow at ten o'clock to accept it or Washington will be attacked and destroyed."

"But commanding generals always take surrenders," Mary said.

Catherine nodded. "Yes, but General Davis knows that Lee was in Drewry's Bluff for almost a day before he left to catch the army on the way to Washington," she said. "Davis says he had intelligence that Lee, Forrest, Hampton and another general were holding talks about what to do. Davis knows he was deliberately excluded. He is almost beside himself."

"Did Lee talk to you about that?" Mary asked.

Catherine thought for a moment. She was so tired of being evasive that she wanted to be open with Mary. "No," she replied. "He said Davis must not be told about the battle because he would call everything to a halt and lose the opportunity. But he said nothing about going to Washington without consulting Davis."

Mary looked worried and disapproving. "Why would they do that?"

Catherine sighed deeply again and turned up her palms. "I don't know, Mary," Catherine said in genuine uncertainty. "Maybe they did not want Davis trying to arrest Forrest until the whole thing was settled."

Mary was dressed in a shabby old housecoat with a tattered hem. Catherine observed her and wondered if all of the goings on had gotten to her. Mary would never win any fashion contests but she always dressed neat and proper. Catherine had never seen her so unpresentable. As Mary leaned back in the chair and tightened the belt, Catherine saw a hole under one of her arms. It only added to her depression. 'Everything is falling apart,' she said to herself.

Just then, Mary sat up and put a finger to her lips. She rose quickly and walked toward the kitchen. Catherine heard he say, "Varina, come in. How long have you been here"?

"About five minutes," Catherine heard her reply. Her heart sank. Had Varina been listening to their conversation?

Mary put the question to Varina. "I guess you heard what we were saying, then"?

Catherine was relieved at Varina's answer. "Oh, no, Mary, I was just…just sitting at the kitchen table crying a little, if you want to know," she said brokenly.

Varina entered the room and sat down. She did not look at Catherine. Catherine decided that if something had arisen between herself and Varina she wanted it out right away. "Varina," she said, "you look so tired.

Varina looked up and gave her a sad smile. "Tired, disappointed, worried, scared, frustrated…you give it a name." Neither Catherine nor Mary said anything. "Well," Varina continued, "I came here to tell you something, and I may as well do it. Someone shot Lincoln last night; he is dead."

Mary gasped. Then she asked, "But I guess…but under the circumstances, will that really matter much to us?"

Varina shrugged her shoulders and made a face. "Jeffy says it will," she replied, "but I don't know. He says Grant will be impossible to work with. Another thing that ties into that is that Grant has signed an agreement giving the South its independence." Catherine and Mary both laughed and clapped their hands.

"This is what we have fought for," Mary said. Isn't it wonderful?"

Varina seemed less than enthused. "I guess, for some people," she said sadly. "I am not sure it will mean much to Jefferson and me."

Catherine was alarmed and saddened. "Varina, why would you say that?" she asked. "I am sure that…"

"Well, that leads to the final thing," she said. "One of the generals is one the way to Richmond to brief Jefferson."

Catherine tried to put a good face on this news. "But Varina, I would think that…"

Varina held up her hand with a dark, almost hostile look. "It is not Lee who is coming," she said with no attempt to conceal the bitter disappointment. "That can only mean one thing. Jefferson is being left out and will probably be forced out." There was a stunned and awkward silence. "Well, I will be going," she said. "I feel as thought I am going to cry again and I do not want to do it here, now." Catherine did not move as Varina started to leave. She stood up as she saw Mary go and put her arm on Varina who turned and looked at them both very searchingly. "Are you still my friends," she asked almost hoarsely.

"Oh, Varina, of course we are," Catherine said emotionally.

"Then why didn't you tell me what was happening?" she asked in a tone betraying deep hurt.

Catherine felt numb from questions of this sort, but Mary answered quickly. "Because we couldn't Varina. You must believe me."

Varina's voiced was quavering and Catherine was alarmed for her and her frame of mind. "I am going to need help in the next few days. Can I come her or am I an outsider now"? She quickly left and Mary followed her out. Catherine sat back down feeling very sad. The victory for the South had not produced any joy yet, but Catherine was determined not to panic. Mary was gone a long time and Catherine, who had brought her girls and come over to stay with Mary until the situation calmed down, was about to go up when she returned. As she sat down, Catherine was reassured to see that some of her self-possession and steadiness had returned.

"That poor, poor woman," Mary said finally. "I feel so guilty keeping all of those things from her. She is about at the end of her rope. I told her to come and stay here but she cannot leave the President alone. He is causing most of her upset. He has accused her of confiding with you and me and shutting him out."

Catherine was incensed. "Oh, no! That man!" she said angrily. "How can he do that to her?"

Mary puffed and put her hands in her lap. "She is about mad," she said. Then she sat up straight. "Oh, she said to tell you to be very careful. Jefferson does not believe you. He thinks you and Lee are conspiring against him."

Catherine felt the tears coming to her eyes. "I almost feel that way myself," she said brokenly.

"Oh, Catherine, don't say that," Mary pleaded. "I can hardly stand myself as it is."

Catherine tried to change the subject a little. "Did you get her to…I mean…"

Mary nodded in understanding. "Yes, she promised me she would come over for the day tomorrow so we can be together and find comfort in one another while we are waiting for the dust to settle," Mary said. "We must try to help her find confidence and assurance. She has given herself for every woman in this town during this god-awful war. I feel so guilty but what were we to do? Hampton told me, and Lee told you, we dare not tell her."

Catherine was fatalistic in her reply. "Some times there is no right answer, Mary," she said, and fell to thinking how she would try to do help Varina.

Mary began to fidget again. "What will happen, Catherine?" she asked.

Catherine rose, her vision blurred. "I don't know, Mary," she said warily. "I just don't know. But I don't think we are going to have to wait long to see. General Lee will be here the day after tomorrow and I hope these mists will begin to clear and we will be able to see the top of the mountain." Then she walked slowly up the staircase to lie down with her children. Sleep, which had almost overcome her when she sat down and relaxed where it was warm, now seemed far from her racing, agitated, and troubled mind.

Chapter Thirty-Nine

Another Giant Falls

As Catherine descended the stairs, she heard excited voices in the kitchen. She crossed the reception hall so she could enter the kitchen by the service door without being seen first. She wanted to know who was there before she made an appearance. It was Varina Davis, but she could not get the sense of what they were talking about. When she entered, they stopped talking and looked up at her. "Good morning ladies," she said cheerfully, "am I interrupting anything?"

"Oh no" Mary said, "We were hoping you would come down. You must hear what Varina has to tell you."

Catherine went to the stove and poured hot water in a teacup. "I think you can tell her best, Mary," Varina said, "I will just listen." Catherine looked at Varina who had a pleasant face and seemed much better than when she last saw her. She seemed to be watching Catherine carefully for her reaction.

"Oh Catherine," Mary said emotionally, "President Davis is dead. He was murdered this morning at sun rise."

Catherine's hands began to tremble. "Oh no!" she said in dismay. The cup slipped from her hands, sending glass and hot water over the kitchen floor. Catherine was horrified. "Mary, I am so sorry," she said, almost desperately, "I will clean it up. Where is the…"

"No," Mary said in a motherly voice. "You sit down before you fall down, Miss Kitty. I will take care of it."

Varina rose quickly from the table. "I will do it while you fill Catherine in," she said. She went to the service porch, returned with a mop, and began swabbing idly at the little spill with the dry threads of the mop. Catherine noticed Varina continuing to watch her closely.

Mary brought Catherine another teacup. As she stirred the leaves, she asked in confused ones. "What happened, Mary? Who would do this?"

Mary was indignant. "That monster Forrest."

Catherine started to protest, then decided against it. "But there had to be something leading up to it," she said. "What happened?"

"Well," Mary said angrily, "there is always something leading up to it, but that is no excuse for him. Forrest arrived yesterday afternoon. He went to Davis' office and accosted him about resigning. The President became abusive. He accused Forrest, Lee, and Hampton of being traitors and conspirators. He told Forrest he was a heathen and should never have been allowed to be an officer in the Confederate army. He was s a poor white, the President told him, who had managed to escape his rightful place by stealing and running slaves."

"But Mary," Catherine asked, "if there was no one but Forrest and Dav…the President in there, how do you know all this?"

"General Bragg was there and heard it all," she said. "He went over and told the whole thing to Varina last night."

"But I thought you said it was this…"

"Catherine, if you do not let me finish this and if you keep pulling me off down rabbit trails, I will never get it told," Mary said.

Catherine realized she must let Mary tell it her way and be patient for the details. "I am sorry, Mary," she said, "Of course it is very rude of me to keep interrupting. I will be quiet until you have finished. But then I may want to…"

"Of course," Mary said impatiently. "Hush, now. Finally Jef…the President told Forest that he was under arrest. Forrest got out of his chair and stood over the president. 'You ain't in charge no more,' he said in his Tennessee cabin boy slang. 'Lee is, and you ain't got no authority to arrest nobody.' Well, Davis really got abusive then. According to General Bragg, President Davis called him things the no man should ever be called. Finally, Forrest had enough and lit into him. 'You ain't got the brains of a bastard rat,' he told the President." Mary stopped and fanned her face with her hand. "Can you imagine such a thing? Catherine. Anyway, Forrest went on. 'You have mishandled this so-called office of yours from the first day. You never should have started this war. We could have got what we got now without it, if we had been patient. You have interfered with and cancelled out your generals in everything they wanted to do except Gettysburg, which was the one time you should have interfered but you didn't have the good sense or the guts. The only way we won this war was to ignore you and go around you.'" Mary stopped to shake her head and get her breath. Then she continued. "General Davis became frantic. 'You are a dishonest, immoral heathen. I have always acted in the highest Christian way and always with the good of the South in mind.' 'Yeh,' Forrest says, 'well what about the hoard of gold you stelt and aimed to make off with, is that part of your Christian character and lookin' out for the citizens of the south?'" Mary stopped again. "Can you imagine him making an accusation like that against our president. You know he did not hide any gold with the intention of taking it if we lost the war."

Varina stopped swabbing and leaned on the handle. "Oh, yes he did, Mary," she said.

Mary looked wild eyed at Varina like she was about to start in on her. Catherine cut in quickly. "Mary, please," she said. "I want to hear the rest of this."

Varina went back to her swabbing and Mary turned to Catherine. 'Well, that was more than Jefferson could take. He slapped Forrest in the face and challenged him to a duel."

Catherine spoke up involuntarily. "Oh, no, General Davis," she said, "No, no, no!"

"Well, I suppose you want to know what weapons that heathen chose?" Mary said.

"Yes, I do, but Mary," she said, "you told me this was murder?"

Mary was firm in her resolve. "It was, wasn't it?" She asked defensively. "I mean, what do you say, Varina?"

Varina stopped mopping, leaned the mop against the wall, and sat down. She looked evenly and calmly at Mary. "It was not murder," she said firmly. "Jefferson challenged him to a duel."

Mary was agitated. "But that heathen chose knives."

"If Jefferson had not challenged him to a duel," she said, "he would be alive today. And if General Forrest had chosen swords, Jefferson would have carved him up just as bad."

"But Varina," Mary said, "You know Forrest was sent down to kill him if he did not resign."

Varian sighed. "No, I do not know that, and neither do you," she said. "I do not believe that General Lee or General Hampton had any part in this."

With that, they all feel silent. Catherine was trying to think her way through this crazy turn of events and not having much success.

After making a quick trip home to see to things Catherine was returning to Mary's when a horse pulled along side. Catherine looked up into the smiling face of Nathan Bedford Forrest. "Well, I reckon I will be sayin' my goodbyes, Miss Kitty," he said. "I am off for Mississippi and home. I will always remember you and I would take it well if you would think a kindly thought of me now and again."

Catherine did not answer. She stared hard and cold into his face and saw the confusion and the hurt. Then he spurred his horse and moved to the tracks and headed south. Catherine felt an acute pain inside. She wanted to go to him the tell him she was sorry and to say a warm goodbye, but she could not, given what she had seen at the Appomattox and after he had cut up her friend and president with a knife. As she neared Mary's house, she waited for that welcomed and telltale indication of some easing but none came.

She entered the house quietly, went in to the fireplace in the sitting room, and plopped down in the stuffed chair. Soon Varina came in and sat down opposite her. "Catherine, are you all right?" she asked. You look terrible, what has happened?"

"Oh, I don't know, Varina,' she said, "I think it is this war and the uncertainly just now."

Varina was not taken in. "What did you just see out there," She asked suspiciously, "or who?"

Catherine was not sure she wanted to talk to Varina about this. "Oh, Varina, I…"

Varina's eyes lit up. "It was Forrest, wasn't it?"

Catherine thought about lying but decided that there had been too much already. "Yes, it was Forrest," she said. "He rode up and said goodbye to me and I…and I slighted him."

Varina was concerned. "Oh no, Catherine you should not have done that on my account," she said, "He is your friend."

Catherine sighed. "It isn't just that," she said. "I cannot forget what I saw from Maynard's Mountain."

"But Catherine," she said, "he had helped you and saved your property and maybe saved your freedom and your life. You love him very much."

"Oh no, Varina," Catherine protested, "I don't love General Forrest."

"Well, 'care for him very much,' or whatever you chose to call it."

Catherine sighed wearily. "Varina, he was shooting unarmed boys who were trying to surrender. I was sick inside. The man is a cold blooded killer."

Varina nodded her head. "Yes, he is," she said, nodding her head wisely. "He is a Plantation owner, a patriotic and loyal southerner, a good friend, a great warrior, a man with his own moral code, and a cold blooded killer."

"Yes, but…well, then…"

"They are all cold blooded killers, Catherine," she said distantly, "don't you see that?"

"Catherine sat up in her chair, turned in it, and stared hard at Varina. "You mean my husband and General Lee?" she asked. "No, I guess I don't see that; not at all." Catherine felt tears of anger, hurt and emotional exhaustion about to spill over. "And I really don't care for…"

"Catherine, do you remember what you said about being sick inside at seeing unarmed boys who were not trying to make war mercilessly slaughtered?"

Catherine calmed down and settle back in the chair. "Yes, yes, I remember that all too well," she said.

"I felt like that once."

"Well, in a way," Catherine said, "I am sure that, during this war, every woman has…"

Varina was looking past her, and did not seem to hear her. "Do you know when?" she asked.

"When? Well, no, of course I do not." She knew she was supposed to ask. "When was it?" she asked cautiously.

"It was the night that Jefferson ordered those hungry, helpless boys at Sumter fired upon."

Catherine was not impressed. "Oh, but Varina…"

"They were no threat to us, Catherine," Varina went on. "Sumter could have sat out there till it rotted, turned to dust on the water, and floated off with the tide and it would never have been a threat to us."

"But Varina," Catherine said, trying to stop her, "it was war, and you above all people know…"

Varina shook her head slowly. "There was no war then, Catherine," she said, "and no one was threatening to start one against us. My husband ordered the killing of unarmed and hungry boys and used that pitiful old fort as an excuse."

"But…"

"General Forrest had an excuse," she said. "If he had not done what he did, the war would have been lost and we would all be occupied by the North."

Catherine was beginning to feel cornered. "Well, but…but what about your husband?" she asked.

"My husband, bless his hot headed little heart, challenged Forrest to a duel. It could only have been an uneven fight, Catherine," she said, "but Jefferson did not think so. From his brawls on the floor of the Senate to the days leading up to the war, Jefferson thought he was the equal of any man who ever lived." Catherine was silent. "But my husband did break the law when he fired on Sumter," Varina said.

"But we were no longer…"

Varina cut her off. "So we said," she replied firmly, "but the Congress and President Lincoln did not agree. Against the nation that all of our fathers fought to help found and to which we swore loyalty, we were lawbreakers. My husband ordered the killing of defenseless men. It was not to protect ourselves from invasion and he did it against the law."

Catherine was confused and worn. "Well," she said, "I didn't know you hated your husband…"

Varina ignored her. Catherine could see that she was driving hard for a point. "And you and I, Miss Catherine," she said, "we are cold blooded killers too."

This was more than Catherine could take. "Oh, Varina," she said indignantly, "I beg your pardon! I…"

"Is that so? What were you doing up on the mountain prepared to leave your babies where they did to want to be and stay two days? Wasn't it to see Grant crushed?" she asked. "Didn't you hope Forrest would be successful in his plan?"

Catherine's head was churning inside. If this was Varina's revenge, it was certainly effective. "Well, Varina, I just have to say…"

Varina ignored her and went on. "Catherine, my husband went through hell the night before Sumter," she said. "He asked me a hundred times, what I thought."

"But you tried Varina," Catherine said, "which proves that you are not…"

"I never said a word, Catherine," Varina said emotionally, her eyes glistening now, "not one word! And do you know why? Because all I would have had to do was tell him not to do it and he wouldn't have. I never said a word because I was afraid he would not do it. I was afraid that, if I argued with him, he would take the opposite side and take himself out of it. That was the condition he was in. I could have helped him and should have helped him but I knew if I kept quiet, he would order it done. I wanted that fort fired and war started with the North upon so badly I was obsessed with it." Catherine was finally stunned to silence. She had not expected this. She felt she was close to tears again. Finally, Varina asked quietly, "What about you, Catherine? Were you afraid the war would not start?"

Catherine remembered her conversation with Colonel Wolf and her feelings the day as she stood at the railroad and shivered from the inner and outer chill wind. "Yes," she said sadly, "I was."

"And so you see, my dear," Varina said with the sharpness of a knife, "we women are just as cold blooded as our men—only in different ways. If we women of the South had banned together in the human compassion we claim to have, we could easily have stopped this war from starting. You know it and so do I. But we wanted war, and in our cute, sweet, and nice little ways, we made sure that their masculine pride would not let them back out. That's cold, Catherine; real cold!"

Catherine blew her nose and rubbed her eyes. "Oh, yes, I see your point," she said. "Now I hate myself for letting Nathan go like that."

Varina moved out to the edge of her seat. "Catherine," she said, just above a whisper, "he only has a little over an hour start and you are known to be one of the best military riders of any woman in the South. Go after him. You can catch him and get back before dark."

Catherine's look of shock turned to one of doubt. "Do you really think I should do that?" she asked.

Varina leaned back, locked her fingers in front of one of her knees, and stared at the ceiling. "I think, Catherine," she said whimsically, "that one day of swallowing your pride and inconveniencing yourself is far better than a life time of regret."

Chapter Forty

Vengeance is Mine, Saith...

Nathan Bedford Forrest left Oxley Manor, rode to the meadow outside Richmond and started down the Danville & Richmond line. At Danville he would take the Southside Railroad to Lynchburg. There he would follow the Orange & Alexandria on south. But as he rode along something was nagging at him that would not go away, even after several hours of riding and leaving Richmond well behind, so he stopped and looked back for a while.

He could not get Catherine off his mind or shake the hurt that the felt. He had never known a woman like her and never had a relationship with anyone like theirs. He was troubled in his mind about her and it aggravated him. He should not have been. He must be getting soft in his old age, letting a skirt like that get next to him.

But there was something else; something that he could not put his finger on. He was not comfortable out in the open. Surely no one was after him, particularly not so soon, but he moved off the railroad and into the woods. There was a small opening into a grove of trees so thickly overhung with mossy branches that it was almost dark. He was secluded in that natural arbor and he liked the cozy feeling. Forrest got off his horse, found a mossy rock, and sat down to think. What was it that was making him restless? Finally, he hit on a thought that seemed to scratch where he itched. He wanted to stay and see that Davis had a decent burial. He knew that that would happen, but still, it seemed like his Christian duty. He did not mind killing Davis—in fact, it gave him more than a little satisfaction. There probably never would have been this long and bloody war if it had not been for that hot-head. And Forrest was sure that the South would fare better with him out of the way.

Anyway, it was Davis who had slapped him and asked for the duel. True, Forrest had made up his mind he would have to kill Davis if he refused to resign, but that did not alter the fact that Davis had asked for it. Forrest felt at ease. No one could blame him for Davis' death. In the South, if a gentleman issued a challenge and was killed, no one dared to pity him or to despise the victor. It was against the code of the South. If Forrest had challenged him, it might have been different, but he hadn't, and there had been a witness.

Nathan breathed deeply and felt strangely good. For one of the few times in his life, he was on the right side of the law, he had no one after him—lawmen, enemy soldiers, Indians, competitors, or vengeful African tribe—and he was praised these days, if not liked.

He wondered about Booth. He was such an unstable soul, but he seemed to have courage and determination. Did he accomplish his mission, or did he take the money and run? It had been two days and Forrest had heard nothing. Perhaps it was a little early, but Nathan would know soon enough, and the South was not big enough for them both, if he had let Forrest down.

Suddenly the amber light of danger flashed in Forrest's head and caused him to break out in a sweat. What was it? He did not wear a pistol for a side arm like most officers, but carried his beloved knife, which he immediately drew. Then he saw him, standing deep in the shadows. Forrest had to look long enough for his eyes to adjust to the darkness of the spot before he could recognize the man. He had a pistol drawn and pointed more or less in Forrest's direction. Had he just come in with his pistol drawn to see who was there—or was it something else?

"Gen'l, I'm surprised to see ya."

"I'll bet you are, General Forrest."

"And what would be doin' here, Suh?" There was no answer. "Why would you be carin' that I killed that wuthless Davis, Gen'l?"

"I don't—not at all."

"Then what's this all about?"

"Wednesday, General. At the Appomattox," the general said ominously.

"Now, see here, Gen'l, war is war," Forrest said earnestly. "I know you are outraged at me for not takin' prisoners. Some folk have a different out look on it, but in the heat of the battle, killin' is what it is all about."

"Killing, General, but not slaughter. Not shooting unarmed boys who are flying flags of surrender. No military code can stand that, General. A civilized world cannot exist with men like you in its armies."

"I have been a good soldier, Gen'l," Forrest said, trying not to sound pitiful, "and I have done my best in this war for the cause of my country. No man can fault another for that."

"Yes, an effective warrior, no doubt," the intruder replied, "but you have also been a butcher, a sadistic man, and one who has shown no mercy."

"But the cause justifies it," Forrest replied, his anger rising a little. "If it were not for men like me, the causes of nations would be lost. It's wrong, out of bitterness, to reward a faithful warrior who was only obeyin' his orders and doing' his duty, with such treatment. The Bible..."

"Let me tell you a story from the Bible, General," his adversary broke in, "since you are so keen on using it to make your case. King David had an effective and faithful general named Joab. He protected David, gave him wise advice that saved the nation, and was the most feared warrior in David's armies, just like you, General Forrest. But Joab was also a bloody and sadistic man. He killed those whom David personally liked and to whom David had obligations and commitments. He scoffed at David, if David did not like it. He thought he had the Indian sign on David, and maybe he did. And he took the law into his own hands. He thought he did not need to take orders or to be governed by the rules of his country and his army. On one occasion, he stayed in Ammon until he had killed every male over the age of twelve in the entire country.

"But when it was all over," the General continued, "and David handed the reigns to Solomon, do you know what the first thing he told Solomon was? He said, 'you kill that bloody, headstrong, sadistic, self-made rebel, Joab. My time has come, and with me, the time of Joab.' David was a man of war and he had to go before the temple could be built and peace could be brought. Joab, who was like him and useful to the old regime, had to go with him.

"I do not argue with you, General Forrest," he said, "if you felt that Davis needed to go for the good of the future of the South. It's cold blooded, but you may have been right there. But if it is right and expedient in the movement and flow of history that Davis go, it is right that you go with him. If Davis was in the way, so are you."

"But Gen'l, I know that story about Joab, and there are differences..."

"It is the similarity that I am interested in, General Forrest," he said coldly.

"It ain't a fair fight, Gen'l; I'm unarmed," Forrest said, trying hard not to plead.

"Executions are never fair fights, General Forrest," the intruder answered. "They are not meant to be."

Nathan Bedford Forrest had killed to keep from being killed in the jungles of Africa, the pirate's dens of Ivory Coast, Gold Coast and Madagascar, on board ship where men had tried to mutiny, among the Indians of the West, and over nearly every inch of the South in the past four years. Nothing was going to deter his stalker from what he had come for. He saw the situation clearly. It was one in which he was at a serious disadvantage, but he was not going to go down without a fight. He sensed what he thought was the slightest relaxation in the man who had come to kill him. Like an uncoiling cotton mouth, he bent at the waist and flung the knife. In unison, the pistol flamed and Forrest could feel the ball tearing though his guts. He staggered for a brief moment and then went to his knees. "Into thy hands, Oh Lord, do I commend my soul," he said hoarsely, his lunges already beginning to fill. Forrest had the sense of waters starting to flow over him—cold, dark, surging billows. A pathetic, hopeless moaning, like slaves in the bowls of a ship, swelled in his ears and sent a chill into his soul. He was going down this time. His luck had run out and his number had come up. He wondered if God had heard him, if goodness was really not required; if grace was really unbounded, free, and all-sufficient; and what he would find on the other side. The light flickered, the darkness followed, and then…

. . . . .

Catherine pulled the horse from a lope to a walk. She looked up at the sun and it was past the mid point. She had been on the trail for about three hours. She had not brought gear to stay over night and she had decided she would not do so. If she did not catch him and an hour, she would turn around and console herself with the knowledge that she had given it a good try. She thought surely he would stop and rest for lunch. As she rounded a wide turn, about two miles from Jetersville, she saw the big wild looking horse with the ring eye standing near some trees with its rump to the track. Elation gripped Catherine's insides. How much she wanted to find him and make it right, only she could know. As she came up and started to dismount, the big horse turned, his ears laid back and his teeth showing. She stayed in the saddle as she called to Forrest. "Nathan! General Forrest, it's me, Catherine…Miss Kitty!"

After a time, she talked to the horse and he seemed to calm down. His ears stood back up and he looked away from her toward the trees. Did he hear something? Catherine dismounted and walked cautiously toward the trees. The horse did not come at her. She entered the grove and looked around. The light was poor and she had to accustom to the dark. She walked around bit and then stopped in shock and fear. There, near the far edge of the small clearing, was a fresh raised mound of earth with a crude little cross, made from two pieces of tree limb, suck in it. Something was on the cross. She walked cautiously over. A little wild flower that had been stuck in the earth near the foot of the cross was beginning to wilt. It had been more than an hour. Who ever made the grave was long gone so her fears began to abate. On the cross was Forrest's old hat, his belt with the knife, and a note. She picked it up and read:

For your brilliance and courage, we were in awe of you.
For your shrewdness as a soldier we feared you.
For the great things you did we admire you.
For the good things you did we thank you.
For the bad you did we fault you.
For the crimes you committed we judge you.
For all lesser things the Lord judge you
    As it is written, "Vengeance it mine…
    they bear not the sword in vain."
    General G.

Catherine covered the grave with a blanket of wild flowers. Then she sat on the ground, lay across it, and wept. In an hour, her tears were dry and she knew she must head back. "Goodbye, Nathan," she said, "I don't know if you can hear me, but if so, thanks for everything. In some ways, I don't think I ever had a better friend in the male world. You stuck your neck out for me when even my friend Colonel Wolf would not do it. I cannot begin to tell you how much I will miss you. I guess, if I get in trouble, I will always be expecting that big ring eyed horse to be standing around the next turn and those very unusual eyes, that I have come to love, staring at me on top of a crooked, twisted, and leering but wonderful smile."

On the way back guilt and remorse tried to push in on her but she fought it off. If he was in heaven, he knew. If not, it would never matter to him anyway. As for her, she knew she had cared and had made the effort. Everything always worked out for the best to God-fearing people, the Bible said. If she had not ignored him in town, she would never have come down here and found him and no one would have known of his fate. Now she could come back each year and put wild flowers on his grave. He probably understood anyway that she was a frightened and confused little girl who had to take a time to sort it all out.

She thought about having the men of the town bring him back for a decent burial but decided against it. The death of President Davis made it too risky. Beside, Forrest would want it this way and so did she.

What a strange life. The man she started out hating and fearing, she ended up loving in a way and adopting as part of her security. Mortality left much to be desired in so many ways. She would never see him again in this life. But she had to stop thinking about it for a while. This life must go on.

Chapter Forty-One

The Mysterious General G

Catherine frowned as she sat in a chair in the White house across the desk from Robert E. Lee and studied him. How haggard he looked and his uniform was almost disgraceful. She knew he had been up for several days without sleep and on the go constantly. Still, it was not the elegant and always impeccably dressed and manicured man she had always known and it bothered her. Then she felt a pang of conscience. She must not start picking at him now just because…just because…Catherine shifted her weight in the chair in a familiar mannerism to help her redirect her thoughts. She looked around the room and tried to envision President Lee instead of President Davis as its resident. He spared her that agony of further thought.

"General G. Hum, that is interesting," he said.

Catherine was impressed with his self-possession. How stunned he had been only a moment ago when she told him about Forrest and skeptical almost of the story about General G. Now a controlled Lee quietly analyzed the situation. She noticed him watching her and she realized she had not answered.

"Yes, General G," she said. "What does it mean to you, Robert? Do you know who it is? I suppose, if the designation is honest, there is probably only one general it would fit?" Lee did not answer immediately. "You are thinking of generals whose names begin with G," she guessed.

"I am thinking of General Gs who could be responsible" he replied.

"But how many could there be?" she asked.

Lee spread his fingers and counted as he spoke. "General *G*rant, General *G*eorge Meade, and General Wade G. Hampton."

Catherine was confused. "Could you explain three-man thing to me?" she asked.

Lee nodded positively. "Yes, I think I can," he said. "Hampton was not as furious as I over what Forrest did last Wednesday, but he was probably more impressed with his duty."

Catherine squirmed and squinted her eyes as she usually did when trying to grasp something. "His duty?" she asked. "I am not sure I…"

She terminated her question when she saw the gentle wave of his hand. Lee began to speak. "You see, there will be a military government in the South for two years," he said. "I am heading it up and Hampton is my…my…my second in command; sort of like a vice president." She started to pursue that but he stopped her. "I will get to that in a moment," he said. "Anyway, Hampton is a true British Aristocrat."

"What do you mean by that, Robert?" she asked.

"Well, the British are less sentimental and much more practical," he said. "We will need trade with England and France," Lee continued. "We will also be faced with putting forth a sophisticated image to prove to the world we are a viable nation. If Forrest is our war hero, we are in trouble with all that. It is much more desirable, given those objectives, to peg Forrest as a war criminal and eliminate him. That is easy to do with the ammunition that Forrest gives you."

Catherine was appalled. "But Robert, that is cold!"

Lee nodded. "Very cold, my dear; too cold for me, but not for Hampton," he said. "To him, Forrest was a remarkable man, an inspiration and a military genius. But he was also a slave trader, a cruel man, a lawbreaker, a mutineer, a despiser of authority, and a violator of war treaties and codes. Each of those is a serious offense and several of them are capital. In England and France he would be tried for war crimes for what he did to Meade's men and either be hanged or shot."

Catherine tried to be objective so she would not become emotional. "So, it would be very like General Hampton to pat him on the back with one hand," she said, "and stab him with the other and feel justified in both."

Lee nodded to her point. "Exactly, Catherine," he replied. "He could easily have left that note."

Catherine was puzzled. "But if that were the case, why the duel?" she asked.

Lee shook his head negatively. "This was not a duel, Catherine, it was an execution. The note makes that clear, it seems to me. Not even Hampton has enough courage to challenge Forrest to a duel and let him choose the weapons."

Catherine wondered if she should ask, but decided to since she wanted his opinion. "So Davis has…had more courage than Hampton?"

Lee proceeded with caution to her question. "I didn't say that…I don't think…I didn't intend to anyway. There is no doubting Davis' courage. But he was a hothead and a person who had to have his way. These combined to drive him to foolishness at times. Challenging Forrest was not so much an act of courage as the as the angry reaction of a fool."

Catherine wanted to mull that over but decided to wait. "So then, back to Hampton," she said, "did he have the opportunity? Surely he was far away."

"No, actually, Hampton was in Richmond on Tuesday, "he said.

Catherine was surprised. "Are you sure?" she asked. "No one saw him."

"I am absolutely positive," he exclaimed. "Davis was dead when he got here but he talked to Bragg. I met briefly with Hampton this morning and have it from his own mouth."

Catherine was silent for a while. "So then that is the answer, isn't it?" she asked.

Lee sighed. "No, not necessarily, as I told you…"

It was she who cut him off now. "So what about George Meade," she asked. "Why would he do that and did he have the chance?"

Lee nodded. "Yes to both," he said. "On the battlefield, Meade told Forrest that he would not rest as long as Forest was alive. Meade may not be much in some ways but I served with him. He may be timid in the putting forth of armies but on the personal level I know him to be a brave and dogged man. And I had the feeling he meant what he told Forrest."

"But when…"

"When I saw Grant on Monday, I was thinking about Meade," he said. "It was not right what happened out there. Anyway, I asked Grant where Meade was. He said that Meade had asked for three days off, starting Sunday, to take care of some personal business."

Catherine thought for a minute. "All right," she said, "but Grant I can't understand at all. Why would he have wanted to do it, and how could he have? Surely there was no time."

Lee looked at her in silence for a moment. Finally he spoke more philosophically than with the others. "Grant may have had the greatest incentive of all," he said. "Here was a great general who only lost one battle—Cold Harbor—in all the war. He had taken over the flagging Army of the Potomac and fashioned it into a great war machine that drove us to tree. The outcome the war had ceased to be in doubt. In all his years in this war, there was only one man he feared and only one he could not best. One man constantly destroyed his supply lines, outsmarted his lieutenants, and eluded the capture and destruction of the best efforts of Grant and Sherman. There was also only one he hated. That was Nathan Bedford Forrest.

"Forrest was his thorn in the side. Now Forrest tricks him into falling for a game that lost the war for the North. Grant is a military man. He can accept losing wars, particularly this one where it is more of a stalemate than a loss, where he never had Lincoln's idealism and it does not change the Union much. The South has been separate nation, except for technicality, for years. But in order for Grant to live with himself, he has to exorcise his personal demon."

Catherine was philosophical too, now. "And that demon was Forrest."

Lee nodded in agreement. "And, by this third scenario anyway, that demon was Forrest."

Catherine sighed. "All right, I can see that," she said. "It makes sense. But what about the time."

Lee nodded and she took it to mean he understood her doubts. "When I met Grant on Sunday, in no-man's land between the river and Washington, he looked like he had been in his uniform for a week."

"They say he always looks like that," she replied.

"Yes, I know, but this was different," Lee answered. "It was dusty and there was straw in his shirt. I can tell when a man has been on a hard ride and Grant, wherever he was, had been ridding all night. He lied to me and said he had been up in his study trying to plan his course. But he did not know Lincoln had died of his wounds. That means he went somewhere Sunday night after Lincoln was shot and did not come back until Tuesday."

Catherine was amazed at the possibilities. "So, which one did it, do you think?" she asked.

Lee shook his head. "I don't know; maybe none of them," he said. "Maybe the letter G is just to throw people off. But it was probably one of them who felt it would be a sin if he tried to hide it but is not anxious to have anyone figure it out. Each had the courage and the ability to do it. It isn't just anybody that would go after Forrest one-on-one in a grove of trees along a railroad track. A man would have to be mightily motivated—driven, almost"

"Are you going to try to find out? She asked.

"No, I am not," he replied. "It is best left as it is. Forrest is a war hero, but he also killed the man who will now also be a war hero since he is dead. Not too many people know about the gold and those who do will keep it quiet. It would be political suicide to bring it out now. No one knows who killed their war hero, the celebrated Nathan Bedford Forrest, but they do know he killed Davis. It is poetic justice. I cannot improve on that." Lee paused, but Catherine was lost in thought and did not answer.

"And now I think it is time to leave the mysterious Forrest and the dark deeds in the spectral wood," Lee continued. "I have many other matters to go over with you and I do not know when I will see you again. But I cannot do it at this moment. I have a few things to get done. Can you come back after the noon meal?"

She said that she could and left immediately so he could get to whatever it was he had to do.

Chapter Forty-Two

The Old Order Changeth

Catherine was back in the armed chair before Lee's desk promptly at 1:00 P.M. The General came in and sat down. "I forgot to ask you earlier," he said. "You heard about Linc…President Lincoln being assassinated?"

Catherine was grim. "Yes," she said, "Who did that, or do you know?"

Lee waved his hand in the air philosophically. "One of Forrest's men—or at least, that's my guess. No one knows for sure. How do you feel about that, Catherine—Lincoln's death, I mean?"

Catherine thought for a moment. Then she replied enigmatically, "I don't know how I feel, General. I find it hard to be joyful. I guess that is not very satisfactory, is it?"

Lee looked up and wrinkled his brow. "I am not sure how to answer," he said. "I guess it is a bit how I feel, too. He was once my Commander and Chief," he added wistfully. "Anyway, it makes it a bit better for me. Grant will be easier for me to deal with."

"Grant surrendered, then?" Catherine asked.

"Yes," Lee replied. "We got there with the whole army in two days. Grant did not have time to regroup and bring people in. He was counting on Sherman and when he found out that story, he had little time to look elsewhere. If we had been one day later, it would have been…when Grant found out that all we wanted was to be let go and that if he did not agree, we would destroy Washington, he signed the papers. He and I had a long talk and I think it helped him to know we do not want to remain enemies."

"Could they have fought on if they had chosen to?" she asked.

"It is hard to say," he replied. "The Union still has four or five hundred thousand men in uniform and armed for battle, but they are scattered from California to Texas. We would have rations, supplies, armaments, and raw materials captured in the Washington area. It is a bit complex, but I think both sides have always felt that if either Washington or Richmond fell, the War would be over, and that is how it worked out."

Catherine could see that she did not have much time. "Did I…did I hear you say there is to be a two-year military government?"

"Yes, I did," he replied. "As the commanding general, I can make that decision after a victory if I think it is necessary for the establishment of stability and order."

"So, it was your idea, then?" she asked.

"No, it was Forrest's," he said.

"And Davis would not have gone along with it."

Lee shook his head no. "Not on your life," he said.

Catherine was getting tense. "Robert, please don't tell me…"

"No, Catherine," he said with emphasis. "No, no, no! I had nothing whatever to do with it. Forrest said he would go to Richmond and force Davis to accept the new regime."

Catherine knew they could run out to time to talk. She had heard enough about Forrest and Davis and she wanted to know all she could about what was ahead. "So tell me about this military interim government," she asked. What is it all about and what is it for?"

Lee sighed as if trying to think how to get into it. Then he answered, "We have to make changes in the South, Catherine, if we are to survive by ourselves. We have to have trade with England and France, and we have to rely on industrial production from the Union," he said. "This is just a stop-gap measure if we try to go it alone."

Catherine saw this as an enormous problem with no obvious starting point. "But how will you do this?" she asked. "Where is the place to begin?"

"One of the ways it has to happen is for us to accept emancipation," he answered.

"Oh, Robert," she said, catching her breath, "that will never…"

"Just wait, now," he replied defensively, "I did not say abolition; I said emancipation."

This was the very thing she feared from her talks with Mary Chesnut. "Oh, but Robert, the South is not ready for something like this," she said emotionally.

She watched him shake his head slowly but deliberately. "I think they are," he said. "Let me lay this out and then we can argue about it if you want. Now that the Emancipation Proclamation has been put out there, the South will have to go along with it or there will never be anything but fighting. The North will never be at peace with the South if we resist the idea of freedom for the Negras."

Catherine could not stay out of it. "But Robert, this is what the war was all about!" she said, the pitch of her voice rising.

Lee set his jaw firmly. "I don't agree with that, Catherine," he said, "and I don't think you've looked at the whole picture. Slavery was not the issue that started the war. It was not why you wanted war. It was the North trying to push the South around and make rules for us that did not fit our way of life."

"But it was over policy about slavery in the free territories, wasn't it?" she asked.

Lee, she saw, meant to be dogged. "Yes, but that is still the issue of self-determination and not slavery," he said. "Human enslavement is another matter and it has been of concern to the South as well as the North. Most every southern Christian and plantation owner has had feelings about, and talked about owning slaves. We all felt that there was something about it that was less than what the Good Lord had in mind when He made us."

Catherine was edgy. "But, Robert," she said, "forced integration will not…"

Catherine stopped in mid sentence. She could see that Lee was getting impatient with her negativism, but she thought now was the time to have her say.

Lee took the occasion of her pause to go on. "I am not talking about forced integration, Catherine," he said, "I am talking about emancipation."

"But Robert," she hung on doggedly, "the South would have to want to. Will the South accept emancipation?"

"Yes, I believe so—the way we will explain it and go about it," he answered.

"Why will they accept it?" she asked him.

"Because they will be doing it voluntarily and under their own laws and direction," he said. "It will appeal to their conscience, their sense of Christian growth, and their basic like for the Negro."

"In the South, Negroes are family and they are friends like your little girl, Tuttle. The Southerner looks to his darkies for advice, for wisdom in practical matters, and he trusts the Negro with his fields and his stock. We leave our children at home alone with them for extended periods of time, and the Southerner believes that the Negro has a basic wisdom about raising children that many aristocratic whites do not have. You leave that young man of yours in charge of your whole estate while you are gone; is that not true?"

Catherine brushed aside his point about Emmanuel because she felt it was not representative. "But General Lee," she said with dramatic emphasis, "the white, southern plantation owner feels superior to the Negro. Surely you cannot deny that!"

Lee nodded in agreement. "That he does," he said, "but feeling superior to someone is not the same as disliking them, and not feeling superior to someone is not the same as liking them. Like and affection, not social caste, must be the visceral force that drives our program of emancipation."

Catherine was prompted to comment again. "So, that makes it sound like superiority is justified in your eyes," she said.

"No, I am not saying it is morally defensible, Catherine," he replied. "I have come to regard it as inferior. And I am convinced the South will change in time, if they are not pushed too hard, and if their better angels are appealed to. But they will have to understand all those things, and they do not now."

Catherine was silent for a long time. Then she said in an even and serious tone. "Though you may not think it from my words just now,

I want this to happen, Robert. I have often felt, in the past several years, that slavery was wrong. I gave my slaves their freedom. But I did not kick them out in the road with no home, no food and no one to look after them."

She could see that she had struck a cord with him. "Of course, Catherine," he said with a forced smile, "that is what I have been saying. We will not do it like Lincoln would have."

She sighed in frustration. "Then tell me how it is going to work, Robert," she pleaded, "because I have thought until my head ached and I cannot see my way through it."

"We do it our own way," he said. "If a slave is faithful and hard working for five years, we give him ownership to his shack. In another five years, maybe we give him an acre of his own and give him time to work it. We can buy what he grows on it, to give him some feeling of getting somewhere. We can tailor the change to suit ourselves and fit our needs. We are not ruled over anymore by the Northern political ideologue who cares neither for the southerner nor the slave."

Catherine could not get inspired. "In the program you outline," she said, "we have not freed the slaves at all. We have just made some token gestures."

"That's where you and I do disagree, I think Catherine," he said. "These are not just words at all. We have officially accepted emancipation. But there is no government in Washington to tell us how to implement it. Surely you must know how many terrified Negras there are in the South right now, wondering what is going to happen to them—where are they going to live? How are they going to feed their families? Without this thing being shoved down our throats, Southerners will take an interest—maybe even pride—in this. They care about their people; at least most of them do. And they will try to help them. But they will do it in such a way that it will give the South time to change its ways and not hurt the Aristocracy or the Negra. Some progress is better than none."

Catherine thought hard. It did make some sense and it was similar to some of the things she had thought before but never thought could be made to work. Maybe that was it? She was afraid of failure. But with Robert E. Lee, the most respected man in the South and one who had a real conviction about what he was going to try to do, it would work. As he had said, it had to work if the South was to survive long. "Well," she said with resignation, "I guess you have won me over to the proposition that we should give it a try, but who is going to put this to the Southerner so that he will understand and want to go along?"

She thought Lee looked as if a great burden had been lifted from him. "That is the reason for the two-year military regime. We are going to get organized, restore order, get horses back on farms, get hungry people food, and get the South functioning again. In the meanwhile, we will have a program to get this information out."

"Will you do it?" she asked.

Lee shook his head negatively. "Not me, Catherine," he said. "I am not a preacher."

"Who, then?" she asked.

"Hampton, I think," he answered, "is the one to do it. He is very eloquent and he has credibility since he is the largest slave owner in the South. Maybe some others will help him."

"Two years," she said, "and then there are to be free elections?"

"Yes, that is the time table," he said.

"Will you run for president?" she asked.

"No." He was emphatic.

"Why not?" she asked. "I thought you would like that."

"Ethics would prevent it," he said. "As a military governor, it would be like putting myself in office. Besides, I hope to have something better to be doing two years from now than being dragged along in this rat race."

Catherine blushed. "Maybe I would like to be a first lady," she said.

Lee wagged his head as if in bewilderment. "You have watched the lives of Varina Davis and Mary Lincoln with some closeness and you could say that with a straight face?"

"Yes," Catherine replied, "but my man would not be like their husbands."

Lee smiled a coy little smile. "No, that is true," he said with a bit of humor. "I would not have Lincoln's great mental powers or idealism and I would not have Davis' fire and ambition. Unless a war started, I would be about the most ordinary man you could know."

It was Catherine's turn to laugh. "Well, I do not want to be the wife of a president," she said, "I was only being…I was only being…silly," she said, which seemed to please him. "So, this is to be your White House or fortress or whatever you will call it?" she asked.

Lee was quick to respond. "No, I am going to make Arlington my headquarters," he said. "I want to be as close to Grant as I can. This is going to be very critical in making this partnership work. Crises must be defused in days and weeks; not months and years."

"So, I will not see you then?" she asked.

Lee did not smile. "You are welcome at Arlington any time you wish to come," he said. "We are adequately facilitated to have you."

"Will you come to Hopemont?" she asked.

Lee was firm in his reply. "Not for one year," he said. "I gave you my promise and I will keep it. It will give us both time to sort everything out. I will not have time to treat you right this first year anyway. I am going to be busier than when I was as Commanding General of the Army of Northern Virginia."

"Well, but you still are, aren't you?" she asked.

"In theory, yes," he replied, "but there is little for a commanding general to do except as I described a few moments ago and those are not military matters; at least I hope they will not be. We have men like D. H. Hill, Heth, Gordon, Bragg, Hood and so on, who will do nicely."

"And Longstreet?" she asked.

Lee sighed deeply and cocked his head. "I don't know about Jimmy; I don't know if he wants to serve under me anymore," he said with a hint of sadness in his voice. "He has never gotten over Gettysburg, I'm afraid."

They fell to silence. Catherine did not know what to say and was determined not to say the wrong thing. Finally, Lee spoke up. "Will you stay here with Mary and Varina?" he asked.

Catherine had never really considered it, but she had thought she might spend a good bit of time there when she could get away. "No, not if you are not going to have your headquarters here," she said. "I thought I might help out as before, but Arlington seems awkward and you are right. I must continue my mourning and we need this year apart to get our lives back together. I would like to go home by way of Arlington, meet General Grant and see your childhood home," she said, "but if I do that, I may get entangled and not want to go back to Hopemont. That would derail the plan we agreed on and I think we both know is best. I will return to Hopemont and spend the next year getting things ready for the future."

She stood up and he stood with her. "If I make my proposal as planned and you decide to accept it, where will you want to live?" he asked.

Catherine looked deep into his eyes for an answer from the soul. She was very undecided about abandoning Hopemont. "I suppose you will not want to leave your roots," she said.

"When you first said that, I was not going to reply," he said, "but now I think I must…I shall. Arlington is not my home. It was my wife's home. I have never felt at home there, to be candid. I am only going there now because it is close to Washington. My childhood home was in Alexandria but…but my father piddled it away."

Their eyes were still locked in a deep intercourse and Catherine felt her affections rising. "Why don't we wait until then to make that decision?" she said. "I know the options now, and I think you do too. It needs thought and I am too emotionally frazzled to think about it now."

"Good idea," he said and started walking her to the door. As he opened it for her, he offered her his hand. She took it and held it warmly. "Dear Catherine," he said with emotion and she thought the tears were not very deep, "thank you so much—so very, very much for the spiritual, secretarial, soldierly, intellectual and patriotic support. I am serious when I tell you that there were times when I am not sure I would have made it without you."

She started to scold him for flattery but decided not to. It was not flattery in one sense; he meant every word—and she liked it. "You are more than welcome, General Lee, and thank you for the friendship, the fatherly advice, the moral support, and for winning the war for me." She felt the tears on her cheeks but she did not care. She wanted to hug him, but she decided it would not be proper. Besides, he looked so ratty and he did not smell particularly good either. It could wait. She wanted to make her decision with the image before her that she saw coming up her walk that day—which seemed like a year ago but was, in reality, little more than a week. The cab was waiting for her but she declined. It was a great day for walking in the free and bustling streets of Richmond.

Chapter Forty-Three

Glory in the Dust

Just after daylight, the train pulled into Lexington Station. Catherine slept most of the way from Richmond. As the train eased to a stop, she rubbed the sleep from her eyes, sat up in the seat, and tried to straighten up her tan, loose fitting, traveling dress. The porter came by with a damp cloth, a towel, and a big smile on his face. Catherine did not thank him—it was not the custom—but she gave him a pleasant look. She bathed her face and handed it back to him. Catherine had not been home since the ordeal with Captain Skinner and she worried that Emmanuel would not be waiting for her as she had instructed in her letter; but he was.

She had not seen such a happy face and radiant smile in months. As they started down the road toward Hopemont, he said, "Miss Cath'n, you is the most beautiful sight in all the world."

Catherine smiled at him. "Why Emmanuel, I didn't know you felt that way about me," she said. "Thank you very much."

Emmanuel's countenance fell. "Aw, Ma'am, I didn't mean nothin' like dat," he said in a troubled tone.

Catherine patted him on the shoulder. "I know you didn't, Emmanuel," she said with a smile, "I know what you mean, and what you meant is what I meant too."

Emmanuel brightened up. "Thank you, Ma'am," he said.

Catherine thought he looked particularly jubilant. She knew they loved her dearly and were glad for the war to be over so she would be home for a while this time, but there seemed to be something else. "Emmanuel," she asked, trying to draw him out, "how is everything?"

Emmanuel grinned from to ear. "Everthin' jis' won'erful, Miss Cath'n; jis' won'erful," he said with a grin.

Catherine studied him for a moment. There was something else and he was trying to tell her. "Emmanuel, you are awfully happy, it seems," she said. "Is there something I should know that you haven't yet told me?"

Emmanuel's big grin turned into a radiant expression of joy. "Yes Ma'am, dey sho' is," he said with a giggle. "Tuttle g'wine to sprout, Ma'am."

When Emmanuel and Tuttle came to them eight years ago, Catherine made a conscious effort to pick up on the vernacular of the servant culture. At times, she felt she did very well, but she drew a complete blank on this. She did not have a clue what he just told her. "Tuttle is going to what?"

Emmanuel seemed almost to break down with emotion. "Tuttle g'wine to sprout, Ma'am," he said, laughing joyfully now. "She g'wine to sprout."

Catherine thought for a moment. 'What is he telling me? I hate to be so dumb.' Finally, she said, "Emmanuel, try to tell me in some other way. Use different words. What is happening with Tuttle?"

Emmanuel grew sober and looked almost frightened. "Well, Ma'am, Tuttle g'wine hab a chile'. I spec I shouldn't a said dat in front of you, should I?"

Catherine put her arm around Emmanuel's shoulder and hugged him. It must have been the strain of past days, but her laughter was mixed with tears. "Oh, Emmanuel," she said with genuine elation, "that is so wonderful. I am so proud for you…for both of you."

Emmanuel was laughing lustily now. In his exuberance, he strapped the horse into a lope. Catherine came to herself in a hurry. "Oh, Emmanuel, no," she said, trying not to ruin his moment, "don't gallop the horse. We want to live to see the baby."

Emmanuel slowed the horse to a trot. "I's sorry, Miss Cath'n," he said sheepishly, "I jis cou'n't he'p myself, it seem like." As

Catherine retrieved a handkerchief and wiped her eyes, she watched Emmanuel grow thoughtful. "Yes Sir, Ma'am," he said proudly, "I figger, now dat I'm free and employed, I got to get me a family goin' hab'nt I?"

"Yes, I guess you do," she said. "Well, be careful not to have too many too fast."

Emmanuel seemed almost insulted. "Oh, no, Miss Cath'n. I don' aim to hab no mo'e'n I kin handle. No use killin' mo'e possum'n you kin eat," he said, shaking his head emphatically. "It jis g'wine spile on ya."

Catherine laughed. "Yes," she said, "I'm sure there is a moral in that somewhere." Then she thought of a question she had long wanted to ask and the moment seemed conducive. "Emmanuel," she said, "Negro families seem to have this figured out better than white families. How do you control how many children you have?"

Emmanuel squirmed and his ears changed color. "Well, it sho ain't dat hard, Miss Cath'n," he said, very ill at ease. "It hab to do wid de moon, and all. Certain times of de moon, you jis' got to leave each udder 'lone in dat way." Emmanuel grew philosophical. "Den, sumthin' differ'nt 'bout each family too. You got to talk to the 'chantress."

Catherine was surprised. She had never heard this before. "The enchantress? Emmanuel, there are no enchantresses around here," she said.

"Oh, yes de is, Ma'am, and dat for sho'e," he said. Then his eyes grew big and his tone very confidential. "Dey don' b'long nowhere; dey stays down in de bottoms and roves about. Sometimes dey comes all de way up de ribber from Luzzyanna," he said, weaving a crooked path like the river in the air with one of his hands.

Catherine worried about this information. "But, Emmanuel," she said with mild scolding, "I thought you and Tuttle were good Christians."

Emmanuel seemed amused. "Aw, we sho'e is, Miss Cath'n," he said. "My women don' talk to no 'chantress bout nuthin' like dat. It's de things you'se askin' me 'bout dat dey knows."

Catherine understood what he was saying. "I see," she said. "In other words, it's folklore…folk medicine, you mean?"

She saw the blank look on his face as he shrugged his shoulders. "I don' know what ya calls it, Ma'am. But dat what you'se askin' and dat what I's tellin' dat we do. You got to ask de womenfolk if you want to know any mo'e. I ain't 'spose to be hoein' in dat row, no way."

At the vehicle shed, Emmanuel helped her down. "You want me to open the house, Miss Cath'n?" he asked.

"Yes, but I want to go see Tuttle first," she said. "Emmanuel, how is she doing? Does she feel alright?"

Emmanuel grew thoughtful. "Oh, yes, I think she is, Miss Cath'n," he answered wisely. "She a little peekud now and den but those Niggers say she doin' fine."

When Catherine entered the cabin, Tuttle was lying down. When she saw Catherine, she began to cry. "Oh, Lawd, Miss Cath'n. Is dat really you? I knowed sho'e 'nuf you was nebber comin' back. God bless you. God bless you."

Catherine was moved by the expression. "Oh, Tuttle," she said, "you know I wouldn't go off and leave you."

Tuttle wiped her eyes on the sleeve of her dress. "You sho 'nuf been gone a long time."

Catherine nodded. "Too long," she said. "So much has been going on. But I am home now."

Tuttle looked doubtful. "How long you g'wine stay dis time, Ma'am?" she asked.

"Oh, well, at least a year, I guess," Catherine answered.

Tuttle and Emmanuel broke out laughing. Then Tuttle grew serious. "Ma'am, if you stay a year," she said as if a great revelation just came to her, "you' be here to see my chile' born."

Catherine smiled from the depths of her heart. "That is a fact, Tuttle," she said proudly, "and I will be right down here helping, too."

Tuttle closed her eyes and began to say prayers of thanksgiving. Emmanuel turned to Catherine. "Yes, Ma'am," he said soberly, "I aim to get me a house for my family to live inside of, one day."

Catherine was cautious. She did not want to do anything to spoil the joy she was witnessing. "Oh, my, Emmanuel," she said, "that is a wonderful goal. But houses cost lots of money."

"I know, Ma'am," he said, "but I's g'wine to save my pay. Me'n Tuttle ain't spent one cent a dat money you been gibben' us."

Catherine was amazed. "You haven't?" she said.

"No, Ma'am, we ain't. I got the whole twenty dollars right here'n dis house in a jar."

Catherine was impressed. "Emmanuel, that is wonderful," she said. "You are to be commended very highly for that."

Emmanuel grew fearful. "What'd I do, Ma'am?" he said, "why de g'wine commend me?'

Catherine did not know what she said to bring this on. "What," she asked. "I don't understand?"

"Dey commenden' a darkie down here to town a while back and 'fo'e de day's out, he wuz hangin' from a tree."

Catherine realized she had confused him with words. "No, no, no, Emmanuel, that is another word," she said. "Anyway, forget the commending. It is a very good thing you have done and I am proud of you."

Emmanuel got over his fright and smiled weakly. "Yes, Sir, Ma'am," he said, "I figger I is got to save 'bout fifty dollar to get me any kind of a house worth habbin'."

Catherine remembered the words of Robert E. Lee on how voluntary emancipation must happen. She acted impulsively. "Emmanuel; Tuttle," she said, "your coming family calls for a celebration. I am going to give you a gift. I am going to give you this house."

Emmanuel and Tuttle looked dazed. Finally, Emmanuel found his voice. "You can't do dat, Miss Cath'n," he said.

"Why not, Emmanuel?" she asked. "It is mine to give."

Emmanuel shook his head in disbelief. "This here wonderful house is too 'spensive, Ma'am," he said. "All those Niggers been jealous ob us ober dis house. We didn't plan on buyin' nothin' dis good."

A question came to Catherine's mind. "Emmanuel, how much do you think this house is worth?" she asked.

Emmanuel scratched his head for a bit. "Ma'am," he said, almost reverently, "I 'spec' dis house wu'th nigh on to a hunnert dollars."

Catherine thought for moment. “Well you might be just about right,” she said. “But Emmanuel, I am not giving you the ground on which it sits, at least not now—just the house; is that understood.”

She smiled at Emmanuel’s effusive reply. “Oh, yes, Miss Cath’n. I does un’erstan’ most well,” he said. “I don’ want no groun’. A house is all I ever dreamed of for now.”

“And I am going to have a paper made,” Catherine said, “and get you a little plaque to put on that wall. It will say: ‘This house is the property of Emmanuel and Tuttle…do you have any last name?”

Tuttle sounded surprised. “Why, ‘Mo’gan,’ Ma’am” she said. “That’s all the last name we ever had.”

Catherine wanted Tuttle to help her with her bath, but decided to manage herself today and leave them to ponder their good fortune of having been given ownership to an old, run down slave shack. And yet she knew it probably meant as much to them as her house did to her. Some things were relative. One thing was for sure. She had not seen as much joy in Richmond in the past year—and certainly not since the war ended—as she had seen in that little cabin this day.

Catherine put on her robe, went out and locked the screen door and critiqued herself in the mirror. It was she first time she had done so since her marriage. At twenty-four, she could not see where she had changed at all. The births of her daughters had been easy and had not left her stretched. She thought of her daughters for the first time today. She left them in Richmond with Varina who was going to bring them and come down for a visit as soon as she set the house in order.

Catherine dressed and went out to the porch. She sat there trying to get accustomed to it so she could think as she used to. It was her place of solitude and meditation then. Would it still be? She looked around at everything. It seemed so familiar and yet so different somehow. It was weird; she could not put her finger on it. While she was thus musing, there was a knock on the porch door. She went and opened it on the two smiling faces of Emmanuel and Tuttle. Catherine knew there was something going on here but she was not picking up on it. She had just come from visiting them in their cabin a few hours earlier.

"Yes?" she asked.

Emmanuel fidgeted a little, then said," Well, Ma'am, us is come visitin'."

"You came visiting,' she repeated slowly, "but you live here."

Emmanuel was laboring but he had his thoughts down. "No, Ma'am, us live out dere in our own house," he said. "I figger now dat we is free and employed and got our own house, maybe we'd come visitin' our neighbors jis' like other folk do."

Catherine was flapped. "Oh, I see," she said, "well do come in and sit down." Tuttle sat on the day bed and Emmanuel on the wooden chair by the stove. Catherine's mind was racing. What had she done now? "Emmanuel—Tuttle," she said cautiously. "I am so glad you have come to see me and…I hope you will do that from time to time—not all of the time, but now and again. But I think it best that you not go to any of the neighbors just now until a little…a lot of time has passed and we see…" She stopped, not knowing just how she wanted to finish the thought.

Emmanuel looked at her with eyes betraying a sad understanding. "I un'erstan' Ma'am," he said. "We ain't goin' off de Mo'gan place. We don't wanna visit no white man but you no way."

Catherine tried to think of something to say. "Well, I think this is going to be just a nice thing, then and…well, what would you like to talk about? I have a little time."

Emmanuel looked grave. "Ma'am," he asked soberly, "what's going' to happen to black folks now? Lots of 'um figured the No'th done won de woe fo' sho'e."

Catherine was sorry for the fears she knew were out there. "Oh, I know, they must be very confused and very worried," she said softly and with sympathy. "Well, let me tell you what I can."

Catherine spent half an hour telling them all General Lee and the transition military government was going to be doing in the next two years. She tried to tell it in words that they would understand but wasn't sure how well she was succeeding. She had most often talked to them like children before. This was her first attempt at talking to them on a strictly grownup level. She saw them steal glances at each other from time to time but could not get a feel for their thoughts. She wound up by saying, "I am sorry, I know that your friends had visions of being released from servitude immediately by an act of abolition from the Lincoln government, but it just didn't happen that way."

Emmanuel smiled. "Ma'am," he said, "I got to tell you sumthin.' All I heard fo' de last year from those Niggers is, 'what we g'wine do, where we g'wine go? Dey ain' g'wine let us stay no mo'e once we is pronounced free.' But now dis here, what you' tellin' us' g'wine put a smile on a lot of faces. You ain't goin'a turn a man and his family out until you sho'e he kin make hisself a livin.' A little bit of somethin' is a lot better'n whole lot of nothin', Ma'am, and sho nuff de firs' concern of ever darkie is to hab a place to sleep, a place to eat and a place to b'long."

Catherine listened in amazement. Emmanuel's words and those of Robert E. Lee were almost identical. Lee understood them better than she thought and better…yes, better than she did…in some ways, at least.

Emmanuel rose out of his chair. "Come on, Tuttle, we is takin' too much of Miss Cath'n time." Emmanuel and Tuttle started out the door. "Thank' you, Ma'am, fer lettin' us visit," he said.

"You are very welcome," Catherine said in a daze, "You come again."

"We sho'e nuff do dat, Miss Cath'n," Tuttle said, "An' you come an' see us."

After they left, Catherine sat long in the dim light of the porch, lost in thought. Could she live up to the promise of hope she had given them? She remembered the day in the woods when she met Harriet Tubman and then the day in Washington. She remembered the speech she made to Sarah Morgan on the way back. "Things are changing and we must change with them or be left behind to dream in a world that doesn't exist anymore and never will again." She wished Robert were there so she could tell him what she had done.

It would not be easy. She had opened herself to them and they felt they knew her well enough to come in. She had to proceed now, but she had to do so cautiously. They would hurt themselves and she would not be able to help them if they went too far, too fast, and dreamed so big that reality discouraged them from taking the opportunities that would be open to them. They must not be given too much freedom too quickly. Then she remembered that she had already given them their freedom and they did not belong to her anymore. Oh, but that was just talk and paper. Of course, they belonged to her…and…and she belonged to them. They were Morgan people. They did not want to be free to go away. It was all very confusing and, for many of her thoughts and doubts, there simply was no answer—but she would keep at it. She remembered her father's old oriental proverb. The journey of a thousand miles begins with one small step. She had taken several small steps and now one bigger one. The journey to discover a new South and a new Hopemont was on its way.

A familiar old sound that she had not heard for a long time brought her back to reality. She went to the screen door and looked out. Tuttle and Emmanuel were rolling on the grass in front of the slave…in front of their house…playing and laughing like children. They had gotten back what they lost.

She sat down on the day bed. Suddenly she knew what was strange about the porch. It was not entirely the same porch of a twenty-year-old maiden and her mother. It was the porch of a twenty-four-year-old widow. It had old sights, old smells, and old memories that were precious and must never be lost. One must retain those priceless things. But one could not live in the past, not even at the home of one's youth in the room that had been her sanctuary and her trysting place with her dreams. Sometimes one must go back. Tuttle and Emmanuel had gone back to the days when they played together and had joy in each other. But they were not living in the past. The greatest time of life and joy for them was now.

Catherine remembered the words of Jesus. A wise householder brings forth out of his treasuries some things old and some things new. Remember the old values, keep old friends, and remember good things and good times and good people. If you have gone away from good habits, reestablish them. If you have lost your faith, return to it—those are the treasures of the past. But live in the present. Seize the moment. As for the future, plan for it, look to it for better things, dream toward it; keep hope alive. But live in the present.

As for the present, Hopemont was a better place because she had done something in it. The porch was the same because it stored old treasures. But it was different because Catherine was different. She was not filled with nostalgic longings for the good old days; she was not an idle dreamer who escaped reality by vain imaginations of the future. She was a 'today' person. She had been a today person with Harriet, with Forrest, and now with Emmanuel and Tuttle. Catherine did not know what slave trader had brought their ancestors to America. She did not know if a future society might make them full participants in the bounty of life. But she knew that their lives were better, their hopes were brighter, they felt good about themselves, and they were happier than anyone she knew. Today they were free, they had money in their little glass bank, owned their little house, and they were going to have a family. And it was because they had a friend who had risked her life and freedom to protect them and keep them together, who loved them and who had now opened her doors to them, not just as servants, but as neighbors. It was a new day on the old porch. That hallowed place would take today's things and put them among its store. As time passed, they too would be woven into the warp and woof of the lore and legend that was Hopemont and the old, honeysuckle-covered screen porch.

The striking clock brought Catherine back from her nostalgic pilgrimage. She rose to go up to the room they had occupied before her husband left Hopemont to go to Richmond. In a few minutes she would be looking at the pictures, holding the objects, reading the old letters, darning a pair of his old socks, and thinking the thoughts that would make her weep. As she glided through the great room on the way to the staircase, she paused beneath her father's picture that hung over the mantle of the fireplace. Beneath it was a wooden plaque. It had been there for many years but Catherine had never paid it much attention. Now she seemed drawn to it. In bold letters, was a title:

Glory in the Dust

Under the title was a verse that read:

From the dust, by God's great hand,
Man's glory did arise.
By the folly of our hand's,
In dust man's glory dies.

On our gave a flower blooms,
More glorious than them all.
It struts its moment in the sun,
And then its withered petals fall.

Back and forth the shuttle moves,
And weaves this fateful story;
From the dust, and to the dust,
And in the dust, our glory.

Catherine stood for a moment and mused on the verse. She thought of the tales her father had told her about the hardship, frost bite, and near starvation in the War of Independence and the glorious new day that dawned. She thought of her mother, father, brother, husband, Jefferson Davis, and General Forrest; all dead. She thought about the glory of the South, dead in unmarked graves in a hundred somber vales and on a hundred battle-scarred hill sides. She thought about the black night of suffering and despair that Emmanuel and Tuttle had gone through and the new life and hope that had come forth. She thought of Harriet Tubman, in the dark of night, crawling through some eerie, snake infested river bottom and the dawn of freedom that had resulted for many. She remembered the travail of child birth and the profound joy her children had brought her. She thought of the crude little grave in the wild wood bower where her friend lay sleeping, adorned only with withered flowers. She thought of what she would soon be doing; embracing death and pain to forge character, find solace, and know peace. She thought of the tide of hope for a better and a glorious future that was blooming in the South just now and the blood soaked ground where its seeds had been planted.

"Glory in the Dust," she said aloud, in a voice where hope was stronger than doubt and understanding greater than confusion. Then she turned and bounded up the stairs.

Printed in the United States
92249LV00005BB/54/A